MEMORY LANE

A SONS OF SCANDAL ROMANCE

BECKY WADE

Romances by Becky Wade

MISTY RIVER ROMANCE SERIES

#0.5 Take a Chance on Me (novella)

#1 Stay with Me (novel)

#2 Let It Be Me (novel)

#2.5 You and Me (novella)

#3 Turn to Me (novel)

BRADFORD SISTERS ROMANCE SERIES

#0.5 Then Came You (novella)

#1 True to You (novel)

#2 Falling for You (novel)

#2.5 Because of You (novella)

#3 Sweet on You (novel)

PORTER FAMILY SERIES

#1 Undeniably Yours (novel)

#2 Meant to Be Mine (novel)

#3 A Love Like Ours (novel)

#3.5 The Proposal (short story)

#4 Her One and Only (novel)

STAND-ALONE NOVEL

My Stubborn Heart

STAND-ALONE NOVELLA

Love in the Details

Copyright © 2023 by Rebecca Wade

Cover Design © Courtney Walsh

Author Photograph by Emilie Haney of EAH Creative

Author is represented by Kristy Cambron

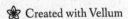 Created with Vellum

For my readers

We booklovers understand each other, don't we? We've experienced the reckless thrill of staying up late reading. We know what it feels like when a romance captures our emotions, when a plot twist blindsides us, when our anxiety mounts because characters are in peril. We cry and laugh over books. We find rest in their pages. Reading is our luxury. Our joy.

I see you! And I appreciate you.

Thank you so much for the support, kindness, and encouragement you've given to me.

Chapter One

The day Remy Victoria Reed fished a drowning man from the Atlantic Ocean began in the most ordinary way.

Her phone alarm woke her at 8:00 a.m. in her cottage on Islehaven Island, twenty-four miles off the coast of Maine. She defrosted her usual breadless turkey sausage egg'wich in the microwave. She consumed it along with one tall glass of water (hydration was key) and one cup of coffee (morning caffeine—also key). She engaged in a thirty-five-minute power walk through mid-September foliage just beginning to shimmer with autumn color. Dutifully, she completed fifteen minutes of yoga on her living room floor followed by ten minutes of meditation. After she showered, it took four minutes to don a gray waffle-knit shirt and jean overalls. She wrestled with her long blond hair for thirty seconds before conceding defeat.

Her appearance would do seeing as how she had no expectation of seeing another human today nor, indeed, for the next few days. Even when she did see humans, they were locals well known to her. Most were much older. All were rugged types who'd be baffled to see her in makeup and disdained the notion that clothing had any purpose other than utility.

By 9:45, she'd entered her studio. After selecting her *Masters of Classical Music* CD, she fired up her boom box, tied on her canvas apron, and settled her safety glasses onto her head. It didn't take her long to submerge into the world of imagination she inhabited when working on her wooden sculptures. Today, she chipped away at a two-foot-long block of lignum vitae, a gouge in one hand, a mallet in the other. She followed the chalk lines she'd sketched on the block, but even more she followed the whispering of the wood—which told her what it wanted to become.

Her next alarm sounded at 12:45, startling her. She switched off her music, then played her frequent game of where-did-I-leave-my-phone?

Her trusty microwave once again defrosted her lunchtime meal. She settled herself and a spicy chicken bowl (nutrition was key) at her kitchen table. As always, she sat in the chair facing her living room. Beyond the large picture window at the living room's end lay her front deck, and beyond that—ocean. Pine trees pressed close on the sides of the house but like polite audience members, they didn't infringe on the scene framed by glass.

As she ate, her attention alternated between two things. One, texting with distant friends and family. Two, staring at the sea . . . which had whipped up considerably since her morning walk.

Her view through the picture window was her constant companion and source of fascination. Incredibly familiar. Endlessly new. It changed with the seasons, yes. But its mood could also change within a matter of minutes, on a quicksilver whim. At times it smiled beguilingly immediately before gnashing its teeth.

She made herself down more water (hydration was key). Just as she set the glass back on the table, a cloud slid in front of the sun, slanting shadows across the floorboards.

An ominous chill slid down the back of her neck. No longer a woman who overrode her instincts, Remy went still.

She heard nothing amiss. Neither did she see or smell anything amiss. Stuffing her phone in her overalls, she neared the window and peered out. The trees rattled and swayed more than usual, but overall, everything was as it should be.

The sense of foreboding remained, insistent.

She played her second-most-frequent game of where-did-I-leave-my-glasses? Once she had her frames in place, she carefully scanned the setting.

A scrap of white out at sea caught her attention. Too far away to tell if it was a wave or . . . something else. She scooped her binoculars from the side table and swept their magnified field of vision back and forth across the water. Where was the scrap of white?

The circle moved to the left, catching a corner of the object she sought. There. She moved the binoculars back to it.

It wasn't an object. It was *a man*. In a white shirt. Swimming with difficulty. Struggling. In clothing, not a wet suit. No boat nearby.

A man. Overboard.

Her pulse leapt into overdrive.

She threw the strap of the binoculars around her neck and rammed her arms into the waterproof jacket she kept on a peg by the front door. Today's temperature had reached the mid-sixties, but the ocean water surrounding Islehaven was dangerously cold. Stuffing her feet into duck boots, she called her friend and nearest neighbor.

"Yep?" Leigh answered.

"I just spotted a man overboard. He's trying to keep his

head above water and he's pretty far out there." Her pitch was too high, her words too fast. "We need to go and—and rescue him. Right now. Immediately."

"I'm still twenty minutes from home."

"No!"

"Yes," Leigh said in her gruff, no-nonsense voice. A lobster-woman, Leigh started her day well before sunrise and drove back from the harbor around this time. "Go and bring him in. I'll meet you at your dock."

"Leigh!"

"You can do this. Keep your phone with you. I'm on my way."

No point calling anyone else because no one could reach her dock in less than the twenty minutes Leigh had quoted. Remy pounded down the dirt path from her deck to the cliff's lowest edge, where her grandfather had built wooden stairs to the dock below. She hardly needed to look as her feet flew along planks her memory knew by heart.

This was terrible! What if the man slipped beneath the surface by the time she got out there? What if she couldn't find him? What if he died? Her brain circled down a toilet hole of horrifying possibilities.

She reached the dock. From the storage chest there she yanked on a life jacket, then tossed a second life jacket and a life-saver ring attached to a rope onto the floor of the only vessel waiting—a small boat with an outboard motor.

Pausing, she shielded her eyes with her hand. She could no longer see the man. She held up the binoculars. There. His head was still above water.

She freed the mooring and clambered inside the boat. It rumbled to life and she took off toward the man's position as fast as the aging boat could go. Not fast enough.

The weather had taken a metaphorical eggbeater to the

water, forming choppy peaks. Overhead, charcoal-tipped clouds rolled toward her angrily.

She leaned forward, willing the boat to go faster.

Twice she lost sight of him and panicked, thinking he'd slipped under the waves for good. Both times she idled the motor and, bracing her legs apart, rose to her full height of five foot seven. Both times she spotted him and continued forward.

Islehaven's residents served as the local emergency rescue force. She'd helped retrieve people from the water a few times in the past. Once after a boating accident and once after a small plane with engine failure had landed on the water. Those times, she'd assisted others.

This time, Remy was it.

She neared the man's position and slowed her speed. "Don't worry," she called in a highly worried tone. "Everything's going to be okay." This situation was not okay. *SOS! SOS! Emergency situation,* her mind shrieked. "Can you put on a life jacket?" If he could, that would keep him afloat and face-up even if he lost consciousness.

He didn't respond. He continued to swim for shore but was so exhausted, he made no progress. Life-preserver ring it was, then.

"I'm going to throw this to you." She brandished the ring. "Hang on to it until we get you on board."

He gave no sign of awareness.

"Sir!"

Still nothing. With shaking hands, she knotted the ring's rope to the metal cleat on the side of the boat, then heaved the ring toward him.

He didn't appear to notice.

"Grab it!" she yelled. "*Grab it!*"

He paused his swimming motion, which caused him to bob

more upright. He was maybe in his mid-thirties. Skin very pale. Short, brownish hair slicked to an angular head.

"Grab the ring!"

At last, one of his arms streaked out of the water and came down on it.

Remy killed the boat's motor. The sounds of sloshing water, squealing gulls, and her harsh breathing filled the void. She towed the rope in, hand over hand. He'd need to enter from the back of the boat via the ladder at its lowest point.

"Sir, can you hear me?"

Apparently not.

Once she'd pulled him close, she leaned her upper body over the boat's edge and gripped the cold fabric of his white windbreaker. "Look at me."

He tipped his face to her profile. His expression was blank. However, his glazed eyes did meet hers. All around him, churning water threatened to suck him down, down, down.

"There's a ladder right in front of you. Climb up. I'll pull as you climb."

No response.

If he couldn't climb, they were going to be in serious trouble. He was much larger than she and she didn't think she could haul his dead, wet weight into her boat.

"Climb!" she ordered, tugging upward on his windbreaker.

He tried to climb, more in a dreamlike state than a conscious one, but his arms and legs refused to work as a team.

She looped the ring's rope around his back. *You are going to survive*, she thought fiercely, the desperation to save herself that had once driven her to this island tangling with her desperation to save him. Remy threw all her body weight up and backward.

One of his feet found the lowest step of the ladder. He straightened that leg, which pressed his body higher.

Remy pulled the rope again and he landed in a heap inside

her boat. Shaking. Waterlogged. In addition to the wind-breaker, he wore black track pants and sneakers.

"Are you all right?"

Chattering teeth were the only answer.

She needed to get him warm and dry as soon as possible. Grunting, she dragged him away from where she'd sit to steer the boat and propped him against the bow.

Instinctively he drew his arms close to his chest.

"Was anyone else out here with you?"

No answer.

She scoured the view, 360. No one was calling for help and she saw nothing except a distant boat—little more than a minia-ture brown smudge—several miles to the southeast.

Remy sent the boat whizzing across the worsening waves toward home. Her urgency to save the life of her passenger distorted time, pulling the minutes unbearably long.

Gradually the façade of her cottage, covered in shingles that time had weathered to gray, drew nearer. She could make out Leigh's stout, reassuring form waiting for her on the dock.

At last, she pulled even with Leigh, who helped her secure the boat. The older woman stepped aboard wearing a green plaid flannel, jeans, and rubber boots. She'd stuffed her three-inch-long ponytail through the hole at the back of a faded ball cap.

"He hasn't said anything," Remy told her friend. "He's semi-conscious."

"Hypothermia can mess with a person's abilities. It mimics drunkenness." Leigh hunched near the man. "There's blood at the back of his head."

"What?"

"I think he has a head injury. Let's lift him out, as carefully as possible. I'll hold under his arms, you get his feet."

Remy followed her instructions.

"One, two, three," Leigh said. They heaved him onto the dock.

He groaned, shut his eyes, and rolled onto his side. His lean, muscular body rattled.

"I'll get one side, you get the other." Leigh braced him into a sitting position and settled one of his arms across her shoulders. Remy did the same, feeling the coldness of it through her jacket. The two women pressed to standing in unison, the stranger staggering between them, head lolling forward. He was over six feet tall and heavy.

They started up the stairs.

Unlike Remy, Leigh had been born and bred on Islehaven. She was forty-eight, with a face that looked a decade older but a body that had the strength of someone two decades younger. Her thighs were the circumference of office wastepaper baskets. Leigh didn't stop to rest and so Remy didn't stop either, despite that her limbs were screaming in protest.

"We can," Remy said between gasps of breath as they pushed through the cottage's door, "put him on my bed."

"Ayuh, but not until we've gotten these clothes off him. Let's lay him on the rug in your bedroom first."

They did so.

Leigh unzipped his windbreaker to reveal a white T-shirt beneath. Remy got out her electric blanket, spread it on the bed, and turned it on high. Then she rushed to the linen closet and returned with clean towels.

Both of them worked to peel the clinging windbreaker and T-shirt from his body. Doing so revealed nasty red and purple bruises across his ribs.

Remy swallowed hard. What had happened to him?

Shivering miserably, he tried to return to the fetal position.

She pressed the towels to his hair and skin while Leigh made short work of his shoes and socks. They'd stripped him down to his track pants, a metal watch, and a platinum wedding band on his ring finger. When Leigh gripped his waistband in preparation to pull downward, Remy focused intently on his clavicles.

"Towel," Leigh said like a surgeon asking for a scalpel. Remy passed her one, then prepared her bed by folding back the covers and stacking pillows so his head would be elevated.

The two women transferred him to the mattress, Remy's vision once again glued to his clavicles.

Leigh drew the sheets and blankets over him. "He might have cracked ribs or a concussion. I'm going to call Michael." She strode from the room.

Islehaven had a year-round population of forty. That number could swell as high as 120 in the summer months, but even then, they had no doctor. Nor did they have restaurants, a gas station, or a grocery store (except for the few items stocked at the post office). Their one-room schoolhouse educated four students. The ferry from the mainland came once a month. The nearest islands—to the north and west of Islehaven—were all smaller, all uninhabited.

Their community's medical needs were served by a ship that carried a nurse to Maine's unbridged islands. However, Nurse Ann was not a maritime emergency room. She came according to a schedule and had been here recently, which meant she wouldn't return for weeks.

The closest thing they had to a medical professional was Michael, Islehaven's resident EMT, who also worked as their air traffic controller and plumber.

The question *What will happen to me if I need medical help?* had plagued Remy when she'd moved here. She'd learned to deal with that fear and many others. Except now, that old question was snapping back like the tail of a whip. *What will happen to him if he needs medical help?*

They'd retrieved this man from the water, but he still might die. If he did, it would happen here. Inside her house. In her bed.

She took a step closer and leaned forward slightly.

The stranger's masculine frame took up the entire length of her queen bed. He was very . . . chiseled. He had a V-shaped jawline. Defined cheekbones. A strong, straight nose and symmetrical brows. His pale brown eyelashes rested against frighteningly white skin. Now that his hair had been towel-dried and stuck up in tufts, she saw that it wasn't brown like she'd first thought but dark blond in color.

Remy caught herself anxiously bending each of her fingers toward her palm. Shaking out her hands, she went to the kitchen to make tea. For the stranger, when he was able to consume it. And for herself and Leigh. She felt wobbly and needed tea right now the way gambling addicts needed Vegas.

As Remy was pouring hot water into mugs, Leigh approached. "Michael's on his way. He suggested we take his temperature. Do you have a thermometer?"

"An electronic one, yes. It's here somewhere." Remy rustled through her messy medicine drawer until she found the thermometer at the back. Did it still have battery? She flicked it on and by some miracle, it came to life.

"Michael says if his temperature's under ninety-six, he'll likely need medical intervention right away."

Remy carried the thermometer to her room and sat on the edge of the bed near the man's waist. Leigh followed, placing the tea tray on the bench at the foot of the bed.

The man's eyelids remained closed. His limbs and teeth continued to shudder.

Remy swiped the thermometer from the middle of his forehead to his temple. It beeped and she read the display aloud. "Ninety-six point seven."

"Good." Leigh leaned a shoulder against the room's wall.

"Sir?" Remy asked their patient. "Can you hear me?"

Several seconds slogged by. "Ico," he slurred quietly.

"What? Please say that again."

He scowled. "Ico."

I'm cold.

"Yes, I know you're cold. I'm very sorry. Hopefully you'll begin to warm up soon. You're dry now and I have the electric blanket going full blast—"

"In . . . pay."

In pain. Empathy gusted within her. "An EMT is on his way. We'll address your pain as soon as we can. I have tea here. If you're able to drink it . . . that will help you warm up."

His hooded eyes cracked open. They were red, no doubt from the salt water. Yet his irises were a rare, first-leaves-of-springtime green. They almost gave the impression of translucence.

Remy lifted his mug. Anticipating that he'd continue to shiver for some time, she'd filled his cup halfway with water that wasn't scalding hot. She scooted closer, her free hand reaching to support the back of his head. Her fingers met the briny strands of his hair then the drying blood Leigh had mentioned, which concealed a lump. Carefully, she positioned her hand below the injury and brought the cup to his lips.

He turned his face away.

She followed his mouth with the rim of the mug and tilted liquid in.

He grimaced. She tried again, but he shook his head. She could smell the ocean on him—that fresh, salty scent.

"This will help you warm up," she repeated, bringing the tea back to his mouth.

He growled and shook his head again. "Sh. Grou. Ara. Fee."

"Hmm? I'm sorry, I don't understand."

"Fres . . . grou . . . n Arab . . . a off . . . ee."

Leigh released her cackle-laugh. "I think he's requesting freshly ground Arabica coffee. I take that as a good sign."

Remy blinked at the stranger in astonishment. Of all the things he could have said in this moment while barely clinging to life, these were the words he'd chosen? He was placing a—a coffee order? As if she was a barista?

"Tea," he gritted out. "Stain . . . d ot . . . ter."

"Coffee is also stained water," Remy pointed out.

"Ara . . . bica," he said.

"I have Folgers coffee and Lipton tea. That's it."

He studied her with groggy outrage.

"I'll be right back with a cup of Folgers," Leigh announced.

His consciousness had begun to return when they'd had him on the rug. All he'd been able to think was that he wanted to go . . . away again. To wherever he'd been. Sleeping? But the way they'd pushed and pulled at him had stolen his ability to go away because pain sliced through his chest whenever he moved. Or inhaled.

What had happened to him? The gears in his head weren't working right. They were turning too slowly, which made the world blurry and gray.

A long, drawn-out curse word dragged through the sludge of his mind.

The blond woman sitting beside him lifted her eyebrows, so he might've said that out loud.

She set his tea aside and reached for a mug of her own. Cradling it with both palms, she took several long drinks.

He tried to shift into a more comfortable position. The movement shot agony through his body, so he stopped. Better to remain motionless. Except he couldn't do that either. His body was shaking uncontrollably.

Frowning, he squinted at the blonde.

Edgy energy radiated from her. She was young but not very young. Late twenties? Medium sized. Plain. Her oval face might be pretty with makeup, but she wasn't wearing any. Bad taste in clothes. Her horn-rimmed glasses had water spots on them that she hadn't seemed to notice. Eyes—no particular color. She'd taken the front of her hair and knotted it on top of her head. It fell wild and wavy in the back.

Where am I?

His line of sight traveled to the closet doors opposite him. Then to the wall that held a window. Rainy weather caused the trees to lean and toss. The bedroom was painted navy blue, the walls covered in stuff. Contemporary art. Metal stuff and wooden stuff. Books had been stacked on the bedside table near the window next to a lamp and wooden head. The head was glaring at him with elongated eyes and a narrow nose.

Cautiously, he looked to the bedside table on the other side and found another wooden head eyeballing him and a lot more junk covering the walls.

The older of the two women poked her head in the doorway. "Anything else I can get you while I'm in the kitchen?" she asked him.

It took him a while to locate the word he wanted. "Morphine."

The older lady with the weathered, rectangular face grinned. "I'm fresh out."

"Then twenty-one . . . year-old rum."

The blonde's mouth tightened with annoyance. "I have one bottle of tequila on hand in case of emotional emergency."

"I'll . . . take it."

"No can do," the lady in the doorway said. "In your condition, alcohol will make things worse not better."

"Then pain . . . killers," he said. "A bottle . . . full."

The older woman disappeared.

"Thanks, Leigh," the blonde called after her.

He was so cold. And naked under cheap, scratchy sheets. He could feel heat coming from the blanket above him so he shouldn't be this cold. "Did you two . . . drug me?"

"What? *No*."

"Kid . . . nap me?"

"Absolutely not. We're trying to help you."

"By taking off . . . my clothes?"

She stiffened. "We had to. I saw you through my binoculars, out in the ocean, swimming in your clothing. I brought you here in my boat but now you have hypothermia from being in the water so long. We needed to get you dry and warm, so we took off your wet clothes. But rest assured, I didn't see anything except your clavicles."

His clavicles? "My chest . . . and head . . ."

"You have bruised ribs and a head injury."

"Only . . . an idiot would swim . . . in their clothes. Why . . . would I do that?"

"I have no idea."

He made a sound of frustration. "I'm going to be . . . . disgusted with myself if it turns out . . . I'm an idiot."

"What do you remember?"

He had a vague memory of sea and desperation, of praying to God and the sense that God was with him, keeping his head above water.

Leigh placed a glass of water, two Advil, and a cup of coffee on the bedside table.

Two Advil? He struggled against a wave of despair. "I'm going to need more medicine."

"When the EMT gets here, we'll give you more if he says you can have more," the blonde answered.

Was this hell? Was he going to spend eternity with wooden statue heads, a woman trying to pour tea down his throat, and not enough medicine to kill the pain?

He wanted all of it gone. The pain most of all. But also this place and these people.

The blonde helped him wash down the Advil with water, then brought the coffee to his lips. The scent of it hit his nose. This time, he cooperated and drank. The coffee was subpar, but better than tea.

Leigh took her tea to the chair in the corner. She sat with her shoulders back, one foot braced on the knee of the opposite leg. He hoped this was her house because she seemed calmer and more normal than the blonde. "Where . . . am I?"

"In my home," the blonde said.

Great.

"On Islehaven Island, off the coast of Maine," Leigh added.

"Islehaven?" he asked.

"Yes."

"I don't . . . know it."

"Can you explain how you ended up in the water?" Leigh asked. "Take your time. I know it's hard to think when your body's that cold."

He searched his fuzzy head.

"Were you out on a boat?" the blonde asked.

He scowled.

"Were you out on a boat?" she repeated.

He opened his mouth to reply . . .

However, when he reached for the answer, he couldn't grab it.

Were you out on a boat?

He could *feel* the answer right there, close. Except he

couldn't pin it down. He couldn't come up with anything, in fact, but blankness. "I don't know."

"What's your name?" she asked. "We should alert your family at once."

Again, he automatically went to pull up the information—

And found that it was gone, too. Missing. He didn't even know his own name.

Chapter Two

A s soon as Michael arrived, Remy and Leigh gave the EMT privacy to examine the stranger.

While they waited, Remy drank tea obsessively and Leigh paced. The time that had passed since she'd spotted the man in the ocean had been so nerve-wracking that it had exacted ten times the toll as regular minutes. She stared at nothing, tasting Lipton, trying to metabolize the stress.

Today she'd *rescued a man* who was currently present in her bed but *absent of his memories.* Leigh had checked his clothes and found nothing. No identification.

At last Michael emerged. At twenty-eight, he was two years younger than Remy. Black curls topped his earnest, pink face.

They congregated near the front door, the spot farthest from the bedroom, and pitched their voices low so the mystery man wouldn't overhear.

Michael listed his accomplishments like a Boy Scout naming the badges he'd earned. He'd checked the patient's temperature, which was almost back to normal. He'd monitored his blood pressure and pulse, which were stable. He'd cleaned and treated the head wound. He'd listened to the man's lungs, observed him breathing, pressed on his chest. "I don't think anything's fractured except for the ribs. But yeah. Broken ribs are very uncomfortable so he's in quite a bit of pain."

"Is there anything you can do for that?" Leigh asked.

"Over-the-counter painkillers." Michael shrugged. "You have some Advil around here?"

"Remy has about a quarter of a bottle left. We gave him two earlier. Can we give him more?

"I'm not a doctor so I can't prescribe more than the standard dose."

"Would it help to wrap a bandage around his ribs?" Leigh asked.

"We don't do that anymore." Michael tugged on a curl, which pinged back into place when he let go. "We want him to be able to breathe deeply. To heal the ribs, he'll need to stay immobile as much as he can."

"Ayuh," Leigh said. "And the head wound?"

"He might have a concussion, but hey. For that, he just needs rest. He asked me to call an ambulance and get him to the hospital. I explained that we don't have an ambulance or hospital and told him I think he'll be fine without them."

"What about the fact that he can't remember anything?" Remy asked.

"Uh . . . I'm not too worried about that. Confusion's normal with hypothermia. It should clear up once he's recovered."

"And where will he be recovering?" Remy asked.

"Well." Michael looked back and forth between them, finally settling on Remy. "Here, I guess. For the moment."

"Here? Who's going to give him care?"

"Well. You, I guess," Michael said. "For the moment."

Remy took a step back, wrapping her hands around her overalls' straps. "The extent of my medical knowledge comes from the healers in the *Merlin* TV series and those healers have superpowers. Without superpowers, I have no idea how to heal a man."

"You don't have to heal him," Michael replied. "You just have to look after him while his body heals itself."

She guarded her schedule and her privacy vigilantly because that's what kept her from feeling overwhelmed. "This is crazy! We need to fly him to a hospital so he can receive professional treatment." The island's dirt airstrip provided the fastest route to shore.

"It's too windy," Michael said. "No flights in or out for the rest of the day."

Remy turned to Leigh. "What about taking him to the mainland on your lobster boat?"

"It would take hours to get him there that way and attempting it might injure him worse. There's a storm rolling in and it wouldn't be a smooth ride."

"Could we at least . . . move him to your house?" Remy asked Leigh hopefully.

"Not with broken ribs," Michael said.

"Here's the deal." Leigh pushed up the brim of her ball cap, then resettled it low. "Having a man who looks like a fallen angel—"

Remy made a scoffing sound.

Leigh's expression turned disbelieving. "You don't agree that he looks like a fallen angel?"

"No, I do not."

"As I was saying, having a fallen angel drop into the sea outside your house is the best thing to happen to me this decade. But I work long hours on the boat. I'll gladly help you with him when I'm off work. But I can't watch him the rest of the time. He's better off here."

Leigh and Michael both knew Remy worked from home.

She went to thrust a hand into her hair and her fingers knocked the side of her glasses. Why was she still wearing glasses? Irritated, she stashed them in her overalls.

"Just give him plenty of hydration," Michael said, "food when he's hungry for it, peace, quiet. Oh, and you know, keep an eye out."

"Keep an eye out for what?"

"A lack of breathing or pulse."

"What!"

"If that happens, give CPR."

"I don't know CPR."

"Well, like I said. His body should heal itself."

Should? *Should?!* She tried to think of any solution that didn't involve a stranger with hypothermia staying in her bedroom—

"Shouldn't be for long," Leigh said. "As soon as his memory comes back, we'll contact his wife. She can take over the decision-making and figure out a way to get him home or to a hospital. Are you okay with letting him stay here just until then?" she asked Remy. The serious look that accompanied the question communicated what she wasn't saying. She knew Remy's history and she knew why sheltering a man here was more than just a logistical challenge.

"Ah . . ." He was too weak to pose a physical threat. And she'd be a terrible human if she refused to serve as temporary nurse to a wounded person in need. "I guess it should be fine for a day or two."

"How'd you find him?" Michael asked.

Remy explained.

"What could have happened to him?" Leigh wondered.

"Maybe he was in a fight?" Michael suggested. "On the boat Remy saw? That would explain the head injury and the broken ribs."

"Then what? He went overboard?" Leigh asked.

"Or was tossed?" Remy offered.

"What about a crash or explosion?" Leigh scratched her wrist. "Could something like that have caused his injuries?"

"Um," Michael said. "Yeah. Maybe."

"Was there any debris in the water?" Leigh asked Remy.

"No. None." Quiet descended and Remy had the sense that their minds were all spinning. "How long will it take his ribs to heal?"

"I googled that when I was in there with him," Michael answered. "About six weeks to heal completely."

Six weeks!

"But I'm sure he'll be gone long before then," he added.

"And what if his memory doesn't come back?"

"Call me."

If the stranger's memories didn't return, what were the chances that Michael—who was relying on Google for medical information—would have the know-how necessary to retrieve them?

For the next several hours, the stranger succumbed to a shaking, exhausted slumber.

Leigh and Remy viewed online tutorials that explained how to check a pulse and how to administer CPR. Leigh obligingly played the part of the victim while Remy practiced her newfound knowledge—without actually compressing Leigh's chest or performing mouth-to-mouth.

When their patient woke in the late afternoon, he was still groggy, but the shivering had finally eased. They brought him more Advil, which he swallowed. And food, which he didn't. They settled for coaxing him to drink water.

He fell back into a heavy sleep.

The two women ate dinner together but eventually Leigh had to leave in order to get sleep in advance of her early morning.

Remy held the door for her. Beyond, stars punctured the dark sky.

"I'll be back after work tomorrow to get him in and out of the tub," Leigh said.

Remy didn't have enough mental fortitude left to even *think* about bathing him. "See you then."

The night closed around Leigh's form as she made her way to her car. Turbulent wind rushed over Remy, pressing her clothing against her. She stepped back inside. Like earlier in the boat, she was once again alone with this unknown man.

Just him and her in this house.

She paused on the bedroom's threshold. Only the light from her lamp illuminated the space.

He cracked one eye open. Then both. "What's your name?" His scratchy voice gave the impression that speech hurt.

"Remy Reed."

He didn't reply.

"And what should I call you?" she asked. "It would be nice if I could refer to you as something other than Sir." She refused to call him John Doe because wasn't that what they called unidentified corpses? Naming him John Doe felt like labeling him as a dead man walking.

"Was there a guy in the Bible who got . . . spit out . . . by a fish?"

"Jonah?"

"That will do."

She pushed her lips to the side. "How do you remember the story of Jonah but not your own name?"

"I'm not sure. I just do."

Suspicious. What if he was pretending not to know his identity? Because he was a . . . crook? Who'd what? Given himself injuries in order to infiltrate her home? Nah. That was too far-fetched.

"Thank you," he said, "for letting me stay here."

"Always happy to entertain houseguests," she responded dryly. Not true. She rarely hosted anyone.

"Remy Reed?"

"Mm-hmm?"

"Can I have your bottle of tequila and the rest of the Advil?"

"No and yes."

He hitched an eyebrow. "You'll give me the rest of the Advil?"

"Absolutely." Then she tacked on, "Six pills, every twenty-four hours until I run out."

He grimaced. "You're torturing me."

"Really? I'm sorry to hear that because I view you as nothing but a blessing and a joy."

"You're about to . . . feel that way even more strongly."

"Oh?"

"Because I need to use the bathroom."

SOS! No. Why couldn't he have mentioned this when mighty Leigh was here to help? "All right," she said courageously.

"Can I have clothes?"

"Yours are still wet. Here." She scrounged through her closet and came up with her largest pair of pajama bottoms—buffalo plaid flannel. "Can you put these on yourself? I hope?" It would be hard to look at nothing but clavicles while trying to dress him in pajama bottoms.

"I'll try."

"Call when you're ready." She bolted into the hallway and opened the closet containing her stackable washer and dryer. Leigh had deposited Jonah's clothes and the towels they'd used on him into the hamper. Remy slid her fingers into every pocket of his garments, going through them to make sure Leigh hadn't missed anything. They were empty. Out in the ocean he'd lost the items a person would normally have on them. Wallet, ID, phone.

The track pants and windbreaker were Nike. The T-shirt, socks, and underwear, Under Armour. Everything looked brand-new. She stuck the clothing and towels in the washer and started a load.

She heard him swear.

"You okay?" she asked loudly.

"No."

"Dressed?"

"Yes."

He sat upright with his legs over the side of the bed, looking sick and dejected. The hem of her pajama bottoms hit him mid-shin. His injuries had rendered his strong body vulnerable.

She supported him as she'd done earlier when they'd climbed the stairs. Except now the arm she wrapped around his waist was touching bare skin. Too intimate. Awkward and triggering.

It took time, but she finally got him propped against the bathroom sink. "Do you . . . need assistance?" she asked. *Please say no.*

"If there comes a time when I need your assistance to go to the bathroom . . . then kill me."

She slipped from the room, waiting a short distance away. "Doing okay in there?" she asked through the closed door after a few minutes. "I'm wondering if I need to bust in to check your pulse."

"I still have a pulse."

"Good to hear." Nervously, she undid then reformed the bun on top of her head as a few more minutes ticked by.

"Remy."

She scurried forward. "I'm here. May I open the door?"

"Yes." He was swaying a little and looked on the verge of passing out.

She helped him back to the mattress. Once there, breath labored, he laid his wrists on his defined abs. "Remy. You know I'm not going to . . . make it on six Advil—"

"This subject again?"

"If you leave the bottle with me . . . I'll take responsibility for my dosing."

"You can't be responsible for your own dosing right now. You're not in your right mind."

"Yes, I am. And I'm clearly old enough to . . . make my own decisions. How old do you think I am?"

"A few years over thirty?"

"Old enough to handle a bottle of Advil."

"Michael didn't condone a higher dose."

"Michael's a child."

"He's an adult."

"He's not as adult as I am." He set his jaw at a challenging angle.

"You can't even remember your name. *I'm* the only adult of sound mind present—"

"Tell me how to sweet-talk you into giving me more drugs."

"I'm immune to sweet-talking."

At this he appeared confused and disgruntled, as if he couldn't imagine a scenario in which a woman wouldn't succumb to his sweet-talking. "I'm in pain."

She clicked off the bedside lamp. "I'll do everything I can to arrange a virtual appointment for you tomorrow with a doctor who can prescribe drugs. Until then, good night."

He responded with a growl.

Remy made it several feet down the hall before realizing she was going the wrong direction. She stopped, reversed course, and settled at the desk in her office adjacent to the living room. Books filled every inch of the bookshelves lining the space. Her mom, dad, and older sister handled the business and marketing side of her art, and thus she mostly used the computer here to watch movies and shows, check her meager email inbox every few days, or research information.

She'd come to the laptop this time for the latter reason. Research. If Jonah's wife and the rest of his loved ones—kids?—hadn't yet realized he was missing, they soon would. She needed to save them that anguish. But how?

She brought up a web browser and hunted for news stories from today about a missing man, a crash at sea, a private plane lost by air traffic control.

She found nothing.

She leaned back in her chair, chewing the inside of her cheek.

He had only two things on his person that might help her identify him. The wedding band and the watch. Could one of them be inscribed with his name? Why hadn't she thought to check this sooner?

She eased back into the dark bedroom. "Jonah?" she whispered.

No reply. He was already asleep.

She delicately loosened the clasp of his watch and slipped it off. He murmured but didn't wake. The ring eased over his knuckle without a yank.

Back in the office, she held the items under the desk light to study them.

Not a single letter had been engraved on either, but the watch's branding proclaimed it to be an Omega. Maybe she could use the watch to somehow . . . figure out more about him? Returning her fingertips to the keyboard, she began searching for this particular style—a diver's watch with a blue face and stainless-steel band.

After several minutes, she located it online. This watch was a Seamaster, Planet Ocean 600M Co-Axial Master Chronometer. Ironic name seeing as how she'd found Jonah barely alive in the ocean, which didn't exactly qualify him as a Seamaster. More like the sea had mastered him.

She skimmed down to the price. Eight thousand four hundred and fifty dollars.

Eight thousand dollars! For a watch? That was obscene.

How many stores carried this? Was it rare?

Not very rare, apparently. Dozens of online stores offered it for sale.

So how could she use a watch to determine Jonah's real name?

She racked her brain. But every avenue she considered ended in a dead end.

Insomnia stunk.

Late that night, Remy lay on her side, knees tucked up, hands under her cheek, ordering sleep to take her away like a taxicab with a customer.

So far, all the proverbial sleep taxis had passed her by.

When her parents or sister visited, she gave them the bedroom, inflated a blow-up twin mattress, and slept on it in the office. But she couldn't listen for Jonah's breathing or check his pulse very easily from there, could she? Thus she'd dutifully wedged her air mattress onto the floor between the bed and her bedroom wall. All lights were off except for one across the hall in the bathroom.

The mugs of tea she'd consumed were jangling in her system. But so was worry.

He was badly hurt and far from civilization. The specter of potential death still loomed.

How could she face his family and friends if he took a turn for the worse and she couldn't rescue him? What would she say then? *Well, you see, I just learned CPR a few hours before his heart stopped and I really didn't know what I was doing. I might have mixed up the number of chest compressions with the number of breaths. So sorry!*

Also, if he'd been beaten, it seemed she should worry that his attackers might come looking for him so they could finish the job. She kept reminding herself that *if* Jonah had been beaten, his attackers had been long gone by the time she'd reached Jonah. They'd have no way of knowing she'd come upon him, or who she was, or where she'd taken him.

Nonetheless, anxiety lingered.

Remy repeatedly lifted up on an elbow and twisted to squint at the clock on her bedside table. 11:52 p.m. 12:30 a.m. 1:28 a.m.

Should she check his pulse?

His breath sounded quiet and steady. But was it *too* quiet? She could no longer hear it. She scrambled upright. Holding her hair out of the way, she craned over him and stuck her ear next to his nose.

There. He was breathing. For long moments she waited. Yes, he was breathing. Almost inaudibly but well.

She resumed her position on her mattress.

2:02 a.m. She peeked over the edge of the bed and squinted

at the dark outline of his chest. Concentrating hard, she could see that it was rising and falling.

2:41 a.m. He shifted, then moaned. "Are you here?" he whispered in a half-asleep voice.

"I'm here."

"Don't go."

"I won't."

She must've eventually fallen asleep because when his voice reached out to her the next time, it took effort to pull herself to consciousness.

"Remy?"

"Yes?"

"Stay."

"I will."

Chapter Three

Beep beep beep. The sound blasted through Jonah's sleep. "What," he rasped, "is that terrible noise?"

Remy jerked to a sitting position on her makeshift bed. "It's my phone alarm. I set daily alarms to keep myself on schedule." She crawled around, patting things, clearly searching for her phone.

He pressed pillows against his ears. The alarm grew louder and louder.

Finally, she shut it off and held the phone high. "Found it."

He screwed his eyes closed and willed himself to go to sleep and wake up in the place where he actually belonged, fit and healthy. What was that old movie with the girl in the curly pigtails? *The Wizard of Oz.* And what was it she'd say? *There's no place like home.* She'd had that right.

If he could remember *The Wizard of Oz*, could he remember his name? Who he was?

He thought hard, but no. He still couldn't take hold of his identity. Worse, trying to do so made his head throb.

"How are you feeling today?" Remy asked.

"Like roadkill."

"Good morning to you, too." She opened the curtains, then left the room. Soon after, he heard her banging around in the kitchen.

Rain pattered against the window. The trees were still shaking and bending the way they had yesterday.

Gloom pressed down on him, making his chest hurt even worse than it already did. He had to find a way to cope with his situation until he could go home.

He staggered across the hall to use the bathroom. After washing his hands, he gripped the sides of the sink and confronted his face in the mirror.

Though he couldn't recall his history, looking at himself wasn't like looking at the face of someone he didn't know. It was like looking at his own face.

His hair was a mess—coarse from the ocean. His features were drained and exhausted beneath the dark gold stubble on his cheeks. If he had to guess, he'd say he usually shaved and didn't often let stubble grow.

His vision lowered to his bare torso. He didn't know what he'd been through, but he did know it had been serious. Vicious bruises marked his ribs and his head wound ached.

He glanced to the side, taking in the small space. One of the bathroom's shiplap walls wore a coat of fresh gray paint but the other three were semi-covered in peeling white paint. The pedestal sink, clawfoot tub, and rusty curtain rod ring above the tub looked ancient. The light fixture was more recent, but only half its light bulbs worked. A packaged toothbrush waited for him in a cup.

He cleaned up as much as possible. With the help of the doorframe, he started the journey back to the bedroom. He was so weak his head started to spin. The remaining distance seemed to be growing longer, like a special effect in a movie.

"Going on an excursion?" Remy asked, hurrying toward him down the hallway. She wore a denim shirt, cargo pants, and scuffed lace-up boots. Her braided hair rested forward over her shoulder. She took hold of his arm, offering support.

"I don't need help."

"I'll be the judge of that."

The headboard in her room was wood, the sheets and comforter white, the floors hardwood, the rug jute.

As he was returning to the reclining position he needed but was already coming to hate, he noticed something he hadn't before. His watch and ring rested on a saucer on the bedside table. Strange. He didn't remember taking them off.

"Have any of your memories come back?" she asked.

"No."

Her forehead lined.

"You're concerned about my lack of memories," he stated.

"Nope."

"You're a terrible liar."

"Michael thinks the hypothermia is the cause of your confusion and that it'll soon clear."

"I'm no longer confused and I'm over the hypothermia." He wanted to be honest so that neither of them could hang on to pipe dreams. "My ribs and head are killing me, but I'm thinking straight."

"I see."

Weren't nurses supposed to be calming and poker-faced? His nurse wasn't either of those things. She was clearly nervous about his lack of memories, which was making him feel more stressed, not less. "Are you a high-strung person?"

"When tasked with keeping strangers alive, yes." She clapped her hands together and gave them a rub. "Ready for breakfast?"

"Only if it's a breakfast of Advil."

"I'm lucky to have such a hilarious houseguest." She gave him a smile too sweet to be genuine. "I'll bring Advil but I'm also going to bring actual food since you didn't eat anything yesterday. How about an egg'wich?"

He wrinkled his nose. "Which is?"

"A frozen breadless breakfast sandwich. Quick and nutritious."

"No, thank you."

"Frozen breakfast burrito?"

"No."

"Then what?"

"I don't think I like frozen food. So . . . anything that isn't frozen?"

"You might want to try frozen food," she shot back, "seeing as how you don't remember your former life or your preferences."

"I know I don't like frozen egg'wich."

She rolled her eyes. "An apple? Oatmeal?"

He looked toward the window. "That will be fine."

"Very good, Duke." She gave a pretend curtsy. "I'll be back with your laundry and your breakfast right away, Duke."

He sighed. This woman took scissors to his patience. Had God stuck him here with her as punishment? If so, what had he done to deserve this?

She sailed back in and left a stack of clothes on the end of the bed. Curtsied again and disappeared.

He fantasized about wrestling the Advil bottle away from her. With his size, it would be child's play to take it from her in his usual state of health. But now? The trip to the bathroom had almost killed him.

He spent several minutes recovering, then attempted the job of changing his clothes. It was more painful than running a marathon, but he managed to strip off the ugly pajama bottoms and replace them with his own track pants. He tried to put on his T-shirt but gave that up almost immediately. No way could he get his arms above his head to slide it on.

Remy opened a lap tray over him, then made a few trips back and forth until she'd assembled oatmeal, slices of apple, coffee, water, and Advil. She carried in a wooden chair and sat near his elbow. "Can you feed yourself?"

"Nope," he answered immediately.

She lifted the glass, and he downed the painkillers. Then she picked up the spoon and started feeding him.

For the first time since he'd arrived at this house, a trace of pleasure trickled through him. Guilty pleasure, because he *could* feed himself. This was payback. If she was going to starve him for painkillers and bully him into eating, let her do the work.

She served him a bite of oatmeal flavored with maple syrup, milk, and cinnamon. He chewed and swallowed. "Is it possible I'm a resident of this island?"

"No. That is, you're definitely not a year-round resident. You might be a vacationer here. I can check today with the owners who rent their properties at this time of year to see if you might be staying at one of their houses." She fed him apple.

It crunched in his mouth, tart.

"I went through your clothing last night," she said, "looking for ID. I found nothing. So I—"

"—stole my watch and ring?"

"—*borrowed* your watch and ring," she corrected, "in hopes that one of them had an inscription. They didn't. But I was able to find information on that model of watch, and it sells for more than"—she lowered her voice as if afraid someone would over-hear—"*eight thousand dollars.*"

She was clearly shocked by that number. He was not. He

put his hands into a praying position. "God," he said fervently, "let me be rich."

She blinked at him. "I'm not a fan of anyone amassing great wealth. It's corrosive. Eight thousand dollars for a watch! A watch!" She brought the water to his mouth while transitioning into a lecture on the importance of hydration. According to her, they hadn't gotten enough fluid down him yesterday so today she was going to be counting every ounce.

Excellent. Something to look forward to.

"Are you married?" he asked, interrupting. He was going to be very surprised if she was, but it might be helpful to know if he was staying in the bed of a married woman. He didn't want her husband to barge in yelling.

She sniffed. "No."

"Boyfriend?"

"No. Did you ask those questions because you're trying to figure out how easy it will be to rob me?"

"Yes. That's why."

"I live here alone. But I've taken several self-defense courses online. So let that be a warning to you."

"Have you ever been married?"

"You're nosy."

"I'd like to know more about my hostess. You're worried I might rob you, but I'm worried you're poisoning me with this oatmeal. You told me you didn't drug and kidnap me, but I have no proof of that." He definitely didn't think she'd drugged and kidnapped him, yet the accusation was worthwhile because it caused her cheeks to turn pink.

"I am not in the habit of drugging and kidnapping men. I can't prove that to you, but what choice do you have but to trust me? If you plan to survive, the food I'm providing is your only option." She popped more apple into his mouth.

Once he'd finished chewing, he repeated his question. "Have you ever been married?"

"I've never been married. But you have as evidenced by your wedding band."

Back when they'd settled on the name Jonah, he'd known that was wrong, not his actual name.

Was he married?

He couldn't attach the idea of marriage to either a yes or a no . . . only to an uneasy shifting within him. Which didn't make sense. If the name Jonah had felt wrong, the idea that he was married should feel right. The ring, his watch, his clothes, his face all gave him an inner sense of familiarity. So why not marriage?

Normal, healthy people could remember. But he could not.

A knife's edge of panic pressed against his throat.

He blocked it. No. No to panic. He didn't think he was someone who usually gave in to fear. Plus, from a practical standpoint, he couldn't afford it right now. He was already in rough shape. Worry would slow his healing. "What do you do for a living? RN?" he asked jokingly.

"I am not a very nurturing person. In fact, I haven't been responsible for any living creature except myself in years—"

"Comforting to hear—"

"And have never even considered getting a pet." She adjusted the neckline of her shirt and sat up straight. "I'm a wood sculptor."

"Ah. A successful one?"

"I don't measure success in terms of income or recognition."

Likely because she hadn't received any of either.

"I'm successful," she continued, "at what matters to me, which is creating art that I'm proud of and contributing beauty to the world."

If she'd made the wooden heads on the bedside tables, he

wouldn't say she'd been a success at contributing beauty to the world, either. "Are you from this island?"

"No, I was raised in Dallas. I moved here six years ago."

"Why?"

Her gaze slid away from his. "I wanted the independence and nature and solitude."

"What made you choose this place specifically?"

"My grandfather built this cottage when my mother was young so that his family could spend time here every summer. Which is exactly what they did. First my mom and then my sister and me. When my grandfather passed away, my mother inherited this place. No one had ever lived here year-round until I asked Mom if I could. She said yes."

"What's it like, living here?"

"Peaceful. Difficult."

"Not at all convenient."

"No," she quickly agreed. "Not at all."

"You don't value convenience?"

She thought about it for a few moments. "Convenience is nice. But I've found that there are things that matter more to me."

"Like?"

"Self-sufficiency. Safety."

Just as she was gathering the last of the oatmeal onto the spoon, he picked up the coffee mug and sipped.

Her lower lip plopped open. "I thought you couldn't feed yourself."

"I'm as surprised as you are."

Her eyes flashed. She tossed the spoon back into the bowl with a clatter. Testy.

He was in so much discomfort that a smile hadn't been possible until now, but he gave her a big one. Both barrels.

He expected her to soften, to smile back, maybe even to get flustered.

Instead, she met his gaze directly, appearing completely and totally unmoved. "You tricked me," she accused.

"Yes."

"I saved your life! I'm basically Florence Nightingale—"

"I thought you were a sculptor—"

"—who is caring for you out of the goodness of my heart. You owe me."

"Take my watch." He gestured to it.

"Stunningly, we do not have a pawn broker on Islehaven, so I have no use for it." She scrambled up, eyes narrow. "You're . . . you're . . ."

"Yes?"

"Ungrateful."

"I'm incredibly grateful."

"Ungrateful *and* untrustworthy." She lifted the tray.

Luckily, he was still holding the coffee, or she'd have taken that, too.

As she was exiting, he spoke. "Could you help me put on my windbreaker? Going shirtless is starting to make me cold."

She paused and eyed him over her shoulder. "To my way of thinking, if you can feed yourself, then you can put on your own windbreaker."

He'd made her mad. Until now he hadn't realized the edgy artist was so passionate. He wasn't sorry for what he'd done. But he did respect her more for her spunk.

Once again, she moved to leave.

"Remy Reed?"

She stilled.

"When's my doctor's appointment?" he asked. "I need hard drugs."

"It wasn't easy to set up a virtual appointment for a man

with no name and no insurance. I ended up having to assure the doctor I'd pay in cash. Your appointment is in an hour and a half. When you speak with him, please ask him about one thing in particular."

"Yes?"

"Ask him if you might have amnesia." And with that, she was gone.

⛵

Remy had been watching for Leigh out the office window. When she saw her beater car pull up that afternoon, she dashed outside.

They met by the front fender. The wind was swirling in such a way that it tossed Remy's hair around her head.

"How is he?" Leigh asked.

"He's crafty, that's what he is. He misled me into hand-feeding him his breakfast."

"Did he?" Leigh cackle-laughed.

"Also," Remy confided in a scandalized tone, "I think he's *wealthy*. His watch costs more than eight thousand dollars."

"Oh, dear," Leigh said with mock seriousness, "that is terrible news indeed."

"I am *not* a fan of him."

The older woman tried and failed to look sympathetic. Today, Leigh's plaid flannel was red, her baseball cap battered beige.

"He's as slippery as an—an eel," Remy pronounced.

"Have you taken the time yet to notice his resemblance to a fallen angel?"

"Do fallen angels wear Under Armour and Omega watches?"

"The lady in *Touched by an Angel* dressed like a civilian."

"I've never heard of *Touched by an Angel*."

"Och," Leigh said sadly. "You're so young."

"His looks are of no consequence to me. He's an injured married man and the only thing I care about is getting him gone. But how am I going to contact Jonah's—"

"Jonah?"

"He still can't remember his name so that's the name we gave him. How am I supposed to contact Jonah's wife so that she can come and get him if I don't know his name?"

"I'm sure his identity will return to him soon."

It infuriated her that no one, including Jonah, seemed as concerned about his lack of memories as she was. "I don't think so. He met with a doctor online today. Though amnesia is rare, the doctor confirmed that might be at play here." It felt ridiculous even to say the word *amnesia* out loud since the only people she'd ever known to be struck by the condition were characters in books and movies. "*Leigh*. I can't be trapped with him much longer without suffocating him."

"Ayuh." Leigh walked toward the cottage. "Did the doctor prescribe painkillers?"

"Yes, as well as breathing exercises. We've already started on the breathing exercises, but the prescription is waiting at a pharmacy in Rockland." Rockland was on the mainland. Not close.

Leigh gave a pragmatic nod. "Is he still in need of a bath?"

"Yes. Though don't believe him if he claims to need your help getting into the tub."

"Remy." A smile broke through. "It would only be in my *wildest dreams* that he asks for my help getting into a bath."

"You're not dreaming big enough, Leigh."

"After he's clean, I'll take my boat to Rockland and come back tonight with his medicine."

"Rockland's more than two hours one way and you've spent your whole workday on the boat already. Plus the cost of fuel."

"I'm happy to do it. We can't allow him to suffer."

Remy thought that, actually, she could.

They entered the cottage. "He only has one set of clothing," Remy said, pulling her friend to a stop near the kitchen table. "My pajamas don't fit him so I was thinking maybe we could borrow some of your clothes for him to wear?"

"Definitely no," came a masculine voice from the bedroom.

The same wisp of Remy's hair kept getting in her eyes today. Exasperated, she blew it off her forehead.

Leigh laid a comforting hand on her forearm. "Sit down, read, take a break. I've got this." She continued into the bedroom.

Remy remained where she stood, listening.

"Jonah," Leigh said warmly.

"Leigh," he returned in a charming tone. "Thank God you're here. I barely survived the night with the quirky blond sculptor."

"You're looking well."

"I feel terrible. See this watch?"

"Yes."

"Is there a pawn shop in Rockland? Because if there is, please take it, sell it, take a cut, and use the rest of the money to get me drugs and cash."

"Ayuh. Happy to."

What? Remy thought.

"And can you buy me some decent clothes?" Jonah asked. "Last night I wore pajamas with red and black checks on them. I'm brave. But not brave enough to deal with physical agony *and* red-and-black-checkered pajama pants."

Cackle. "You don't seem to be in *that* bad of shape—"

"I'm in black and red pajama pants shape, Leigh."

"I'll do my best."

Confounded *Jonah* had made a conquest of *her* friend.

"How about we ask some of the island's male residents if they'll lend you clothes?" Remy called out. The median age of their population was fifty-five and most of the men she knew were either much larger around the waist than Jonah or shorter than Jonah. But beggars can't be choosers and the residents of Islehaven were a generous group.

"Definitely no to that, too," he said.

Apparently borrowed clothes weren't acceptable for the Duke of Nowhere.

Remy watched as Leigh crossed into the bathroom.

Remy followed her in, closing the door behind them. "Were you coming in here to run the tub?"

"I was."

"Here. Let me." You had to open the left knob a tiny amount and the right knob a tremendous amount to achieve the correct temperature, plus the plug was wonky if not positioned just so, and one had to make a wish with her eyes closed for the faucet to work properly.

Knowing the water sound was loud enough to mask their voices, Remy whispered, "Did you just agree to sell his watch?"

"To ease his mind. I'm not going to sell it. The watch might have—"

"Sentimental value," they both said in unison.

"When I come back, I'll pretend I sold it and give him some clothes and cash," Leigh said. "That'll help him feel a little more in control of a terrible situation."

"You're more noble than I am. Do you want to take him?"

Leigh winked. "If only I could."

While he bathed, the two women stripped the sheets and pillowcases and put on a clean, alternate set. He was going to come back to the bed salt-free, so they wanted him to have salt-free sheets.

After that, Remy busied herself in her studio but found she couldn't tap into the vast concentration she usually accessed when working. Instead, she used the time to straighten up, then to sharpen, clean, and organize her tools.

After a time, Leigh ducked in to say that she was heading to the mainland. Remy walked her out, then peeked in on Jonah.

He was sleeping.

Amber afternoon light burnished his skin and picked out different shades in his damp, finger-combed hair. Thanks to her years on the island, she was well acquainted with the look of at-home haircuts. His haircut was not that. It was fashionable and had been accomplished by a professional who knew exactly what they were doing.

He was still reclining on pillows, but Leigh must have helped him into his windbreaker because its collar now framed his jawline. Even from here, she could smell the scent of the lemongrass, pine, and sage soap she kept near the tub.

His profile—which was turned to the side—was an artist's master class in firm, decisive lines. If those angles told the full story, his face would be one of empty handsomeness. She wished that were the case. Instead, his face held an endearing quality she couldn't quite put her finger on.

It might be the softness of his lips. Or his slightly overlong lashes. Or the set of his hooded eyes.

Whatever it was, that quality gave his face poetry.

The air seemed to thicken.

Her mouth went dry, and she jerked back as if scalded, then returned to her studio.

After dark that night, Leigh returned from her long journey to bring him his medicine. *Thank God*, Jonah thought, when he heard her enter Remy's small house. She'd arrived with the good stuff.

Leigh came and went without visiting the bedroom, so it was Remy who handed him the pills. He downed them while his host looked on like an annoyed schoolteacher.

Sometime later, Remy came in to turn off the bedside lamp. By then, the pain had drained from his body. Sweet relief. He was floating. For the first time since he'd been pulled from the sea, he didn't care about anything. For the first time, she wasn't frustrating him.

He heard himself ask, "Will you sleep here again tonight?"

"I will."

She would be nearby.

It eased his mind even more to know . . . she would be nearby.

Chapter Four

Many miles to the west, Fiona was feeling smug.

Smug because she'd been born in Maine. Smug because she had the good sense to live here still, in Maine's prettiest and most charming town, no less. Whenever anyone tried to say Groomsport wasn't best, she leapt in to argue. Because, obviously, it was.

The weather. That was the thing making her especially secure in her choices on this autumn morning. Fog hovered over the ground, magical, but low enough that she could glance to the side down alleyways and streets to catch glimpses of the harbor.

Fiona made her way down Main Street like a toned and curvy eighteen-wheeler, dressed in chic business clothes, high heels clicking smartly on the sidewalk, hair salon-fresh.

On Tuesday and Thursday mornings, she arrived to work early, parked her car in the lot there, then walked to her favorite coffee shop for breakfast. Had she walked to the coffee shop every weekday morning, it might have begun to seem like a compulsion. But walking on Tuesdays and Thursdays without fail? Not at all.

Settlers had first come to Groomsport in 1770. Because many were Irish, they'd named the town after a seaside village in the old country. Initially, their economy had depended on shipbuilding and fishing. But by the late 1800s, wealthy Americans had discovered Groomsport's beauty and begun flocking here and building summer homes purely for pleasure. Almost all the historic buildings, mansions, and cottages had survived—giving the blocks and blocks of the downtown area a time capsule feel.

The surrounding hills formed a V—with the harbor at the V's base. Thus Main Street started high on one end near the library. It dipped down from there past numerous restaurants and boutiques before rising again up the opposite hill toward the opera house.

Fiona's town had everything a coastal Maine town should have. A dock made of wood. A lobster shack. A fleet of windjammers. Taste and class. A lighthouse minutes away. And plenty of tourists to properly admire it all.

She breezed through the front doors of Java Junkie. Minutes later, she was carrying a saucer and cup of skinny cappuccino in one hand and a gluten-free, sugar-free nut bar (better than the green smoothie she consumed most mornings of the week) in the other. Her only sorrow? That she was forced to sit at her least favorite table because all her favorite ones were taken. Why would anyone build a table so tall that your feet didn't touch the ground and you were obliged to perch them on a little metal protrusion?

Sipping her coffee, she slid her iPad from her Hermes bag and skimmed through the day's news stories. Weather drama, political drama, international drama, celebrity drama. Usual, usual, usual—until she suddenly came upon a scientific article about the total solar eclipse scheduled to occur in Maine one year from now.

Memory collided into her and she set her coffee cup down with a *clink*.

Her father had once dreamed of becoming an astronomer and was fond of saying he would've gotten a degree in that field had he possessed either the brains or the means to attend college. Absent those things, he'd contented himself working as an electrician and indulging his love of astronomy by traveling whenever possible to the sites of solar eclipses. Because the family's budget was tight, he typically drove alone to eclipses in the continental United States. But there had been one time, back when Fiona had been eight years old, when the whole family had journeyed to Suriname in South America to view a total eclipse and to vacation.

Everything about the experience—visiting a foreign country, holding a paper apparatus to her eye, watching the moon move across the sun until the daylight faded to darkness—had been memorable. As was the promise she'd made to her sister, Isobel, that day.

Isobel was the second-oldest child and first girl in their family. Fiona had followed fifteen months later. They'd shared a room. They'd played and fought in equal measure—driving their parents crazy and exhausting their siblings.

Fiona was big enough to admit that she'd been the instigator of most of the problems. She'd been too intelligent and crafty for her own good, born with a deep sense that she wasn't being treated fairly even when she was being treated fairly by all. Isobel was good-hearted, but also staunch. Had Isobel been a doormat, the two of them would've gotten along famously. As it was, Isobel stood up for herself, which led to frequent confrontations between the principled older sister and the fiery younger sister.

Immediately following that South American eclipse, when the sunlight had returned, bathing them like a fairy spell, their love for each other had reigned above their competitiveness. They'd looked at each other with awe, then chattered, talking over each other in their excitement, about the miracle they'd just experienced. The moon had come in front of the sun! And it had been scary, how everything had gone dim and still. And they—the O'Sullivan sisters from Maine who never got to go anywhere or do anything—had seen it.

Isobel asked their father when a total eclipse would come to their part of Maine. He named a date so far in the future that it made Fiona's mind spin. She'd be an adult then. Seeing that eclipse in Maine felt unreachable—as real as pulling Excalibur from a stone.

Isobel turned to her. "Let's make a promise," she said gravely.

"About what?"

"Let's promise each other that we'll watch that total eclipse in Maine together. Just like we did this one."

Fiona immediately felt the genius of the idea. "*Yes.*" She was honored to be asked. Flattered. Eagerly, she extended her pinky finger. "Pinky promise."

Isobel locked her pinky around Fiona's. "Pinky promise."

They bobbed their joined hands a few times to seal the deal.

And now here, on her iPad, was a reminder that the eclipse of the pinky promise was no longer wildly far in the future. No longer an imaginary thing.

She needed to experience it with Isobel and fulfill their girlhood promise.

They must.

Problem was . . . she'd done something unforgiveable to Isobel.

And they'd been estranged ever since.

By the following afternoon, Jonah could no longer stand his imprisonment in Remy's bed. The only entertainment he'd found inside this room had come from two things. One, her stack of fantasy novels. Two, the small TV/VHS combo she'd plugged in for him and the six VHS tapes of fantasy movies that went with it.

He couldn't remember his past, but he'd learned two things about himself. Isolation made him itchy, and he was not a *Lord of the Rings* fan. So he went on a mission with one goal: *get to a view of the ocean.* Which would be much better than a view of Frodo.

Dressed in some of the new clothes Leigh had brought him —a pair of black basketball shorts and a long-sleeved athletic shirt—he made slow progress on bare feet, doing his best not to jar his cracked ribs. The clothes had come with TJ Maxx tags on them, and he was pretty sure he wasn't a TJ Maxx shopper and usually paid more than $12.99 for a pair of shorts. But since his choices were A) wear the stuff Leigh bought, or B) wear black and red pajama bottoms, he'd go with the TJ Maxx wardrobe.

Remy's kitchen looked like a throwback to the 1960s with its wood cabinetry and white Formica countertops. Her stand mixer had been taken apart and the missing sections never reinstalled. He opened the pantry door and regarded the depressing contents. The only thing that appealed was her stockpile of chocolate pudding cups. He snapped one free, grabbed a spoon, and continued on.

The walls in the living area were jammed with art, just like her bedroom. So much art it was like wallpaper. It stabbed his eyes. The beige sofa and chairs had navy-and-white-striped throw pillows on top. An unfinished puzzle covered the coffee table. More books on the side tables. A long piece of knitting—a scarf?—draped over a basket.

He let himself outside and found the view of the ocean he'd been searching for. Carefully, he eased his weight onto one of the two Adirondack chairs.

He'd made it. It had hurt, but he'd made it.

He drew in a breath as deep as he could manage, bringing cool, fresh sea air into his lungs.

It was breezy but not stormy like the past two days. Sun sparkled against the water spreading toward the line of the horizon. To the right of Remy's house, land jutted out a short distance. To the left, jagged coastline stretched a long distance. He couldn't see any other houses, just trees pressing close to the rocky shore.

His shoulders relaxed, and he tilted his face toward the sky. Here the only soundtrack was wind in the trees and water pounding rhythmically against the cliff below. This felt right. He must be someone who liked the water or who was accustomed to it or both.

Minutes passed.

"Jonah?" Remy called from inside the house.

"Out here."

She walked onto the deck and planted her hands on hips covered by overalls. Today she wore a soft-looking black T-shirt beneath. She'd stuck half her hair in a bun and left the other half down. She wore her glasses like a headband. "Now you're a pudding stealer?"

"Yes. Now I'm a pudding stealer."

She tutted. "You should have asked for help getting out here."

"I wanted to make it on my own."

"When I saw the door open, I worried that you might have thrown yourself back into the ocean."

"If I had, why would that have worried you?"

She smiled. "You're right. That outcome should have no reason to cause me concern." She took a seat on the remaining Adirondack.

For long minutes he said nothing. And, a rare gift, she also said nothing.

He ate the pudding, enjoying every bite.

"The weather is better," she said.

All good things, including the pudding cup and her silence, must come to an end.

"We could fly you to a hospital on the mainland," she finished.

"No. I barely made it to your porch. I'm not up for a car ride, a plane ride, and another car ride. Plus, Leigh must have taken a big cut of the profits from the watch because I've only got three hundred dollars in cash. That won't cover a plane ticket and pay for my hospital stay."

"I can loan you—"

"No. You said you researched cracked ribs, and all it takes to heal them is time. So there's nothing a hospital can do for me now."

"I'd feel better if you were examined by experts."

And he knew she'd also like to get him off her hands. He met her eyes. "I don't want to be a burden to you. But even if the hospital could help me and I had money, I'm not strong enough to go anywhere right now. I can't."

Her chin inclined a fraction of an inch, indicating acceptance of her sad fate.

"When I'm able," he told her, "I'll pay you back. For your time and the expense of my room and board."

"One Omega watch does not a rich man make."

"No. But I'm a man who pays my debts. I'll pay mine to you."

"How would you know what kind of man you are?"

"I know I'm someone who pays my debts because the idea of not doing so turns my stomach."

Remy nodded but didn't appear to care much whether he did or didn't reimburse her. *"I don't measure success in terms of income,"* she'd told him. Everything he'd observed about her so far supported the idea that money wasn't what motivated her.

She rested her head and shoulders against her chair's back, her attention on the ocean. "I contacted the people who rent houses on the island. None of them have guests this week. Which leads me to the conclusion that your presence in the water didn't originate on land, but at sea."

"Okay."

"And seeing as how your memories haven't returned, I think we need to proceed as if you have amnesia."

Amnesia. The word weighed five tons.

He still had the sense the memories were right there, waiting. But every time he tried to retrieve one, he'd come up blank. He didn't want amnesia but at this point it was the explanation that made the most sense.

"I've already spent ten hours researching the condition," Remy announced.

"Ten hours?"

"Yes. I can follow a rabbit hole obsessively if a topic interests me. Amnesia interests me. So I've been reading and taking notes—last night and all day today."

"When you weren't monologuing about the importance of hydration, I assumed you were working."

"When I'm working, you'll know because I play music."

"Can you afford to take time off work to research?"

"Yes and no. Yes, because I don't believe in deadlines. No,

because I do believe in making enough income to pay my bills. I'll get back to work soon."

He glanced toward the water to see a brown pelican glide in an arc then dive. "Look." He pointed.

She patted her overalls' middle pocket. "Where are my glasses?"

"On your head."

"Oh!" She located them and slid them on, watching the bird with wonder. The breeze danced through her hair, and the direct light illuminated her face. He had to admit, her skin was a beautiful shade, creamy with peach undertones.

"After studying your condition in great detail," she said in the direction of the pelican, "I think you have dissociative amnesia—likely a result of both psychological stress and physical trauma. A patient's memories can return all at once or gradually. Most commonly, they come back in days, but it can take weeks or months. The prognosis is good but there's no medicine for it other than relaxation, a peaceful environment, and psychotherapy."

"Well. One out of three isn't bad."

"Here you have two out of three," she corrected. "Relaxation and a peaceful environment."

"One out of three. I'd have a peaceful environment except that you're here." He shot her his dimples.

She rolled her head toward him and held a hand horizontally a few inches in front of her chest. "This is my last nerve." She positioned her other hand above it and poked down on her lower hand repeatedly. "And this is you."

He chuckled, which turned into a wheeze.

"I've been reviewing case studies of people," she said, "who turned up with amnesia in order to see how the police or FBI figured out their identities."

"And?"

"If the police or FBI were here, they'd fingerprint you. They'd check DNA. They'd use facial recognition software."

"But since they're not here, what can we do?"

"Look at your clothing and belongings for clues, which I've already done. Look for tattoos. Do you have any distinctive tattoos?"

"You've seen most of my body."

"Just your clavicles!"

"I don't have any tattoos."

"Some people with amnesia are able to bring up fragments of information. For example, parts of their Social Security number. Places. Images from their childhood. Has anything come to you?"

He could see how much she wanted him to give her something to work with. Clearly, she was not willing to sit on her hands and wait for his history to come back to him. He wished, for both their sakes, he had information to give. "Nothing has come to me yet. If anything does, I'll tell you."

The bun on top of her head unwound. Almost unconsciously, she piled it up again. As soon as she finished, it started to come undone again.

The sound of an approaching car reached him. "Is that Leigh?" he asked.

"Yes."

"Her brake pads are worn down."

She gave him an inquiring look.

He shrugged.

A short time later, Leigh appeared. He started to rise to give her his seat, but Leigh placed a hand on his shoulder. "Don't get up."

"Take my chair." Remy relocated to a cross-legged position on the deck as Leigh sat.

"Before I forget," Leigh said to Remy, "Wendell called me today. He's on island, staying at Harry's."

"Aw." Remy's expression softened. Clearly, she liked this Wendell a thousand times more than she liked him. "I'll go by and check on him tomorrow."

"Who's Wendell?" he asked.

"Our elderly friend," Leigh answered. "Wendell Reeves. He used to live here but had to start getting dialysis so he moved near the hospital in Rockland." She rubbed her chapped hands together, looking between Remy and him. "Where are we on our search for Jonah's identity?"

"We were just saying that we're going to move forward as if he has amnesia," Remy informed her.

"Okay. How?"

"Well, one man I read about revealed a clue to his past while doodling." Remy considered him. "Maybe, if you let your mind go while sketching, you'll draw something that will give us insight into your past."

"I'm willing to doodle."

"Other amnesia patients have had success with hypnotherapy," Remy said.

"Maureen does hypnosis," Leigh suggested.

"Is Maureen also the mayor here and the tax collector?" Jonah asked. He'd learned a few things about island life.

"Something like that," Remy confirmed.

"If I don't have to do anything except lie on a couch, then I'm fine with hypnotherapy. Does she do house calls?"

The deck creaked as Leigh crossed her rubber boots. "Nah. You'll need to go see her."

"Getting there will be an issue," he said.

"She's only twenty minutes away," Remy told him, "and the drive's not terribly bumpy."

"What type of car do you have?" he asked.

"Chevy Silverado truck."

"How good are its shock absorbers?"

"Just good enough to transport a duke."

"I've been on the same tank of gas," Leigh said to Remy, "for a month. You?"

"Three months," she said proudly.

"You people are barely civilized," Jonah stated.

"When should I schedule a trip to Maureen's for hypnotherapy?" Remy asked him.

"A week from now? I might be able to make it if I take medicine thirty minutes before we go and if I drive."

"You can't drive if you've taken pain medicine thirty minutes before we go," Remy pointed out.

"If it takes you two months to go through a tank of gas, who am I going to hit?"

"Ayuh." Leigh grinned. "Good point."

Leigh was smart enough to have a soft spot for him.

"I'll call Maureen," Remy said, "and set up an appointment for three days from now."

"I said a week."

"Three days. We need to do everything we can to figure out who you are."

"The people who love you must be worried sick," Leigh added. "Remy and I have both been checking online daily, trying to find missing-persons postings or news stories about an emergency at sea. We haven't found anything yet."

"Maybe there aren't any people who love me." He scratched the scruff near the hinge of his jaw. "It could be I'm disconnected from other humans. Or hated."

"Yep. That's probably it." Remy's eyes glittered mischievously.

"That's not it." Leigh's boots hit the deck. She leaned

toward him, planting her elbows on her knees. "Of course people love you. You're married and charming—"

Remy snorted.

"—and I'm sure your absence has been noticed and they've posted about it. It's just that we haven't been able to *find* their postings yet. Your detective team is made up of a lobsterwoman and a sculptor." She shot Remy a stern look. "We'll continue looking. Any day now something will turn up."

"If one of you will loan me a computer," he said, "I'll look for clues, too."

"I doubt my laptop is up to your standards," Remy murmured.

"You can borrow mine." Leigh winked at him. "Remy, can I speak with you privately for a minute?"

Reluctantly, Remy agreed and the next thing she knew Leigh had taken hold of her elbow and was steering her through her house. Leigh didn't let go until she'd ushered her into the studio.

Leigh was stoic, always. Except for this present moment. She glared at Remy from beneath the brim of her baseball cap. "Be kind to him! He's hurt."

"He's exasperating."

"He's recovering."

"He's wily."

"He's defenseless."

"He's spoiled."

Leigh shook her head, circled the studio, and returned to face Remy. "Tomorrow's Friday. If I'm very careful, I think I can drive him to my house without causing him too much pain. I'll keep him over the weekend."

Resistance pressed upward within Remy, immediate and

strangely strong. "That won't be necessary. I don't want him to impose on you."

"He won't."

"I don't think he's well enough to make the trip."

"I just heard you tell him he'd be well enough to make the trip to Maureen's in three days. If so, he can make the trip to my house in one day. I live much closer."

Remy straightened her posture. "Jonah and I drive each other crazy, but we have a routine. He's accustomed to things here. He'll stay here this weekend."

Leigh surveyed her. "Ah. So you've finally realized that God tipped an angel into the ocean outside your cottage?"

"Please stop with the angel nonsense. He's nothing but an underwhelming, generic man."

"There's nothing generic about him." Leigh peered down her nose at Remy from her superior height. "He's the freshly ground Arabica of men. The twenty-one-year-aged rum of men. He's quick-witted and humorous and so dazzling to look at I feel like I need to wear sunglasses."

"I disagree with"—Remy made an emphatic circle in the air —"*all* of that."

"Then why are you insisting on keeping him with you this weekend?"

She honestly didn't know. She only knew that she wasn't sending him to Leigh's house. *She* was the one who'd rescued him. *She* was the primary good Samaritan here. *She* needed to be the one who reunited him with his wife (and kids?).

Also . . . fine. Maybe she did harbor one cubic inch of protectiveness toward him.

"I'm insisting on keeping him with me," she lied, "for the reward money his wealthy wife will surely provide."

The next morning, Remy found Jonah sitting in her living room, doodling. "I'm heading off to see Wendell. Sure you're fine here alone for a while?"

He looked up from the sketch pad. "I'm sure."

This was the first time she'd left him alone here and was feeling strangely hesitant. "You'll refrain from going into cardiac arrest until I get back?"

He looked right into her eyes and gave her a small, slow smile. "I will postpone cardiac arrest until you get back."

"Very good. I'd say call me if you need anything—"

"But I have no phone."

"Precisely."

"I think parchment and quill is more my style of communication anyway," he said, perpetuating their running Duke joke.

"In that case, if you need anything, send a parchment message to me via pigeon."

"Will do."

Their exchange had ended on a humorous note yet as Remy drove Islehaven's bumpy roads, worries over Jonah kept rising to the front of her thoughts. Repeatedly, she pushed them down.

Stop chewing the inside of your cheek, Remy. He's fine. Think about one of your story worlds instead.

She felt safest when deep in her own mind, pondering one of her three favorite things to ponder. One, the narrative she was weaving in her mind about her sculpture in progress. Two, the narrative of the book she was reading. Three, the narrative of the show she was watching. Like the stories she created to inspire her art, her books and shows typically fell into her treasured fantasy genre. Thus there were always juicy places of myth, magic, legend, and action to visit in her imagination . . . .

Yes, but what if Jonah took her absence as an opportunity

to down all of his prescribed pills? She should have brought his pills with her! Why hadn't she brought them along—

Stop it, Remy.

She parked, then knocked on the door of Harry's spartan cottage.

Wendell answered. "Remy!"

They shared a hug that gave her impressions of brittle bones and the faint scent of his English Leather cologne.

"Harry's out," he said when they pulled apart, "helping Kitty pick the rest of her apples." He shepherded her inside and to the kitchen.

Wendell had the face of a leprechaun. His cheerful, pointy features would have been more at home on a short, young man. Yet, Wendell was eighty and tall with lanky limbs. His receded gray hair stood out from his scalp a few inches in every direction, and he always dressed in patterned sweaters and khaki trousers. Today's sweater featured foxes chasing one another around and around his torso.

He made small talk as he prepared Irish tea and served her store-bought butter cookies from a tin. But just like something was off with her (concern about *confounded* Jonah) she sensed that something was off with Wendell, too. He was doing and saying the usual things, but it was as if a light had gone out inside him.

Remy took stock of him as he settled across from her at the well-worn table, backlit with views of ocean and tumultuous sky.

When she'd moved to Islehaven, Wendell and his wife, Ruth Ann, had immediately befriended her. She'd been a newbie with a lot to learn about life on Maine's most remote island. They'd known everything there was to know about life here. The difficulties of numerous harsh winters had sowed in them both a calm, "we'll get through it" capability that had been medicine for her soul.

Once upon a time, Wendell had written theological nonfiction tomes for a living. After he'd retired from that, he'd volunteered as their local pastor. He was gentle, slightly mischievous, and given to speaking in superlatives. Ruth Ann had been opinionated, quick to laugh, and a terrific cook.

Week after week, they'd invited Remy into their home for Sunday lunch. Remy had never turned them down. She'd loved the lively conversations that had circled meals of corned hake, chowder, crab cakes, and whoopie pies. Those lunches had been a golden spot of interaction. Through them, she'd come to know all the year-round residents of Islehaven and many of the summer people.

A heart attack two years ago had suddenly and heartbreakingly ended Ruth Ann's life. Soon after, Wendell's kidney disease had grown more acute, and dialysis had become imperative. He'd had no choice but to sell his beloved home here and move near a medical facility. Now, when he visited Islehaven, he stayed in the homes of friends for no more than a few nights at a time before having to return to the mainland for more treatment.

"When were you here last?" she asked.

"Five months ago."

She lifted her brows. "Did something keep you away longer than usual this time?"

"It's not easy to get here and back."

"Right, but even so, you used to come every two months. Has something changed?"

"I suppose"—he scratched behind his ear—"I don't come as often as I used to because leaving Islehaven is harder on me every time."

Her heart twisted with sympathy. It seemed her "we'll get

through it" friend was losing the ability to get through it without his wife and without his island. Ruth Ann wouldn't have wanted Wendell's sorrow to cause him to flounder, of that Remy was certain. "Surely there are things to love about your life in Rockland?"

"Hmm." He appeared to think it over. "No."

His dissatisfaction couldn't be rooted in the town itself. Tourists flocked to Rockland because it was so picturesque. "How do you spend your days there?"

"When I'm not at the medical center, I watch a lot of TV. I never miss *Days of Our Lives, Jeopardy*, or *Wheel of Fortune*. I read my shipment of Harlequin Love Inspired romances every month." After a lifetime of heavy writing, he'd come to adore light reading at this stage of his life.

"What else?"

He shrugged. "The things I listed are about it."

Remy knew him well enough to know he flourished in the company of others. His life on the mainland sounded relaxing but entirely too lonely. "What can you and I do to make your life in Rockland worth loving?"

"Eh?"

"What can we bring into your life there that would add meaning and joy?"

A pause. "I have no idea."

"There must be something that you want. Right? What is it that you really, really want?" He needed to see he still had things to live for.

"I can't think of anything."

"Then think harder, please."

He munched on a cookie morosely. She sipped her tea. Beyond the cabin, a seagull flapped past.

"There is one thing," Wendell said reluctantly.

"I'm listening."

"I'm afraid to say it. You'll think I'm a foolish old man."

"No. I won't."

He bought himself time by piling his hands in his lap. "There was a woman, once. Her name was Marisol."

Remy worked to keep her expression placid and encouraging. This, she had not anticipated. "Tell me about Marisol."

"I was eighteen when we met. She became . . . everything to me. Softhearted, wise, generous. The best person in the world. I fell in love with her, and I asked her to marry me. She said yes." He appeared to lose himself in memory.

"What happened?"

"She was a few years older than I was and had had a child out of wedlock—a two-year-old boy. She was Hispanic. My family didn't approve of her. Her family didn't approve of me. My parents insisted I was too young to marry and too young to know what I wanted." He sighed. "Maybe I *was* too young to marry. The fact that I let them come between Marisol and me indicates that. But time has proven them wrong when they said I didn't know what I wanted. I *did* know. I knew then and I've known for the sixty years since that I loved her." He frowned. "I should have fought for her, you see. Instead, we went our separate ways."

Remy was no stranger to living with regret. She understood how it could drag at every step you took.

"I met Ruth Ann years after Marisol," he continued, "when I was finishing my graduate degree. We made a wonderful life together. We raised a wonderful family."

"You definitely did."

"I was very loyal to Ruth Ann."

"I know you were. You made her happy. She couldn't have asked for a better husband."

"Since Ruth Ann died, I've been wondering more and more about Marisol. If she's still alive. If so, how she is. Whether she married a spouse who was as good to her as Ruth Ann was to me."

She confronted him, eyeball to eyeball. "Obviously, we need to find Marisol."

He blanched. "Oh no. I'm scared to do that."

"Why?"

"What if we find out she's married, or dead?"

"What if we find out she's single and alive?"

"A sad outcome would be worse than not knowing."

"Is that really true, though?" Remy leaned forward, stacking her forearms on the table. "It sounds like the not-knowing is pretty sad for you."

The pendulum clock in the hall sounded like a metronome. Ticking.

"I'm scared," he repeated.

"You're a brave man, Wendell. You've shown that to me a hundred ways." She reached across the table and squeezed his hand. "We'll try to find out what happened to her for the sake of closure." She owed Wendell that much. She owed Ruth Ann, too, a debt she could try to repay by looking after Wendell.

"I'm not sure if we should do that, Remy."

"Then I'll be sure for the both of us." It was highly nuanced and complex for *her* to think about stepping out from behind her past and her fears. But in Wendell's case, the need to do so was as clear as sunlight. "What's Marisol's last name?"

"Soto."

"Do you remember her middle name?"

"I remember everything she ever said to me," he replied simply. "Her middle name was Ramona. Marisol Ramona Soto."

Remy typed the information into a note on her phone. "Birth date?"

"May fifth, eighty-two years ago."

"And where were you living when you met?"

"Belfast." He was referring to Belfast, Maine, about thirty minutes up the coast from where he currently lived in Rockland. "That was where I was born and raised. Her family had moved there four or five years before we met."

"And her son was named?"

He went on—providing Marisol's son's name, her hometown, her parents' and siblings' names, her friends' names. Remy jotted it all down.

"Do you think this might work?" he asked. "Do you think you'll be able to find her?"

"I have to admit that I've spent the past few days trying to locate the identity of a missing person online and have come up empty. Since that situation"—Jonah definitely qualified as a *situation*—"is demanding most of my attention, I won't be able to start looking for Marisol just now. When I do start looking for her, I'll give it my best."

"I'm worried."

"That I'll find her or that I won't?"

"Both."

Chapter Five

R emy had told Leigh that she and Jonah had established a routine. The next forty-eight hours proved that truth.

Each night before bed, Jonah asked if she would stay and every night, she said she would. In the middle of the night he'd wake at least once and ask, "Remy?" From her pallet she'd answer, "I'm here."

She'd bet money that in his usual state he was the type of man who never asked for anyone in the middle of the night. But on this island—not just this physical place but also this island of time surrounded by the sea of his regular life—he was not his usual self. He was injured, mentally and physically.

She fed him three meals plus four pudding cups a day, forced him to consume a great deal of water, and badgered him into reducing his reliance on painkillers and doing his breathing exercises.

An *adult man* had been thrust into her space, which continued to demand enormous adjustments from her. With him in the house, Remy guarded her time, energy, and privacy like a dragon protecting a treasure chest of gold. She and Jonah interacted often, but not more than necessary. And since he no longer required close supervision, she resumed yoga, walking, and meditation. She also returned to work, retreating to her studio for hours each day. When her trusty phone alarm signaled quitting time, she ate dinner with him, then retired to her office to hunt for his identity, voraciously read, or voraciously watch shows. She did her best not to let him stir emotions in her, which was the hardest part of all, because for some maddening reason he had the power to rile her up with a simple sidelong look.

For his part, Jonah staggered to the bathroom for showers and staggered to the deck to sit for long periods. He searched and searched for his old life on Leigh's borrowed laptop. Or he read books from her library or watched movies or sketched.

Unfortunately, Remy's doodling plan hadn't yet paid dividends. So far, he'd drawn happy faces, suns hovering above mountains, stick figures, cars that resembled Hot Wheels, and one-dimensional houses like kids drew—a square front topped by a triangle roof. He was laughably bad at drawing. Every time he handed his creations to her, his mocking features said, *Excellent plan, Remy.*

Leigh continued to show up, to coddle him, and to search the web for leads.

No luck. The theory he'd raised—that no one was looking for him—started to seem like a possibility. Privately, Remy agreed with Leigh on the wrongness of that. Jonah was uppity and a handful. But surely, he had a whole network of family, friends, co-workers, and acquaintances. Surely.

"You drive *this*?" Jonah asked as they approached Remy's red truck.

It was Sunday, five days after she'd rescued him, and they were on their way to his hypnosis appointment.

"Not all of us are able to ride around in phaetons."

"How old is this truck?" He was walking upright and without assistance, but still painstakingly slow.

"Seventeen years old. We make do with clunkers here. There's no sense in bringing expensive cars into these conditions."

He looked like someone who'd just smelled sewage. "There isn't even a license plate."

"That's because this is an island-use car. It can't be driven on the mainland, but all I need to drive it here is a decal from the state."

He opened the driver's-side door and eyed the distance to the cab as if eyeing whether it would be possible to swim from here to England.

Had she made a mistake? Maybe it was too early to test his ribs like this.

As he began to pull himself up, she lifted her hands to offer support, but they hovered in midair because . . . where to place them? His elbow? His lean lower back? Now that he was recovering, it no longer seemed as if there was a safe place to look or touch. "Need help?"

"I need help getting my hands on better coffee, better food, better alcohol, better sheets, better clothes, and better Wi-Fi. But I don't need help getting into this piece of junk." Moving at a snail's pace, he made it to the driver's seat.

She circled the hood and shut herself in on the passenger side.

"You keep the key *in* the ignition?" he asked.

"Yes. For one thing, no one here is going to steal this car because where would they go with it? For another thing, the key can no longer be pulled from the ignition."

He started the engine, wincing at its uneven sound.

"Also," she announced, suddenly relishing her vehicle's deficiencies because they seemed to needle him and she liked needling him, "the radio's broken and only the high-beam lights work."

He stared at her across the interior.

She fidgeted slightly but held his gaze.

His stubble had grown in. It wasn't a beard yet. But it did make him look disheveled, which somehow highlighted his bone structure and perfect hair.

Like those silver scratch-off squares that hide information on a lottery ticket, Jonah's injuries had initially hidden some aspects of his personality. Time was scratching off those squares.

When she'd brought him to her house, he'd been mentally sluggish. No longer. His true demeanor oozed lazy, easy confidence. Which could make a person suspect that he was laid-back. He was and he wasn't. You had to look closely to notice the intensity shimmering in the depths of those green eyes. Turned out, he was an observant man, alert, with swift and assessing intelligence. A man naturally very much in control of himself.

"Why are you driving this terrible car?" he asked.

"Because it's serviceable and because I'm on a budget."

"Do you really have *no* money, Remy?"

"I have more than you."

"How much do you have?"

"None of your business."

He moved his mouth as if chewing gum though he was chewing on nothing but annoyance with her. "Why are you living on Islehaven?"

"I've told you why."

"You didn't tell me the full story."

"The full story is also none of your business."

"I want to know. I'm curious."

"Well. Like with the"—she made air quotes—"*better* coffee, food, alcohol, sheets, clothes, and Wi-Fi . . . you can't always get what you want."

Shaking his kingly head, he steered the truck down her pock-marked driveway.

"It will smooth out soon," she said, "but we're going to be late for your hypnosis appointment if you continue driving at two miles an hour."

"Is Maureen booked solid with hypnosis appointments today?"

"It's the principle of the thing. I don't like to be late."

He'd set his shoulders in the way that indicated he was bracing for discomfort.

"I respect that you're trying to protect your ribs," she continued, "but we could probably stand to go as fast as seven miles an hour."

"This is why I insisted on driving. Two miles an hour is as fast as I can go on this track that can't even be called a road. What did you do, come out here with a pickaxe to make the surface as rough as possible?"

"Yes. That's what I did."

"The tire pressure is all wrong. The truck's alignment is way off. The brakes are shot. And it's not responsive at all."

"You know," she mused, ignoring his grumbling, "I can walk more than two miles an hour."

When they hit a more level stretch, he visibly relaxed and accelerated. Then accelerated more.

She wrinkled her nose. He'd been so slow at first that it was shocking to discover he had a lead foot. He was going fifty. She'd never gone over thirty-five here. "Not to be a pest, but I now think you're going a little too fast."

"Women. Impossible to please."

Thanks to the very fast driving that followed his very slow driving, Jonah was pleased to see that they'd arrived at Maureen's slightly ahead of schedule. One less thing for Remy to nag him about.

Maureen met them at the door of her small house and waved them inside. No taller than five foot one, she looked to be around seventy, with a round white face and short hair dyed black. Her living room was covered in shades of brown and dotted with chicken statues, a chicken print throw blanket, a chicken vase on top of a chicken coffee table book.

Remy remained behind as Maureen led him to a back room. More brown, except here she had a desk, sewing machine, chaise lounge, and shelves holding a collection of teapots shaped like chickens.

"So." She spoke in a kind, reedy voice. "Go ahead and make yourself comfortable here." She indicated the chaise.

He did so, feeling like an idiot. His feet hung off the end.

She pulled the squeaky desk chair even with his face. "Many years ago, I benefited from hypnosis when struggling to quit smoking. After that, I began an in-depth study of it. Though I'm not a certified hypnotherapist, I really love it. And chickens."

A bubble of laughter caught in his throat. How was this his life? Stuck on this island with these females? Being put under by an amateur hypnotherapist?

What. Was. Happening.

Was it possible Remy had drugged and kidnapped him after all? Was this an elaborate prank? Purgatory?

"Anyway," she went on, "I like to think I've brought some healing to people here on Islehaven."

"I'm sure you have," he said politely, though he couldn't imagine that outcome.

"I've never encountered anyone with amnesia before."

"Is that so?" he asked, deadpan.

"I want to be sure you understand that you shouldn't hang your hopes on me."

The laughter threatened again. But he managed to keep a straight face as he said with absolute honesty, "I won't hang my hopes on you." He was here because Remy had advocated for hypnotherapy. Remy was the one in need of this speech.

He interlaced his fingers over his stomach.

She switched on calming background noise and asked him to do things like breathe and relax.

He did his best. He felt sleepy but still fully conscious.

This was a bust.

Jonah saw a woman in his mind's eye. A beautiful brunette with long hair, curves, and upturned eyes.

He was responsible for her, was supposed to be taking care of her, yet she was . . . locked away somewhere here and he couldn't find her.

He began to search the big, sophisticated house, room by room. He knew this place. It was expensive. Old. No, new. No . . . an old house that was new inside.

His heartbeat thudded sickly, then gained in speed. *Where is she?* He opened door after door. Empty rooms. Empty. Empty.

He climbed the stairs.

He was supposed to have . . . to have set the brunette free.

Days ago. But he'd forgotten. She would have needed food and water to survive. Why hadn't he come for her sooner? He'd failed.

She must've died by now and it was all his fault. How could he have made such a mistake? Terror and shame chased him. He pushed himself to move faster but couldn't. His limbs were trapped in wet concrete. He dreaded what he would find and yet, at the same time, urgently needed to find her.

Where is she?

"Jonah?"

He squinted toward the sound.

The lady . . . Maureen . . . sat in her chair, watching him. "How do you feel?"

"Unsettled." He rubbed his eyes, then scrubbed his fingers over his forehead. "Did you hypnotize me?"

"Yes. Do you remember what you experienced?"

Pieces of the dream remained, overlapping with reality, churning anxiety inside him. "Yes. I do remember some things."

"Would you like to talk about them?"

"No, thank you."

"That's perfectly fine."

Was the brunette his wife? If so, had he . . . done something to her?

This was the first time that any person had risen from the mist of his history. He couldn't be pleased about that because the nightmare-type vision was such a bad omen.

They met back up with Remy in the living room. His thoughts rattling around his skull, he stood motionless while the women had a conversation about the island's upcoming Sunday bean supper.

He fixed his concentration on Remy and, to his surprise, felt a circle of ease open inside him. The more he focused on her and not the nightmare, the more that circle expanded, calming him.

When he'd first seen Remy, he'd viewed her as plain.

He'd been wrong then. He didn't know if that was because the hypothermia and pain had distorted his perception. Or because her looks were the type that snuck up on a person slowly.

Remy wasn't a beauty in the same commercial way as the brunette. Yet her looks *were* fascinating. Layered.

She had an old-fashioned face, the type of face that should have belonged to someone who lived three hundred years ago. Her wide mouth hinted at her passionate personality, but her ordinary nose did not. The apples of her cheeks were defined but only when she smiled, and she rarely smiled at him. She didn't have enormous eyes made bigger with false lashes. Her eyes were dainty, the irises a gray that reminded him of fog over ocean, marked with a few lighter slivers like lightning and a few darker dots like storm clouds.

None of that explained her appeal, though. Her appeal was more about the energy that hummed beneath her skin. Sometimes that energy was soft and dreamy, when her mind went away to her art. And sometimes that energy was sharp and spiky.

When they were finally in her truck and he was driving them back to her cottage, she angled toward him on the bench seat. "What did the hypnosis reveal?"

He shifted uncomfortably. "It was depressing."

"I'm just glad something came to you. Tell all."

She'd worked harder than anyone, including him, to uncover his identity. He owed her this information, so he listed everything he'd seen and felt in the vision. "Do you think the brunette is my wife?"

"Probably so."

"What does it mean? I definitely didn't lock her up and forget to bring her food and water."

"Don't be so sure."

Ordinarily he valued Remy's sass, but he didn't have the bandwidth for it right now. "Remy. The vision was genuinely disturbing."

"Jonah," she said, matching his seriousness, "you did not lock up your wife and forget to bring her food and water. I'm sure what you experienced during hypnosis was more like a dream in the sense that it personified your fears."

"If so, why do I have fear tied to my wife? I mean . . . my head kills me every time I try to remember my past. Do you think that's my body's way of warning me that I won't like what I learn when my memories come back?"

"I'd think not."

"Then what?" The sound of the truck's engine was like sandpaper to his ears.

"I think the part of your memory you can't access right now knows how much you love your wife. Maybe the vision was about how deeply that part of you wants to be reunited with her. Subconsciously, you're eager to release her from the separation between the two of you caused by your amnesia because you understand the pain she must be going through."

He cut a quick look across at her. Remy dashed hair behind her ears. He refocused on the road.

Her theory struck him as over-the-top. But Remy's interpretation was plausible, and, in it, he was more of a hero than a villain. So in the interest of his sanity he'd go with it.

"I view myself as a champion of your marriage," Remy stated. "I'll keep looking for her until we find her."

If his subconscious self was desperate to find his wife, his conscious self was oddly detached from that goal. He wanted to remember his identity in general. Yet the subject of his wife in particular left him indifferent. He couldn't remember her. He didn't know the woman in the vision.

"Today was a success," Remy announced. "Not only because of what you saw during hypnosis but because we've learned that you seem to be unusually knowledgeable about cars."

"Don't a lot of people know about cars?"

"I suppose. But ordinary people don't have a sense for the tire pressure or mention things like responsiveness. Maybe you're a mechanic."

"A duke mechanic?"

"Well . . . yes. Now we have new angles to research. A man who might be a mechanic. A brunette woman. Whether or not any men with estates named Pemberley or Mansfield Park have recently gone missing."

Remy seemed enthusiastic, but apprehension curled in the pit of his stomach. Was his brain refusing to remember because forgetting was to his benefit?

That night, the same vision from hypnosis visited him in his sleep.

The panic, the searching, the failure to find the brunette—

When Jonah jerked awake, he was panting. He lay on his back, fists gripping the sheets. "Remy?" he whispered raggedly.

"It's all right," she said at once. Her voice wasn't even sleepy. "You okay?"

"Yes." Because *she* was the one beside him instead of the brunette.

Thank God this was real, and the nightmare wasn't.

Only . . . what if that was wrong?

What if the nightmare was a real memory and his existence here with Remy was a passing dream?

Two days later, just when Remy was congratulating herself on her outstanding amateur nursing skills, her patient started coughing.

The two of them were cleaning up after dinner. Remy paused in the act of doing dishes, one hand holding a plate, one hand gripping a scrub brush, water running. "What's with the cough?"

"It's nothing."

She gave him a look like, *It's not nothing.*

"I think I'm allergic to something in the air today. It'll pass."

What if it didn't? Her brain spun.

She'd gathered enough information on rib fractures to know every possible complication. Foremost among those?

Pneumonia.

Chapter Six

"Jude? May I have a word with you?"

Jude looked up from his desk at the FBI office in Bangor. "Sure." Supervisory Agent Dixon Martin had spoken, and Jude always made time for the guy. For one thing, Jude liked and respected him. For another, Dixon was his boss.

He followed Dixon into his office and saw that Shannon Bailey was already inside. Jude took the chair next to hers.

Dixon lowered into his desk chair across from them. He was fifty-five with brown skin, an oval head, and short, graying hair. His long nose and recessed chin made him look like what he was, a person of patient intelligence. "We've received approval to move forward with a new op. Shannon will be Case Agent."

Shannon was a tough veteran who'd been on the job for fifteen more years than Jude. Jude nodded at her, and she nodded back.

Morning sun was brightening the office, which made the room seem even plainer than usual. Dixon wasn't much for decorating. Nothing hung on the walls except for a painting of a mallard in flight that looked like it had cost $5.99.

"Two wealthy executives from France," Dixon said, "have been putting out discreet feelers to see if they can find a buyer over here interested in their employer's trade secrets."

The feelers had not been discreet enough, apparently, to escape the notice of the FBI's network.

"The executives work in the perfume field. Have you ever heard of a perfume called Rhapsodie?" Dixon tried to pronounce the word with a French accent but ended up butchering it.

"I have," Jude answered. "I'm not a perfume person myself but my mother is, and she told me about it once."

"What do you know?" Shannon asked.

"I know a perfumer began making it in a French convent hundreds of years ago."

"Right," Shannon said. "The nuns invited an herbalist to move her business into their apothecary in the 1600s. Legend has it that either the space and quiet of the convent or divine inspiration enabled her to create Rhapsodie soon after she arrived there."

"And ever since," Jude said, "the business has been in the same family. Right?"

"Exactly." Shannon tapped her armrest twice for emphasis. "It's one of the most exclusive fragrances in the world. The company's notoriously protective of the recipe and method. Those things aren't written down *anywhere*. They're saved in memory and at any given time, only two family members know the recipe and method. Each one who's given that honor has to swear a vow of silence regarding it in a church packed with family members and employees."

"So one of the French executives you mentioned is a family member?"

"Yes," she said. "His name's Cedric Bettencourt."

After four hundred years of loyalty, Cedric was willing to sell his family's secret? "How can I help?"

"Our plan," Dixon said, "hinges on this woman, Gemma Clare." He opened a file and spread out three large photos of a beautiful redhead. One shot of her looked like something taken from a LinkedIn profile. The other two were surveillance shots. "She's Cedric's cousin and lives near here, in Bayview. Gemma's a perfumer and she's dating a guy who works in the perfume industry in New York. Cedric trusts her. He's already asked if Gemma's boyfriend might be willing to buy the secrets he's selling. So far, Gemma hasn't given Cedric an answer."

"We want to intervene," Shannon said, "and see if we can gain her cooperation before she broaches this subject with her boyfriend and before she gives Cedric an answer."

"What kind of cooperation are you hoping she'll provide?" Jude asked.

"We're hoping she'll tell Cedric that her boyfriend is interested in buying. Then we'll send you in undercover as her boyfriend."

Her boyfriend? Jude looked between them. "Cedric doesn't know her boyfriend's name or what he looks like?"

"Fortunately for us," Shannon replied, "no. Gemma's private. She's not on social media. She keeps the details about her romances to herself."

Dixon tilted back his chair. "Gemma will introduce you to Cedric and his sidekick."

"We're thinking of presenting you as someone who's wealthy, runs in the same circles as numerous CEOs, and isn't afraid to bend the law," Shannon added.

"You establish a relationship with Cedric," Dixon said. "And eventually offer to buy the secrets on behalf of one of your contacts."

"I'm tracking with it," Jude told him.

"Good"—Dixon spread his hands—"because you're the only one in the office who's right for the role."

In fact, he was one of the few in the office even eligible for the role. He'd completed undercover training two years ago. Since then, they'd only tapped him for a couple of short-term UC ops so he'd mostly been doing casework like the other agents.

"Gemma's thirty," Shannon said. "You're the right age to be her boyfriend."

Jude was thirty-two.

"You look the part," Dixon added. "Gemma's gorgeous and none of the rest of the jokers in this office are good-looking enough for her."

"You speak French," Shannon pointed out.

"I took French in middle school and high school but I don't speak it fluently."

"You speak it better than the rest of us," Dixon said.

Shannon cracked a rare smile. "Best of all, you know how to act rich."

Inwardly, Jude flinched. He'd done everything he could to separate himself from his past. Even so, he was reminded often that there would never be any true escape from it.

"As always, it'll take us a while to lay the groundwork and do our research," Dixon said. It wasn't easy to establish a UC identity. It required documentation, a digital history, IDs, evidence to support an entire fictional life. "Are you interested?" Dixon asked.

"Absolutely," Jude said without hesitation.

Jonah woke from a nap the following afternoon to classical music that sounded like it had been written by a Spaniard who wanted people to dance to it while clamping a rose in their teeth.

The music meant Remy was working.

He sat up and carefully swung his legs over the side of Remy's bed. He'd been on the island eight days now and his rib pain had decreased to about a five out of ten.

Last night, he'd informed Remy that he would sleep on the pallet so that she could have her bed back. She'd flatly refused. When he tried to be noble and insist, she got angry the way she had the day he'd tricked her into handfeeding him. Her cheeks turned pink, and her hand gestures jabbed the air. Her irritation was the best entertainment he had on Islehaven.

He now washed his own clothes and had started showing up to help make and clean up their meals. Remy didn't welcome his presence in the kitchen and if he was really lucky, she'd even stick her chin in the air and huff.

Quietly, he made his way toward the studio.

She usually kept that door closed and locked. But today, it stood half-open. He could see her back, but also part of her profile and one hand. She'd tied a leather apron over a work jumpsuit and captured her hair—which usually went in every direction—in a messy ponytail. Goggles covered her eyes, and he knew her well enough to know she'd likely forgotten that her glasses were positioned on top of her head. Her weight seemed to be divided between the boot she'd planted on the wooden floor and her stool's rung. A clamp secured a block of wood to a worktable. She was bent over it, absorbed in chiseling.

She didn't let him watch her work. But fate had given him a chance to do just that without her knowing. He set his shoulder against the doorjamb and leaned into it, crossing his arms.

Her studio was simple. White walls. No curtains over the

window that let in sunlight. The large, utilitarian light fixture here put off more light than the other fixtures in the house because, unlike the rest, all its bulbs were working. She'd mounted a row of tools on the wall behind the worktable and taped pencil drawings of abstract forms to the other walls.

Three finished sculptures occupied the corner. They ranged from about two feet tall to about four feet tall. To his surprise he saw that they were . . .

Good. Excellent, in fact.

He'd assumed she wasn't great at this.

Why? Because she wasn't old and male like most well-known artists? Maybe part of his assumption had been about that, but also, she didn't seem to have earned much money, couldn't even make oatmeal well, and he didn't like the artwork she'd hung in her house.

The pieces sitting in the corner, though, he liked. They were freeform, modern shapes. Their smooth, gleaming lines called attention to the beauty of the wood. His favorite piece rose from a squarish base. It slid in and then out, forming a rounded section at the top with an opening carved through.

His attention moved from the art to its creator, and he was struck by the sight of her, intently focused on her work with music all around. Had he ever been as dedicated to anything as she was to her art?

He stayed where he was for long minutes. Twenty? Forty?

It was starting to hurt his chest to stand this long but he refused to go.

It was only when one of his inhales resulted in a cough that her chin swung toward him. His cover was blown.

Behind her goggles, her eyes narrowed. "You're not allowed in here."

He eased into the studio. With a wheeze, he gladly lowered onto a supply crate. Next to him sat several blocks of uncarved wood—different colors, heights, thicknesses. A glass jar holding steel wool topped the block closest to him. "I won't bother you. Keep working."

"I can't work with an audience."

He didn't move. "You've been keeping secrets from me."

"Many. Which one are you referring to?"

"Your talent. I'm impressed with your finished pieces."

She set her tools aside and tilted her head. Her ponytail fell forward down her chest. "You are?"

"Very. What kind of wood did you use?"

She pointed to his favorite piece. "That one's lignum vitae. That one's rosewood. That one's beefwood. They're all hardwoods, which I prefer."

"How come? I'm guessing softwoods are easier to carve."

"True. Hardwoods are more stubborn. But when you put in the effort, they're also more rewarding because they reveal gorgeous color."

"Do you have a specific inspiration for each sculpture when you start?"

"Absolutely. I begin with one wisp of inspiration, then build on that, spinning an elaborate story around the piece as I work."

"Explain."

She rose and rested a hand on his favorite sculpture, which came up to around her waist. "My initial inspiration for this one was the female form. To be precise, a woman standing with her feet together turning at the waist and looking up."

It hadn't occurred to him that the sculpture represented a person.

"From there, I imagined a young woman who was caught in a difficult life, caring for her ailing father and scraping by to earn money. I pictured them living in a fictional world that looks something like the Black Forest region of Germany a few hundred years back."

Talking about her process animated Remy in a way he hadn't seen until now. She sparkled.

"The woman has the ability to read people's thoughts and she's coming into her powers more and more as she ages," she went on. "As the story evolves, a group of gypsies ask her to lead them because they revere her for her abilities. But she can't leave her father, so she toils on until she comes across an evil plan to kill the king of the land."

"The plot thickens."

"She goes to the castle and attempts to find someone who will take her seriously. None will. So she calls on the gypsies to spirit her inside the castle, then risks her life by revealing her powers to the king's court. Because of her, the assassination plot is foiled."

Remy had built this whole story around a wooden circle with a hole through it? "Then she and the king marry and live happily ever after?" he predicted.

She appeared insulted. "No. Better. She becomes the king's right-hand advisor. She and her father move into the castle, where they earn the respect of the court."

He didn't think he was a creative type because he couldn't imagine making up a scenario like this. "What was the young woman's name?"

"Emiline. There's no detail about her that I don't know. As her journey unfolded in my mind, I responded to what the wood told me it wanted to say."

"Huh."

"Yeah." With a trace of uncharacteristic self-consciousness, she rubbed her thumb against the top of the statue.

"Is it because you get lost in your work that you have all those alarms set throughout the day?"

"Exactly. When I first started this, I'd get swept away and forget to eat and drink and sleep. Which didn't end up going very well for me. So I tried the alarms and found that they don't hinder my creativity. I'm always able to disappear right back into the carving when my work hours start."

He nodded. "You love your job."

"Yes," she said simply.

"How long does it take you to complete a sculpture?"

"It varies. Anywhere from two weeks to two months."

"Do you have an art degree?"

"No." She returned to the stool, facing him, hooking the heels of her boots over the rung. "I was always artistic but when it came time for college, I had no idea what I wanted to do jobwise so I went with a marketable degree in Human Resources. It wasn't until I moved here that I started doing this."

"Why wood sculpture?"

"My grandfather, the one who built this place, enjoyed wood carving. He taught me the basics when I was little. Back then we made small birds, fish, boats, trees—that type of thing. He passed away before I moved here, but I found out from Leigh that he'd taught her everything he knew. Leigh caught the woodcarving bug. She went to conferences and took online classes and practiced. She doesn't do much woodworking anymore but when I first came to Islehaven, she was still going strong."

"Did she sell her pieces?"

"No. She'd tell you she had two of the three important components of a professional artist. She had dedication and passion."

"What's the third component?"

"Talent. She came to the conclusion that she didn't have enough talent. But she saw something in me and so, for two years, she taught me. Which shows you how generous she is. She was determined that I'd become a professional artist, even if that wasn't in the cards for her." She crossed her legs, causing her apron to bunch. "Leigh gave her pieces away to loved ones. The heads on my bedside tables are hers."

That explained a lot. "Was the rest of the art in the house made by your artist friends?"

"Much of it. My collection includes pieces of sentimental value and pieces that speak to me because of their fearlessness or uniqueness. I love a wide variety of art. The only stuff I can't stand is the tepid commercial stuff. Like Siley. Or Dartin. They're just in it for the money."

"Where are your electric tools?"

"I don't use any. My grandfather and Leigh were both purists in that way. So am I."

She'd made *Emiline* using only her small hands? "Isn't it exhausting to carve blocks of wood without power tools?"

"I'm stronger than I look."

He pointed at *Emiline*. "I want to buy that one."

Her eyes widened. "No," she said immediately.

"Why not?"

"Just no. That one is not . . . *for* you."

"Not *for* me?"

"You don't appreciate it properly."

"Yes, I do."

"No. Also, you can't afford it."

"One day I'll be able to afford it—" A cough interrupted his words.

"I really don't like the sound of that cough."

"It'll be gone tomorrow." As he shifted to rise, his elbow collided with the jar on the nearby block and sent it flying. His hand shot out and he caught it in midair.

Remy gasped.

Gently, he replaced the jar.

"Your reflexes," Remy said, "are incredibly fast."

"Are they?"

"Yes."

"What is your background?" she wondered out loud.

"I wish I knew."

The next day Jonah's cough wasn't gone.

In fact, as Remy sat across from him at the breakfast table eating an egg'wich while he ate oatmeal, she noted that in addition to the cough, he looked flushed. It was chilly inside this morning, but he wore only a T-shirt and joggers. "Feeling all right?"

"Fine." He nudged his chin toward her coffee table. "How come you haven't added on to your puzzle lately? It's been at that stage since I got here."

She waved a hand. "I haven't added to it in more than a year."

"And the knitting?"

"Two years. Maybe three."

"The stand mixer in the kitchen? The one painted wall in the bathroom?"

She took a sip of coffee. "I can become very . . . *devoted* to a project. Sometimes I stay devoted long-term. Like with my work. Or reading. Other times, I only stay devoted for a little while before losing interest."

He turned to the side, coughing.

Fear turned the coffee in her stomach to ice. "I'm going to take your temperature."

"No need."

Despite his words, she retrieved the thermometer and ran it

across his forehead. Her heart dropped like a rock when she saw the read-out. "Ninety-nine."

"You look upset but that's in the normal range."

"It's higher than it was after you recovered from hypothermia." She'd invested so much in getting him to this point. As he'd improved, she'd let herself believe that he was going to be fine. Suddenly, she wasn't so sure.

She *must* get him to full health. *For his wife,* she hastily tacked on. For his wife and kids, she needed to get him to full health.

She hurried to her computer and ran a search for pneumonia symptoms. "Do you have sweating, shaking, or chills?" she called.

"No."

"Shortness of breath or stabbing chest pain?"

"No."

"Loss of appetite or fatigue?"

"No. This isn't a big deal, Remy."

She returned to her spot at the table but couldn't force herself to consume more food. The world outside was gray today, which cast a pall over the interior of her cottage. Even so, *he* shone. Jonah was masculinity and athleticism and easy grace. She couldn't allow his health to slide on her watch. "I'm going to schedule another virtual appointment for you today."

Looking put out with her, he set his spoon in his oatmeal. "An appointment will cost money."

"Fine. I'm the one who makes the medical decisions concerning you."

"*I* make the medical decisions concerning me."

"You have amnesia."

"Which doesn't mean I'm stupid."

"You're attending an appointment this afternoon and that's final." She jerked up her plate and carried it to the kitchen sink.

She'd spoken with more fire than she'd intended, but concern was morphing quickly into anger. She'd related to the sense of responsibility he'd said he felt toward the brown-haired woman in his vision because it was the same responsibility she felt toward him. It was imperative they get the advice of a doctor regarding his new symptoms.

"Don't forget to drink your water, Remy," he said silkily. "Hydration is key."

"Jonah." She swung toward him and held out her hand in front of her chest. "This is my last nerve—"

"Yeah, yeah." He grinned and he was just so . . . so . . . She let loose a strangled sound. He was just so *impossible.*

"If there's a church on the island," he said, "I'd like to go today."

"But . . . it's not Sunday."

"They probably leave the sanctuary open. I just want to go and sit."

"Why?"

"I have the sense that faith is important to me. I miss church."

"Your doctor's appointment—"

"Won't take all day. I can go to church and to a virtual appointment."

"We have one church on the island," she admitted, "but it's a thirty-minute drive, farther than you've gone before."

"I'll drive there alone," he said, "so you can work."

What if he got lost? Hurt? His condition worsened? How would she know? "I'll go with you."

He drove even faster to church than he had to Maureen's house despite the helpful comments she'd given, encouraging him to slow down.

The first available virtual appointment hadn't been until four this afternoon. So here they were, arriving mid-day at Isle-haven's wind-beaten green clapboard church. It sat on a rise, overlooking the cluster of colorful buildings fronting the harbor.

Jonah skidded the truck to a stop, and they climbed down. Overhead, charcoal clouds dripped rain. He reached behind the seats and pulled free an umbrella. After opening it, he surprised her by holding it over her head and not his own.

"You can have it," she told him.

"No." Droplets speckled his face and gold-brown hair.

She caught herself staring up at him in a swoon-daze. Mortified, she startled and set off toward the church's front door. But not too fast. She didn't want him to strain to keep up. The umbrella remained above her. "This is silly," she pronounced.

"Why is this silly?"

"Because it feels like you're my footman."

"And?"

"I should be the footman here."

"Aren't footmen male?"

"You," she said, "should be bundled in a great coat and top hat with spaniels at your feet."

"And you should be wearing an art smock and holding one of those painters' palettes."

"Even though I'm not a painter?"

"You with a painters' palette makes as much sense as me with spaniels."

She rolled her eyes. "You're *clearly* a spaniels man."

They stopped beneath the portico. Jonah collapsed the umbrella, then leaned over, coughing.

It physically pained her to watch him coughing. "Here." She took the umbrella from him. "I'll wait. Call if you need anything."

"You're not coming inside?"

"No."

"Why?"

"I'd feel uncomfortable."

He waited for her to elaborate.

She looked toward the sea, annoyed with her own awkwardness. "I don't go to church anymore."

"Any specific reason?"

"Yes, but I don't want to go into it."

Quiet lengthened. Then lengthened further. Why wouldn't he just go inside?

"I know something happened to you," he finally said. "And I think it was bad."

"It's complicated. I'll wait here."

His attention remained on her for a torturous amount of time, then he disappeared into the church.

Peace came over Jonah as soon as he stepped inside the little building. He took a seat in a pew on the right, halfway back.

He didn't remember much about his time in the ocean, fighting for his life. It was mostly a blur. But he did remember praying. And he remembered knowing that God was there. A power much greater than him, keeping him afloat.

Since he'd returned to consciousness, in the worst moments of pain and in the best moments, he'd had an awareness of God.

God was close. And God was real.

He'd wanted to come here today because he couldn't shake

the sense that he was heading for a collision. Again last night, he'd dreamed of the brunette and woken in a cold sweat, terrified. Plus, despite what he was saying to Remy, he knew his health was slipping away from him. He was worse today than yesterday.

Hadn't he suffered enough? What would he do if this sickness was a chest infection? He'd have to leave for a hospital. This island was not his home, but it was the only place familiar to him.

Most of all, this was Remy's place.

She was here. Though she was prickly and quirky, she was also the person who reassured him, centered him, and gave him strength. She was his lifeline. He needed to be where she was.

God, he prayed silently, his gaze fixed on the simple altar, *I trust you. Will you help me again?*

Remy kept butting in on his virtual doctor's appointment. She hadn't butted in on his first appointment, days ago. But this time, she'd insisted on being present.

When he tried to downplay his cough, she leaned into his video feed and told the doctor, "The cough is increasing in severity."

"Whose appointment is this?" Jonah grumbled.

"His fever was ninety-nine this morning," she announced, "and is still ninety-nine."

"That's within the range of normal," the doctor responded via the computer screen.

"That's what I said," Jonah whispered under his breath to Remy.

"However, the cough combined with that temperature is

worth watching," the doctor continued. "Pneumonia can be an issue for patients with fractured ribs."

"That's what I said," Remy whispered under her breath to Jonah.

"If your temperature is higher or the cough is worse tomorrow," the doctor continued, "you'll need to come to the hospital for treatment."

Light pressure slid across Jonah's forehead the next morning, waking him. It was followed by a soft electronic sound.

He moaned in protest and opened his eyes.

Remy hovered over him, thermometer in hand. "It's eleven in the morning and you're still sleeping. Also, your temperature is higher today—one hundred degrees. You're going to the hospital."

Disappointment socked him in the stomach.

"I'll call the airstrip and book you a seat on a flight out." She started pacing up and down the side of the bed.

What a lousy way to start the day. He pushed onto his elbows, struggling to throw off the confusion of sleep. "Are you coming with me?"

"I don't have to, no. I can figure out a way to get you from the airport to the hospital—"

"No. Remy."

She paused.

He put all the force of his will behind his words. "I am not going to the hospital unless you're coming with me."

It was the truth. He was going nowhere without her.

Nowhere.

Chapter Seven

"I've packed some things for you," Leigh said to Jonah shortly after they'd entered the building next to the airstrip several hours later. She passed over a brown paper sack. "Folgers coffee, some chocolate pudding cups, and a carving I made. I also put a slip of paper in there with my cell phone number on it, in case there's ever anything I can do for you."

"Thank you. For this and everything else." He wasn't leaving with much—a carry-on containing his small amount of clothes and the items in this sack. But it was more than he'd arrived with.

"C'mere." She motioned him forward and hugged him. He could tell she was using only a percentage of her strength in awareness of his healing ribs. Pulling back a little, she regarded him with gruff affection. "Promise me you'll come back. I'm determined to see you again fit and well."

"I'll come back."

She hugged him again. When they separated it took him off guard to spot moisture in the eyes of such a practical woman.

Leigh thrust it away with her wrist, then went to give Remy, who was talking with an employee, a hug.

"Love you," he heard Remy say.

"Love you. You two be on your way now. He needs a hospital."

"I'll get him there," Remy promised.

Leigh jerked a nod and walked out the door without looking back.

Remy crossed to him. "Ready?"

No. "Yes." How expensive was this flight? He hated that she was having to pay for him.

The pilot led them outdoors to a prop plane.

They buckled into seats behind the pilot.

Jonah looked over at her, breathing in the scent of her soap —lemon, sage, sweetness. Her hair was down today, parted in the middle. She wore a V-neck gray shirt, black jeans, flat black lace-up boots.

Internally, he cursed the fever and cough. He'd been making steady progress, but then, as if he was playing a board game, he'd drawn the wrong card and been sent several spaces backward. He couldn't recover here any longer. He had to leave.

Resistance overwhelmed him as the plane raced down the dirt airstrip, gathering speed. It lifted off. Soon after, Islehaven slipped from view. He twisted in the seat, trying to keep sight of it.

Too soon, it disappeared.

Be careful what you wish for, Remy thought grimly. Stress tightened her posture as they prepared to land in Rockland after their twelve-minute flight.

When she'd found Jonah ten days ago, her first goal had been to ensure that his vitals stabilized. Once that had been achieved, her goal had been to reunite him with his family and get him gone. She'd wanted him out of her house.

All of a sudden, she'd gotten her wish.

It's just that she'd never wanted it to be like this. For this reason.

As challenging as having him as a houseguest had been, she was realizing that she perhaps hadn't *completely* loathed having him around. She'd just mostly loathed it. Because now that their time at the cottage had come to an end, some very tiny part of her was . . . sad.

When Jonah had insisted that she accompany him here, she hadn't put up a fight because she needed to see her duty to him through and because he wasn't up to making this journey alone. He needed her . . . . Well. Not *her* exactly. But he did need someone capable to go with him and get him safely squared away.

After landing, she called a cab. Then watched Rockland's sunny streets slide by from the cab's backseat. It always jarred her system to return to the mainland. There were *so many people*.

"Does anything here jog your memory?" she asked.

"No."

She'd called Jonah's doctor this morning to tell him the fever and cough were slightly worse and that they were heading to the mainland. He'd assured her he'd speak with hospital admin in advance of their arrival.

When they reached the medical center, the doctor's legwork saved them from much of the bureaucratic nightmare that would normally accompany the arrival of a man with no ID, name, health insurance, or memory.

They waited an hour—*so many people*—then a matronly

nurse showed them to an ER exam room. Jonah sat on a bed on wheels. His legs hung off the end and he looked disgruntled as the nurse flitted around him.

At the very least, she'd succeeded at getting him under the care of qualified medical professionals. Which was something.

Fifteen minutes after the nurse left, a thirty-something man with tidy brown hair entered. His name tag read *Dr. Denny.* As soon as he saw Jonah, he came to a stop, staring in shock. A huge smile broke across his face. "I'm a big fan." He released a disbelieving laugh. "What an honor to meet you."

Everything inside Remy stilled.

Jonah's face had gone expressionless. Except for his eyes. They resembled the eyes of a hiding lion the moment before it pounces. "Do you know who I am?" he asked the doctor.

"Yes. You're—Ah! I'm sorry." Dr. Denny shook his head wryly. "I lost my focus there for a second. I did read in your chart that you're suffering from amnesia."

"Correct."

"I do know who you are, yes. Your name is Jeremiah Camden."

Wait. What? The implications of the surname Camden collided with Remy like a breaking wave.

"Jeremiah." Jonah spoke the name slowly, as if testing its syllables.

"Yes," the doctor confirmed.

"The name feels right," Jonah said. "How do we know each other?"

"We don't know each other personally," Dr. Denny answered. "You're famous."

"I'm famous?"

"You were a Formula One race car driver. A . . . legend. You're from here, Maine. And you're the only American driver who's won two driver's championships as well as the only American who's been active on the circuit in recent years."

Remy's balance careened as if she was falling, though she was still sitting squarely in the chair against the wall. A legend? His fast reflexes and the speed at which he'd driven her truck now made sense. She knew nothing about Formula One except that it might take place in locations like Italy and Bahrain. "Is he . . ." Remy cleared her throat. "Is he from the well-known Camden family?"

"Oh, yes." The doctor beamed at Remy, then Jonah. "You retired almost a year ago after . . ." His face fell a little. "Anyway, you retired."

Jonah held up his palm. "That's enough for now, if you don't mind." She could tell by the harsh set of his lips that the new information was giving him a splitting pain in his head.

"Certainly. I'm glad you're so recognizable. We should be able to contact your family and confirm your identity right away. First things first, though. Let's check on your lungs so we can get you feeling better."

"When I found him," Remy said to the doctor, "he had an injury to the back of the head. You might want to check that, too."

"Will do." Dr. Denny listened to Jeremiah's breathing through a stethoscope, examined his head, informed them that he was going to request some scans, then excused himself.

When the two of them were alone, he met her gaze. Beneath the flush of his fever, he'd paled. "Can you pull up a photo of Jeremiah Camden online to confirm I'm who the doctor thinks I am? Maybe I just look like this Jeremiah, and he's mistaken."

She pulled her phone from her purse. Seconds later, she whispered, "He's not mistaken." She passed the phone to him so he could study the photo of himself in a one-piece uniform leaning against a narrow race car that pointed down in the front and had giant wheels. In the picture, his head was cocked at a victorious angle, a satisfied smile on his face.

His childish sketches that had reminded her of Hot Wheels had actually been clues! He'd been drawing Formula One cars and she'd missed the hint.

He ran his hand through his hair and clasped the back of his neck. The sleeve of his T-shirt rode up, displaying the pale underside of his bicep. "It's strange to see a picture of myself in a past I don't remember."

"I can imagine. Overall, though, the fact that we've finally pinned down your identity is excellent news." Privately, she wasn't so sure. *The Camdens?* She was pretending to take all this in stride, but her head felt like a scary carnival. "We finally know who you are."

"Jeremiah." He tried out his new name again.

"Coincidentally, we selected a temporary name for you that starts with a *J* and ends with an *h*—just like your real name."

He brought his arm down, leaving his hair rumpled. Her phone looked small clasped in his big, elegant hands. "Have you ever heard of Jeremiah Camden?"

"I haven't heard of you specifically. I don't follow racing. But the Camden name is a name all Americans know."

"Why?"

"Certain surnames became very famous because they belonged to the robber barons of the 1800s. Vanderbilt, Carnegie, Astor, Camden, and more." She shifted, uncomfortable with the idea that so much had been concentrated in the hands of so few and unwilling to tell him that she both suspected and dreaded which Camden branch he belonged to.

"Okay." He passed her phone back. "I can't hear any more right now. My head's killing me."

"Let me know when you're ready and I'll google you. And your wife. And your parents."

He coughed several times. "I'm not ready."

She needed to respect his pace and not hijack his story just to satisfy her own curiosity. However, she was itching to look up info. On Jonah— Not Jonah. *Jeremiah.* It was going to take effort to replace his false name with his real one. She wanted more info on Jeremiah but also his wife. Was his wife the woman in his nightmares?

"I feel sick," he said.

"You are sick. But you are not, apparently, a mechanic."

"The race car driver part sounds good. That feels like it fits. But if I'm a recognizable person from a recognizable family, how come no one reported me missing?"

"I don't know." They'd looked high and low for missing-person reports.

"Do you think I'm estranged from my family?"

"You *are* difficult to get along with, so maybe."

"*You're* difficult to get along with. If I was difficult, it was only because I was in extreme pain. What was your excuse?" He lifted a teasing eyebrow.

"I was afflicted with a man in extreme pain."

The nurse returned to escort him to the scans. Jeremiah stood to follow. "Please don't look up more about me while I'm gone."

"If you don't want me to, I won't."

"I don't want you to."

"Then I won't."

Remy was left alone in the exam room. Twining her hands together in her lap, she let her thoughts unspool.

He'd said he felt sick. She felt a little sick herself. Why was she so rattled to discover he was famous? He'd worn that expensive watch. His haircut, his bearing, his vocabulary, his accent all spoke to the fact that he'd come from prestige and money. Which was why she'd called him Duke. He'd turned out to be precisely the type of man she'd suspected him to be.

She was rattled because she deeply mistrusted fame and money. Jeremiah had both. Which meant he truly, *truly* wasn't Jonah anymore. Jonah was lost to her. Jonah had never existed, truth be told. Her houseguest had been Jeremiah all along.

Now, thanks to Dr. Denny, his past life was coming for him. She could feel it rushing up—about to crash into his present. Soon he'd have an endless supply of the things he'd been deprived of with her—credit cards, clothes, expensive food, luxurious lodging, his loved ones. Soon his family—most notably his wife—would arrive.

Grief lumped in her throat.

Remy! Don't be ridiculous. You've spent untold hours trying to find his family. At last, they would be told that Jonah—Jeremiah was alive. She'd be able to surrender custody of him, which was what she'd wanted all along. He would rightfully be surrounded by the people closest to him. He'd no longer need her. And she'd no longer have to deal with the most infuriating and spoiled of men. She should be rejoicing.

So why was it that, in her heart of hearts, dejection reigned?

Be careful what you wish for.

Jeremiah was procrastinating.

Clearly, though, Remy wasn't going to stand for it much longer. Any second now she was going to demand he give her the go-ahead to look up details about himself and his wife.

He watched her pacing, pale hair fanning out, arms crossed. Her quick footsteps communicated her stress.

The scans had returned good news and bad. The good news—his head wound had healed. The bad news—he was suffering from pneumonia, so he'd been admitted to the hospital. They'd sent him to this room on the fourth floor, forced him to change into a hospital gown, and predicted that he'd only need to stay for a night or two. It was now late afternoon, and the light had begun to fade from the sky beyond his window.

He was sick of being stuck in beds. In this particular bed, the top half elevated so that he was reclining, he was also saddled with an IV dripping drugs into his system.

Remy came to a halt and faced off with him. "Jeremiah."

"You've said *Jonah* with irritation a lot of times. But this is the first time you've said *Jeremiah* with irritation." What was wrong with him that he actually *liked* it when she said it that way?

"I'm sure it won't be the last."

"Good." The name Jeremiah felt right. So did the job of driver and the famous family. He was glad he wasn't a pauper but for some reason, learning of his profession and family hadn't brought him comfort. Instead, it brought the sensation of weight, lowering down on him pound after pound.

"Your family members are going to walk through that door any second." Remy gestured toward the hall. "And we're not going to know anything about them."

Once Dr. Denny had given hospital staffers his name, it hadn't taken them long to locate records concerning him. He'd been seen at this hospital a few times in the past. Also, this hospital was part of a larger network of regional doctors' offices of all specialty types. Apparently, he was a patient at two network offices in a town called Groomsport. At one office, he saw a GP. At the other, a PT. He'd signed annual forms just nine months ago at his GP's office listing the two people his doctor was allowed to share his medical information with.

Someone named Fiona Camden. And someone named Jude Camden. The hospital staffer had asked him if she had his permission to contact them both.

He'd hesitated.

Remy had glared daggers at him. "I'm so thankful," she'd said meaningfully, "that we finally have the opportunity to let your family members know you're alive. I've lost sleep over my inability to contact them."

He'd known he was being a jerk for delaying consent. Thing was, he resented his family for not making it easier for Remy to find them for the last ten days.

When he'd remained silent, she'd added, "I'm relieved that they won't have to languish in despair for another minute." Her expression had said, *Give consent now or I'll hit the ceiling with fury.*

Though his gut instinct was to delay, he'd given the staffer permission to contact Fiona and Jude. That had been twenty minutes ago, and Remy was right. Fiona or Jude, whoever they were, might walk in at any time.

"When your wife—Fiona—walks in, it will be better if you're able to at least recognize her from a photo online. It will help ground you if you know how long you've been married, how many kids you have, where she's from, and where you live. At the moment, you won't know your wife from your sister and if you mistake your wife for your sister that will be hurtful to her."

"I have amnesia. It's not my fault if I don't know who she is."

"It *is* your fault because you have access to Google! Why are you dragging your feet on this?"

"I'm going to be straight with you."

"Please."

"I'm dragging my feet because I don't want you to leave."

For a moment, her mouth softened, her lips parting. Then her shoulders drew back into a fighting posture. "Don't blame your procrastination on me! I have nothing to do with this."

"I'm not blaming you, but you are the reason. If we googled Fiona Camden and found out we've been married five years and have two kids and we live ten minutes from here, you'd already be gone. Wouldn't you?"

She spluttered. "Yes! And you'd want me gone—"

"Except I don't—"

"—because it's going to be very awkward if I'm sitting here when she arrives. Talk about a third wheel! Put yourself in her shoes. She's been worried sick about you. And if your night-mares are any indication, your subconscious has been worried sick about her. I'd never want the two of you, who are very much in love, to have your grand reunion with me in the room!" Her voice was rising, high-pitched.

"I am not very much in love with her. I don't even remember her." He could easily tap into the sense of failure he'd experienced while searching and searching for the brunette of his nightmares. The idea of her showing up here in person gave him the same feeling of doom he'd had in the dream.

"We both need to prioritize how *your wife* feels," Remy insisted. "How you feel doesn't matter at the moment—"

"It matters to me."

"I have a sneaking suspicion that everyone in this hospital is whispering, 'Formula One champion Jeremiah Camden is here!' to each other. Already, they all seem to realize who you are. What if word reached your wife that a strange woman is at your bedside?"

"I don't care about gossip."

Remy yanked out her phone and tapped the screen.

"Don't look up Fiona Camden," he growled.

"I've respected your feet-dragging as long as I can. I'm looking her up."

"My head can't take it, Remy."

"I've noticed that you have quite a hard head."

He wanted to wrestle the phone away from her the way he'd once wanted to wrestle the bottle of Advil away. This time, his IV restrained him.

Remy froze, head bent.

A sinkhole opened in the center of him. "What did you find?"

"Fiona Camden is not the name of your wife. That's the name of your mother. Hang on. I'll google Jeremiah Camden's wife."

"Don't."

"Yes."

Time scraped by. Probably just seconds but it felt like minutes.

Remy made a soft, sad sound . . . the kind of involuntary noise people make when hit with terrible news.

He didn't ask what she'd found because he was sure he didn't want to know.

She hauled her attention up to him. He'd seen many different moods cross that face, but this was the first time he'd seen this mixture of regret and sorrow. "Your wife, Alexis Camden, passed away fifteen months ago."

Again, rightness echoed within him at the news. But it only brought more weight. Pound after pound. "How did she die?"

"It says here that she committed suicide by jumping from a cliff into the lake below. She was only thirty-one." She bit her bottom lip.

He'd felt guilt in the dreams. Was *he* the reason she'd jumped off a cliff? "Did we have kids?"

"No. You don't have any children." She swallowed hard. "I'm sorry. I'm sorry she's dead and now I'm also sorry that I insisted on looking her up. It would have been better for you to find this out in a more compassionate way from someone who's close to you."

"You're the only person who's close to me."

"I'm very sorry."

"I don't know her," he reminded her again. "I've never even heard the name *Alexis* until now."

"I was so certain that the two of you were living an epic romance . . . ."

"You made that up," he pointed out gently. "Just like you make up the stories surrounding your sculptures."

"To me, your dream really did indicate an epic romance. In fact, your romance probably *was* epic. Which is why you still wear your wedding ring. I'm sure you've been devastated over the loss of Alexis ever since her passing."

It was clear to him that *Remy* was the one devastated by Alexis's passing. She'd told him once that she saw herself as the champion of his marriage. She was very attached to the fiction she'd created around him and his wife. "Can you pull up a picture of Alexis so I can see if she's the one in my dreams?"

Remy found an image on her phone and displayed it to him.

He could hear a cart hissing down the hallway and the sound of a door closing. His headache turned unbearable as he squinted at the photo. "Yeah. She's the one I dreamed about." Long and flowing dark hair. Blue eyes. It was awful to look at this healthy, young, beautiful person and know that she'd killed herself.

In some strange way, his amnesia had been acting like an

anesthetic, protecting him. When the anesthetic wore off, what level of destruction would be waiting for him?

A knock sounded. He and Remy looked toward the door.

An older man swept inside as if he owned the building.

"Are you Jude?" Jeremiah asked.

"No," the newcomer answered. "I'm your father."

Chapter Eight

Remy swung toward the stranger.

He wore sleek pants and a pale blue dress shirt opened at the throat one button. His gray-blond hair had been slicked back with comb tracks. He was likely in his late sixties, which didn't diminish the vitality and magnetism flowing from him. His resemblance to Jeremiah was evident in their firm jaws, straight noses, fit bodies, and the rare shade of their pale green eyes.

The newcomer bent down to clasp Jeremiah in a swift hug.

Jeremiah didn't push the stranger away nor did he reach up to return the hug.

The older man straightened. "How are you, son?"

"I'd say I've been better, but I don't remember if I have."

Jeremiah's father stretched out his hand to Remy. "I'm Felix Camden."

So Jeremiah does belong to the most notorious branch of the Camden family. She was beginning to relate to a boxer trying to absorb punch after punch. "Remy Reed." They shook hands.

"A pleasure to meet you." His eye contact was direct. His confidence towering.

"How did you know I was here?" Jeremiah asked. "The hospital told me they'd notify Fiona and Jude."

"Your mother called me as soon as they called her and, by the looks of it, I got here first. I have," he said dryly, "a very fast car. I hear you have no memory and a lung infection."

"That's correct."

"I'm not familiar to you?"

"No."

Felix Camden probably rarely-to-never came into contact with anyone who wasn't familiar with him. The least famous thing about Felix Camden was his iconic last name. The most famous thing about him—his career as an NFL quarterback.

Remy had grown up in Dallas, Texas. Her parents had watched Cowboys games on TV and occasionally seen the team play live when gifted a ticket by a friend or business associate. Remy was no football expert, but she didn't have to be to know the name Felix Camden. He'd become a part of the culture. Like Terry Bradshaw or Joe Montana.

"I'm glad you're safe," Felix said to Jeremiah. "We've been worried."

"Have you?" Jeremiah asked evenly. "Remy and I have been searching for missing-person reports and no one posted one about me."

"You left ten days ago for a week of vacation on your boat. You'd told us you were going off the grid. You'd have your phone with you but shut off and stowed away only to use in case of emergency. For the first week, we had no cause for concern. Then you didn't return to port as scheduled three days ago and none of us could reach you. That's when we got worried. Had we announced publicly that you were missing, it would have created a firestorm. Instead, I hired two private detectives. They, and the rest of us, have been making inquiries the last few days."

Jeremiah regarded the older man the way people at galleries regarded art they were trying to understand.

Just then a woman sailed in.

She looked to be around Felix's age with defined cheekbones, a sharp jaw, and perfectly placed eyes. Her clothing communicated wealth. Her skin was as smooth and glowing as Botox and facials could make it. She'd twisted her ash-blond hair into an updo in the back. In the front, curtain bangs framed her face.

"Sweetheart," she said to Jeremiah.

"This is your mother," Felix said. "Fiona."

This time, Jeremiah returned her hug.

When they parted, Felix motioned to Remy. "Fiona, I'd like to introduce you to Remy Reed."

Fiona glanced across at her vaguely, as if she'd only just registered her presence. "Hello."

"Hi."

"She's been taking care of Jeremiah for us."

"Oh, how kind. *Thank you.*" As her focus returned to her son, her brows twitched toward each other. "What happened to you? I've hardly slept the last couple of nights. The only thing that kept me going was the possibility that you'd decided to extend your vacation without notifying anyone."

"That's not what happened." Without emotion, Jeremiah recounted how and where Remy had discovered him and the days since.

"No one on the island recognized you?" Felix asked Jeremiah.

"I was laid up with fractured ribs. I only saw three people on the island."

Felix looked at Remy with a polite expression, yet she could feel his disbelief percolating under the veneer.

"None of the three of us are Formula One fans," Remy explained. "I'm into art and fantasy novels. Leigh's a lobster-woman. And Maureen's into chickens and hypnosis."

Felix and Fiona were peering at her as if she was an oddity —which she knew she somewhat was—Jeremiah was scowling, and Remy was wondering how she'd landed in the epicenter of these grandiose people. The journey from her cottage to the hospital suddenly felt like a journey of a million miles.

"Are you two married?" Jeremiah asked Felix and Fiona.

Surprise stamped their faces. "No," Felix said.

"We were married for sixteen years," Fiona added. "But we've been divorced now for eighteen."

"How old am I?"

Felix appeared bemused but Fiona appeared dumbstruck. Her expression said, *You really don't know the answers to these questions?*

"Look, I understand this must be weird for you," Jeremiah told them. "The fact that you know me well but that I don't know you or anything about myself. But that's the deal. My memories begin ten days ago."

Fiona was clearly struggling to process that bitter fact. What must it be like to learn your child's experience of you had been wiped away? Upsetting. Disorienting. Incredibly sad.

"No memories of me from your childhood at all?" Fiona asked. "No memories of the things we've done together in recent years?"

"No."

"Your memories will come back," Felix stated with conviction. He was a cool customer, the type of man who believed he could go to battle with his son's amnesia and win. "We'll do everything we can to facilitate that."

"To—to answer your earlier question," Fiona said, "you're thirty-four years old."

"Do I have siblings?"

Fiona dipped her chin. "You have a younger brother, Jude."

"And another brother, Max," Felix tacked on.

Jeremiah's forehead lined. "How come you didn't mention Max?" he asked Fiona.

"You and Jude are my sons. Max is your father's child with another woman." Fiona was dignified. Even so, a light blush rose on her cheeks.

The family dynamics here were very dangerous, like a plot of land with patches of quicksand.

"Apparently, I see a doctor and physical therapist in Groomsport," Jeremiah said. "Is that where I live?"

"Yes," Felix said. "Groomsport is where both you and I were born and raised. It's about fifteen minutes up the coast."

"I didn't grow up there, but I live there now, too." Fiona's manicured hands balled around the strap of her purse. "The three of us all have houses there."

A tense gap opened in the conversation.

"Do either of you," Jeremiah said, "have any idea why I was floating in the water off the coast of Islehaven Island on Tuesday, September thirteenth?"

"You left on your boat trip that day." Felix slid his hands into the pockets of his suit pants. "You sent me your itinerary, so I know your course would've taken you past Islehaven."

"Can I get a copy of my itinerary from you?"

"Absolutely."

"What type of boat do I have?"

"You have two," Felix replied. "A speedboat. And the one you took on your trip, which is a thirty-five-foot Commander by Chris-Craft. It was built in 1953 and you'd had it restored. You named it the *Camdenball* after the nickname the F1 commentators gave you."

Jeremiah punched a button to bring his torso more upright on the motorized bed. "Have I taken the boat on trips like this before? Alone and unreachable?"

"Yes. Without incident."

"Where's the boat now?"

"We don't know," Felix answered. "When you didn't return, that's one of the things we were trying to determine. So far, there's been no sign of it."

"Perhaps it sank?" Fiona suggested.

"If that's the case," Jeremiah said, "it seems like I would've had time to send an SOS message on the radio or put on a life vest at least."

"He wasn't wearing a life vest when you found him?" Fiona asked Remy.

"No. Nor was he in a wetsuit. He was swimming in his clothing. My guess is that he went overboard for some reason."

"Does anyone want me dead?" Jeremiah asked his parents.

Immediately, the silence turned explosive.

"No," his mother said, eyes flashing with protective anger at the very idea.

"Like any famous person," Felix said more diplomatically, "you have your . . . detractors. But you never gave me reason to think that any of them might be dangerous."

"Maybe we underestimated my detractors."

"Angel of God," Fiona breathed. Then, louder, "You're very popular. I don't think anyone wants you dead."

Jeremiah lifted a skeptical eyebrow.

Felix turned to his ex-wife. "I'm inclined to think private care for Jeremiah might be superior to this—"

"No," Jeremiah said flatly. "I'm satisfied with the level of care I'm receiving here. I'm not going anywhere."

Amusement crinkled Felix's eyes. "You might've lost your memory, but it seems your personality is very much intact."

"It's important to us that you receive exemplary care," Fiona said to Jeremiah. "Also, we don't want your story leaked to the media and we can't be assured of your privacy here."

"I don't care about the media."

"When your memories return, you might care," Felix commented drolly.

"I might. But I'm not making decisions based on what my former or future self might want."

"There are a number of laws surrounding the confidentiality of medical information," Felix said to Fiona. "We might be fine on the privacy front. Or we might not. I'll have my lawyers look into it."

Fiona gave a refined nod. She was definitely the composed queen to Felix's bold king.

"Have the doctors said when you'll be able to go home?" Felix asked Jeremiah.

"Tomorrow, I hope. If so, I'll need someone to tell me where I live and how to get inside."

"I have a key to your house," Fiona said, "and so does Jude. I just talked to him. He works for the FBI in Bangor but he's planning to drive here tomorrow, to be with you over the weekend. He's already said he wants to take you home whenever you're able to leave. But, of course, both your father and I would also love to do so."

"I'm going to speak with the top experts in the field of amnesia," Felix announced, "and gather information about the most effective treatments."

Jeremiah shrugged. "Remy's done a lot of research. It seems like even the most effective treatments are only slightly successful. I'm not going to submit to therapies that I think are a waste of time."

Mortification inched its way up Remy's cheeks at the memory of the homespun amnesia treatments she'd administered. Maureen's hypnotherapy. The sketch pad. She very much hoped he didn't mention any of that in this company.

Felix's attention swung around, landing on Remy. "Thank you for rescuing Jeremiah and taking such good care of him. We will, of course, compensate you for your time as well as the expenses involved—"

"Do I have money?" Jeremiah asked his father.

Slowly, one edge of Felix's lips curled up. "There's forgetting and then there's *forgetting*. Come now, Jeremiah. You expect me to believe you don't know the answer to that question?"

"You do have money," Fiona said, "yes."

"Then I will handle reimbursing Remy for my care."

Felix neither argued nor showed surprise. "You must be very tired," he told Remy, "after spending ten days looking after Jeremiah. You're a heroine."

True, Remy thought. Also true: She was being dismissed.

"We'll let you get back to your life," Felix said.

It was the face-to-face equivalent of when people said "I'll let you go" over the phone, when what they really meant was, *I want to hang up now*. Of course Jeremiah's parents would want her out of the picture. She was a complete stranger to them. An unknown quantity. Who might jeopardize their son's secrecy—which they esteemed so highly.

She should *want* to go and never look back. Except for some unfathomable reason, she wasn't ready—

"Remy is not leaving," Jeremiah said.

"Jeremiah—" his mother tried.

"No."

Felix cleared his throat. "In that case, Remy, would you

please excuse us for a few minutes? We'd like to speak with our son privately."

"Certainly." No doubt they wanted to speak to their son privately *about her*.

"You don't have to go," Jeremiah said.

"I'd like to." She owed it to herself to show them that while they had wealth, she had wealth of character. "I could use a cup of coffee. Can I get anyone else a cup?"

The three Camdens gave identical shakes of their heads. Probably because hospital coffee was not freshly ground Arabica.

She scooped up her purse and slipped out.

Jeremiah considered his mother and father. They stirred an echo of familiarity inside him—similar to déjà vu. Their presence was also causing his head to throb. Did he love them? Did he trust them? What was his history with them?

"I feel obligated to point out," Felix said, "that Remy might be playing you. It's possible that she did recognize you or learned of your identity after taking you into her home. Then decided to run a long con on you. She might be trying to earn your loyalty in order to worm her way into your heart or bank account."

Fury swept up Jeremiah's body.

"It sounds cold, I know," his mother hurried to add. "But your father's warning is valid. We've learned this lesson the hard way. We've both trusted people we shouldn't have trusted."

The force of his emotion shocked him. Since regaining consciousness in Remy's house, he'd experienced annoyance but nothing close to this red-hot anger. He hadn't known he was capable of it. "I have no actual memories of either of you. Right now, Remy is the *only* person I trust."

Felix stepped closer to his bedside. "We can prove our relationship with you through hundreds of photos and videos. She can't."

"Only because she and I just met." A chilling thought occurred to him. His father had mentioned hiring private detectives and lawyers. There were things in Remy's past she'd kept from him, and he didn't want his father unearthing them like worms beneath rocks. "Don't turn your private investigators on Remy. I don't want her ruined because she was stupid enough to show me kindness."

"Jeremiah," his father said, "be sensible—"

"Right now, I have one inch of faith in you. Investigate Remy and you'll destroy that inch."

"We're trying to protect you," Fiona said.

"Get out. Both of you."

Hurt dawned on his mother's face. "We're only trying to help—"

"I've got a splitting headache and it's time for you both to leave. If you throw suspicion on Remy, I'll make the separation between us permanent."

He could tell his words had shaken his mother. "I'll check on you soon," she said as she moved toward the door.

"Don't check on me," Jeremiah said. "I'll reach out to you both when I'm ready."

"*Felix*," Fiona said in a meaningful way.

His father exited the room behind her.

What kind of parents were these?

What kind of family was this?

Remy stayed away for an hour and a half.

Once she'd reached the hospital cafeteria her stomach had reminded her that it wanted food. In all the hubbub she'd missed lunch and now it was almost dinnertime. So she'd eaten and tried in vain to gather her thoughts.

When she returned to Jeremiah's room, she entered quietly, half expecting him to be dozing. No. He was looking right at her with a frown. He clicked the remote in his hand, silencing ESPN on the TV. "You were gone so long, I was afraid you went home."

"I thought about it."

"Remy." He sat upright on the mattress, one bare calf and foot dangling over the edge. "I need for you to stay."

"That's not technically true. You know your name. You're in good hands here at the hospital. You've been reunited with your family."

He bent over, coughing. Straightened. "If you're concerned about my health and recovery—"

"I've devoted the last ten days to your health and recovery."

"—then you'll stay." A muscle ticked in his throat.

They locked metaphorical horns.

"I can recover," he said, "and I can face . . . whatever is in my past if you are here. But not without you. You're the only ally I have."

"*We're* allies?"

"Yes."

"Crises make strange bedfellows."

"Tell me you'll stay."

She hesitated.

"Please," he said.

"For how long?"

"Until I'm settled and doing fine on my own. I'll pay for your hotel room—"

"I am so weary of you—and more recently your father—assuming that I'm motivated by money! It's insulting. I am not motivated by money."

"Then spend the night here in the hospital room—"

"Absolutely not. I won't be camping out at your bedside through the night anymore. You have nurses for that now."

"Fine. Remy. What I want is for you to remain on the mainland for a while. Apparently, I have a house. You're welcome to it."

She looked out the window at the nocturnal scene, looked back to him. "Wendell lives here in Rockland. It would probably do him good to have me as a houseguest for a bit."

"So you'll stay on the mainland?"

Now was the time to tell him no, that she was returning to her beloved, isolated existence on Islehaven.

Now was the time.

Yet the words wouldn't come.

She wanted to return to her isolated existence. But for the first time in six years, she wanted something else a little bit more.

She wanted to remain here with him. Just a while longer.

Why?

Because the two of them had come this far together and she refused to sabotage his progress. Plus, she had questions that needed answering. How had he ended up in the ocean? And why had his wife jumped off a cliff?

Based on her photo, Alexis was precisely the type of woman Remy would have expected him to marry. Alexis's heart-shaped face had been strikingly, unbelievably beautiful. Her makeup looked to have been applied by a pro. In fact, the only thing that seemed completely wrong about Alexis was the fact that she'd died by suicide at such a young age. Even hours after learning that Alexis had passed away, Remy still felt dazed by that information.

Jeremiah was not going to receive the fairytale Remy had concocted for him. Instead of embracing a happy ending, he was slated to wrestle with a tragedy.

"Will you stay?" he repeated.

"Just until you're settled and doing fine on your own?" she asked, quoting him.

"Yes."

"Okay. I'll stay until then." She spoke lightly, trying to downplay it, pretending that following men to the mainland and making the impromptu decision to linger was something she did with casual ease.

In the middle of that night, Jeremiah came up from sleep toward the surface of waking. "Remy?"

The hum of a commercial heating system answered.

Disappointment and confusion shifted inside him. "Remy?"

"No, hon," an older nurse said as she noted his blood pressure. "It's just me. I'll be gone in a sec."

Several miles away, Remy lay awake in the guest bedroom at Wendell's.

Her aloneness blanketed her more heavily than the darkness. How was she supposed to sleep without the sound of Jonah's—*Jeremiah's* breathing? Without the rustling of his covers? The male scent of him? His nearness?

What if he was struggling tonight? What if his pneumonia was worsening and she wasn't there?

That's ridiculous, she told herself impatiently. *He'll do just fine without you.*

But would she do just fine . . . without him?

Chapter Nine

The following day, Saturday, Remy and Jeremiah sat on the loveseat in his hospital room, waiting for him to be discharged. He'd just given her a bite of the chocolate pudding they'd brought him on his lunch tray. She was tasting its flavor and consistency, pretending to be a pudding connoisseur, arguing with him about its strengths and weaknesses relative to the chocolate pudding she stocked on Islehaven.

A day's worth of antibiotics and fluid had gone a long way toward curbing the chest infection. The doctors and nurses had tripped over themselves to flatter Jeremiah, citing his "outstanding fitness" and status as an "elite athlete" as contributing factors in his A+ response to treatment.

She'd rolled her eyes at Jeremiah behind their backs. Yes, his physique made it clear that he kept himself in great shape generally. But he was actually a *retired* athlete with fractured ribs who'd spent the last eleven days as a couch potato.

They'd recently unhooked his IV and allowed him to put on his own clothing. His fever had gone and with it the flush.

"Hold on," he said. "There's a drop of pudding on your lip." He reached a blunt thumb toward her mouth.

Her thoughts blanked for a second before her brain sent a message to intercept his hand. Remy found herself cupping his fingers inches from her mouth, his profile very close to hers.

He met her eyes. She was so near she could hear his inhales and exhales. Smell the Tide laundry detergent he'd used on his clothes back at the cottage. See at close range the way his lips tipped up on one side—a subtle challenge.

Desire kicked at her, taking out her knees with tingles. She would have gone down had she not already been sitting.

What is this?

This was physical awareness, rolling over her the way nighttime rolls over the continent. It had been so long since she'd felt this response that she'd forgotten how forceful it could be. Skin-rushing, blood-pumping power. Terrifying.

She pushed away his hand. "I can remove chocolate from my own lip, thank you very much." But when she attempted to do so, she found none. He'd invented the drop of chocolate in order to touch her! He was toying with her for his own entertainment. Just as she opened her mouth to accuse him, a handsome blond man around their age entered the room.

She shut her jaw with a *click*.

"I'm Jude." The newcomer stopped a few feet in front of them. "And you're the older brother who's been a pain in my butt for the last thirty-two years. However, it sounds like I'm the only one of the two of us who remembers that."

"You must be an imposter," Jeremiah told him. "I have a hard time believing I was ever a pain in the butt."

"I don't have a hard time believing that," Remy said with feeling, "at all. Clearly, you *are* Jeremiah's brother."

"Yep. I'm the boring, dependable, rule-following one." Jude

motioned to Jeremiah. "You're the daring, ambitious, pain-in-the-butt one."

Jeremiah made a sound of amused acknowledgment. Remy noted this family member hadn't caused Jeremiah to wince in the way that indicated a headache.

Remy and Jude exchanged introductions and a handshake.

Jude's face was slightly more thoughtful and poetic than Jeremiah's. The brothers' eyes were the same shade of green that had obviously been their father's legacy. They were the same height and both exquisitely masculine. Jude had on semi-casual gray pants and a startlingly white business shirt. None of his clothing revealed a single wrinkle or smudge.

"I hear you're getting out of here today," Jude said to Jeremiah.

"Yeah. Any minute."

"Mom told me that you've temporarily banned her, so I thought I'd drive you to Appleton—"

"Appleton?"

"Your house."

"My house has a name?"

"It does. I'll drive you there and stay until tomorrow to help get your life back up and running."

"Okay." Like with his parents yesterday, Jeremiah seemed indifferent, failing to offer the appropriate amount of gratitude.

"They're discharging you just in time." Jude flicked a humorous glance down to Jeremiah's chin. "You'd never want to be caught dead with a short beard."

"At least I'm no longer wearing a hospital gown."

"That's not as big of an improvement as you might think."

A knock sounded, then the doctor stepped in to say Jeremiah was free to go and to provide instructions. Jeremiah would continue on a course of oral antibiotics and could soon begin ramping up his aerobic level. He should make his "coughs count" to clear the remaining congestion in his lungs and watch for signs that he wasn't getting enough oxygen. The doctor finished by telling Jeremiah he'd been an all-around excellent patient—Remy had found the opposite to be true when he'd been *her* patient—and thanking him for coming by, as if Jeremiah's hospital stay had been a social call.

"Remy," Jude said when the doctor left, "will you be coming with us to Appleton?"

"No," she answered at the exact same moment that Jeremiah said, "Yes."

Her face turned toward Jeremiah and his turned toward her and she felt breathless all over again. What was the matter with her?

She lifted her chin to Jude. "I will not be coming with you. I need to spend some quality time with my friend Wendell."

"Understood. I'll get my car," Jude said to Jeremiah, "and pick you up at the front entrance." Then he disappeared into the hall.

"Your brother seems much more agreeable than you," Remy remarked.

"Am I going to have to fight him for your affection?"

It was preposterous of him even to joke about a circumstance in which either of these two would be interested in her romantically, let alone both. "That question presumes I have affection for you," she said tartly. "Which I do not."

"Yes, you do."

"Is this a good time to confess that Jude has already stolen my heart?"

"He was only here for five minutes."

She winked. "When you know, you know."

"Suddenly, I hate his guts."

"That'll be awkward, once Jude and I marry."

He grunted and pushed to standing. As soon as she rose to her feet, he opened his arms in an invitation for her to hug him.

"What?" she asked, indignant. "We don't hug."

"Bring it in."

"We don't hug."

"I want to give you a thank-you hug before you leave me for Wendell and maybe also my brother."

"Send me a fresh supply of oatmeal to thank me."

"Bring it in," he said stubbornly. His fingers curled a few times.

With a huff, she stepped forward stiffly.

He gave her the first bona fide hug they'd ever shared.

The warmth of his skin radiated through the smooth texture of his athletic shirt. She could feel the contours of his muscles and torso. This was heaven, undiluted heaven.

"Once Jude gets me set up with a phone—" he started.

"You mean once *my future husband* gets you set up with a phone—"

"I'll text you," he finished.

"Except you don't have my number."

"Here." He grabbed a pen from beside the phone and a napkin from the lunch tray.

As she stooped to jot down the digits, he spoke with the false gravity of a knight swearing fealty. "I'll guard this napkin with my life."

Eleven days with him—he was still insufferable.

"We're here." Jude eased his black Ford Bronco to a stop at an electronic gate a few miles outside the town of Groomsport.

Jeremiah watched his brother punch numbers into a keypad.

"The code is two two two two," Jude said. "That's in honor of the two F1 championships you won. In fact, as far as I know, all your four-digit passcodes are two two two two. Not extremely original."

"Nor humble."

The gate slotted to the side. Boundary walls continued in both directions from the gate, disappearing into the trees. It seemed his property was large in size. It also seemed his house was located on top of a hill, because the paved drive took them up through woods yellow and orange and burgundy with autumn leaves. Through the foliage, a meadow came into view. It rose toward a big red-brick house that was obviously over a century old. "This is where I live?"

"Yes. Is it different from what you were expecting?"

"I guess I was expecting something modern."

"The inside's modern but the outside's historic. You like old things."

He did? "It looks more . . . grand than what I would want."

"Grand is your style. You and Dad are similar in that way. The bigger, the better." They parked outside a four-car garage and Jude killed the engine. "I'm sorry you're having to go through this. Your amnesia is strange for me, so I can't imagine how strange it must be for you."

"Very."

"I read up on the condition last night and almost everyone gets their memories back."

"Yeah."

"You'll be one of those. Until that happens, I'm happy to do anything you need."

Jude didn't have a garage door opener, so they followed a stone path to the front where white columns held up a deep covered porch that spanned the length of the house. An outdoor dining table occupied the porch as did fire tables on both ends surrounded by seating. Jeremiah turned to take in the view. Hills curved down to the town of Groomsport and its horseshoe-shaped bay, which glittered navy in the sun.

"What's the population of Groomsport?" Jeremiah asked.

"Five thousand." Jude unlocked the front door. The house alarm beeped so Jude disappeared into the office on the right to deal with it.

Inside Appleton, the floor was pale, wide-plank hardwood. The walls—dark gray. Unlike Remy, it appeared that he preferred uncluttered spaces and had good taste in art.

When Jude returned, he seemed to get that Jeremiah needed time to take it all in. They stood side by side for long seconds.

"Do I like chocolate pudding?" Jeremiah eventually asked.

Jude released a bark of laughter. "What?"

"Here are the things I think are true about me. I think I like chocolate pudding. I have faith in God. I'm a fan of nice cars, nice rum, nice coffee."

"These days you eat food that's healthier and more sophisticated than pudding. We used to go to church regularly as kids. But as far as I know, you've fallen away from that as an adult, maybe because of your schedule. You're right about the rest."

What had he become? "Am I a jerk?"

"No. You're a good guy. Just . . . driven." Jude had the type of demeanor that put a person at ease. He seemed calm and capable. Much easier to take than their father and mother.

"You and Fiona were listed as medical contacts. Felix wasn't. What's my relationship with him?"

"Similar to my relationship with him. Good but not necessarily close. Dad's a complex person. He has his strengths, but unselfishness isn't one of them."

"What's my relationship like with Fiona?"

"Solid. She's complex, too. Intelligent, strong, protective.

Sometimes pushy. When it comes to you and me, she's unselfish because we're her two favorite people in the world. She's from a big family, the third of seven kids."

"What's my relationship with you like?"

"We get along well. We're both independent but we text or talk whenever something comes up. Here. You can take a look at our texts." Jude passed over his phone, open to their messages.

Jeremiah took his time scrolling back through them. He and Jude communicated frequently—checking in, joking, reminding one another about family obligations.

"While you were driving F1," Jude said, "you were pretty busy. After you retired, your pace slowed way down, and we saw each other more."

He'd been too busy for important things, it sounded like. Jeremiah handed back Jude's phone. "When did I start driving?"

"You moved overseas to drive when you were thirteen."

"Thirteen?"

"That's when you went to Europe to compete in the karting circuit. Dad paid Uncle Mike, Mom's younger brother, to live over there with you during the season. After you started driving professionally, you got your own place in Monaco."

"But this house is my home base?"

"In recent years, yes."

Jude took Jeremiah on a brief tour of the downstairs rooms —living room, office, library, kitchen, dining room, media room.

"How many bedrooms and bathrooms?" Jeremiah asked.

"A lot."

A curving staircase led them upstairs. Remy's whole house could fit inside his master bedroom, bathroom, and closet. It didn't suck to find out he lived in a mansion. On the other hand, this place was far too big for just one person. It felt wasteful and kind of lonely. What had Jeremiah 1.0 been trying to prove when he'd chosen this as his home?

Downstairs, he followed Jude into the kitchen. Like the rest of the place, it was new and spotless. White tile, white marble countertops, black cabinetry. Nothing about the house felt lived-in. Either he was a clean freak, or he had a fanatical cleaning crew.

Jude handed him a bottle of beer. Its simple white label read *Dinner*, by Maine Beer Company. He popped the top and took a long sip.

"Almost as good as chocolate pudding?" Jude asked.

"Almost." Jeremiah extended the neck of his bottle and Jude tapped it with his own—which brought on another flash of déjà vu. They'd done that before. Many times.

"I couldn't tell how things stood between Felix and Fiona." Jeremiah leaned a shoulder against the fridge. "I know they're divorced but beyond that, what's their story?"

"You're going to need more than one beer in order to face our family story."

"Am I a drinker?"

"Not that much of one anymore. In your late twenties, you were relying a little too much on hard alcohol. Nowadays, you just drink beer occasionally."

Fantastic. He'd been a widowed workaholic who'd had a problem with alcohol.

"Let's move this party outside." Jude grabbed several things out of the fridge, tossing them to Jeremiah. Bags of organic baby carrots. Hummus. Olive tapenade. Crackers. Almonds.

Was this the kind of food he ate now? He hadn't been here in a week and a half, so he checked expiration dates. All still fresh.

They set the snacks and beer on the porch table and took chairs facing the ocean.

"How much of your past have you looked up?" Jude loaded hummus onto a cracker, then popped it in his mouth.

"Very little. Trying to think about my past makes my head literally hurt."

"Is your head bothering you now?"

"Not really. With you, it's more like a dull, mild ache."

"Flattering."

"After we learned my name," Jeremiah said, "Remy ran a few searches about me. Which is how I know my wife was named Alexis. And that she died fifteen months ago. I know that I retired from racing. And I know that the Camden family is a famous American family. That's about all."

"It's true that the Camdens are famous. We have been ever since the 1800s, when a great-grandfather of ours named Finbar Camden came over from Ireland and made his fortune in banking. His sons established more banks and enlarged the empire. Many of the families from that time weren't able to maintain their fortunes over the generations. They gave a lot of money away to philanthropies and the heirs spent the rest. But the Camdens were good with money from the start. To this day, we all receive a large sum at the age of twenty-five from the family trust. We're expected to be entrepreneurial with that money and grow it."

Jeremiah downed more beer, then nodded. "What did I do with my inheritance?"

"Invested it. By the time you were twenty-five you were already making a huge salary driving."

"Ah."

"Many of our Camden relatives still work in banking but Dad was never interested in that. He was a great athlete—a college quarterback at Notre Dame. He was picked in the second round of the draft and went on to play for sixteen years and win three Super Bowls. Now he's a commentator for one of the networks on Sundays."

"And his personal life?"

"Eventful. Soon after he started playing in the NFL, Dad fell in love with a model named Isobel O'Sullivan. They were both already celebrities. They allowed their wedding to be broadcast live, which doubled their fame. The media dubbed it a wedding of American royalty." Jude sighed. "The whole thing was a debacle and I wish Dad hadn't made it so public."

"Why?"

"Because the fact that they were such a well-known couple made the scandal worse."

"Scandal?"

"It came out that our mother, Fiona, who is Isobel's younger sister, had been having an affair with Dad. That affair resulted in a child."

A pit formed in Jeremiah's stomach. "Me?"

"Yes. I'm sorry to saddle you with this." Jude gave Jeremiah a level look. "It's hung over both our heads all our lives. The fact that we're the sons of scandal is a part of our identity."

He missed Remy. The realization came to Jeremiah clear and certain.

He hadn't been apart from her during the day for longer than a few hours since the part of his life he remembered had begun. He was at his own house talking to his own brother. Yet he wasn't going to feel like himself again until he was with her. "Would Remy have known all this about our family when she found out who our parents are?"

"Ninety percent likely."

That type of notoriety was exactly the kind of thing she hated.

How was he supposed to deal with all of this without being

able to look at her hair, flying seven directions at once? Without the distraction of sparring with her?

"What did Isobel do," he asked Jude, "when she found out her husband had been cheating on her with her sister?"

"Immediately left Dad and filed for divorce. She excommunicated her sister. The two of them haven't talked since. Mom and Dad married shortly before you were born. I was born two years later."

"What happened to Isobel?"

"She's done well. She's had a long modeling career. She married a man who loves her and is faithful to her. They have two grown kids."

Jeremiah chewed a bite of carrot. "I can see why that would hang over our heads."

"Unfortunately, that's not the only scandal."

Jeremiah shot his brother a glance like, *You're kidding, right?*

Jude's expression said that he was not. "We were raised on an estate near here called Maple Lane that Dad inherited from his family. There was a separate caretaker's house on the grounds and a woman named Nicole lived there. She worked for Mom and Dad doing a lot of things—cleaning, cooking, babysitting. She and Mom were around the same age and became good friends. When Mom was pregnant with me, Nicole was also pregnant, due a few months after Mom. Nicole had a son named Max. He and I—well, really, all three of us grew up together. We played together. We shared the same land. We drove to the same school in the same car. Max and I were best friends until we were fourteen and it was discovered that . . ." Pain tightened Jude's features.

"It was discovered that Felix was Max's father," Jeremiah guessed.

"Yes."

"Felix enjoys adultery, apparently."

"Felix enjoys excitement. Especially the forbidden kind. The affair with Nicole went on for a few years under Mom's nose. But he hadn't been with Nicole for a long time when the truth came out. Even so, it ended our parents' marriage and Mom's friendship with Nicole."

"Fiona lost her sister and her friend because of the same man."

"Right. I will say that at least Dad's had the grace not to marry again." Jude paused. "This is hurting your head, isn't it?"

"Starting to," Jeremiah confirmed. "I have a couple more questions."

"Sure."

"Were Alexis and I happy?"

"Yes."

"How did I take her death?"

"Very hard. It was after you retired from F1 as the crowd favorite, in November of last year, that her death seemed to hit you the worst."

"What type of work do I do now?"

"You work some with your old team as a consultant. It's flexible. You have an open invitation to contribute whenever you have time. You also do some marketing event driving for Mercedes, Ferrari, and Lotus. You'll show up and they'll film you driving their newest, fastest cars. You also do occasional speaking engagements. That kind of thing."

Jeremiah scooped up several almonds. "Who are my friends?"

"Anton Quintrell. He was your performance coach the whole time you were driving."

"What does a performance coach do?"

"He's a best friend, physiotherapist, personal trainer, assistant, psychologist. All twenty of the drivers have one.

When you left racing, your gift to Anton was a house here in Groomsport."

"That was generous of me."

"You are generous."

Good to hear he had one decent quality.

"You're friends with some of the people in town you knew growing up," Jude continued. "You're tight with one of our cousins. Once we download the backup of your old phone onto a new one, all your friends and acquaintances should be in your contacts. I'll write out a list for you, so you'll know how you're connected to each one. FYI, I know Mom and Dad reached out to a few of the people in your inner circle when you went missing and have since let them know that you were found." He pulled a few more crackers from the box. "Any other questions for me?"

"Just one. Do you have any idea who might've wanted to kill me?"

Jude's expression turned instantly serious. He set aside the crackers. "You think you ended up with amnesia because someone tried to kill you?"

"I do. When Remy found me, I'd sustained a blow to the back of the head and I had cracked ribs. Which makes me think I was beaten."

Jude studied him. "There was something you were fixated on before you left on the boat trip. I wasn't sure if or when I should bring it up. But if you were beaten, it might be relevant."

"What was I fixated on?"

"The idea that Alexis's death wasn't a suicide like the police ruled it to be."

Agony cut through Jeremiah's skull. "I suspected that someone killed her?"

"Yes."

"Why?"

"You didn't go into it. You just told me that the idea that she'd committed suicide didn't sit right with you. You started investigating the whole thing and came to me for pointers because I'm with the FBI. I tried to help. But to be honest, I didn't think there was evidence to support your theory. I thought that compiling notes and research was your way of working through your grief . . . and that you'd give up the investigation when you were ready. I don't know how far you got with it." For a few seconds, Jude appeared lost in thought. "If you were right about the fact that Alexis was killed and that you were beaten—then I'm tempted to think the same person might have been behind both things."

"Right," Jeremiah said. "What if I got close to the truth about Alexis, so her killer decided to take me out?"

Chapter Ten

Several miles away, Remy was gearing up for a difficult conversation of her own. "Wendell. We need to have a talk."

She'd been too tired to confront him last night and by the time she'd risen this morning, ElderTransport had already taken him to dialysis. After leaving the hospital, she'd decompressed over a lobster-roll lunch eaten solo on a bench facing Rockland's lovely bay. She'd chased that with a large amount of tea and an M&M cookie.

But now she was back at Wendell's house. He was back. And she could no longer ignore the obvious.

She stood, hands on hips, in the living room. Wendell looked owlishly up at her from his recliner, wearing a sweater patterned with golf clubs, trying to soften her with his cuteness. She would not cave. "Your house," she stated, "is in a state of extreme mess."

"I gave up cleaning."

"You can't give up cleaning."

"I can. I'm eighty."

"You're eighty and plenty healthy enough to clean. When you lived on Islehaven you did your part and helped keep the house straight."

His darling face pruned. "This is the worst house I've ever seen in my life."

"This is a charming Cape Cod–style home!" His white front door was flanked by gray siding and windows on each side accented with maroon shutters. The two-bedroom, one-bath-room house had been updated in the past decade. The interior bones were promising. "You're located in a historic neighbor-hood just a five-minute walk to shops and restaurants. What more could you want?"

"My life on Islehaven back."

The wreck he'd made of this place verified the concern she'd experienced when she'd seen him on Islehaven more than a week ago.

An untold number of items encircled them: newspapers, mail, clothing, books, lone shoes, bags of new purchases from Marden's that hadn't been unpacked, and miscellaneous trash.

Obviously, the contents of his larger Islehaven home had been shoved into this one. Now this square footage was straining to contain three times as many things as it should hold. So many cardboard boxes and pieces of furniture had been jammed into her guest bedroom that she had to sidestep through a canyon to get to and from the bed.

Remy dropped to a seat on his coffee table. Old magazines and empty wrappers crinkled under her butt. "Is there anything other than cleaning you've given up recently?"

"Groceries, cooking, driving, and laundry."

"*Excuse me?*"

"I order take-out when I'm hungry. When I run out of things to wear, I send the laundry to a service."

"Is there anything you haven't given up on?"

"Showers and Indian food."

It was almost as if Ruth Ann had conspired to bring Remy here, to show her the state of things. Remy could hear her saying, *Do you see what I see? This is not okay with me, Remy. Not at all! He needs encouragement and a kick in the pants.*

Wendell and Ruth Ann had two children who lived out of state. They'd honored their father's wish to remain in Maine as close as possible to Islehaven and set him up beautifully here. But without his wife, Islehaven, or the community there he'd loved, his heart and spirit had been broken.

"Wendell?"

"Yes?"

"You can't give up on the hard and necessary business of living."

"I'm living," he said half-heartedly.

"No. Not really. You're marking time. You're existing."

Tears gathered in his rheumy hazel eyes. "Existing is the only thing I have left."

"That's not true. You're very fit, for a man with kidney disease. You have an excellent brain. You have family and friends who love you. For more than fifty years you and Ruth Ann took care of each other. She cooked and ironed your pants, and you did the dishes and bought her candles. Remember how she loved candles?"

He nodded.

"Ruth Ann would want you to take care of yourself now that she can't." She stood and extended a hand to Wendell. "I haven't found a lead on Marisol yet. But I will. And the two of us together are going to clean your house."

He eyeballed her hand but didn't move. "I don't care about a little bit of clutter. There's only me to see it."

"Except that I'm standing right here, seeing it."

"What's the point of working so hard every day to make the house tidy? It gets messy again a few minutes later."

"The point? The point is that neatness helps you find things when you need them. And it's better mentally and physically to live in a tidy environment." She waggled her fingers. "Come on. You can work alongside me for an hour today, an hour tomorrow, an hour the day after that, and so on. I'm not going to push you to exhaustion but I'm also not going to do this all by myself."

Finally, Wendell took hold of Remy's hand, and she pulled him to his feet.

⚓

When Remy's phone alarm went off, signaling dinnertime, she mounted a search and eventually located her phone in Wendell's kitchen drawer.

Several text messages had come in from an unknown number that clearly belonged to Jeremiah. He was putting his new cell phone to good use. She created a contact for him and in the name field input *High Maintenance Duke.*

The gist of his messages: He wanted her to join him and Jude for dinner at his house. Or a restaurant. Whatever she'd prefer.

It worried her, how much she wanted to say yes. Separation from him felt uncomfortable and impossible to ignore, as if she were suddenly missing a limb. She'd like to have her limb back.

She'd been telling herself, as the day had worn on toward evening, that she was simply undergoing an adjustment. Every time she came to the mainland, she had to adapt to the people, the buildings, the bustling pace. In the same way, it was normal to enter a brief transition period while she adjusted to living without Jeremiah. She'd do well to remember that life without him was her regular, beneficial setting. He'd no longer be present to grate on her nerves all day!

Also, what was her end game here? She was beginning to detect flirtation between them. Maybe? But there was no chance of the two of them . . . dating. It felt ludicrous even to broach that possibility in her mind. Were Jeremiah to date someone, it would be a supermodel. And she wasn't looking for a relationship. *Certainly* not with a man like him. If she was ever to date someone again, Jeremiah was the opposite of the kind of man she'd consider. His life was too big, too rich, too famous, too complicated. He was smooth and untrustworthy. When she thought about a future potential boyfriend—which she almost never did because the creation of her sculptures took up almost all the space in her mind and heart—she imagined someone understated, patient, kind.

If she missed Jeremiah—which she *did not* because that would be so, so stupid—it would pass.

And, very soon, she'd stop thinking about him 24/7.

REMY

I'm enjoying a well-deserved break from you. So, no thank you to dinner. But please tell Jude that we need to set aside time soon to decide on a wedding venue.

JEREMIAH

I'll kick Jude out, if he's what's keeping you away.

REMY

On the contrary. Jude was the only thing that tempted me to say yes to dinner. Also, since you don't appear to have a sensitive bone in your body, let me inform you that it would be shockingly rude to kick your brother out. Jude's generously dedicating his weekend to helping you reclaim your life.

JEREMIAH

As far as you know, he might be pretending to help me just so he can steal things from my house when I'm not looking.

Remy laughed. She tucked her phone in her pocket and went back to sorting piles of junk.

Her phone buzzed.

JEREMIAH

When can I see you?

REMY

Maybe tomorrow. I have my hands full here. Wendell's house is less organized than a landfill. Making it livable is going to be a huge project.

JEREMIAH

See you tomorrow. Until then, have you considered stealing things from Wendell when he's not looking?

The next afternoon, Jude rolled his carry-on to the media room at Appleton and found his brother there, as expected. Jeremiah's feet were crossed on the coffee table and he had football playing on the big screen.

Jude was planning to head home soon, but he could spare thirty minutes for Sunday football. He lowered onto the leather sofa a few feet from Jeremiah, mirroring his brother's pose.

Born two years after Jeremiah, Jude had literally looked up to his older brother throughout his childhood. Jeremiah had been taller, stronger, braver. Full of big plans and good ideas.

Like a cargo ship, Jeremiah had cut a path through stormy seas. Jude had been the smaller, simpler boat—following in the quiet center of the cargo ship's wake. Jeremiah's doggedness had made Jude's life simpler, a fact that had pleased them both. Jude liked simplifying his life and Jeremiah liked that Jude had the good sense to take advantage of his effort.

The two of them were very different, but in ways that had made them more compatible, not less. Jeremiah had street smarts; Jude had book smarts. Jeremiah was ambitious, Jude strategic. Jeremiah could be wily in pursuit of what he wanted; Jude was firmly ethical. Jude was the one who got the boring things done, the one everyone else relied on, the one who picked up the pieces.

Back when the revelation that Felix was Max's father had detonated, Jeremiah had been sixteen and living overseas. Fiona had slid into depression following the scandal and Jeremiah hadn't been there to function as the cargo ship. Out of necessity, Jude was the one who'd ensured their mother survived.

His memories of his high school years didn't include sports and friends and parties and girls. He'd pretty much given up those things—and lots of days he'd given up school attendance, too—in order to keep an eye on their mom.

Too many nights to count, he'd lain awake, gripped by anxiety, terrified that his mother's sorrow would lead her to suicide. On his watch. Thank God, it hadn't. If it had, he'd never have forgiven himself.

He rolled his face toward Jeremiah and saw that his brother was scowling at his phone. "Why are you frowning?"

"Because Remy. Let me ask you a question."

Jude nodded.

"Are women usually impressed with me?"

It was weird to explain Jeremiah to Jeremiah. Overall, though, this situation mostly left Jude grateful. Jeremiah had been found in open water, injured, with hypothermia. They were all lucky that Jeremiah was alive. Yes, he had amnesia and needed extra support right now. But Jude knew his brother's strong-willed personality too well to doubt that he'd recover quickly. "Yes. Women are always impressed with you."

"Do they ever give me a hard time?"

"Never."

"I'm . . . good with women?"

"Very." In fact, had Jeremiah been the one who'd been asked by his employer to go undercover as the boyfriend of a beautiful woman, Jeremiah would have had no problem executing that assignment.

Jude fulfilled his work responsibilities with excellence. That's what he did. And that's what he was determined to do with this upcoming op. Unfortunately, a few factors were working against him. One, he had zero experience at the role of fake boyfriend. Two, he knew enough about Gemma Clare to know she was the type of woman he'd never date in real life.

"If I'm good with women," Jeremiah asked, "then how come I'm no good with this one? Remy gives me nothing but a hard time and she's not impressed with me at all. She's driving me crazy because she won't say when she'll see me again."

Jude couldn't help but smile. He wanted to get to know Remy better. And maybe give her a certificate.

"This is not amusing," Jeremiah said.

"It's highly amusing to me. I've waited my whole life for a woman to treat you this way."

"It's the worst."

"It's the best. Propose to her. She's one in a million."

Jeremiah made a derisive sound, letting his head fall back against the cushion. "Propose to her? She's not even civil."

"You have a crush on her."

"I do not."

"Mm," Jude said noncommittally.

"I don't."

"Okay." Though Jeremiah absolutely did have a crush on Remy.

Seconds later, the brothers yelled, "Fumble!" in unison.

Jude stuck around long enough to watch the recovering team connect a thirty-yard pass to the end zone, then pushed to his feet. "I'm taking off."

Jeremiah moved to stand.

"Don't get up."

"I'm getting up."

"Broken ribs."

"Which are improving." Jeremiah extended his hand, and they shook.

"Thank you," Jeremiah said.

"You're welcome. If there's anything else I can do, call me."

Jeremiah watched Jude go. Remy had been correct when she'd said that Jude had been generous to dedicate his weekend to helping Jeremiah reclaim his life.

Gaining access to the computer in his office had been the easiest part—they'd unlocked that with Jeremiah's fingerprint so hadn't needed a code. Emails had revealed which bank he used. They'd driven to the local branch and validated his identity there. Bank statements showed which credit cards he carried. They called each credit card company, cancelled the old cards, and requested new. They located his phone backup on the cloud, bought a new phone, then downloaded the backup. They requested a new driver's license online. Incoming email from business associates had enabled Jeremiah to send them all an outgoing email, letting them know he was extending his vacation for personal reasons.

This morning, he and Jude had gone through his list of

phone contacts. Jude knew who more than half of them were. For those, Jeremiah added the details Jude supplied to each contact's information. Things like, *Aunt on Fiona's side. Friend from my driving days.*

Jeremiah's phone chimed to signal a text. He checked it, hoping it was from Remy. It wasn't. It was from someone named Gigi Kaminski. Jude hadn't been familiar with Gigi. Jeremiah's plan for the people Jude wasn't familiar with: ignore.

He tossed his phone to the side and massaged his temples.

Remy wasn't warming up to the idea of simply hanging out with him, so he needed to change his strategy. She'd agreed to stay until he was settled and doing fine on his own. Which meant he needed to give her a reason to think he wasn't settled, wasn't fine on his own, and required her help. That's what had done the trick on Islehaven and that's what might do the trick here on the mainland.

About an hour before sunset the following evening, Remy carried trash bag number eight thousand to the driveway beside Wendell's house. She'd deposited the first few bags in the city trash bins. Quickly filling those, she'd been depositing subsequent bags near the bins. Soon, she wouldn't be able to park her rental car in the driveway, so she spent time dragging several out of the way.

As she skirted the front corner of the house en route back to the door, she saw that a man was standing, hands in his pockets, on the front stoop. He was facing her and staring straight at her.

She jerked to a halt. Jeremiah.

A *clang* went through her. His eyes, though the coolest shade of green, blazed hot.

He wasn't the same. The scruff on his cheeks was gone, as

were the familiar clothing items he'd worn and reworn on Isle-haven. Until now she hadn't realized just how much those things had combined with his weakened physical state to make him seem . . . approachable. Human?

He was a self-controlled man but today he looked more in control of himself than ever. The smooth lines of his cheeks and jaw were unforgivingly handsome. He'd dressed in a simple dusky blue sweater, jeans that fit him like a dream, European-looking sneakers. Every item gave off an expensive vibe.

"How'd you find this place?" she asked.

"I looked up Wendell Reeves's address on Whitepages.com."

She raised a fist and shook it.

"What does that mean?" he asked.

"I'm shaking my fist at Whitepages.com."

He chuckled, then followed her inside.

Wendell was sullenly going through one of the cardboard boxes left over from his Islehaven house.

Jeremiah introduced himself.

"Are you the Indian food delivery guy?" Wendell asked.

"Afraid not. I'm a friend of Remy's."

"I wouldn't say friend," she whispered.

"I'm an *acquaintance* of Remy's. And, Wendell, I have a lot of sympathy for you now that you're the one having to live with her. The work she's making you do looks like it stinks."

"It's the most awful thing in the world."

"Yeah." Jeremiah nodded sadly. "I'm sorry, buddy."

"I am not an albatross to either of you!" Remy proclaimed. "I'm an asset."

"Right," Jeremiah said. "Which is why Wendell here is stuck sorting pink glassware."

"It's for his ultimate good."

"And his temporary misery." Jeremiah lowered to his

haunches next to a box. "I'll help. I'll go through these"—he tipped a flap open—"jars of spare change?"

"No. You will not be lifting heavy jars of spare change! You're an invalid." It was far easier to think of him as such.

He peered at her for a protracted moment, head cocked. "You're right. I'm much too weak to spend my time sorting through fifty years of"—he rolled his lips inward as if curbing a bad word—"things."

"Might be best for you to leave, in that case."

Setting his hand on top of a tall jar of change, he used it to lever himself to standing. "I came because I need your help with something."

"Oh?"

He drew near so that they were out of Wendell's earshot. His body suddenly contained such tremendous magnetism that she had to consciously hold her ground instead of retreat.

"Jude told me that, before I went on my boat trip, I was investigating Alexis's death."

"Investigating it? Why?"

"I didn't believe it was suicide."

His words struck, capturing her full attention.

"It's important that I find," he went on, "whatever research I'd gathered about her death so I can know what Jeremiah 1.0 knew."

"You're Jeremiah 2.0?"

"Yeah."

"Where have you looked so far for this research?"

"The electronic files on my computer and the drawers in my desk. No luck."

"Did Jude say *why* you suspected Alexis's death wasn't a suicide?"

"No. I'd simply told him that I knew something about it wasn't right."

She pushed one finger at a time in toward her palm, thinking.

"If someone caused her death," he added, "then my disappearance makes more sense because the same person could be behind both things."

She turned that around in her head, examining it critically the way she would a sculpture in progress. "That feels like a stretch. Everything that I've read about Alexis's death online points to suicide."

"You've read about her death online since we left the hospital?"

"Yes. At length." She might have gotten a wee bit obsessed. "Also, if a killer succeeded in taking her out and tried the same with you, why did he fail in your case?"

"Because I'm an athletic specimen."

She snorted. "And why would someone try to kill you by dumping you in the ocean? That's an impractical way to kill someone."

"I hear you. But isn't it harder to believe that Alexis jumped off a cliff and then, fifteen months later, I'm coincidentally found bobbing on the ocean with amnesia?"

He had a point. "All of it is hard to believe." Remy frowned. "If Alexis's death and your injuries are connected by the same villain, that means the villain is still on the loose."

"Unless I killed him in a fight the day I went overboard. I'm an athletic specimen."

"You were the kind of athlete who was good at turning a steering wheel." She swept toward the back of the house. "I'll get my jacket, then we'll go to your house, and I'll help hunt for your research."

Inside the guest room, she caught her reflection in the mirror that balanced on top of cardboard boxes like a cherry on top a sundae. She scrunched her nose. Her white T-shirt and olive-colored cargo pants looked rumpled and dusty from the day's work, and why were her glasses hiding in her hair? She plucked them free. After finger-combing the wavy strands, she secured her hair in a side ponytail. Then she applied the lip gloss she found rattling around at the bottom of her purse. This would have to do.

She did not want to look appealing for Jeremiah Camden anyway.

Obviously.

When she returned to the living area, she heard Jeremiah saying, "Perk up, Wendell. You can stop sorting glassware because I'm going to take her off your hands."

The degree of gratitude in Wendell's voice as he thanked Jeremiah was not complimentary to her in the least.

Jeremiah led the way to a sleek, royal blue car parked at the curb.

"What's this?" she asked.

"A 2017 BMW M5." He opened the passenger door for her. Once she was settled, he took the driver's seat.

"A bit . . . showy, don't you think?" she asked.

"This is the least showy car I have." They zoomed off.

She clutched her purse against her torso as the speedometer climbed. "Why would anyone need more than one car?"

"You're adorable."

He commanded his phone to pull up directions to Appleton, which reminded her that his amnesia would have stolen his memory of how to get around Groomsport just as surely as everything else.

After several minutes, they flashed by an open gate and followed a private drive uphill. Appleton introduced itself to her in fleeting glimpses. Then, gradually, made its full magnificence known. The mansion was as self-important as a

Downton Abbey butler, bristling with the secrets of its past residents.

"A fitting home for a duke," she remarked. "Is there a pond nearby? If so, all that's missing is for you to dive into it wearing breeches and a white shirt."

"I have no idea what you're talking about."

"That's a Mr. Darcy reference."

"I'm proud to say I don't get it."

They parked and approached the front. "Are the servants going to be standing in a line outside to greet us?" she asked.

"I think I might have a cleaning crew, but as far as I can tell, no servants."

She stopped to crane her neck up at the façade. "*Why* would any sane person choose to live in a building of this size? It's ludicrously enormous."

"I've been asking myself the same question. The short answer is that Jeremiah 1.0 chose this place because he liked it." He held the door for her, and she stepped inside a cavernous living area.

Jeremiah closed them in, stilling the wind that had been riffling through her hair. She took in her surroundings, appalled. "Your art!" Her fingers jutted toward a nearby painting. "It's all by *Dartin*. I should have known. You're a Dartin collector," she accused the same way she'd have accused him of being a redcoat spy.

"Who's Dartin?"

"One of the painters I told you I loathed. This art is drivel, created by a sell-out."

"Doesn't all art have merit?" he challenged.

"Not this stuff."

He went to the nearest painting and reached as if to lift it off the wall.

"Don't!" she ordered.

He paused.

"Your ribs," she explained. "Also, you shouldn't be handling these pieces. While they are not a valuable contribution to the art world in my eyes, they are of sizeable monetary value."

He stood nonchalantly next to his Dartin, looking every inch like American royalty. *This* is who he was. This is how he dressed. This is where he lived. Descendant of a storied family, son of an infamous father. Successful race car driver. He was a prominent man caught up in the pursuit of worldly success.

Seeing him here was like seeing a cougar in its natural habitat. You didn't want to *be* the cougar. But you didn't exactly want to be the bunny, either.

She moved to slip out of her jacket and felt his hands behind her, helping her off with it. That perfectly polite, not-sexual courtesy sent a cascade of goosebumps down her neck and arms.

Remy! Stop this. She'd invested years in her hard-earned recovery and had no interest in jeopardizing that in any way. So how come her body's ability to experience physical desire was coming back now with this most ill-advised man?

He hung up her jacket and purse.

"Your home office, I presume?" She moved toward the room separated from the living space by interior French doors.

"Yes."

"You said you've already looked through your computer and desk for your research on Alexis's death?"

"Right."

"I vote we start here. With these cabinets." The wall opposite the window held built-in cabinetry below and shelving above. She sank to her knees next to the first cabinet. He began to kneel. "Don't even think about it," she told him before he'd lowered five inches. "You have fractured ribs, so sit on a chair, Duke."

"As you command." He sat and then rolled the desk chair toward her, executing a spin on the way.

The cabinet held a slide-out filing system. She handed him half the files and started making her way through the rest.

"Financial documents here," she said.

"Employment documents here."

She rapidly scanned each page. Then moved to the next file. "Contracts."

"Property records," he said. "It says here I bought this place three years ago." He unfolded architectural blueprints. They were clearly new, no doubt commissioned when he'd bought this house. It showed room after room, three stories worth. Really, it was absurd that Jeremiah lived here. An insult to decency and frugality.

Once they'd gone through the files in the first cabinet, they tackled the second.

"Legal documents in this file," she murmured. "Including a copy of your will."

"That, I'd like to see."

She set the papers on top of the counter above the cabinets. He slid his chair close.

"I'll excuse myself so you can read your will in private," she announced.

"You really think there are any secrets between us after you saw me naked on Islehaven?"

"I only saw your clavicles!" Her cheeks heated.

His lips quirked as if to suppress laughter and she had the impression she'd reacted to his question just the way he'd hoped.

"Please stay and help me translate this legalese." He patted his lap. "You can sit here."

"Absolutely not."

"To staying or sitting here?"

"Sitting there."

"Your loss."

They worked together to understand the meaning of his will. Essentially, he'd specified that upon his death a charity called Global Citizen should receive two million dollars and someone named Anton Quintrell should receive two million. A lot of stipulations followed about what was to happen with the money he'd received from the Camden family trust. Finally, his mother, Jude, and Max should split the remaining (largest share) of his assets.

They continued through the rest of the cabinets, then moved on to other downstairs rooms. They opened every drawer, looked in every container in every closet.

Nothing about the interior of the house made her think Jeremiah or Alexis had furnished it themselves. It smacked of professionals who'd mastered the art of design and organization. He had everything a man his age could want, grouped together in logical and practical ways.

However, the whole thing felt . . . highly impersonal.

She skated her fingertips along a bookcase shelf in his library. Difficult to imagine paying for hardbacks when paperbacks were so much cheaper, yet all Jeremiah's books were hardbacks. In addition to hundreds of books, the shelves held decorative objects and framed photos.

The photos provided a fascinating glimpse into his former life. Jeremiah traveling in exotic places. Jeremiah surrounded by people in the colorful matching uniforms of his racing team. Jeremiah with trophies and race cars. Family photos old and new. Photos of him with friends. "Does it strike you as strange that Alexis isn't in any of these pictures?" she asked.

"It does strike me as strange."

"How many of the downstairs rooms have we searched so far?"

"About half."

Good grief. Tiredness was gnawing on her because she'd spent most of the day attacking the chaos of Wendell's house. As soon as they finished this room, she'd call it a night. "Are the photos of you and Alexis grouped together somewhere else?"

"No. I've been in every room. I haven't seen a picture of her anywhere."

Turning toward him, she found him so close that their eye contact caused her heart to thump, then pick up speed. She cleared her throat. "D—do you think you put away pictures of her because they caused you too much pain?"

"I don't know."

"That's probably why you did it. When I was sixteen, our wonderful family dog, Buttercup, passed away. We had to put his bed and bowl and toys in a box in the garage because it was too painful for us to see them. Not that I'm comparing the magnitude of your loss to ours."

"Huh."

"I mean . . . you wouldn't have spent time investigating Alexis's death if you didn't deeply love her."

His scrutiny of her didn't waver. "I don't know what it was that drove me to investigate Alexis's death. I don't know how I felt about her or why there's no pictures of her here. I only know that she's not here now. That she's been gone for quite a while. And that she isn't coming back."

"Yes, but it's important to honor the fact that Alexis still owns your heart. Soon, you'll remember your grief."

And as soon as that happened, he'd revert to being Jeremiah 1.0 who had loved and married Alexis.

Chapter Eleven

"Remy?" In the middle of that night Jeremiah started speaking her name sleeping and finished the syllables waking. "Remy?" he repeated, hopeful even though clarity was returning, and he was realizing he was in his big house in Groomsport—a place where she was not.

Only quiet reached his ears.

His sheets were not scratchy. This cover was just the right weight and thickness. His body was warm, and he was not wearing hideous black-and-red-checkered pajama pants.

He should be content. Yet he kept waking through the night, discontent, missing Remy.

The two of them were very different.

He was controlled. She was unfiltered.

He was moderate. She was obsessive.

He was a spender. She was frugal.

He was pragmatic. She was artistic.

He was conventional. She was eccentric.

He had something to prove. She did not.

His motives were selfish. Hers were pure.

He should not want her close as much as he did. But an ache for her had lodged itself between his healing ribs and wouldn't go away.

It felt as if Appleton went upward and outward for miles, separating him from all other human beings, isolating him when he already felt isolated because he had no memories of the people he loved.

He was alone.

Fear came for him then, cold and immediate. It spiked adrenaline into his heart, which started racing. He sat up in the dark, hands braced on the mattress behind him, panicking.

What was happening?

His brain scrambled. He . . . he'd shoved down his worries about the amnesia. That had been necessary because concern about his physical health had been most urgent. Now that physical concerns had lessened, his body was reminding him that worry about the amnesia had only been pushed away. It wasn't gone.

In fact, it was viciously strong now that he no longer had Remy.

He hated the things he was left with. A whitewashed past. This house. Loneliness.

He couldn't remember. Not his childhood, not his family, not his career, not Alexis. Why couldn't he remember?

Jeremiah rushed to his feet next to the bed as a way to escape the fear. But it was no use. The fear came with him.

He needed to hang on to the fact that he'd see Remy again tomorrow. When she was near, he'd be able to breathe.

And he needed to begin therapies that might help treat the amnesia. Not so much because he wanted his biography back, which he did. But because he *needed* to access one particular memory.

If someone had done Alexis harm and then tried to do

him harm, they would have done so on his boat the first day of his trip. As soon as humanly possible, he had to recall what had happened on the boat. And even more importantly, he had to recall the face and name of the person who'd done this to him.

Remy split her time four ways.

One, she waded deeper into the gargantuan job of sorting Wendell's belongings. Right off the bat, his house got worse when its contents were vomited out. It was like living inside of a junk drawer and it was giving Remy hives.

She wasn't the most organized person herself. That said, she considered her cottage mostly clean with a cozy dash of clutter. Her elderly friend, on the other hand, was burying himself in a tomb of mess.

Two, she sat in front of Wendell's computer, trying to figure out how to locate Marisol. She checked for her on search engines, social media sites, genealogy sites—and made zero headway.

Three, she helped Jeremiah search Appleton for his mysterious notes regarding Alexis's death.

Four, she and Wendell spent the late-evening hours in his living room. Him in the recliner, reading Harlequins. Her curled on the sofa next to the lamp on the end table, reading fantasy novels. It was during those moments, when she'd look across at Wendell in companionable bookworm silence, that she loved her old friend best.

On the third day of searching Appleton, Remy wondered aloud to Jeremiah whether someone might have gotten inside his house and stolen the notes. He pointed out that there'd been no sign of a break-in. Besides, it was likely that no one knew about his investigation into Alexis's death other than the few people closest to him.

When she returned to Wendell's that night, she took a hard look at her bank account. She'd taken a break from work when Jeremiah had first come to stay with her. And now she'd taken another six days away from her studio.

Her last vacation had occurred almost a year ago and she was due for time off, definitely. Yet the Remy of a month ago would have scoffed at the idea of spending her "vacation" assisting a man without a memory who could not be her boyfriend and helping another man with a messy house hunt for his lost love. This wasn't exactly Tahiti, was it? Even so, she wasn't ready to end her time here which is why it was disconcerting to watch her balance tick lower and lower. She figured she could afford to stay another few weeks—tops. As soon as Project Wendell ended, she'd go.

On the fourth day of searching, Jeremiah suggested that he might have saved his notes on a digital platform. They pulled chairs up to his computer and visited the most prominent cloud storage sites to see if typing his email address into the log-in screen revealed that he had an account at any of them. Remy was infuriatingly distracted by how sinfully good he smelled and the sight of his adept hands moving over the keyboard. They located an account at Dropbox. After resetting his password, they accessed the account. There were documents there but none pertaining to Alexis.

On the fifth day of searching, they combed his bank statements to see if he paid either for office space outside his home or storage space anywhere. He did not. Though it was intriguing to see where he spent his money. On normal things, it turned out. Food, clothing, his house, utilities, entertainment, travel. It was *how much* he spent on those things that left her breathless.

September had given way to October and where were his notes?

Also, would he notice if she disposed of the soap he used here at Appleton? No woman could be expected to be productive in the company of a man who smelled that enticing.

Remy wished she could hit a button and an automated voice would respond by asking, "What about this?" so she didn't have to voice the words. She'd spoken the sentence on repeat to Wendell as they'd continued their donate/keep/store sorting process.

She held up a wooden box after lunch on Sunday. "What about this?"

"That," Wendell replied with gravity, "is the cleverest box that ever was."

It didn't help that Wendell was sentimental and wanted to hang on to much more than he should have. From where he sat, on a chair in his bedroom, he extended age-spotted hands to her.

She passed the box over.

He cradled it. "This belonged to our son Elliot. It was passed down to him by Ruth Ann's father. And it had been passed down to Ruth Ann's father by his grandfather. It's a feat of workmanship that you'll appreciate, seeing as how you're a woodworker yourself."

Remy, sitting cross-legged on the floor, pushed her tongue against her back teeth to keep herself from saying that the box did not look to her like a feat of workmanship. It looked like a simple rectangle with a hinged lid and a piece of trim at its base.

"Elliot used to keep his bottle caps in this." He opened the top and his leprechaun face creased with delight. "They're still here. It's good to know that some things don't change." She sensed Wendell's thoughts traveling back in time to when Elliot had been young enough to collect bottle caps in his bedroom on Islehaven. Elliot was now fifty and a city controller in Maryland. "This box has a secret. It's not as it appears at first glance. See if you can figure it out." He handed it down to her.

Remy poured the bottle caps onto the floor, then took her time examining the box. She tested the different surfaces, tugging gently on the flat planes. The inside right wall of the box slid upward. She drew it higher until the piece of wood came out in her hand. On its bottom edge, a metal column similar in size to the point of a tack protruded. Now that she'd removed this piece from the box, she could see two depressions in the bottom corner of the box that awaited metal columns.

She chewed on her lip, thinking.

"You're on the right track," Wendell encouraged.

"Don't tell me the answer."

"And ruin your fun? I wouldn't dare."

So . . . if she turned the piece of wood around, then fit it back into place, the column would slot into the hole it had not been resting in before.

She tried it and *there*.

A *click*. Instantly, the piece of trim on the right side jutted out, revealing a shallow hidden compartment. Inside, Elliot had kept his most prized bottle caps. One orange Fanta and one root beer.

Wendell clapped. "Well done."

Remy revised her earlier mediocre opinion of the workmanship involved in creating this box. Hats off to the person who'd had the imagination to add a secret drawer.

A niggle grew at the edge of her mind, whispering to her

that there was something more here—a connection she should see.

What did an old box, bottle caps, or a secret storage space have to do with anything relevant to her?

And then in a wash of tingles, the answer occurred to her.

Jeremiah was in his home gym—riding his Peloton, listening to indie rock, and watching sports—when he registered banging coming from somewhere else in the house. He slowed, silencing the music.

Yeah, definitely banging. On his front door.

He wiped his face, hair, and hands with a towel, then made his way toward the sound.

When he found Remy on his front porch, dark satisfaction rose in a rush. He was so, so glad she'd come. She'd never shown up here without him nagging her to do so. And yesterday she'd refused to see him at all because they'd finished their failed search for his notes.

The only people he'd interacted with yesterday were the strangers at the grocery store. Several had recognized him and introduced themselves. Two had wanted to take selfies with him. Another asked if he'd sign the back of a grocery store receipt to his grandson.

They'd been nice people, but the conversations had under-scored the strangeness of his situation. He didn't remember being well-known. Worse, he didn't remember doing the things he was well-known for. He'd come home from the store feeling hollow. Like an imposter. Not like a person who'd earned the right to take selfies and sign autographs on the back of receipts.

"Are you wearing overalls again because you know I can't resist them?" he asked as she walked inside.

Remy made overalls sexy. Today she wore a tank top under them, which gave him glimpses of the curvy body beneath.

"I'm wearing overalls again because I didn't bring many outfits to the mainland. Are you exercising just to make me mad? You aren't strong enough for exercise."

"Remy, I'm healing fast now. My cough's gone and my rib pain is a two out of ten—"

"Look here." She lifted the wooden box she carried. "This is a clue. I think. I hope." She set the box on the entry table. "Watch." She pulled up an interior section, turned it, and pushed it back down, which popped open a hidden drawer. "Well?" Expectation rolled off her in waves. She'd piled all her hair on top of her head today.

He wanted, with an almost overpowering urge, to plunge his hands into that hair, pull her against him, and kiss her. Wanted that more than he could remember wanting anything. Words fled and he stood there, struggling to get a hold of himself and control his sudden hunger. He noted the shade of her pink lips. The flutter of her pulse at the hinge of her jaw, the sage scent of her—

"Well?" she demanded again.

"Did you," he said slowly, racking his brain, "come to tell me that you spun a story around this wooden box the way you did around your wooden Emiline statue? Is this box . . . a wizard or a mage or something?"

She made a sound of frustration and raised her hands high. "My plane of thinking is up here. And yours"—she plunged her hands low—"is down here."

"And now I'm jumping on your last nerve." He poked at the nearest hand.

She jerked it away and leveled him with point-blank exasperation. "This box has a secret compartment. It's over a hundred years old. Appleton is over a hundred years old. This box makes me wonder if Appleton has a secret compartment, too."

"A secret compartment one inch deep isn't large enough to store my research on Alexis," he said, to needle her.

"You're being deliberately obtuse." She went to his office and rifled through files. Soon, she'd extracted the house's blueprints. She smoothed them across the surface of his desk. "I'll start looking on the third floor. You start looking on the first floor. We'll meet in the middle. We're on the hunt for a small room or closet that we didn't search this past week because its access point is hidden."

He leaned over the drawing. She leaned over it, too, causing a lock of her hair to trail against the palm he'd placed on the desk's surface.

His instincts surged again. He swallowed and briefly closed his eyes.

She lived on Islehaven. He lived here. She'd never agree to date him, which was for the best because he shouldn't date anyone until he had his memories back and was his whole self again.

"See anything?" she asked.

"Not yet." He scanned the drawing as seconds ticked by. Then he pointed to a spot. "Here." There was a closed-off room around the size of a walk-in closet near the kitchen, behind the butler's pantry.

Like a bird, her head cocked to assess what he'd found. Then she let out a whoop. "I'm brilliant! My plane of thought, Jeremiah, is way up here." She gestured.

"This secret space might be filled with canned green beans."

"No. I have a good feeling about this."

"Or it could be empty. What if 1.0 didn't even know about

it? I'm not sure I pay enough attention to detail to spot that on the drawings if I wasn't looking for it."

"A secret space is noteworthy. Surely someone pointed it out to you when you bought this house."

Was it noteworthy, though? Maybe only to creative people like her. Remy hurried out of the office.

He followed. "Not sure where you're headed, brilliant one, but the butler's pantry is this way."

She turned on her heel, and he led her to the butler's pantry. One wall held a counter and sink with storage above and below. The opposite wall held shelves stocked with liquor bottles.

"According to the plans"—Jeremiah pointed to the liquor—"this is the wall that becomes a door."

"Good hiding spot because I'd never have thought a wall full of breakable bottles would give way."

"Me neither."

They pushed and prodded every inch of the trim, shelving, and the lip at the front of the shelves that kept the bottles secure.

"Surely," she said, "there must be someone on the internet who's posted videos about how to enter secret rooms like yours."

He pulled his phone from the pocket of his basketball shorts. Sure enough, several YouTube videos populated in response to his search. Most had been created by people trying to master "Escape the Room" challenges.

They watched three videos in a row before implementing the suggested techniques.

No success.

They watched another video. Tried the technique. No.

"How come mysteries never take this long for Nancy Drew to solve?" Remy wondered.

"Who's Nancy Drew?"

"A girl detective in a series of novels."

"Wish Nancy was here now."

Next, they watched a video that had just 127 views. In it, a man suggested they hunt for an item that was permanently affixed. That, he said, would be a lever.

One by one, they tested the bottles. They seemed too fragile to function as a lever. The items used as levers in the video—a book, a small statue—had been more substantial—

"*Jeremiah,*" Remy said.

"Did you find it?"

"Look. This one can't be removed." She'd wrapped her hand around a matte black bottle of Scotch whiskey positioned near the height of her shoulder. She stepped aside to let him try.

He couldn't lift it upward, either. But when he tipped it to one side, it leaned smoothly. With a *shlick*, the entire wall of bottles swung on a central hinge. One side of the wall turned in, the other side turned out. Behind lay a short passageway that ended in an old-fashioned wooden door.

He glanced at Remy. Her hands lifted to cover her mouth.

"Would Nancy Drew be proud?" he asked.

Slowly, she dropped her hands. "Yeah. She would."

They walked into the hallway. He tried the door.

Locked. "Maybe 1.0 was very protective of his green beans," he said.

She visibly deflated.

The historic door was clearly original to the house. So was the keyhole below the knob. As he hunched over to look into the keyhole, realization tripped in his brain. He reversed out of the space and went to the mudroom next to the garage, Remy hot on his heels.

"What are you thinking?" she asked.

"My plane of thought is so high that you wouldn't understand if I tried to explain." During their searching of the past several days, Remy had looked through the cubbies in the mudroom and he'd looked through the storage bench and also the contraption mounted to the wall. The contraption had a mirror, a rectangular drawer, and a row of hooks where jackets, sweatshirts, and umbrellas hung.

He opened the drawer. "This is where 1.0 kept his keys." A key ring for his house keys that snapped open and closed. One key for each car that he could add to the main ring depending on which car he took. Plus a few miscellaneous keys. Jeremiah picked up the old-fashioned metal key he'd remembered and grinned at Remy.

"Locating a key in a key drawer? That's the extent of your high-plane thinking?" She shook her head but was doing a bad job of hiding her pleasure.

It would take her down a few notches to learn that the secret room *did* contain green beans. But he couldn't make himself hope for that. He wanted her theory to lead them to his notes about Alexis. For both their sakes.

They returned to the historic door.

The old key slid into the lock without a problem but didn't easily turn. He jiggled it, adjusted its position, attempted to twist it again and again. Finally, the lock gave way with a rusty wheeze.

Remy gasped.

Jeremiah pushed the door inward. Light from the butler's pantry revealed a tiny room and an even smaller table that supported only one item—a manila envelope.

He pulled the dangling cord overhead and the bulb flickered on.

Remy came to stand at the table next to him, hands wrapped around her overalls' straps.

"Do you want to do the honors?" he asked.

"No. This is your envelope. Yours to open."

"Except that we're a team."

She shook her head. "I'm a lone wolf."

He paused. "You do that a lot, you know."

"What?"

"Put distance between us."

"Distance is good."

"Except when it isn't."

"Jeremiah! We're standing in a secret room in front of a mysterious envelope. This is not the time for introspection."

He freed the envelope's flap and pulled out a stack of paper and more. Photos? Clearly, they'd found his missing notes. "How about we move into the kitchen? We'll have better light and more space."

"'Kay."

In the kitchen, he set the stack on the marble surface of the island. They pulled up barstools.

The top-most piece of paper was a printed email from someone named Fred Kimley dated two and a half years prior.

March 23

Dear Mr. Camden,

I've completed my work on your case. You hired me to determine whether or not your wife, Alexis Camden, was engaging in an extramarital affair. According to the evidence I uncovered through financial forensics of her accounts, analysis of the activity on her phone, and visual surveillance, the answer to that question is yes. She engaged in an affair with Sabato Messina for three months.

You can view the evidence I compiled via this link. I will also mail physical copies to you shortly.

I've attached a detailed report of the hours billed on this project and my activities during each of those hours. I've also attached an invoice for the remaining portion of my fee.

Sincerely, Fred Kimley

The email ended with a logo that included Fred's name followed by *Private Investigator*.

Jeremiah held himself perfectly still while pain carved into his skull and the taste of betrayal rose like bile up his throat. Even though his memory had wiped Alexis away, his body bore the scars of her infidelity and death. His physical self—muscles and bones and blood—remembered and was rebelling.

"*No*," Remy whispered in a shaken voice. She looked horrified.

Tenderness for Remy shoved much of the darkness aside. He wrapped an arm around her shoulders and pulled her near. Her head tipped against his shoulder, and he rested the side of his head on top of hers.

He closed his eyes and soaked in the feel of her. "It's okay."

This might be hitting her even harder than him. From the start, Remy had concluded that he'd loved Alexis. But the whole happy newlywed thing had never resonated with him.

Nor had the idea of himself as the grieving, heartbroken husband.

That had just never . . . felt like it fit. But this information about Alexis?

As harsh as it was, it did fit. And explained why his dreams of Alexis had not been happy.

His brother had told him his marriage to Alexis was solid. Which suggested that he'd told Jude about his suspicions regarding Alexis's death but not about her affair. Why? Because he'd been too proud? Too private? Had he been protecting Alexis or his own reputation?

Remy moved to straighten.

He immediately let go. "Ready to continue?"

"Yes."

He placed the first page to the side, facedown. Below it rested bank statements. Pages and pages worth. Kimley had highlighted certain transactions. Hotel rooms. Dinners. Travel. Lingerie purchases. Huge amounts of money had been deducted. "This must be the physical evidence he said he'd mail," Jeremiah said.

Next came phone records with highlighted calls and texts.

Then photos of Alexis with a good-looking, black-haired guy. One photo captured the two of them snuggled into a corner table at a fancy restaurant. One of them walking into a hotel. One of them sitting at a bar facing each other and leaning in for a kiss.

He cut a glance in Remy's direction. She looked pale and grim. He raised a questioning eyebrow.

"I'm just . . ." She dashed a tendril of hair off her forehead. "I'm just disappointed, I guess. I'd been imagining Alexis as this wonderful, loyal, devoted person."

"Are there very many wonderful, loyal, devoted people in the world?"

"I *have* to believe so." She said it in a way that made him think it really was necessary for her to believe that.

"Maybe Alexis was wonderful, but also made some mistakes? Or maybe I cheated on her first? Like father, like son. And this was how she paid me back."

Remy's expression told him that the possibility of that, him cheating on Alexis the way his father had cheated on both his wives, made her nauseous. "If you were a cheater, why would you have gone to the trouble of paying a private investigator to catch Alexis in the act?"

He ran a hand through his hair. "I might have been a

cheater who was fine with my own affairs but jealous of hers? I mean, I hope not. We don't have all the facts." What kind of person was 1.0? What kind of person was Alexis?

He continued through the stack until he reached another letter from Fred Kimley. This one was dated more recently— fifteen months ago, over a year after the first letter from Kimley, one day after Alexis died.

June 25

Dear Mr. Camden,

I've completed the investigation you requested. As before, you will find an electronic file containing the evidence I've compiled online here and can expect to receive hard copies in the mail.

It is my opinion that your wife is engaged in another affair, but I was unable to prove it conclusively this time. Mrs. Camden has learned how to evade detection. When she did not wish to be followed, she took public transportation.

For example, you'll see in the log that on one particular trip she drove from Camden to Brunswick and bought a ticket on Amtrak's Downeaster train. Because Brunswick is the northern-most stop, I purchased a ticket going as far as the final stop, Boston. I was at a disadvantage because I didn't know where she was exiting. Moments before the doors closed at Wells, she disembarked and hurried to a taxi she'd pre-scheduled. She was gone before I could secure a taxi and follow. The next time she took the train, she drove farther south to its Freeport stop. I booked a ticket south again, but this time she stepped onto the northbound train at the last second.

She no longer uses her credit cards to make purchases linked to her secretive behavior. She now withdraws cash. See the attached bank statements.

On March 19-22 she told you she was traveling with her friend Naomi Nomura to the Outer Banks of North Carolina. On April 29-

May 2, she told you she was on a trip with her cousin Bree Whitcomb to New York City. Both those women were quiet on social media during the days of the supposed trips. Alexis did post during those time windows. However, when I ran the images Alexis said were taken at the Outer Banks through reverse image search software, I was able to confirm the photos she posted were not taken at the Outer Banks. The photos in New York were taken there, but none of them included Bree, which makes me doubt whether she was in New York with Bree. She may have been there with a man.

I completed the number of hours you requested for this case and only regret my investigation was not able to yield more concrete information.

Sincerely, Fred Kimley

More bank statements followed. More photos, this time Alexis behind the wheel driving, then walking onto a train. She wore big sunglasses on her beautiful face. Her dark hair was thick and long. Her clothes elegant.

She looked like a confident woman bent on accomplishing her goal. Apparently, in these photos, her goal had been to sleep with another man. She did not look, at all, like a woman about to throw herself off a cliff.

Near the bottom of the stack they found a desk calendar with the year of Alexis's death embossed on the front. Jeremiah flipped it open, revealing feminine handwriting in different colors of ink. She'd written in appointments. Restaurant reservations. Parties. Lunch dates with friends. Workouts with her trainer. Tennis matches and more.

He turned to the page that showed the week of her death. "She died on this day." He tapped it.

"It's eerie to see the days leading up to it. It looks as if she was living a full life with no knowledge of what was coming for her."

He flipped ahead. Alexis's appointments continued.

"And it's even eerier," Remy continued, "to see the plans she'd made for the days following her death."

Her life had stopped midstream.

Beneath her calendar, he found pages of notes in his own handwriting. He'd clearly been trying to construct a timeline of the last two weeks of Alexis's life. Under a heading for each day, he'd scribbled names and places. Occasionally, he'd added questions. Some things were crossed out, some underlined twice. At the bottom of the final page, he'd written the name *Detective Phillip Holland* and a phone number.

"Even if your marriage was troubled . . ." Remy said softly.

"Understatement."

"You went to a lot of effort to try to figure out how she died. Which suggests to me that you really did love her."

"Remy, it's time to set aside the idea that I loved Alexis. I might not have at the end. That would explain why I have no pictures of her displayed in this house."

"You didn't file divorce proceedings."

"I didn't have time to. I would have received this second report from the PI right after her death."

"You were still wearing your wedding ring when I found you. And you're still wearing it now."

He hadn't taken off the ring because doing so had seemed disrespectful toward Alexis and like he was going against what 1.0 would have wanted. But now? In light of Alexis's affairs, he had no problem pulling it off his hand. He walked to the nearest drawer, dropped it in, and shut it out of sight.

"*Jeremiah.*" Remy spoke in a scandalized tone.

"Good riddance."

They gazed at each other across several feet of charged

silence. "Let's think about why I left this evidence"—he nodded toward the items on the island—"locked in a secret room before leaving on a boat trip."

"In order to protect it while you were gone."

"Which makes me think I had reason to worry that someone would try to take it from me."

"True. Someone might still try to take it from you. May be best to continue to keep it in the secret room when you're not at home." She consulted one of the papers. "Who is Detective Holland?"

"Good question." He pulled out his phone and dialed the number he'd listed for the man.

As it rang, she murmured, "It's Sunday. He might be off."

No answer, so he left a voice mail, then added the detective to his phone contacts.

"Well." She slipped from the barstool and crossed toward the entry where she'd left the wooden box. "That was exciting. And then dismaying."

"You don't have to go."

"I do, though."

"Please stay." The words were an echo of what he'd said to her in Islehaven when he'd felt awful and needed to know she'd be close through the night. They were also an echo of what he'd said to her in the hospital in Rockland.

Her nearness had become the thing he prized most in his life.

"I'm going," she said.

It was dead true, what he'd told her earlier. She put distance between them at every opportunity.

She scooped up the wooden box and let herself out. A few steps onto the porch, she stopped and looked back. "It sucks, the things we found out about Alexis just now. You have every right to be upset. Once, someone I thought was good turned out to be bad—"

"Who? What happened?"

"My advice is to experience the feelings," she went on as if she hadn't heard his questions. "Sit with them and let them settle."

He watched her go.

He *did* feel upset. About Alexis, yes.

But more so about Remy.

Chapter Twelve

"Hey Siri," Fiona said the following day in the direction of her dashboard. Smoothly, she steered her Aston Martin SUV along the country road leading to her house as sunset painted the sky with shades of pink and blue. "Send a text message to Jude Camden."

"What would you like to say?" Siri prompted.

"Badmouth your father to your brother all you want but be sure to convince Jeremiah that I am stellar." Jude was such a straight arrow that she knew he wouldn't badmouth Felix to Jeremiah. He'd tell Jeremiah the truth about his father. Problem was, he'd tell his brother the truth about her, too, which left her on edge. No one knew your faults as well as your closest family members. And she really, really needed her oldest child to reestablish contact with her.

As soon as she'd realized that Jeremiah had not returned to civilization when he was scheduled to do so, fear had erupted inside her like lava—neon red and seething. She'd told herself that he was fine, a grown man in his thirties who was entitled to extend his vacation if he wanted. If only she'd learned how to *believe* the healthy things she told herself to believe. Instead, she'd slept little and popped some anti-anxiety pills to get by until the hospital had called to say that Jeremiah had resurfaced. But then she'd arrived in his hospital room and her son did not remember her. Her! The person who'd given him life. He also didn't appear to trust her or like her. He'd gone so far as to *kick her out*. Since then, he hadn't contacted her, so the lava remained stubbornly in the pit of her stomach. No longer erupting, but definitely bubbling.

How much longer was this going to go on? Both his ban of her and his amnesia?

Patience had never been her strong suit.

And now she also had her epiphany regarding the eclipse and Isobel to deal with. For thirty-five years, she had not reached out to Isobel. Not once. Partly because of her pride, partly because of her guilt. But as the days had passed since reading the article about the eclipse, she'd grown more certain that the time had come to break the stalemate. As the party who'd wronged the other, she, of course, must be the one to act, to extend a humble olive branch, to apologize.

Writing a letter seemed best. So now it was just a matter of gathering her courage and making it happen.

Two turns later, Siri read Jude's reply text aloud. *You're stellar?*

Children. So foolishly slow to appreciate their parents' merits.

As she slowed to turn onto her drive, she saw a bike propped on its kickstand near her entrance. A fit man with pale gray hair and a pale gray beard leaned against the stone wall that housed her gate, arms crossed.

A loitering stranger was the very last thing she needed on

this Monday evening. What to do? Opening her gate would grant him access, which she did not want. However, she was on her way home after a long day of work. Hesitating outside her own property? Also something she did not want.

She came to a stop and, with a pang of comprehension, realized that this was not a stranger. This was Burke Ainsley. It had been three or four years since she'd seen him. The beard was new and his hair was more silver than she remembered. He'd dressed in a long-sleeved gray exercise shirt pushed up at the forearms and lightweight hiking pants. God bless him for having the sense not to wear biker shorts, which were, to her way of thinking, nothing more than elongated Speedos.

She tapped a button and her window zipped down. "Are you a stalker or are you Burke Ainsley? Please confirm so I'll know how to proceed."

A smile etched lines and warmth into his tanned face. "Do you want me to be a stalker, or do you want me to be Burke Ainsley?" He walked up to her car. "Your answer will help me know how to proceed."

"I'd prefer for you to be Burke Ainsley."

"Lucky for me, that's who I am. Do you want me to present my driver's license?"

"That won't be necessary. I recognize your irreverence."

He chuckled. "I was out for a ride and this stretch of road started to look familiar. I remembered coming to that dinner party you hosted years ago. I needed to stop for a minute and hydrate anyway, so I rang the bell."

"I'm glad I caught you. Would you like to hydrate up at the house?"

"I would."

"Then come." She punched the clicker to open the gate. "Can I give you a lift or are you going to pedal there?"

"Pedal there." He trailed behind her on the bike.

She'd met him and his wife, Kay, back when Jeremiah had entered The Kellan School as a kindergartener. Burke's daughter, the younger of his two kids, had been in Jeremiah's class. Kay was an attorney. Burke's schedule, as the only architect at a firm he'd founded, had been more flexible. He'd become involved in the PTA and the school moms had begun referring to him as Nice Dad. Calm. Genuine. Understated. Good-looking. Not as good-looking as Felix, of course. But then, no one was as good-looking as Felix.

She and Burke had interacted quite a bit as their progeny had promoted through the grades side by side. There'd always been a zing of chemistry between them. All very chaste, yet enough of a zing that his presence had made volunteering at the school more enjoyable.

When Fiona had learned of Felix's affair with their house-keeper, she'd vengefully imagined the affairs she'd have in return to give Felix a taste of his own medicine. Vividly, she recalled thinking, *I'll have an affair with Burke!* From there, her schemes had become more far-fetched. *I'll have an affair with my golf pro who's a decade younger! No, I'll have an affair with Tom Cruise! He presents himself as straight via his marriages but is he really? I know, I'll have an affair with Liam Neeson! He's definitely straight.*

Those fantasies had remained fictional.

Long, long ago, at the age of twenty-three, she actually *had* engaged in an affair. With Felix. For a good long time after that, she'd been optimistic or naïve or deluded enough to think that she would be able to repair her reputation. But no. She now deeply comprehended that the public's opinion of her would stay the same throughout her life and after her death. That long-ago affair had remained the one and only affair of her lifetime because it had done more than enough damage, thank you very much.

Now, at the age of fifty-eight, her affair was very far back in her rearview mirror. Her divorce from Felix, eighteen years back. Since then, she'd had a handful of romantic relationships. None serious.

She left her car in the garage, passed through the house, and waited at the front door for Burke to catch up.

It didn't take him long.

Like a lot of Mainers, he had a granola vibe to him. She recalled that he'd enjoyed spending his free time hiking, biking, rock-climbing, or camping. He was probably the adorable type who collected stamps from the national parks in a little "passport" booklet. No doubt he was far more fervent than she was about composting and ensuring the survival of bumblebees and earthworms.

"Your garden's incredible." He paused at the base of the steps that led to her landing.

"Thank you. I do all the gardening myself. Not the lawn mowing, mind you. Just the planting beds and pots."

"It's amazing, what you've done."

"I enjoy it. Out here, I have control. I can plant what I want and make it look how I want." It was terribly nice when work and skill paid visual dividends.

She held the door open and he entered, carrying his water bottle.

"Your house is great, too." He followed her to the kitchen. "Even though the way you've decorated it is a flashing neon sign telling men they don't belong here."

She laughed. "Sounds like the flashing sign is saying exactly what was intended."

The prenup she'd agreed to before marrying Felix had

ensured that he retained Maple Lane, the house where they'd lived together. An impressive, masculine mansion, that estate had been in his family for generations, and she'd been fine with him keeping it. When she'd moved out, she'd swung in a completely different direction and purchased a storybook cottage. Unapologetically feminine, this house had cobblestone pathways, soft rooflines, wooden shingles, round-topped windows. She'd done the interior in cream and dreamy pastels. Though Fiona was not as white as snow, Snow White *could* have lived here.

She motioned for him to pass over the bottle, filled it with purified water, and handed it back. Propping her weight against her farm sink, she slid her hands into the pockets of the gray dress she wore with hose and heels.

As their kids aged, her path had crossed less with Burke's, though she'd still seen him socially from time to time because he and Kay were two of the people of her generation in this town that she liked. Then Burke and Kay had followed Kay's job to Boston.

"It's been a long time." She spoke the perfunctory thing you had to say when you saw someone after the passage of years.

"It has been," he agreed. "You look great." With that, he'd voiced the second perfunctory statement.

In her case, she expected a "You look great" from just about everyone. She'd become accustomed to it now, to the point that if people failed to say it, she felt miffed because she put a lot of time, money, and effort into looking great. "You look great, too." It was true. He'd become a bit brawny. He must be lifting some pretty heavy weight because his muscles were large for a man over the age of sixty.

It appeared they were both battling the paunch that often came with aging. Most men and women their age had surrendered to it because it was exhausting to keep fighting it as the years went on.

"Was the dinner party I hosted here the last time we saw one another?" she asked.

"Yes, and that was four years ago. I remember, because Kay and I moved to Boston soon after."

"How is Kay?"

"She passed away two years ago."

Fiona's face fell. "Oh no."

"Cancer."

"I'm so sorry." Even though Burke and Kay had moved away, she was surprised she hadn't heard. It was shocking how many people in her circle were dealing with cancer and other serious conditions. "What happened?"

"Did you remember that she had cancer when our kids were in college?"

Fiona nodded.

"It stayed in remission for several years. But when it came back, it came back with a vengeance."

Kay had been pensive and studious. Basically, nothing like Fiona. "That's terrible. I wish I could take a machine gun to cancer and just mow it down."

"I wish you could, too."

"How are you and your kids doing?"

"It's been a hard two years, but we're doing all right. How are your sons?"

"Jeremiah has amnesia and doesn't remember me."

His eyes rounded.

"I know," she said. "Who gets amnesia? And who tells their mother a version of 'Don't call me, I'll call you'?"

"It's hard to believe that anyone couldn't remember you," he said with a perfectly straight face.

"Precisely. Also, Jeremiah's enamored with the woman who

served as his caregiver and may or may not be a con artist. In my opinion, she wears too little makeup to be a con artist. But one can never be too careful."

"Ah." His light brown eyes were warm and sweet as cinnamon rolls.

"Jude got a law degree from Columbia. He worked for the DA for a few years, then decided to become an FBI agent. I'm still stupefied by that because who takes a law degree from Columbia and decides to earn peanuts with it working for the FBI?"

"Public servants?" he proposed mildly. "People who have family money?"

"My son falls into both categories. I just . . ." She flung up her hands. "*A law degree from Columbia*, Burke."

He shrugged like, *There's no accounting for what our kids do now that they're adults.*

She'd been so proud when her boys had become adults. *Look*, she'd thought, *I'm sending excellent and independent men out into the world!*

But then those excellent men had proven *so* independent that they rarely came to stay with her here. Nor did either one seem inclined to fulfill her dream of becoming a young grandmother still active enough to dazzle her little grandbabies.

There'd been a season, after Jeremiah had married Alexis, when she'd believed the dream of grandchildren was within her grasp. But Jeremiah and Alexis had no children before their marriage ended with Alexis's death. She prayed every day that the Camdens would not go the way of the Kennedys—stricken by tragedy after tragedy.

"Neither of my sons," she announced, "are doing anything to ensure that I become a grandmother before I'm in a wheelchair and wearing bifocals."

"Shame on them."

"Yes! Thank you." She was remembering why she'd always liked Burke. They had an easy rapport. Sometimes her personality rubbed up against other people's personalities like sandpaper. But not with him. "Did you come to Groomsport for a visit?"

"I moved here about a month and a half ago. I've been wanting to come back to be near my kids and grandkids. I finally made the jump."

"You were always the consummate family man."

"Is that a compliment or a criticism?"

"A compliment. If I sound bitter saying that, it's only because my husband was so much the opposite. Which is exactly what I loved about him at the start and loathed about him at the end."

She'd been raised in a lower-middle-class family. In her early twenties, responsible men, exemplified by her father, had seemed boring. She'd wanted thrills and glamour and everything that glittered. She'd gotten exactly what she'd wanted, and, in the end, it had ripped her heart out. "Are you going to pick up where you left off, working for yourself?"

"I decided to retire."

She arched a sculpted brow. "Why would you do that?" she asked in the scandalized tone she'd have used if he'd announced he wanted to become a swamp person.

"I take it you're not a fan of retirement?"

"Goodness, no! Why would anyone give up meaningful work?"

"To do other meaningful things."

"How old are you?"

"Sixty-four."

Far too young to retire! "What do you do with your time?"

"Spend it with my kids and grandkids—"

"Braggart."

"—Volunteering, exercising, reading, hanging out with friends."

"Hiking and camping?"

"Yes."

"I knew it." Granola.

"I saw your hand creams on display in a store window downtown last week. The salesman said your company's a huge success."

After two years of wallowing in romantic movies and wine following her divorce, she'd gone on a spending spree. She'd dumped swaths of Felix's money into luxurious spa getaways, Botox, designer clothes, shoes, handbags, and lingerie.

Her revenge had proven empty. Ultimately, she'd realized that the only true and lasting revenge would be to make something of herself. Even as a preschooler, she'd had the soul of a business tycoon. Combining that with her love of hand creams, she'd started Lavish.

Gradually, she'd grown her company the old-fashioned way —beginning small and scaling it through hard work. She'd kept her persona away from her business. Only the people of Groomsport and her employees knew that *the* Fiona Camden was Lavish's owner and CEO. That way, her image couldn't tank her company. More than that, the separation between her identity and her business ensured that no one, especially not her, could say that Lavish's success had anything to do with the Camden family or their money.

"My company's doing very well," she said modestly. She always downplayed verbally the success that she was, privately, fiercely proud of. "It keeps me busy, so now that you're retired maybe I can hire you to be my cook and grocery shopper." She was only half kidding.

"I hate to ruin my image as the consummate family man, but I don't cook very well."

"How are you at grocery shopping?"

"Average."

"Housekeeping? I could hire you to do that."

"Are you offering me employment because you're concerned about my financial status?" he asked with obvious amusement. "To put your mind at ease, I don't need to take on work as anyone's housekeeper to make ends meet."

"Pity."

"But I really am glad I had the chance to reconnect with an old friend."

"Just so you know," she said, "I don't approve of the word 'old' attached to me in any way. I turned my back on that adjective in 2013."

His amusement grew. "Noted."

Remy hadn't seen Jeremiah for three days.

She'd intentionally put space between them and focused instead on Wendell. She'd been taking her friend to dialysis, taking him to a diner for blueberry cobbler, taking him to Marden's because he loved the store even though the last thing he needed was more stuff. Also working on his trainwreck of a house and his hunt for his lost love, Marisol.

While she'd succeeded at taking time away from Jeremiah, she only wished she'd been as successful at putting a stop to thoughts of him. At that, she'd utterly failed. And now—*today*, ready or not—she was about to see him again. Thus, she was emotionally girded for battle.

After letting herself through Appleton's gate with the code Jeremiah had supplied, she parked outside his garage and stepped from her rental car. She was immediately assailed by the beauty all around. The calendar read October fifth and

Down East fall was at its finest. Tourists flocked here at this time of year with good reason. The sixty-degree air sang crystal clear. The pale blue sky stretched endlessly. The foliage blazed color. And all of that was emphasized by the charm of Jeremiah's property—his woods, the old house, the sweeping view down to the ocean.

Pushing her hands into her pockets, she stayed right where she was—internalizing the glorious weather, using it to steady herself.

The connection between herself and Jeremiah was becoming more complex and dangerous. Complex because of the mystery of Alexis. Dangerous because of the rising physical chemistry she felt for him.

When they'd found proof on Sunday that Alexis had been unfaithful, the story Remy had invented regarding Alexis had cracked. She could make the stories in her head more real than reality. She could make those fair, and noble, and inspiring. She didn't like having to acknowledge that one of her stories was broken beyond repair. And she was struggling to accept Actual Alexis because she'd liked Fictional Alexis so much better.

In truth, she felt personally betrayed by Jeremiah's wife. Which was ridiculous. She and Alexis hadn't known each other. Alexis owed her nothing. Alexis had died young and potentially not of her own will so Remy should feel compassion toward her. And she did! It's just that . . . Remy valued honor. Alexis might not have had any of that. Which left Remy feeling let down by the woman she'd worked so hard to find for Jeremiah's sake.

As for the Duke himself . . . he'd been texting and calling her the past few days, asking for her assistance finding answers. She'd put him off. Turned out, though, it was genetically impossible for her to permanently ignore someone in need of her help.

"Hey." Jeremiah's voice drifted to her from behind.

Pleasure slid over her like liquid chocolate over ice cream.

She wished she could keep him at arm's length the way she'd done on Islehaven. That was no longer so easy. He was drawing frighteningly close to her gun-shy heart.

Chapter Thirteen

Remy angled toward him. She'd chosen some of her better clothes today—wide-legged white pants and a button-up denim shirt knotted at the waist. But he effortlessly made her attempt at dressing well seem pitiful.

Jeremiah approached wearing a burgundy shirt and dark jeans. His cheeks remained clean-shaven. His hair, which had been perfectly trimmed back when they'd met, was now over-long and rumpled. It was equally sexy both ways.

He'd told her, *"I'm healing fast now,"* the last time she'd seen him. The truth of that was impossible to miss. He still moved more carefully and slowly than other men of his age and fitness. But he was reclaiming more of his strength and health every time she saw him.

"I was working on the cars in the garage," he said. "I heard you drive up."

"Ah. Did your valet not answer the call of the bell when you rang for him to work on the cars?"

"Nope." He made a study of her face, his gaze appreciative. Her skin prickled with warm sensitivity in response.

"I missed you," he said.

"What? No. You're not allowed to say that."

He shrugged, unconcerned in the face of her scolding. "It's the truth, Remy. I missed you."

He was wrong-footing her right off the bat, the villain. "So! I'm here to help out. Explain more fully than you did over text what our goal is today."

He mimicked her body language, hands in his pockets. "I spoke with the PI, Fred Kimley, and the detective, Phillip Holland. The detective is with Groomsport PD and he's the one who investigated Alexis's death. Apparently, 1.0 met with him three months ago to share suspicions about her cause of death. According to Holland, he told me then that he'd need additional evidence before they'd have a reason to move away from the medical examiner's ruling of suicide."

"What kind of evidence is he wanting?"

"Signs of a struggle. Fingerprints. Motive. Proof that someone had threatened her life."

What chance did she and Jeremiah have of unearthing evidence like that fifteen months after Alexis's fall?

"He said," Jeremiah continued, "that families of people who take their own lives sometimes invent theories to explain how it could have been anything other than suicide. Holland thought that's what was going on with 1.0."

"And the PI?"

"I called him around the same time that I met with the detective. 1.0 asked Kimley for advice regarding how to go about my own investigation."

"What did he suggest?"

"Create a timeline of Alexis's final two weeks. Return to the scene of the crime. Check her email."

"And today we're working on the timeline?"

"Right. Based on my notes, that's what I'd been doing before my boat trip."

"Are we simply looking at Alexis's calendar and trying to figure out where she went and who she saw?"

"Yes, because Kimley says that can reveal inconsistencies and gaps in time that raise valuable questions. Kimley also suggested I call everyone she saw during those two weeks."

"And ask them what?"

"What they talked about with Alexis, how she seemed, whether she mentioned anything unusual."

"Can we expect them to remember after all this time?"

"That's what I asked. Kimley says yes. He told me that people often recall in detail the things that happened the last time they were with a friend before their friend died."

"Okay, but you're not going to be able to call any of the people listed in Alexis's calendar because you can't remember them."

"I might ask Jude to make the calls—"

The sound of a car coming up the drive reached Remy. "Expecting someone?"

"Only you."

"Do you think this might be the person who tried to off you? Not that I blame them. Offing you has crossed my mind more than once."

"I'd be surprised if the person who tried to off me knows my gate code."

A boxy, hunter green Mercedes SUV came into view. After it stopped, doors opened on both sides, emitting a man and woman. They looked to be in their late thirties. The woman was an all-American type of pretty with brown, shoulder-length hair. The man wore Adidas from head to toe. Tall and handsome, he kept his ginger hair tidy and his ginger beard close-cropped.

The man walked straight to Jeremiah. "Memory still gone?" he asked with a British accent.

"Yes."

"You don't recognize me?"

"I don't."

"I'm Anton Quintrell."

Jeremiah inclined his chin. "Jude told me about you."

Remy knew enough of Jeremiah's history to place Anton at once as Jeremiah's former performance coach, his right-hand man and friend.

"This is my wife, Camille," Anton said. "Your mom brought us up to date on some of what's happened, so we came by to see how you're doing."

"Thanks." Jeremiah introduced Remy to the couple.

Anton was a direct sort of man. Direct eye contact. Direct body language. Seeing him and Jeremiah side by side threw their differences into light. Jeremiah had an ease about him, a natural charisma. He was like cheese and fig jam on a cracker. Anton was just the cracker. No embellishment.

Camille appeared unable to decide who presented more of a spectacle. Remy (who'd suddenly materialized in the life of their long-time friend) or Jeremiah (who had amnesia).

"Is there anything we can do for you?" Anton asked Jeremiah.

"I do have a few questions for you."

"Sure."

"We'll give you some space," Remy announced. She might have hovered over Jonah back on Islehaven but that's because she'd been scared of pulse stoppage or loss of breath. She would not be caught dead hovering over Jeremiah now. "Camille and I will . . ." Her mind blanked. Sort the pantry? Compare bra sizes? This was when her lack of a social life on Islehaven showed.

"Take a walk?" Camille suggested, coming to her rescue. "You up for that?"

"Yes," Remy replied gratefully.

⛵

Anton might be 1.0's best friend. Yet Jeremiah hadn't seen Remy in days and Anton had interrupted his time with her just minutes after she'd arrived. Because of that, as he watched Remy walk away, what he mostly felt toward the guy was irritation.

"I'm sorry about your amnesia," Anton said. "You've been through an ordeal."

"Yeah."

Jeremiah sized Anton up, weighing his own response. A low-level headache had arrived. That symptom reminded him of how he'd first reacted to Jude and was a sure sign of Anton's involvement in Jeremiah's forgotten past. "I know that I retired from F1 in November of last year."

"That's right."

"Can you explain why I retired?"

"Last season was the final season on your contract with Mercedes. After the first few grand prix on the circuit, you told me your reflexes had slowed, just a fraction. It wasn't discernible to me or to anyone else, but it bothered you. At that point, you'd been driving F1 for thirteen years. You were growing weary of it. At the same time, you'd given your life to it. So, if you were to retire, you wanted to do so at the top of your game instead of going into a slow decline."

Yep. That information fit like a jacket that had been tailored to him.

"Then Alexis died midway through the season," Anton went on, "which was terrible for everyone, most of all you. You kept it together because the team and all the fans were relying on you. You finished the season in Alexis's honor and drove brilliantly, coming in fourth in the drivers' championship."

All of a sudden, Jeremiah saw himself standing on a track, raising his arm to acknowledge the cheers of thousands of fans in the stands. He could hear the roar of their applause. Feel his sweat and gratitude. This was the send-off after his final race.

Goosebumps rose on his skin. A memory. He attempted to draw it out and expand it forward or backward. But that's all his brain would give him. Just that small slice.

Jeremiah started walking and Anton matched his pace. They passed the front porch, stopping at the point where the meadow began to tilt downhill. Arms crossed, they both faced the Atlantic. Breeze moved around them as if stirred by a giant, invisible spoon.

"What can you tell me about my marriage to Alexis?" Jeremiah asked.

"You two were the couple everyone wanted to be."

"What was our relationship like?"

"Good for the most part."

"What does that mean?"

"It means that you had some issues but no more than any couple."

"What were our issues?"

"I know you and Alexis argued occasionally and that there were things about your marriage that made you sad at times. But you never told me specifically what you argued about or what made you sad. You kept those details private."

"Before my boat trip, did I tell you that I was looking into Alexis's death because I didn't believe it was suicide?"

Anton's expression turned troubled. "Yes."

"Who would have wanted Alexis dead?"

"No one. She was admired. Extremely popular."

"Who would've wanted *me* dead? I ask because I was found injured at sea."

"Like any Formula One driver, you had your share of haters. A few of them made death threats over the years, but there was never anything of legitimate concern."

"No one stalked me? Or tried to hurt me?"

Anton shook his head. "The only person I can think of who'd want you dead is the person who'd benefit the most financially from your death. You're a rich man. Which, in a way, makes you a target."

⚓

Remy suspected that Camille had been a gymnast during her adolescent years. She had the body for it and the cheerful, energetic personality to match.

So far the two of them had been trading abbreviated life stories while following a trail through the forest.

Camille had been born and raised in Michigan. She'd then followed a job in hospitality to London for a two-year stint, which was when she'd met Anton at a pub. They'd been married nine years and their sons were seven and five. These days Camille was a busy, thriving, contented mom.

"Are you and Jeremiah in a relationship?" Camille asked Remy.

"Only if uneasy allies counts as a relationship. I intend to go back to Islehaven very soon. I've stayed on in Rockland mostly because my friend Wendell needed a hoarding intervention." She was staying on for Jeremiah, too, but the Wendell angle was an easier motivation both to publicly verbalize and to privately accept.

"You're not interested in dating Jeremiah?"

"No. If I had to summarize my feelings toward him, I'd use the word ambivalent," she lied.

Camille laughed. Evidently the prospect that anyone could feel ambivalently toward him was hilarious. "Do you follow F1 at all?"

"Not at all."

"I wish you could've known Jeremiah during his driving days. He was incredible. Charming with the media, always outwardly relaxed. Underneath, though, he was full of fierce concentration. Once he got out on the racetrack, he was ruthless. Competitive and fearless."

Remy gave a sound to acknowledge Camille's words but made sure that the sound wasn't fawning.

"I sometimes joke that Jeremiah is the trifecta of desirability," Camille continued. "Talented, wealthy, famous."

The scent of pine hovered thick in the air. Beneath it lay the tang of salty sea and a whiff of distant wood fire. "Talent I appreciate, but I think it's debilitating to receive too much money and fame. It's far better to pursue the thing you were meant to do strictly out of dedication and love for it."

"In addition to the trifecta, Jeremiah is also, of course, better looking than any man has a right to be. The Camden eyes are legendary." Camille stepped over a fallen log, clearly rejoicing in her role as informant about all things Jeremiah. "So is the Camden swagger and the Camden smile. They're all lethal."

On the surface, it certainly did seem that everything in life had been handed to Jeremiah on a silver platter. However, Alexis's infidelity had cast new light on him.

He'd been handed some things, yes, thanks to the privilege of his birth. But he'd worked very hard to achieve other things. And many important things had been taken from him. His career was over. His wife was gone. And he'd been robbed of his memories, which left him isolated.

He wasn't the happily married man Remy had assumed when she'd first spotted his wedding ring. And he might not be the brokenhearted husband in love with his dead wife that she'd supposed him to be after learning that Alexis had died.

Remy would have found Jeremiah much easier to resist if she didn't feel sympathy toward him. But she did sympathize.

"Jeremiah was already a shooting star when he met Alexis," Camille was saying. "Did you know that she was a famous Instagram influencer?"

"I did."

"F1 collaborated with Alexis on a promotional campaign several years back. They gave her access to interview some of the top drivers. When she interviewed Jeremiah, sparks flew."

This topic was disturbing enough to counteract the calming effect nature typically had on Remy. She jerked her hair into a braid as they crunched onward.

"Alexis's family is from Belgium," Camille continued. "Her mother was a diplomat, so Alexis and her siblings were raised in several countries around the world. Alexis spoke flawless English. You could barely hear an accent." Camille fell into a few moments of reverie. "She was wonderful. Anton and I spent a lot of time with them. We even went on vacations together. I . . . still can't believe she's gone. It's heartbreaking."

"Yes." No matter what, Alexis's death at the age of thirty-one *was* heartbreaking.

"Their wedding was lavish but relatively small." Camille plucked a dangling orange leaf from its branch and twirled it as she walked. "It was kept secret. No press at all. Afterward, Jeremiah and Alexis sold exclusive photos of the ceremony and reception for a small fortune. F1 is such an international sport. And Alexis was an international influencer. As well-known as they are here in the States, they're even better known around the world. At times, being around them felt like being around movie stars."

The more she learned about Alexis, the more certain Remy became that she was not Jeremiah's type.

The pathway looped around and brought them back to Appleton.

By the time she spotted Jeremiah on the front lawn, he was already motioning for her to come nearer.

The four of them went inside and it felt awkwardly like she and Jeremiah needed to play host to Anton and Camille even though they didn't know them and hadn't invited them.

Jeremiah brought out beer and wine choices. Camille—who knew her way around Jeremiah's kitchen—arranged snacks on a tray, then announced that the library was her favorite room in the house. They moved the food and conversation there.

Remy melted with inward delight at the taste of good-quality butter on crusty sourdough bread. Best food combination ever? In her mind, it was. Though it felt disloyal to acknowledge that anything about the mainland was superior to Islehaven, the food here definitely *was* superior to what she subsisted on there.

Anton and Camille were young-people-with-money types and certainly not as down to earth as Remy's friends. However, they were more normal than she would've expected Jeremiah's friends to be. They weren't arrogant, nor were they wearing Izod shirts with the collars turned up, nor did they talk about golfing and trips to Belize.

As the four of them chatted, Remy glanced at Jeremiah and caught him gazing at her in a level, I-could-look-at-you-all-day-long kind of way.

Contrary to what was wise and safe, the awareness between herself and Jeremiah was growing electric. It didn't help that Jeremiah's attention strayed back to her repeatedly. Obviously, he didn't care that his behavior was stirring the notice of Camille, who kept looking speculatively between them.

Remy had no idea what he was thinking and feeling. She only knew that, on her end, she was attuned to every word he spoke, every movement he made. She cataloged the timbre of his voice. She noted when he resettled his position or set down his beer or ran a hand through his hair.

About an hour after they'd entered the library, they walked Anton and Camille out so the couple could relieve the babysitter. By that point, Remy was so edgy and overwhelmed by the heated vibe between herself and Jeremiah that she did not trust herself to stay. Too much emotion! Too much . . . extroverting. She needed to be alone somewhere. Which is why, once they'd said their goodbyes to Anton and Camille, she crossed to her own car.

"Where are you going?" Jeremiah asked, clearly confused. "We planned to work on the timeline."

"Rain check on that." She turned her key in the ignition. "Sorry. I'm tired." Which was a lie. What she actually was? Nervous and fighting an overactive libido. She rolled down her window.

"Would caffeine help?" he asked. "I can make you coffee. Or tea."

Caffeine would not help what ailed her. "No, thank you."

"Remy." He looked worried and a little . . . lost.

"I'll return soon to help with the timeline."

Driving away, she glanced back at him in the rearview mirror. The man with everything. And nothing. American royalty who somehow needed . . . *her*, of all people.

Shame twisted inside her for bailing on him.

It couldn't be helped.

She could not be alone tonight with the Camden eyes and the Camden swagger and the Camden smile.

The following day, Jeremiah steered his Ferrari F12 east, shooting past a minivan and flying around a wide turn. He'd lost his memory, but his instincts remembered exactly how to drive a car like this one.

He hadn't lied when he'd told Remy the BMW was the least showy car he owned. In addition to the BMW and this Ferrari, two classic cars occupied his home garage—a Mercedes gull wing and a Shelby Cobra.

He'd chosen the Ferrari this morning because he'd had an hour and a half of roundtrip driving ahead of him—to Augusta and back for an appointment with a psychologist followed by an appointment with a hypnotherapist. He was now heading home and wishing the appointments had been more successful.

Using voice controls on his phone, he connected a call to his brother.

Jude picked up right away. "Hey."

"Hey. I met Anton yesterday. Can you tell me more about him?"

"Sure. What would you like to know?"

"His background?"

"One sec." Rustling noises on Jude's end, then a door closing, then quiet. "Anton grew up in a working-class family in London. He and his father were both huge F1 fans. They dreamed that Anton would become a driver and both tried to make that happen."

"But?"

"But they didn't have the money or the sponsors to continue karting."

"Why no sponsors?"

"Because Anton was good, but he was never great. He became a physiotherapist and went to work for Mercedes, which is based not far from London, in Brackley."

"And Mercedes assigned him to me."

"Yes. You'd made a name for yourself in karting and then in Formula Two. Mercedes promoted you to Formula One when you were twenty. Anton's four years older than you are. They assigned him to you because he was young enough to be relatable but responsible enough, they hoped, to keep you out of trouble."

"He seemed like a straightforward guy. Serious."

"He is. Anton's a hard worker and not the type to waste his time flattering you. He'd tell you things straight and sometimes you'd butt heads because of that. But at the end of the day, you appreciated his honesty."

"How often did we butt heads?"

"Rarely. I've never seen you truly lose your temper in your whole life and Anton almost never lost his. When that did happen, though, you used to say everyone would duck and run for cover."

"Huh."

"I was jealous of him at first," Jude admitted, "because it felt like he'd taken my place as your brother. I got over that pretty quickly, though, because I didn't want to spend my life doing what Anton did—flying around the globe, working to motivate you to the top of podiums."

"Anton and I were like brothers?"

"Right. Closer than friends but too argumentative to be colleagues."

"When I asked him if he had any idea who might want to kill me, he suggested I find out who'd benefit the most financially from my death. My will names you, Fiona, Max, and Anton. Do you or any of those other three want to kill me?"

Jude laughed. "I'm certain we've all wanted to kill you from time to time. But Mom, Anton, and I are also the closest people to you, which is why we're the least likely to kill you even when you make us crazy."

"And Max?"

"There's sometimes friction between you two but also a lot of affection and history. You're half-brothers. You share blood. I'm sure that's why you included him in your will."

"Is there enough friction between Max and me that he'd want to kill me for the money he'd inherit from me?"

"Max doesn't need money. He owns a successful company."

"In my will it mentioned what was to happen to my share of the Camden family trust money in the event of my death. That section was hard to follow. Can you put it in plainer words?"

"Sure. If a recipient of the Camden trust dies without having children, any unused funds in the trust go to another Camden family member. In your case, since Dad's living, the funds would have gone to him if you'd died."

"So Felix is the person who'd have benefitted the most from my death."

"Financially, yes. But Dad would never hurt you. Plus, he needs your money even less than Max. He made a fortune playing football, he received his share of the family trust, and now he makes a great salary commentating. He's a smart investor. He's got more money than he knows what to do with."

"What if it just appears that way? What if he's somehow lost it all?"

"Nah. Dad has too much pride and is too dependent on luxuries to lose it all."

"He's the type of person who's at the center of scandals. Maybe he's done something terrible and somebody's black-mailing him?"

"Dad's arrogant enough to think he can weather scandals. And the truth is, he has. A lot of people can't stand him, but a lot of people idolize him. If he'd been susceptible to blackmail, our mother and Max's mother would've made out like bandits."

"Okay. Thanks."

"You bet. Anything else I can do?"

"Help me figure out how Alexis died," Jeremiah answered.

"I'm game. How?"

"I'll think on it and call you back."

He gripped the steering wheel as the sports car shot down a straight stretch of road bordered by trees. His muscles recalled this sensation—the solidity of the wheel against his palms.

The psychologist had provided a great deal of information about amnesia. The causes of it. The mechanics of it. The reassurance that his memories would likely come back soon, especially now that Jeremiah's brain had retrieved one memory. They'd worked on EMDR therapy the remainder of the session, which hadn't loosened up any more memories. Even so, Jeremiah had booked follow-up appointments when the psychologist suggested he try more EMDR, cognitive therapy, and neurofeedback.

During hypnotherapy, he'd experienced a vision similar to the one he'd experienced with Maureen on Islehaven, except today's vision had taken place in a different setting. This time, he'd been climbing a mountain at night, pushing branches to the side as he'd searched for Alexis. Like before, he'd had the overpowering sense that he'd made a terrible mistake. Urgency had driven him to move as fast as he possibly could but, once again, his limbs had been weighted and slow.

After hypnosis he'd woken to the same sense of dread. Why did his dreams of her come with so much guilt?

Today had confirmed that he was a shell of a person because of the amnesia. Inadequate. At a huge disadvantage with Remy.

She wasn't impressed with any of the things that impressed most people. But at least if he'd met her when he'd been 1.0, he'd have brought his whole self to the table. He'd probably have been mentally sharper. More appealing to her. More able to see how to soften her toward him. More willing to thank Remy for all she'd done for him and let her go.

As it was, just the thought of letting her go caused his heart to rebel. He was too selfish to stand to the side and let her return to Islehaven without a fight.

Islehaven valued her. But he valued her far, far more.

Remy sat back in astonishment, blinking at the screen of the library computer.

The Groomsport librarian had spent close to an hour giving Remy a mini class in the library resources that might aid her search for Marisol Soto. Remy had been putting her fledgling knowledge to use for most of the afternoon and now, right here in front of her, she'd found mention of a Marisol Soto on the Newspapers.com site the library subscribed to.

Sitting up straighter, she clicked the link.

A digitized article from a small-town newspaper appeared. Remy read it quickly. The article featured a non-profit used clothing store called Threads that provided jobs and housing to formerly homeless people.

"This organization does so much good for our community," says

Marisol Soto, a volunteer who assists with training and stocking shelves. "It's rewarding to be involved."

That was the only mention of Marisol in the article.

Still! *Marisol Soto.* Right there in black and white.

Remy collected her things, strode several yards onto the grassy park outside the library, and called Wendell's landline.

"Wendell speaking."

"I just found a Marisol Soto quoted in an article at the library. The article's only two years old."

"Oh?"

"She volunteers at a non-profit in Belfast called Threads. Belfast, Wendell! The town where the two of you met."

"My, my," he marveled. "Truly?"

"Yes!"

"What should we do?"

"We should drive to Belfast first thing in the morning and visit Threads."

Chapter Fourteen

If Wendell had gotten his way, he and Remy would have arrived at Threads at 5:00 a.m. in advance of their 9:00 a.m. opening.

As it was, Remy was the person with the car keys and thus the person with the power. She refused to leave until 8:00. Then made a stop at the diner so they could grab breakfast. They arrived at Threads, which occupied an unassuming slot in a strip mall, at 9:20.

Remy peeked across at Wendell once they'd both exited the car. He smoothed his best sweater—the one with a pattern of small nautical flags—and took a deep breath. He appeared pale and more wobbly than usual.

"Ready?" she asked, hoping against hope it had been a good idea to bring him here, that it had been a good idea to try to find Marisol in the first place. Should Marisol no longer volunteer here, surely someone at Threads would remember her and be able to provide additional information about where and how to contact her.

"Never more ready," Wendell said. He held the door for

her, and they made their way to a large cash register and the grizzled, middle-aged man working behind it. "Anything I can do for you?" he asked.

Wendell blanched and didn't seem capable of speech.

"Yes," Remy said to the employee. "We know that a woman named Marisol Soto used to volunteer here. Does she still?"

"She sure does."

"Any chance she's here this morning? We'd like to say hello to her."

"You bet. I saw her in the back five minutes ago. Let me go get her."

"Thank you."

The employee left and Remy mouthed *Oh my gosh* to Wendell. Not only did Marisol still volunteer here, but she was actually present—an amazing stroke of good luck.

"I've never been so nervous in my life," Wendell said.

They waited, eagerness snapping and fizzing the air around them.

A few minutes later the grizzled employee returned with a young, heavy-set woman with dark, curly hair. "Hi," she said shyly, with confusion.

"Is Marisol not here today after all?" Wendell asked.

"I think"—Remy's heart was sinking—"this is Marisol."

"No, I'm afraid not," Wendell said.

"Marisol Soto?" Remy asked the young woman.

"Yes. Darrell told me you . . . wanted to say hello?"

Wendell had gone stiff, mouth set. She rested a steadying hand on his forearm. "My friend here knew a Marisol Soto once," Remy said. "We saw you quoted in an article, and we thought you might be the Marisol he knew. But that Marisol would be over eighty now. Sorry for the misunderstanding."

"No problem." She looked between them, her focus snagging with compassion on Wendell. "I hope you find your Marisol."

"Thank you." Wendell tried to smile at her, but his mouth wasn't cooperating. "It's a treat to meet another Marisol Soto. God bless you."

"Are there a lot of Soto family members in this area?" Remy asked. "And do any of your relatives share your name?"

"No, none of my family members share my name. I came to Maine for college three years ago but I'm from Arizona. So . . . I don't know if any other Sotos live here."

"Okay. Thank you." Remy turned Wendell and steered him from the store. On the sidewalk, he went as still as a tree trunk, staring hard at nothing.

Remy squeezed her eyes closed for a few seconds before opening them. She'd been too rash. She should have called Threads and asked to speak to Marisol. Had she done so, she'd have quickly realized this woman wasn't Wendell's Marisol and could have saved him this trip and the anguish he was enduring now.

Instead, she'd fallen victim to the romantic idea of surprising Wendell's Marisol with a reunion.

"I'm very sorry," she said.

He looked down at her as if he'd forgotten she was there. "It's all right, Remy. You've done a whole lot for me. A whole lot. I appreciate it."

"I'll keep looking for her."

He nodded, but the twinkle in his eye had disappeared. This setback had hit him hard, and he was losing his faith that Marisol could be found.

The instant Jeremiah opened his front door that night, Remy comprehended that the Camden eyes and the Camden swagger and the Camden smile had only gained in power since she'd seen him last.

He wore a blue logo T-shirt beneath an open chambray shirt with jeans. His soft lips and eyelashes combined with his hard jaw and cheekbones and—SOS—that endearing quality about his face that she was still trying to articulate. For a few seconds, the sight of him stole all her air.

"You're here." He gave her a slow grin.

It was half-dark on the porch where she stood, but all warm, amber light inside his house.

"Yep!" she said hoarsely, then cleared her throat. "I'm here."

But really, how was that possible? How could her life have brought her *here*?

She was isolated Remy Reed of the tiny cottage on Isle-haven, who made sculptures and rarely saw humans. Yet she was currently entering the mansion of this larger-than-life man and following him toward his kitchen, where he was asking what he could get her to eat or drink.

She set aside her purse and accepted a glass bottle of Perrier. Valiantly, she tried to ignore how simply, honestly *good* it felt to be near him again. No one else around. Just him and her.

Remy liked to think that she had the ability to view herself objectively. For example, she understood that she possessed an unusual ability to fixate on things. A topic, an idea concerning her art, a book, a project. If it caught her fancy, she'd become highly curious and highly invested in that thing. And whatever she felt toward it, she'd feel *fervently*. To the point that it could be hard for her to understand when others didn't see/think/feel the same way about it that she did.

She'd gotten herself into a predicament because Jeremiah had caught her fancy. Remy could sense her enormous capacity for curiosity and investment tipping toward him. And when that happened, it could be difficult for her to disengage, keep her head, and make the moderate choice.

She was, after all, the person who had to set timers when working so she'd remember to eat. It was of the utmost importance that she exercise restraint with Jeremiah.

"I had a memory," he said.

"What? Tell me everything."

He relayed the memory. They talked it over, then discussed his appointments in Augusta, and the progress of Project Wendell and the search for Marisol.

When their dynamic began to feel a little too intimate, she polished off her Perrier and announced it was time to get down to the business of the night—working on the timeline of Alexis's final two weeks.

He provided his notes. She took the liberty of creating a rainbow of papers on the living room floor and they sat side by side in the center of the rainbow.

They looked up the addresses of every place Alexis had gone. They noted gaps of time that she hadn't filled with activity. They tried to confirm the identities of the people listed in her calendar using the input Jude had given Jeremiah regarding Jeremiah's phone contacts. That method only helped them figure out who about a third of the people were.

"It's not like you can call Alexis's sister"—Remy tapped the name *Francesca* on one of the papers—"and ask her about the last time she talked with Alexis without actually remembering Francesca yourself. As mentioned the other day, you're going to need help."

"I agree."

"Wait. Did you just *agree* with something I said?"

"Yeah."

"Well, that's a first." Their eyes met and held. Illumination from the nearby lamp glimmered in the strands of his hair.

"I . . ." Her pulse sped up. "What was I saying?"

"I don't remember." His eyes went smoky.

Her hormones heated to a boil.

"Are you experiencing this sexual tension between us?" he asked bluntly.

"Nope." But the word came out thready.

"Because I am. Big time."

"I'm sure it's a passing thing. Hang on five minutes and it'll be gone."

"I don't think so. For me this has been going on for days and days."

She pushed one finger at a time toward her palm. "I really have no idea what you're talking about. Let's get back to brainstorming—"

"I want to kiss you." He said it just like that. So simple and so complicated. So plain and so powerful.

Her skin rushed and desire curved hot in her abdomen. She should leave right this minute. Instead, she rose up onto her knees.

Fast and coordinated as a panther, he rose to his knees, too. Now they were facing each other, him gazing down at her.

"Admit that you feel the pull between us," he said.

She shook her head in a jittery type of way.

"You don't feel it at all?" he asked, incredulous.

"No." The lie caught in her throat, and she couldn't say any more.

She was mesmerized by his face, undone by her biology. The next thing she knew, without planning it or sanctioning it, she was pressing her lips against his and locking her arms around his neck.

He responded instantly, his hands coming to her lower back and drawing her body against his. He made a guttural sound of masculine pleasure as he kissed her.

All at once, nothing in the world mattered more than this. No concerns had the power to stop her from grabbing this scrap of pleasure.

The contact between them was raw . . . then tender . . . then needy. It was like being inside a snow globe of wonder—just the two of them exploring their magnificent chemistry. An interaction of bodies and souls.

He pulled back a tiny distance. Both their chests were heaving as he briefly looked into her eyes. Then he returned, funneling his tremendous will into their kiss. It was as if she was the center of his universe, his sole focus.

He was all experience and confidence, by far the best kisser she'd ever—

A wicked shard of memory intruded. Another man's hands pressing onto her head and neck. Another man's mouth and tongue pushing into her—

She wrenched away and fell back, catching herself with her arms against the carpet. Looking to the side, she pressed the back of one wrist against her lips.

"Remy?" he asked, concerned. "You okay?"

Parting from him that way had been involuntary, stunning her slightly.

Her brain fought to function while submerging in the quicksand of fear. *What . . . What am I doing? Kissing Jeremiah?*

He was reaching down, offering her a hand up.

This was crazy! So stupid!

Ignoring his hand, she scrambled to her feet. She strode toward the back of the house as if chased by demons. Made it through the sliding door, then she was walking blindly into the night with some vague idea of needing more oxygen than she'd had in there where the strength of Jeremiah's presence thinned the atmosphere.

A panic attack was thundering toward her like a runaway train. She'd learned techniques for this. She could head it off. Maybe.

She halted near a fire table circled by chairs and focused her whirling thoughts on the details of the nearest chair. Adirondack. Brazilian walnut. Warm, rich color tone.

She counted as she inhaled, *one two three four five*, retained the breath for a few seconds, counted as she exhaled. Concentrating, she relaxed her muscles and made herself breathe deeper.

She knew Jeremiah had followed and was standing nearby. But he seemed to understand the silent message she was sending not to speak and not to touch her.

She hovered on the edge of a panic attack for a few agonizing minutes. Then spent a few more minutes recovering and gathering courage to face him.

At last, she straightened.

He looked stricken, pale. "Someone hurt you," he said quietly. "Didn't they, Remy?"

All of a sudden, she wanted to cry. To scream. To shake her fists at the heavens.

She did none of those things. Said nothing.

His hands dangled at his sides. "Please tell me."

Should she tell him? She typically discussed it only with her inner circle. People she'd known longer than she'd known Jeremiah.

Yet staying silent was what an ashamed person would do, and she had no reason to feel ashamed. Even so, shame always, *always* tried to score her with its talons. She loathed shame.

"Let's sit," she said. That would help slightly. She'd feel less exposed if she didn't have to look at his face while talking about this. Also, her legs were wobbly.

They sat, his chair just a few feet from hers. His back muscles lengthened beneath his clothing as he leaned forward to flick a switch on the fire table. Flames danced from granite stones.

She'd just kissed him.

He'd kissed her back. Thoroughly. Expertly.

Earlier this very evening she'd told herself to exercise restraint! Yet she'd been the one who'd initiated the contact. Which had been a terrible decision . . . that had resulted in something addictively wonderful.

She knew why the ugly memories had intruded. Because that was the first kiss she'd experienced since . . .

The temperature was dropping, and she wrapped her arms around herself in an effort to stay warm.

"I have throw blankets inside. Hang on a minute." He disappeared into the house.

Her mind skittered in circles as she stared up at blinking stars.

When Jeremiah returned, he handed her a downy men's jacket and a throw blanket that must have been knitted from angel fluff. She pulled on the jacket and inhaled the scent of his soap. Warmth cocooned her as she tucked the throw blanket over her legs.

He returned to his seat and thrust his long arms into what looked like a black snowboarder's jacket. It had several zippers and pockets and a high neck that accented his profile.

Remy waited for him to say something. He didn't. He was using the power of silence to coax her to speak.

After a time, she forced out the hardest sentence. "I was raped."

She looked across at him just as he looked across at her.

His expression revealed sympathy and also a reassuring kind of constancy. That look said, *Whatever you have to say, I won't flinch from it.* She hadn't known what sort of response would give her the green light to continue. Turned out, this was it. Without saying a word, he'd helped her find stable footing.

She fixed her attention on the flames. "It happened six years ago. I was twenty-four. I'd graduated from TCU two years before that. I was living in Dallas, doing the career-girl thing, and happy with it." She shifted, pulling the throw blanket under her chin. "Up until that point I'd led a fairly charmed life. I had a secure, loving family. Wonderful friends. My college years were great. I got the job I wanted. I enjoyed dating along the way. Never anything super serious but the boyfriends I did have were all decent guys. Nice guys. I expected that I'd meet my husband one day, that we'd marry, have kids. I had faith in that because my life up until that point had led me to believe that I could count on good things."

She felt fondness toward the person she'd been, maybe in the same way that mothers felt fondness toward memories of their children when they were small.

"I met a guy named Gavin," she continued. "He was good-looking, charming, intelligent, from a wealthy family. He'd been a Division One soccer star before going pro. He was playing for the Dallas team when I met him."

She paused to collect herself. Even after all this time, she had a visceral reaction when recounting these events. Her muscles tightened defensively against the sensation of being trapped.

"Gavin and I went out a couple of times," she said. "I was still trying to decide if I was interested in dating him or if friendship was a better fit. On paper, he was impressive. But, looking back, I think my instincts were warning me away. One night we had dinner with a group of his buddies and my

216

friends. It was a long, loud dinner. Lots of laughter. We both had quite a bit to drink, him more than me. Afterward, we walked from the restaurant to my apartment. I didn't think twice about inviting him up. I expected we'd hang out for a little while, then he'd call a taxi and go."

Vitality flowed from Jeremiah. Which was perhaps why she'd never realized he could be so still when he wanted to be. He remained silent, but it wasn't a hostile silence. It was a respectful one. She knew she had a supporter in that quiet.

"Gavin and I started making out," she said. "I liked it for a short period of time. But when he tried to take things further, I'd had enough. I pushed against his chest, never thinking for a second that he wouldn't immediately back away. Except he didn't back away. So I pushed harder. I told him no. I told him to stop. I told him to get off of me. He wouldn't. And the next thing I knew, he was holding me down."

Remy had been over this many times. In therapy. Via journaling. Through two separate trips to trauma camp where she and other survivors practiced the experiential model of reliving the trauma, feeling the emotions, and filing them away. Remy wished speaking about this event was like riding a rollercoaster along a familiar track—rote. Instead, it stirred complex emotions every time.

"He pressed a hand over my mouth, and I started to panic. I'd never been assaulted before and was horrified. Shocked. Scrambling to comprehend what was happening. I went into fight mode, but his physical strength was much greater than mine." She took a few seconds to inhale, exhale. "It was the single most terrifying and demeaning thing I've ever experienced. When he was finished, he kissed me on the cheek. He checked his phone, said he'd call me soon, and walked out humming. *Humming.* I was left there, broken and sobbing."

"I hate him." Jeremiah spoke with deadly calm. "I'm so sorry."

"Once I had a hold of myself enough to find and dial my phone, I called my best friends. They rushed over to comfort me. They're the ones who took me to the hospital. The staff there administered a rape kit exam."

She rubbed a fingertip back and forth against the texture of the blanket. "The aftermath felt surreal, like I was separated from my body. My charmed life had ended. Suddenly, I didn't know myself anymore. I didn't recognize this circumstance. I—I didn't know how to deal with this thing I was supposed to deal with. My friends and family and counselors helped. A lot. I pressed charges against Gavin." Her words ebbed away.

"And?" he asked.

"I mentioned earlier that he was from a wealthy family, right? He had a team of attorneys. They put me and my morals on trial. They claimed that I was his girlfriend, that I was drunk, that I wanted sex, and liked it rough. It's true that we'd gone out a few times and that I was tipsy. But I wasn't his girlfriend, and I wasn't drunk. The fact that it was consensual was absolutely false. Despite my testimony and the evidence, the jury found him not guilty."

She drew the sounds of nature into herself. "That verdict made me feel like I'd been violated twice. I went to trial because I thought I was doing the right thing. But when they set him free, I had to wonder if going to trial had been the correct decision after all, because it sure seemed like I'd dragged myself and everyone who cared about me through something unbelievably painful for no reason."

"You should have received justice."

"I should have, yes. But a lot of people don't." She closed a few of the snaps on the jacket she wore. "My only consolation is that his soccer career ended when his team learned of my accusations."

"You moved to Islehaven following the trial."

"Yes. I couldn't go on living the life I'd been living. Everything felt shallow and empty, and I was afraid a lot of the time. I moved to Islehaven for the same reason that people decide to climb Mount Everest. It was a test of my own inner strength. At that point in my life, I needed to find out what I was made of."

"And you found out that you were made of steel."

"I found out that there was just enough steel to get me by. Moving to Islehaven distanced me from all the people I love. But it connected me to myself."

"I promise you that I will never use physical force in any way."

"I appreciate that. However, I no longer put stock in words." Long seconds rolled past as they considered each other. "I haven't had a single romantic interaction since I moved to Islehaven." She bent her legs up, hooking her heels on the front edge of her chair's seat. "When you and I were kissing, I remembered . . . pieces of what Gavin did to me that night. That's why I broke it off so abruptly. It had nothing to do with you."

"Okay." He held her gaze. "I want a chance with you. We can go slow. At your pace."

"It's just . . . the pace I want is no pace at all. I can't afford to mess up my current state of wellbeing by attempting a dating relationship. When it comes to the question of *us* or *me* . . . I choose me."

He didn't flinch, just as his demeanor earlier had assured her he wouldn't. "Are you never going to have a dating relationship again?" There was no condemnation in his tone.

"Never's a big word. I wouldn't say never. I'd say *not now.*

Living on Islehaven suits where I'm at with this because there's no one there to date."

"There's Michael."

"I'd rather embrace lifelong singlehood."

"What would encourage you to consider dating?"

"More time and the right guy."

"I'm the right guy and more time isn't a problem."

"You're completely wrong for me."

"Why?"

"For one thing, through no fault of your own, you share many characteristics with Gavin. You're both athletes, both wealthy, both handsome, both confident."

"I am nothing like Gavin."

"Maybe not in the ways that matter. But you do have enough in common with him to scare me."

"I hate that I'm similar to him in any way. I wish I wasn't."

"Also, while I do find that I'm . . . attracted to you, if I have a relationship with someone, it won't be with a man who himself is in crisis and who's"—she gestured toward the house—"wrapped up in materialism."

Normally, he'd have taken that type of bait as an invitation to defend himself with a comeback or joke with her. This time, he did neither. "Is what happened with Gavin why you didn't want to come inside the church on Islehaven?" he asked.

"After I was raped, I begged God for justice that didn't come. But I was still hanging in there with Him, by a thread, after the trial. I prayed and prayed for Him to remove my feelings of betrayal and anger and shame. Based on everything I knew about God, that's a prayer He should have wanted to answer. For months I prayed. But all those things continued to strangle me. God just sort of . . . left me there. Abandoned. So I stopped praying and believing."

The quiet whooshing sound of the gas that fed the fire

reminded her of the sound she'd heard from God in response to her prayers during those barren, devastated months.

"Do you still feel betrayal, anger, and shame?" he asked.

"For the most part, no."

"So is it possible that God did answer your prayers eventually?"

His gentle question took her off guard.

Wait. Could that be true?

Her brain spun for a few seconds but then, to her relief, gained purchase. "No. It's not thanks to God that I don't wallow in those emotions anymore. It's thanks to the fact that I created my own solutions."

Chapter Fifteen

The things Remy had suffered wrecked Jeremiah.

Mid-morning Saturday, the day after she'd told him about the rape, he sat alone in the sanctuary of a church on the outskirts of Groomsport. He'd asked his phone's GPS to locate the church nearest his house. It brought him here—to a small brown-brick structure with a tall steeple. The interior had pews with green padding, wood floors, and rectangular windows.

Unfortunately, the peace of his surroundings hadn't yet rubbed off on him.

While Remy had been telling him about the assault last night, he'd been gutted. He hadn't known how to respond in the way that would be best for her. He doubted he'd ever known that type of thing, but if he once had, he'd forgotten it.

The one thing he had been aware of? That showing too much outrage on her behalf might make things worse. Her story wasn't about him, so he'd tried to get out of her way, tried to stay calm. But he had been—was—outraged.

A man held Remy down and raped her.

Remy, with the huge imagination. Remy, with the overalls

and the crazy cottage and the flowing hair. Remy, the sculptor. Remy, who'd taken him—a stranger—in. Remy, who was smart and feisty and unique.

This Gavin person had forced himself on her using brute strength. Then allowed his attorneys to tear Remy's character down while he'd been busy lying under oath.

The thought of it stirred fury into a hurricane inside of him. In the middle of last night, he'd shoved aside his covers and gone to his office. With only the glow of his computer screen to force out the dark, he'd typed *Gavin soccer player rape trial Dallas* into a search engine. That's all it had taken. He'd received pages and pages of results.

He wanted to *kill* Gavin. He couldn't stand his smug face or his long hair. He couldn't stand that he'd been found innocent.

Remy had been honest with him and now a new level of understanding existed between them. But so did the heavy reality of the thing that had happened to her.

He had more of a buffer toward the hard things that had happened to him than he did for what had happened to her. With her, he had no buffer. He wasn't dealing with this well.

He kept trying to think of ways to make it right and remembering again that he couldn't and simmering in his own powerlessness. She'd already done what could be done—she'd made a new life for herself. All that was left for him to do was support her.

His world was small, and she was the person at the center of it. He trusted her the most, liked her the most, and respected her the most. More than he wanted answers about his history, more than he wanted his memory back, he simply wanted . . . her.

But he couldn't have her.

Jeremiah thought and prayed, prayed and thought.

Eventually he heard footsteps and turned to see an elderly Black man approaching down the church's center aisle. "Hello there," the man said warmly. "Welcome."

"Thanks. Are you the pastor?"

"No, no. Just a member."

"Is it okay if I sit in here?"

"Absolutely. I'm here because I like to come and sit once or twice a week myself." He took a seat across the aisle, interlacing his hands over his potbelly.

"Are there a lot of things that go on here during the week?" Jeremiah asked.

"Oh yes. We've got two services on Sundays, Sunday school, a men's group, Wednesday night service, ladies' Bible studies, and more. Would you be interested in attending any of that?"

"I'm interested in attending all of that." His calendar was too empty.

The man's face sagged with surprise. "You are?"

"Well," Jeremiah clarified, "not the ladies' Bible study."

"Excellent, *excellent*. We'd love to have you. And may I just say how thrilled I was over your championships?" Wrinkles folded across his skin like an accordion as he smiled. "And not just the championships, but the way you handled yourself in that final, painful season. Pure class. Inspirational."

Remy walked atop the breakwater that jutted out from the Rockland harbor's northern edge. Almost a mile long, it had been completed in 1901 to safeguard the ships and industry of the town from storm-driven waves. Seven hundred thousand tons of granite blocks had been used, which now formed a wide walking path to the lighthouse perched at the breakwater's end.

On her left, more than ten miles of water separated the mainland from North Haven and Vinalhaven Islands. On her right, the harbor stretched wide and deep. Then came the town, tucked against a backdrop of hills. The heavily clouded sky seemed to pause to watch the progress of boats of every shape and size—sailboats, commercial barges, tourist schooners.

This was the first time since moving in with Wendell that Remy had made this walk. She'd have liked to look up and admire the views while moving forward. As it was, the cracks between the boulders and their uneven tops meant she had to keep her eyes down. She counteracted this by stopping often to enjoy the vistas.

When she reached the picture-perfect lighthouse—a quintessentially New England creation of red brick and white-painted wood—she walked around it, then up the exterior staircase to an outdoor landing. Wind tugged her hair behind her like a banner as she faced in the direction of Islehaven.

Soon, she'd need to return there. Not only because she missed the power it had to restore and protect her, but also because her checking account balance was beginning to demand it. During this trip, her rental car was her largest expense. Next to that, food. She'd been frugal, but still. She flatly refused to dip into the savings she'd worked so hard to grow.

The simple financial realities of her chosen profession of artist were these . . . It had taken her a long time to create sculptures worth buying. Now that she'd reached that point, she was limited income-wise by her own output. Her creative process took time and could not be rushed. While she had amassed a following of collectors willing to buy her pieces, that following was relatively small. A lack of great demand combined with her unwillingness to over-charge combined with the fact that she compensated her mother and sister for running the business side of her art meant that she was not a person who could afford to tarry here much longer.

In a few days she'd return home and resume work. And that was for the best, except . . .

Jeremiah.

Every time she thought his name it was like a screw twisting into her heart. She'd been in communication with him since their kiss, but she couldn't bring herself to see him today, which was cowardly and unfair because he'd been wonderful to her.

Truth be told, she was embarrassed by her freak-out last night. She shouldn't be. People who'd experienced trauma sometimes found themselves in situations that shoved them close to or over the edge of a panic attack. That wasn't her fault. That was just trauma, and she shouldn't be embarrassed, and she should give herself kindness and acceptance.

And *yeah yeah yeah* . . .

She was embarrassed.

By the freak-out and by the fact that she'd kissed him ardently then just as ardently yanked away. Worse, if she was to see him again—this evening, for example—she had no reason to trust herself to behave better. Because that kiss . . .

That kiss had been a masterpiece.

She'd lain awake last night thinking about it. Today she'd been daydreaming about it.

Remy started back across the long line of boulders. *Think on this inspiring walkway*, she ordered herself, *and what a wonderful addition it would make to one of the stories surrounding your pieces.*

An orphan girl could cross it holding a sword. And on both sides seething fog could shelter dragons. The girl could be on a . . . a quest to free a knight on the other side. He could be held captive behind bars.

Remy pictured it, her heroine drawing near the captive and the captive turning toward her in his suit of armor. Pale green eyes, dark blond hair, a knowing smile—

She broke off the reverie with frustration.

Things were dire indeed if Jeremiah didn't have the good taste to leave her alone even in the inner chambers of her imagination.

By sunset, Jeremiah was going crazy from inactivity. He finished every possible piece of work connected to Alexis's timeline in an attempt (that failed) to distract himself from Remy. Then he texted his brother.

> **JEREMIAH**
>
> I don't remember the people Alexis saw during the final two weeks of her life. Would you and Anton and Fiona be willing to call them for me?

Jude replied almost instantly.

> **JUDE**
>
> Definitely

> **JEREMIAH**
>
> When can you come to Groomsport?

> **JUDE**
>
> Tomorrow night, seven o'clock at Appleton?

> **JEREMIAH**
>
> Good

> **JUDE**
>
> I'll contact the others.

Jude's drive to Appleton was longer than both his mom's drive and Anton's drive. Even so, when he pulled up to Jeremiah's house the next night, he saw that he'd arrived first. Which pleased him but did not surprise him. He always ran at least fifteen minutes early for any non-FBI event, and for FBI events he arrived forty minutes ahead of time because all his co-workers arrived thirty minutes ahead of time. Knowing Anton, he'd arrive one minute early for the meeting tonight. Knowing Mom, she'd arrive twelve minutes late.

Using his key, Jude let himself through the back door. "I'm here."

"In the living room," Jeremiah called.

Jude found his older brother standing on the area rug, hands pushed into the pockets of his jeans. He hadn't shaved for a few days, and he looked exhausted.

"Everything okay?" Jude asked.

"I'm worried about Remy."

"Ah. Worried why?"

A pause. "Just worried." Jeremiah pressed his fingers against his temples as if he had a headache. "What would 1.0 have done to convince a woman to give him a chance?"

Jeremiah was finally admitting what Jude had known all along. His brother was falling for Remy. "1.0?"

"That's how I refer to my former self."

"As far as I know, convincing women to give him a chance wasn't really an issue for 1.0." Jude had spent a lifetime watching Jeremiah react with polite indifference toward women who were infatuated with him. "But if it had been an issue, the old you would have used charm and persistence. If something was important to 1.0, he never gave up."

"You make it sound like 1.0 was the better model."

"No way. 2.0 likes chocolate pudding and God, so 2.0's obviously the better model. If you're having trouble convincing Remy to hang out with you, it's only because she's a very rare type of person."

Jeremiah's face softened. "She is rare. And there are . . . some things in her past that make her cautious. I can't pressure her."

"Then hang in there. Be patient."

"Was 1.0 the patient type?"

"No."

"Neither is 2.0." He headed toward the stairs. "I'll go get my notes and Alexis's calendar."

Jude went to one of the living room windows overlooking the hillside. He knew this part of Maine better than any place on earth. Groomsport was *his* town and returning here always unloosened tight places inside him.

It was full dark out, but clear. Lights from homes and streetlights dotted the hillsides, congregating in numerous points of light in downtown Groomsport. Tonight the sea was made silvery by the moon sitting low in the sky.

That big moon reminded him of the time Uncle Jack O'Sullivan had taken him and Jeremiah night fishing when they were kids. Jeremiah had reeled in an eight-pound large-mouth bass with a lure he'd made himself. Even back then, Jeremiah had made everything look easy, including things that took strength and a will of iron to accomplish.

Jude had always regarded himself as the less flashy, less successful, and less handsome Camden brother. For the most part, that had been just fine with him. His father, his mother, and Jeremiah were all driven toward big achievements and big glamour. But through a trick of genetics, he was not.

He was dedicated to his work because he wanted to do the

right thing and do it well. Not because he wanted recognition or money for it.

Jude avoided the spotlight. In fact, he hated fame—the thing that had brought stress and misery to his family members. He definitely didn't want scandal. He didn't even want to be recognized as a Camden. When he was ten, he'd asked his parents never to allow another photo of him to be published—not in magazines, not in newspapers, and not on websites. The family attorneys had been busy ever since warning and suing entities that attempted to take and post photos.

Even though he didn't want the public at large to connect him to his family, he did love his family. They were his priority, which was why he was glad Jeremiah was about to give him something tangible to do to help.

Jude registered the sound of Jeremiah coming downstairs just as he spotted Anton approaching the front door. He checked his watch. One minute ahead of schedule.

The three made themselves comfortable on the living room furniture, talking sports, until Mom's voice reached them.

"Hello," she called. She, too, had come through the back door. Only six minutes late, which showed how much she valued this gathering.

They stood to welcome her, and she arrived the way she arrived at all places—as if she was a queen and the activity could begin now that she had come. She was carrying a bottle of red wine and wearing a wool coat, an ivory sweater, tailored pants, and high heels. She approached Jeremiah first. "Good to see you, darling. Is it all right with you if I give you a small hug? I promise not to draw it out and make it awkward for you."

"That'll be fine."

She hugged him. "Thank you." Jude knew she was referring to more than the hug—she was thanking Jeremiah for inviting her back into his life.

Next, she came to Jude, and he registered her crisp perfume as she leaned in to hug him. Then she moved on to Anton, giving him double air kisses. "I brought wine! Who else would like some?"

No one, apparently. "I'll get you a glass." Jude was back with a glass and a wine opener in seconds. By that time, Mom had settled onto the couch, pushing her coat back so that it pooled around her.

Jeremiah eyed Mom suspiciously as she crossed her legs and took a long sip.

Jude bit back a smile. Since the amnesia, this brother was both familiar and slightly unfamiliar to him. But to Jeremiah, they were all completely unfamiliar. If you hadn't built up experience with Mom you would find her to be a lot. Jeremiah was probably second-guessing his decision to include her.

"Have you already started discussing the help that we can provide?" Mom asked Jeremiah.

"No."

"Oh, good. I'm glad I didn't miss that. I'm all ears."

"I'm trying to reconstruct the last two weeks of Alexis's life," Jeremiah said.

"Why's that?" Mom asked.

"Because I discovered that's what I was working on when I disappeared. Apparently, I doubted that her death was a suicide."

Mom's face blanched, though her posture remained straight. "The police—"

"—aren't budging off of their suicide ruling until new evidence is uncovered. I'm hoping you can help me uncover new evidence. I need to . . . deal with this before I can move forward."

"I'm in," Jude said.

"Same," Anton added.

"Yes," Mom told Jeremiah, though there were a hundred questions in her eyes. "Absolutely. Anything for you."

"Just so you're all aware," Jeremiah said, "Alexis had an affair with a man named Sabato Messina about a year and a half before she died. She was having another affair at the time of her death. I don't know with whom. It may have been Messina again."

His words froze Jude with shock. Mom and Anton also looked stunned.

"I'd hired a private detective and he compiled evidence on the affairs. I'm telling you about them because if we find out who she was in a relationship with when she died, that'll give us a more complete picture." Jeremiah spoke without emotion. "I've put together a list of the people she saw those last two weeks. I thought we'd divide the names between you three, then you can call each of them." He outlined the types of questions they should ask.

"I'll create a worksheet for the interviews," Jude offered. "We can fill out one worksheet per person as we're having conversations. That'll keep us on track and give us a consistent framework for organizing information."

"Good." Jeremiah slid a sheet of paper from beneath the calendar and read off the first name. "Naomi."

"Naomi Nomura," Fiona supplied. "She was Alexis's friend and part-time assistant. I can give her a call."

"Renee," Jeremiah said.

Anton shifted forward in his seat. "She and I are both members of the country club. I'll speak with her."

Jeremiah ran through several more names, including her personal trainer, Hank.

"I'll reach out to him," Fiona offered. "He's my trainer, too."

"Do you think Alexis could have been having an affair with Hank at the time of her death?"

"No," she answered immediately. "He's excellent at his job but he's older than I am and not at all her type."

"Okay," Jeremiah said. "Kelly?"

For the first time, they were stumped.

"Even though," Jude said, "we don't know who Kelly is, it's likely one of the people we'll be talking to will know who she is. I'll add a question about her to the worksheet."

And so it went. "That's all of them," Jeremiah finally said, setting the paper aside.

"I'm going to need more wine," Mom stated.

Remy checked the time. Very soon, on this mid-morning Tuesday four days after The Kiss, Jeremiah would arrive at Wendell's. She and Jeremiah were going to hike to Maiden's Cliff—the spot where Alexis had either jumped or been killed. They'd be out in a public place. That and the seriousness of the location would bolster her control.

She was prepared!

This was fine. She was sitting calmly at Wendell's kitchen table, very much over whatever temporary insanity had possessed her at Appleton when she'd kissed him.

Wendell wandered in and opened his bread drawer.

"There are no more donuts," she informed him. "I bought frozen bran muffins for you instead."

His shoulders slumped. "Why would anyone freeze a muffin?"

"Convenience and nutrition."

"But not tastiness." He stuck a bran muffin on a small plate and put both in the microwave.

"Can I talk to you about something?" she asked as he waited for the muffin to thaw.

"Of course."

Wendell had been a theologian and pastor, which made him her resident expert in matters of faith. She relayed to him what she'd explained to Jeremiah the other night, about how she'd distanced herself from God. "Jeremiah asked me if I still struggle with the emotions I asked God to take away. I said no and he wondered aloud if it's possible, then, that God *did* eventually answer my prayer by taking the emotions away. My knee-jerk reaction in the moment was to tell him no. But I've been thinking about it and now I'm not so sure."

"Ah." He carried his muffin over to the table and sat across from her, his adorably pointy face empathetic. Today's sweater was green with a lawnmower stitched into the front.

"I hate thinking back on the months following the assault," she confided. "The feelings were so huge, it was like they became my whole identity. I was nothing but atoms of rage, bitterness, and humiliation. At the time, I believed I'd never get free of them." It had been skin-crawling, panic-inducing terrible.

"I understand," he said simply. "As you know, I've been struggling with sorrow and grief. I don't have any quick fixes. But I can tell you what I know, if you want me to."

"I do."

He stacked his long hands on the table. "I know that God has a soft spot for those of us who feel like we've been thrown onto the garage sale pile. A giant soft spot for us. He's never closer to us than when we're beaten up, unloved, betrayed."

"Then why, back then, did He seem so far away?"

"I don't know. Sometimes the way things seem isn't the way they are."

"I was right to pray for Him to remove those feelings, so why didn't He go ahead and remove them sooner?"

"I don't know," he said again. "I've been asking Him to remove my sadness. And what did He do? He sent you."

She released a surprised laugh. "I'm not an answer to prayer! I'm making you clean your house."

"Answers to prayer don't always look the way you expect them to. My sadness isn't gone but it's much better, you know. Because you're here, Remy. And now I have company."

She reached over and squeezed his hand. He squeezed back. This moment of solidarity and affection was her reward for all the days of work. She'd been right to spend time here. Right to help him.

"I've learned in my eighty years," Wendell said, "that seasons of emotional hardship are like storm fronts. Powerful, yes. Damaging, yes. Scary when they're on top of you. But also *passing*."

She sat back in her chair and took a look at her life from way high up, from the view used by TV weathermen when they showed graphics of storm fronts. Over the years, she'd experienced so many sunny, temperate, quiet days. But there'd been vicious storms, too. "Rape should not have been a part of my story. It should not be a part of any woman, man, or child's story."

"You're right."

When Gavin had attacked her, he'd forced rape into her story. "That's not what I wanted for myself." With effort she kept her voice level. "That's not how it should have gone."

"I know," Wendell said with all the compassion of a grand-father. "That's not the way God wanted it to go for you, either."

Many trauma survivors reached for drugs and alcohol to numb the pain. She'd reached for an island, solitude, and art. After enduring something brutal, it was so much harder to trust God because trust, in general, was no longer an easy thing to give. Not to God. Not to Jeremiah.

Knock knock.

She jumped.

Jeremiah was here. She made her way to the foyer and could hear Wendell ambling behind her as if she were in high school and he was coming to meet the boy who was picking her up for a date. Which was not at all the vibe she wanted here. But she couldn't very well tell Wendell to hide himself away in his own house after he'd just been so kind.

She swung the door open and there was Jeremiah. More than six feet of lean muscle. His exercise clothes fit him like a dream, but it was his eyes that wielded the lion's share of the power. They were slightly hooded and communicated equal parts strength and vulnerability. As usual, it was the vulnerability that got her.

This was fine! Everything was fine.

"Did you bring me Indian food this time?" Wendell asked, crowding next to Remy and winking at Jeremiah. He was referencing the fact that he'd asked if Jeremiah was the Indian food delivery guy the first time they'd met. "Chicken tikka masala is the most delicious dish ever created."

"I'm afraid that I'm fresh out of tikka masala, Wendell." Jeremiah grinned. "I'll bring it next time."

"Actually," Remy announced, "I'm canceling Wendell's imaginary Indian food order. Tikka masala is not a friend to his kidney disease." She scooped up the credit card, ChapStick, and hairband she'd deposited on the entry table in preparation for the trip.

"You two kids be safe now," Wendell said as she exited.

"Yes, sir," Jeremiah said at the same time that she said, "We're not kids."

"What time should I expect you home?" Wendell asked Remy, mischief in his eyes.

236

"Very shortly, since Jeremiah and I can only get along for abbreviated periods."

"Call me if you need anything," Wendell said.

"And you'll what? Come get me via ElderTransport?"

"If you two arrive home after dark and I turn the porch light on and off, that'll be your signal to stop kissing and come inside."

"This is not a date, Wendell!"

Chuckling, Wendell retreated into the house. They continued to Jeremiah's BMW. Once inside, he looked across the interior at her with deep affection and amusement, though she'd done nothing funny.

Butterflies flapped tiny, tingly wings within her stomach. "Are we leaving now?" she asked impatiently.

They started off.

"Do you realize what today is?" she asked.

"The one-month anniversary of the day you rescued me."

"Drat. I wanted to make you guess."

"I remember everything about you, Remy."

So, okay. Maybe she wasn't completely over the temporary insanity that had possessed her at Appleton. "If it wasn't for the fact that I rescued you one month ago, you'd be fish food."

"You're still rescuing me."

"Stop saying endearing things!"

"You don't like it when I say endearing things?"

"No! It's off-putting. Inauthentic."

"These are the most authentic things I've ever said to you."

"Let's discuss what we know about Maiden's Cliff and Alexis's death." Just as she'd known it would, the subject change thrust his deceased wife between them. Which put things back on familiar footing that she could navigate.

Finally. Jeremiah was with Remy again.

They parked at the base and set off on the trail toward Maiden's Cliff. Before leaving home, he'd read about the hike. He knew it was two miles long, which would have been easy on flatter ground. This was a lot steeper than he'd expected. Not easy, especially on his healing lungs. He pretended that the elevation gain wasn't a problem, but Remy had a sixth sense about him. Halfway up, she started asking if he was all right. Three-quarters of the way up, she started insisting on stopping for water breaks.

More and more sky began to show through the branches as they finally approached the cliff. Here bare mountain jutted out like a stubborn chin. The forested arms of the land reached down on both sides to embrace the dark blue lake eight hundred feet below. Clouds threw uneven shadows over miles of hills and water.

This spot had been named Maiden's Cliff in honor of a girl, Elenora French, who'd died here in 1864. She'd been just eleven years old when a gust of wind had blown off her hat. She'd caught it successfully but as she'd tried to put it back on, she'd fallen over the edge. They'd placed a cross and a plaque here to remember her by. The elements had destroyed several crosses over the decades, but new generations had replaced them all. The current cross was large, made of steel, and painted white.

Looking over the edge caused a sick feeling to jump in the pit of Jeremiah's stomach.

It was hard to imagine the terror of falling through inky black air, knowing that death was rushing up toward you. Then the unimaginable impact. Awful enough if Alexis had chosen that fate, but much worse if she'd been shoved to it.

He felt Remy's attention on him and glanced down at her.

Her expression was serious, as if they were standing at some-one's graveside. Which, in fact, they were.

Her beauty stilled his thoughts and stole his words. The better he knew her, the more stunning she was. Creamy skin. The face of an artist. Gray eyes lit from within by intelligence. She carried herself like an independent woman who'd embraced who she was.

Remy's phone alarm sounded. It took her at least twenty seconds to find it in her pocket and silence the thing.

"Time for lunch?" he asked mildly.

She tucked her phone away. "It is, indeed, time for lunch, Jeremiah."

"Good to know."

"Hey," she said softly.

"Yeah?"

"No one should die the way Alexis did."

"No. They shouldn't."

"Are you glad you came here? Or is this too hard?"

"I'm glad." *I'd go to every sad place in the world if it meant you were next to me.*

"Good. Does anything about this site help illuminate your investigation into what happened?"

"It's more difficult than I'd realized to get from the parking lot to here."

"And in the dark, when Alexis came, even more so."

"Right. So if she came here intending to commit suicide, it wasn't a spontaneous choice—she'd have had a lot of time to think about it on the way up. And if someone brought her here to kill her, they couldn't have hauled her—either conscious or unconscious—all the way from the parking lot."

"Which means if she came here with someone or met someone here, she did so willingly."

"Yes."

Down to the right, hikers walked along a trail. To the left, a reflection flickered—sun bouncing off a person's cell phone or sunglasses or a metal water bottle. This place wasn't uninhabited in daylight but no doubt it became isolated after dark.

What happened to you, Alexis?

Jeremiah's cell phone rang, and he connected the call. "Hello?"

"Is this Jeremiah Camden?"

"It is."

"This is Seaman Collins with the Coast Guard. We've found your boat."

Chapter Sixteen

Anton called Jeremiah three days later. "I learned who Kelly is."

"Oh?"

"Remember me offering to reach out to Renee, one of the women listed in Alexis's calendar?"

"Yeah."

"Well, I just got off the phone with her. Turns out she knows Kelly and that Kelly is a guy. He and Alexis were mixed doubles partners in tennis."

A guy? "I assumed that Kelly was a woman."

"Same here."

So, there had actually been two men listed in Alexis's calendar during those final two weeks—her trainer and her doubles partner.

"Renee mentioned," Anton said, "that Kelly always plays in the drill that starts at five thirty. Want me to swing by and pick you up? There's just enough time for us to drive over and chat with him before it starts."

"Sure."

Several minutes later, Jeremiah slid into the passenger seat of Anton's Mercedes and they set off. A sense of familiarity washed over him, which jogged a memory. He saw himself, sitting in the passenger seat of another car as they inched along crowded city streets. Anton driving, profile serious.

"Did you drive me places a lot?" Jeremiah asked.

"All the time. To and from the hotel and the track. To and from your apartment. To where we trained. To press conferences." A pause. "All the time."

"What kind of work do you do now?"

"At the moment I'm writing a book about my time in Formula One."

Anton played relaxing indie folk music. They spoke little. Jeremiah's subconscious recognized both things—that style of music and the easy silence between them.

They passed the country club's iron gates and followed a road that snaked past manicured flower beds and ancient trees. Inside the clubhouse, the timber beams, stone accents, and thick carpets smacked of luxury.

Anton greeted the young woman at the reception desk. She brightened, obviously familiar with Anton. When Anton asked if she remembered Alexis Camden, her pretty face immediately showed sorrow. "I do, yes."

"This is her husband, Jeremiah."

She turned awestruck eyes in his direction. "It's so nice to meet you."

"Likewise."

"While we're here," Anton said, "I thought I'd introduce Jeremiah to Kelly Dupont, Alexis's doubles partner."

"Oh! Sure." She consulted her computer. "He's signed up for the five-thirty drill so he should be here any minute."

"We'll wait for him in the pro shop." Anton gestured

toward the retail space filled with golf and tennis products. "Will you tell him where we are when he gets here?"

"Of course, Mr. Quintrell."

They sat in leather armchairs while a handful of customers browsed and chatted around them.

Learning Kelly's identity was the first real lead he'd had, in addition to the discovery of his boat off the coast of Cape Hatteras.

A commercial fisherman had reported the *Camdenball* to the Coast Guard, who'd then investigated. They'd discovered it unmanned and adrift. Because the fuel had been spent, they'd towed it to their base. Then they'd looked up the registration papers he'd filed and pinpointed him as its owner.

In the days since he'd received the call from the Coast Guard, he'd made arrangements to have the *Camdenball* transported back to Groomsport. He'd also spoken with Detective Holland, informing him that a crime may have been committed on the boat and asking if he'd sweep it for evidence. Holland had told him the Feds had jurisdiction over crimes at sea and given him a number to call. Jeremiah had called it. The man on the other end of the line had been polite and sympathetic but had stated that unless Jeremiah could offer proof that foul play had occurred on the *Camdenball*, they could not intervene.

Jeremiah had hunted for a solution online and found one in the form of a freelance forensics expert named Eleanor Dobbins. The references she'd provided checked out, so he'd explained to Eleanor over the phone that he suspected he'd been attacked on his boat and wanted evidence gathered off it. Eleanor had asked him follow-up questions in a voice without inflection. She frequently let long pauses sit between them. At the end of the conversation, she'd offered her services.

He was willing to pay for quick answers, so he'd used his checkbook to convince Eleanor to drop everything and fly here from her home in Phoenix. His boat would arrive the day after tomorrow and Eleanor would arrive that same afternoon—

Jeremiah watched a twenty-something man enter the country club's foyer. He checked in with the receptionist, who gestured toward where they were sitting. The man made his way in their direction.

In unison, Jeremiah and Anton pressed to their feet.

Nothing about Hank's description had led Jeremiah to think that Hank could have been Alexis's lover. But this man? Yes. Kelly was as tall as Jeremiah. He had an athletic build and a tan. His brown hair was trimmed in a modern cut and held in place with gel. His Adidas clothing looked as new as the racquet bag he carried.

"Jeremiah and Anton?" Kelly asked.

They introduced themselves and shook hands.

"I haven't had a chance to give you my condolences," Kelly said to Jeremiah. "About Alexis. I'm sorry. She was great."

Jeremiah nodded. "I wanted to meet you because of her. You saw her a few days before she died. Is that right?"

Kelly set the tennis bag on the floor and crossed his arms. "Yeah. We hit for about forty-five minutes one night after I got off work."

"How did she seem that night?"

"Seem?"

"Yes. How was she acting? Like her usual self? Unlike her usual self?"

He took a breath and raised his brows. "It was more than a year ago."

"I know. I'd still like to know what you remember."

"If you don't mind my asking, is there a particular reason why you'd like to know?" He glanced at Anton, then back at Jeremiah.

"Just trying to find closure," Jeremiah said. That answer

was vague but believable enough that Kelly would be rude to question it.

"She seemed normal," Kelly said. "That night when we hit. She acted one hundred percent like her usual self." There was a hint of defensiveness in his body language.

"Do you remember what you talked about that night?"

"I don't. We typically talked about regular stuff, though. Tennis. The town, the weather, restaurants, movies. My job. Her life."

"Would you say you were close?" Anton asked.

Kelly frowned. "I'd say we were friends. We'd been mixed doubles partners for a while."

"How long?"

"Like a year. At least. We were both competitive. We made a good team."

"Did you see each other outside of tennis?" Jeremiah asked.

"After matches we'd sometimes grab a drink or a meal with the team."

Then head to a hotel together? Jeremiah wondered. There was something about Kelly that read as shifty. He didn't trust him.

"Do you keep a calendar on your phone?" Jeremiah asked.

"Yeah."

Jeremiah pulled out his phone and double-checked the notes he'd jotted down based on Kimley's investigation into Alexis's second affair. "Can you do me a favor and give me a sense of what you were doing on the following dates?" He read off the dates of Alexis's mystery trip to the Outer Banks.

Kelly blinked at him. Asking without words why he wanted to know.

"Again," Jeremiah said evenly, "I'm just trying to get closure."

Kelly checked his watch—a silent signal that they were

245

going to make him late for his drill. He pulled free his phone and flicked its screen with impatient expertise. "I was here that weekend."

Jeremiah read off the dates of the mystery trip to New York.

"I was visiting college buddies in Boston on those dates. Look, I've got to go." Kelly hauled the tennis bag over his shoulder and backed away. "I wish you all the best." Turning, he jogged away.

"I don't like him," Anton said.

"Me neither."

On the ride home, Jeremiah found Kelly on social media. As far as he could tell, he was single. And very much into beautiful women.

⛵

On Tuesday afternoon, Remy followed Jeremiah along Groomsport's dock toward where the *Camdenball* was moored. Eleanor, the freelance forensics expert he'd hired, plodded alongside.

Light sleet pinged against the wooden boards and crackled against the hood of Remy's jacket. The ocean frothed steel gray and forbidding. But even if there'd been a hurricane afoot, she wouldn't have missed this outing because—and she hadn't told this to Jeremiah yet—it was likely the final thing she'd do for him.

Her work on Wendell's house was, at long last, very close to completion. Plus, she'd finished setting up systems for Wendell that gave her faith that he'd be able to keep things organized after she left.

She'd go back to the simple life she'd lived before Jeremiah. Where she could protect her time and energy. Where she felt safe.

So how come preemptive grief tugged at her whenever she thought of how little time they had left?

The three of them stopped before the *Camdenball*. It looked like a relic from the glamour days of the 1950s—the type of boat Marilyn Monroe and Cary Grant would've taken out for a spin. It had been exceptionally restored, though at the moment it looked dirty and parched by the sun thanks to its weeks of drifting.

Jeremiah stepped back to allow her and Eleanor to precede him onboard.

Eleanor's stout, rectangular head topped a stout, rectangular body. She'd donned a navy windbreaker, khaki pants, and sturdy black tennis shoes closed with Velcro straps. Her prematurely gray bob had been parted straight down the middle. "How do you theorize that your attacker boarded?" Eleanor eyed the deck critically through large glasses.

"Remy and I have two theories." They'd talked through this at length. "One, that the attacker hid himself on the boat before I arrived."

"How long of a trip had you planned?"

"One week."

"For a week-long trip, wouldn't you have used every storage compartment large enough to accommodate a hiding person?"

"I don't remember that day so I'm not sure. But my brother told me that on trips like this, I typically pack light and pick up more food and water in various ports."

"Hmm." She turned in a slow circle. "If someone did stowaway, where did they go after they attacked you?"

"My guess is that they stayed with the boat until someone came and picked them up."

"What's your second theory?"

"That my attacker flagged me down while we were both at sea, maybe pretending a crisis."

"You're suggesting that person was lying in wait for you with the intention of boarding this boat and causing you injury?"

"Yes."

"Then they must have known your plans and where to intercept you."

"Or," Remy said, "were lying in wait for anyone with an expensive-looking boat. And Jeremiah happened along."

"Hmm," Eleanor said again.

"I think it's more likely," Jeremiah told Eleanor, "that I was their intended mark. And I think what happened to me is somehow connected to my wife's death fifteen months prior."

"In this second scenario, are you supposing that your attacker then got away on their craft?"

"Exactly."

She nodded, her lips an almost invisible line. "Take your time, both of you, and look at everything carefully. Does anything look wrong to you? Off? Tell me what you notice, no matter how small."

In silence, they studied their surroundings.

Remy's attention kept going renegade and returning to Jeremiah. He'd dressed in all black today—track pants and his snowboarder-style jacket. Water was darkening his hair, and a few droplets were suspended like crystals in the strands. The cold had brought color to his hard cheeks.

Though she remembered their kiss often and with startling clarity, she also found it hard to believe that had actually happened.

"Nothing looks off to me," Jeremiah said, startling her out of her reverie.

"Nor to me." Remy tried to look like someone who'd been giving the area a proper amount of study.

Eleanor slipped on plastic gloves, then opened the door

248

leading to the area below. Pausing, she pointed to a smear of rusty red high on the right side of the jam. "At first glance, this resembles blood."

Remy's eyes widened. "Jeremiah had a head injury the day I found him. It had been bleeding."

"If you please, Mr. Camden, will you stand next to the jam so we can approximate whether this blood might have come from your head injury?"

He moved to do so.

"Do not touch anything," Eleanor cautioned.

He was careful to stand close without touching.

"That stain lines up with where his injury was," Remy said, "on the back of his head."

"Good to know." Eleanor tugged three sets of paper booties from her bag. They put them on and descended the stairs. The dim cabin smelled of sea salt and new carpeting. Immediately to her right was a dinette followed by a tiny kitchen. On her left, a built-in sofa gave way to a bathroom. A bedroom occupied the bow of the boat.

"Anything here look wrong or off?" Eleanor asked.

"There's a spilled bottle of something near the berths." Jeremiah pointed.

Remy made her way deeper into the interior. "There's food on the floor of the kitchenette. It looks like he was interrupted while making a sandwich." Two slices of bread stood upright in the toaster. Closed containers of mayonnaise, mustard, deli ham, and cheese had fallen to the floor. A head of lettuce, now wilted, remained in the sink.

Eeriness brushed like a feather down the insides of her arms. This setting held gravity, just like at Maiden's Cliff. Both sites had witnessed brutal things and the echoes of them remained.

Jeremiah squatted close to the small, spilled bottle. "'Clean all-day energy,'" he read. "Native Vitality is the brand name. Blackberry." He straightened. "There's its top." The screw-top had rolled into the bathroom. "I recognize the bottle. Some of this flavor and a few other flavors were in my refrigerator at the house."

Eleanor opened the fridge. "You stocked them here, too."

Native Vitality drinks slotted next to bottled waters, milk, cold brew coffee, beer, eggs, bagged veggies, and fruit.

Eleanor faced them, spine straight. "I will handle this boat as I did crime scenes back when I was on the force. I'll gather as many samples as possible. I . . ." She peered at Jeremiah and suddenly appeared to lose her train of thought. Pink bloomed on her cheeks.

Oh, Eleanor. Not you, too. If sensible Eleanor wasn't immune to Jeremiah, then what chance did the rest of them have?

How Remy wished she was the one woman in the world immune to him. Why? Why couldn't she be that one? Everything would be so much easier for her and better for him seeing as how the effect he had on womankind wasn't doing his humility any favors.

Eleanor cleared her throat. "As I told you over the phone, the fact that the boat was exposed to the sun, water, and wind for such a long time will make things difficult above deck, where weather conditions have had their way. Below deck, we may have a greater opportunity for success."

"When will I receive the report of your findings?"

"Once I'm done here, I'll return with the samples to my lab in Phoenix. I'm just one person, and I have other jobs in the queue before you so my report will take anywhere from four to six weeks."

"I'm not an expert in forensics," he told her. "Will you interpret your findings for me?"

"I will."

"We'll leave you to it, then," he said. "Thank you."

Two days later in the late afternoon, Remy sat beside Jeremiah as he drove them up his drive toward Appleton. This was the first time she'd ridden in this particular car. He'd said it was something called a Shelby Cobra. She could tell it was old, which hopefully meant this was more modest and less stupidly expensive than his other cars.

Project Wendell was done and at least five times, she'd picked up the phone or surfed to a website to buy her ticket home to Islehaven. Each time, she'd hesitated for reasons she couldn't fully explain to herself.

Jeremiah had stopped by Wendell's unannounced just now with a fragrant bag full of chicken tikka masala. Wendell had been overjoyed. Jeremiah had ignored her scolding regarding feeding Wendell rich food and asked if she'd come to Appleton to look over the spreadsheet on which he'd been recording the data coming in from the conversations his mother, brother, and Anton were having with the people Alexis had seen before her death.

Remy had heard herself say yes because this *really was* the last thing she'd have the chance to do for him.

As they neared the house, she noticed a white Lexus SUV parked outside.

"Who's this?" she asked.

"I have no idea." They exited the Cobra and Remy followed Jeremiah along the path toward the front door.

A brunette came into view. She sat, legs crossed gracefully, on one of the porch chairs.

Alexis?

That fanciful thought sent ice water whistling down her spine before rationality returned. This was a lovely brunette. But not all lovely brunettes in the world were Alexis. This was someone else entirely. The stranger had a heart-shaped face, makeup that highlighted her dramatic eyes, clothing that flattered her curves, expertly styled long hair.

The woman came down the porch steps toward them, distrust and anger overcoming her features. Halting, she slanted one foot and knee to the side.

Jeremiah and Remy stopped, too.

"Do we know each other?" Jeremiah asked.

Her gaze homed in on him. Then Remy. Then back to him. "Is this a joke?"

"No," Jeremiah said calmly. "I'd genuinely like to know. Do we know each other?"

"I'm Gigi," the woman said. "Your girlfriend."

Chapter Seventeen

Outwardly, Remy froze. Inwardly, her heart plummeted.

His girlfriend.

He'd moved on to a new woman after Alexis?

Her emotions wailed even as her reason asked, *And why not?*

Alexis had been gone more than a year and Jeremiah's relationship with Alexis had been rocky long before that. So it wasn't beyond the bounds of possibility to think that, yes, he'd have moved on romantically, seeing as how he must be a target for thousands of women.

Gigi was an ideal representation of his type. She knew her way around a cosmetics counter and probably read *Vogue*.

Why hadn't Remy anticipated this? Why had it never once crossed her mind, after learning that he was a widower, that he might have been dating someone when he'd left on his boat trip?

Her stomach felt as if it was trying to digest sticker burs.

Jeremiah gave no outward sign of surprise, stress, or dismay.

"Are you going to pretend that you don't know me?" Gigi asked Jeremiah in a disbelieving tone.

"I don't have to pretend," he answered. "I have amnesia and so I literally don't know you."

Her face blanked. "You have amnesia?"

"I do."

"What . . . ?" She stammered. "How?"

"I'm not sure how, but it occurred the first day of my boat trip."

"I've been trying to contact you. When I couldn't get through on your cell, I finally decided to drive over."

Jeremiah gave a short sound of acknowledgment but no explanation as to why he hadn't responded to her attempts at contacting him.

"Are you . . . okay?" Gigi asked. "Other than the amnesia, I mean?"

"Yes."

"I'm sorry." Her tone was quickly turning sympathetic. "Amnesia. That's awful." She moved toward Jeremiah with her arms outstretched as if to hug him.

Jeremiah stiffened and Gigi must've seen it too because midstride she changed course and opted to squeeze his shoulder with a manicured hand. She stepped back. "I'm Gigi Kaminski," she said to Remy.

"I'm Remy Reed, Jeremiah's friend." She'd added the title of *friend* for Gigi's benefit. There was no reason to torture the woman into thinking she was Jeremiah's girlfriend when she wasn't. But she'd also said it for her own benefit. Best to continue to keep things clear—most especially in her own head.

Jeremiah scowled at her. Clearly, he didn't like that she'd demoted him to the status of mere friend.

Whatever. It was for his own good and hers.

254

"If it's all right with you," Remy said to him in the most level voice she could manage, "I'll borrow your car and drive myself back to town."

"You don't need to leave."

"I don't need to, but I do want to." Stubbornly, she extended her palm for his key.

"Remy. Please stay—"

"I'm going to give you two a chance to catch up privately," Remy said. "And I'm going to give myself permission to take it easy. I'm hungry and tired and I'd like some downtime."

His beautiful mouth set.

She kept her hand outstretched. Why did he have such terrifying power over her? He was looking at her with sadness and her knee-jerk reaction was to move heaven and earth to erase that sadness.

He had a girlfriend! A quaking was beginning deep within her.

He had a girlfriend and there was no telling how serious these two were about each other. Gigi looked like the type of person who could fit into his life seamlessly. Gigi was probably a huge fan of fame and material possessions and Formula One.

Reluctantly, he set his car key on her palm.

"Thanks," she told him. Then, to Gigi, as she was walking (bolting?) away, "Nice to meet you."

Gigi responded in kind and Remy picked up her pace as she continued toward his car.

"Do you know how to drive a stick?" he asked.

"Absolutely!"

"I'll call you."

She didn't respond.

As she reversed his car, tears began to push their way into her eyes.

Crap, Jeremiah thought. Gigi had upset Remy so much that Remy had left.

Gigi was looking at him with affection and it sounded like he may have felt affection for her at some point in the past. But the only thing he felt toward her right now was sharp annoyance. "Would you like to come in?"

"I would. Yes."

In his living room, she slipped off her high heels and tucked her legs beneath her on the sofa. She settled a throw pillow on her lap and her fingers toyed with its texture.

She looked more comfortable in his house than he was.

He switched on lights and took a seat in the armchair facing her. "I appreciate you coming here to check on me." It was taking effort to be civil. "I'm sure this is weird for you."

"It's so weird. I can't believe you have amnesia."

He let that pass. "None of my friends or family told me that I had a girlfriend. Can you explain that?"

"Our relationship was still kind of new. We hadn't gone public."

"How long ago did we meet?"

"This past June."

"How did we meet?"

"We met at a bar called Blyth and Burrows in Portland."

"What was I doing in Portland?"

"Speaking engagement."

"And what were you doing there?"

"I live there. That bar is one of my favorites."

The internal compass that sometimes gave Jeremiah a sense of rightness stayed silent. "When did we start dating?"

"Well, that first night was pretty hot." She smiled. "So . . . we started dating the same day we met, I guess."

"And after that? We saw each other often and communicated frequently?" He was trying to get a sense of how seriously he'd taken Gigi. Three months wasn't a very long time to date someone and yet she'd confidently stated that she was his girlfriend.

"Yes, we saw each other often considering that we live an hour and a half apart and that my schedule is demanding. I work in finance." She rolled her shiny lips inward. "And, yes. We communicated frequently."

"Do you have photos of us together?" Since Jude hadn't known who Gigi was, he wanted evidence.

"I do." She bent her head over her phone, then leaned forward, revealing cleavage, as she handed it over. "I named you in my photos app and just ran a search for all the photos of the two of us."

He clicked through the images. He and Gigi dressed in formal clothing. Walking on the beach. At a restaurant. In Cape Cod. The photos backed up her story because they'd been taken over the span of time she'd said they dated.

He passed the phone back. "What was the status of things between us when I left on my boat trip?"

"I'd say we were both very much into each other."

"Yet I went off on a boat trip alone?"

Her frown indicated hurt. "You're an independent man. You told me that you'd gone on this type of trip before. You said you liked to get away by yourself to clear your head. I understood and respected that completely."

She was a beauty, he'd give her that.

However, she left him cold. There wasn't a drop of space left in him for any woman except one.

"I'd be happy to tell you more," she said. "Is there anything else I can fill in for you? Anything else you'd like to know?"

257

"Just one thing. Did I tell you about a . . . project that I was working on during the months that we were hanging out?"

Her penciled eyebrows drew together. "You were consulting with the Mercedes F1 team. You were updating your boat for the trip. You were hoping to acquire more pieces from this artist you like." She flicked her fingers toward the piece behind her on the wall. "I can't remember his name, but his paintings are brilliant."

He hadn't told her about his research into Alexis's death. Why? Because he hadn't trusted her?

"Did you come here today thinking that we'd pick up where we left off?" He held her gaze, putting her on the spot.

"I hoped . . . we'd pick up where we left off. But, of course, I haven't talked to you in ages, so I didn't know where I stood."

"Where do *you* stand?"

"My emotions toward you . . . run deep. I'm committed to seeing where this relationship leads." She swallowed but kept her chin up. "What about you?"

"As of now, you're a stranger to me. I'm sorry about this but I don't remember our relationship."

Her face fell. "If we spend time together and I tell you all about us, do you think that might help your memories return?"

"No."

She nodded slowly. "The woman I met outside . . . ?"

"Remy."

"Remy said that you were friends. Are you more than that?"

"Not in her eyes. But in my eyes? Yes. She's been my anchor."

Her lips tightened and he could see that his honesty had caused her pain. "I wish I could have been there for you," she said, "when you found out about the amnesia. I would have been honored to be your anchor."

He kept his mouth shut, but he didn't think that if Gigi had been the one to rescue him, she would have become his anchor. Remy wasn't what she was to him only because she'd been close at hand when he was injured. She was what she was to him because of *who* she was.

"I should go." She put on her heels, then paused. "Unless you can think of something I can do to help you?"

"I can't think of anything," he answered. "If I do, I'll let you know."

"Please do."

They both stood.

"I hope your memories come back soon," she told him. "When they do, and you remember what we had, feel free to reach out to me. If I'm still unattached at that point, maybe we'll get our second chance."

He smiled noncommittally.

He already knew there would be no second chance for them.

The short drive to Wendell's house seemed to take Remy forever.

How had she allowed herself to become so enamored of Jeremiah that the appearance of his girlfriend had the ability to cause her true pain?

Heartache formed a ball of fire in her chest.

If someone was going to be his girlfriend, she wanted that person to be her—

No!

Yes. She wanted him to be her Jeremiah. Because she loved him.

Remy!

She didn't love him. She'd never been in love in her life.

Except now, she was.

She loved him. She absolutely did.

She brought Jeremiah's old car to a jerky stop in Wendell's driveway. She killed the ignition and sat, her mind shell-shocked and her body agitated.

She, who prided herself on her uniqueness, had gone and done the most predictable thing ever. She was a quirky, average-looking sculptor who'd fallen prey to the Camden eyes and the Camden swagger and the Camden smile. Like millions of other women, she loved Jeremiah Camden. Jeremiah Camden! Son of Felix Camden.

This was a catastrophe. SOS. She'd played with fire for too long and this was the result.

Gigi's arrival was a wakeup call. She should be grateful.

She wasn't grateful. At all.

She needed to leave the mainland and go home.

She dialed the plane service to Islehaven.

No flights scheduled today or tomorrow.

She dialed the boat service. A tourist boat was scheduled to leave tomorrow morning at nine. They were taking passengers to Isle au Haut but for a fee that made her wince, they'd add a stop at Islehaven to the itinerary.

She read off her credit card details and booked a seat. Then entered the house, bypassing Wendell, who was watching TV. Once she reached her bedroom, she started folding clothes and jamming them into her suitcase.

A few minutes later, her phone rang. She eventually found it in her purse.

Jeremiah.

Ordering herself to sound calm, she answered. "Hello?"

"Gigi's gone," he said without preamble. "I'm really sorry about how that went down."

"Quite all right! Not your fault or hers."

"Yeah, but I know it bothered you and I regret that. I hate that my past keeps coming back to bite you."

"What did she have to say?"

Remy listened without comment as he filled her in on his conversation with Gigi. He finished with, "She showed me pictures of the two of us, so I don't think she's lying about the fact that we were together. On the other hand, we couldn't have been very serious. We were only together three months."

Remy refrained from pointing out that Jeremiah had known her less than six weeks.

"I told her that whatever we had is done," he continued, "and that you're the one I'm into."

"What?" she squawked. Her motion ceased, except for her scrambling heartbeat. "Why did you say that? We're not a couple!"

"But you *are* the one I'm into."

"Jeremiah 1.0 is going to be so angry at you for pushing Gigi away when you get your memories back!"

"Jeremiah 1.0 is not my main concern. You're my main concern."

She blocked the swoony melting that wanted to happen inside her chest. "Duke," she said sternly, "recovering your memories should be your main concern right now. Your past is not going to stay in the past. It will keep finding you and it will demand to be reckoned with."

"Are you mad at me?"

"No."

"You sound mad."

She'd meant what she'd said earlier. Gigi's appearance was not his fault. It's just that she was *so* weary of his past loves! Alexis and now Gigi. Who knew how many more girlfriends might come out of the woodwork? It was too much. Over-whelming.

"Are we good?" he asked. "You and me?"

"Yes."

"When can I see you again?"

"I'm not sure." If she told him now that she was leaving, he'd mount a defense against that and she didn't have the energy to battle a will as strong as his. "Tonight I'm going to stay here and rest."

"I'll see you tomorrow, then."

"Good night." She added warmth to her tone to mask the fact that she had not agreed that she would see him tomorrow.

An hour later, Jeremiah was brooding over Remy when a text came in from his mother.

FIONA

> Darling, my family (the O'Sullivans) is getting together for lunch tomorrow. Is it too much to ask for you to drive over to Jefferson with me and eat with us? Everyone would love to see you.

He ran a search to see how long it would take him to drive to Jefferson. No way was he accidentally getting roped into a whole day of driving with Fiona.

Eyeballing the GPS map, he texted Remy.

JEREMIAH

> My mom invited us to the town of Jefferson for lunch with her family tomorrow. It's about a thirty-minute drive. Are you up for that?

No answer so he sat in his media room and tried to distract himself with college football.

A text from her came in twenty minutes later.

REMY

No, thanks. I wouldn't want to butt in on a family lunch. However, it's wonderful that you and your mother have plans. I'm sure that will make her happy.

JEREMIAH

I couldn't care less about going. If you're not up for it, then that gives me a reason to say no.

REMY

Say yes, please. You're not allowed to make me feel guilty about turning her down simply because I'm not going. Plus, family's important. You need to go.

He groaned. Despite what Remy had said on the phone earlier, he knew she was mad at him. He needed to make things right and it sounded like turning his mom down wouldn't be a step in that direction.

JEREMIAH

Fine, I'll go. I'll see you after the lunch.

She sent back a smiley face emoji, which did nothing to reassure him.

When Remy stepped back from hugging Wendell the next morning, a gust of emotion caught her by surprise. She felt a mixture of pride for all they had accomplished, deep fondness for this lonely man, and a chaser of sorrow over saying goodbye.

"I'm sad to see you go." His lips quivered. "It's been the best thing in the world to share a house with someone again."

"I've enjoyed it, too. Thank you for hosting me."

"Thank *you* for making this place nice for me."

"Do you promise to utilize the organizational systems I set up and stay on top of everything?"

"I promise."

"And you'll take your medicines and vitamins and stick to your kidney-friendly diet?"

"Yes, ma'am," he said as if he were a schoolboy and she, his principal.

"I regret that I haven't found Marisol yet."

"I probably shouldn't have mentioned her to you in the first place. That was just the wishful thinking of an old man."

"I'm not giving up, Wendell. I'll keep looking for her."

His head moved in a small *no* motion. "I knew back then, and I've known every day since, that I ruined my chance with her. It's a mistake that can't be undone."

By 9:00 a.m., Remy was pulling her rolling suitcase over the planks of the dock. It made an uneven *bump bump bump* noise behind her.

She kept looking over her shoulder, unreasonably concerned that Jeremiah would come running toward her, ordering the boat's captain not to pull away. And, of course, the captain would bow to his wishes as if Jeremiah were a prince and the rest of them were commoners.

So far, no sight of him.

They climbed aboard and the mellow conversations of tourists ebbed around her. The first mate loaded their belongings, then unwound the rope that bound them to the mainland. The boat eased away.

She looked back once again.

No Jeremiah.

She'd gotten away successfully, and this was absolutely the right thing for her. She was certain of that. So she should be feeling relief instead of this dragging sense of loss.

She missed him already.

Chapter Eighteen

Fiona knew exactly where to stand inside her living room—just back from the glass and sheer curtains—to observe someone's arrival without being observed in return. Thus, she spotted Jeremiah as soon as he pulled up to take her to lunch.

She still hadn't wrapped her mind around the fact that *her* Jeremiah had no memories of being Jeremiah. No recollection of her, his brother, his childhood, any of it. The millions of beautiful and heartbreaking (but mostly beautiful) moments he'd lived—*gone*.

Would he come to the door or honk? Would things be closer to normal between them today? Or uncomfortably strange? If the latter, she mustn't let that get her down. He was physically safe. His past would return to him. All *would* be well.

He did not honk. He got out and approached the door, just as she'd taught him to do from a young age.

An excellent sign.

He knocked.

She waited a few seconds before opening the door. "Hello,

darling." Since he'd let her hug him the last time, she took the liberty of another brief hug. Then she swept up her coat and purse and they walked to his 1950s Mercedes. It had doors that opened upward like wings. She lowered into the passenger side —very gracefully for her age seeing as how the car was just inches from the earth—and they were off.

Today, he wore a navy sweater with a short zipper at the front beneath a beige corduroy jacket that fit him beautifully. Dark jeans. He'd trimmed his hair since she'd seen him last.

He could have made a living as a male model had he not become a driver. In fact, he *had* been invited to model for dozens and dozens of brands but had only taken one up on the offer. Omega watches. She had his Omega ads preserved in a binder that also contained hundreds of articles about him.

Her oldest son had been gilded by angels from the start. The first time she'd looked into the beautiful face of her pale-haired newborn, her life had changed forever. He'd made her a mother, and she'd loved him ferociously. It hadn't mattered that he had not been the long-awaited, well-planned child of committed parents, like many firstborns. He, and later Jude, were the two very best gifts of her life.

Her boys were a study in contrasts and similarities.

Even as a baby, Jeremiah had instinctively understood how to gain everyone's favor. He'd been endearing and confident. A natural-born leader. He'd managed to get what he wanted from her and Felix while somehow making them feel that what he wanted was exactly, coincidentally, the very same thing they wanted to give him. When Jude arrived, Jeremiah had dealt with his little brother the way a CEO deals with a promising new hire.

Jude had been a kindhearted baby, but a little on the suspicious, introverted side. Observant. The quieter of the two. The rule follower. The dutiful one who, when asked to go upstairs and make his bed, would go upstairs and make his bed.

Jeremiah was the son who'd stepped into the limelight. Jude was the one who'd stepped away from it.

Jeremiah had the face of a race car driver. Jude, she'd thought since the day he'd written a brilliant poem in kindergarten, had the face of a writer.

She had the report cards and glowing comments from Jude's English teachers to prove just how excellent he'd been at writing all through school. For years, she'd fancied that he'd become a bestselling novelist or nonfiction author. He'd aced college and when he'd decided to go to law school afterward, she'd amended her projections and begun to picture him as a judge who wrote verdicts instead of novels. But right when he could have transitioned into a plum private practice job, he'd made the baffling decision to go into the FBI.

She didn't have a doubt, of course, that he was outstanding at his role. It's just that working for the FBI wasn't a very high-paying job and didn't come with as much positive feedback as he deserved.

Both of her sons had passionate, loyal hearts. Both were smart. Both had a great sense of humor. Both honorable. Both good to her and the rest of the family.

To this day, she could picture with precision Jeremiah and Jude, ages four and two, standing on a strip of beach in Groomsport's harbor. Holding hands, the boys jumped over each incoming rush of tide while the summer sun glinted in their fair hair.

Tears misted her eyes. She earnestly missed those little boys, who'd lavished her with love and trust. The cruelest trick of motherhood was that your children exhausted you when they were small . . . which hindered your ability to appreciate them at that age as much as you should. She deeply appreciated them at that age *now*. But now those little boys were gone. They'd grown into capable, headstrong adults who didn't require much from her. She'd grown into the one who required things of them—their presence, communication, and fondness.

"Can you tell me about your family?" Jeremiah asked, his words bringing her back to the present.

"Certainly. My parents are named Patrick and Mary and they still live in the same house where I grew up. Fun fact— Felix is also from an Irish-American family and his parents are *also* named Patrick and Mary. You have grandparents on both sides with the exact same names."

"I do?"

"Yes. Additionally, your father has three siblings named Mike, Elizabeth, and Jack. Believe it or not, I also have siblings named Mike, Elizabeth, and Jack."

"What?"

"Whenever we talk about them, we say 'Aunt Elizabeth O'Sullivan.' Or 'Uncle Mike Camden' to avoid confusion."

"Ah."

"Of course, Felix's Patrick, Mary, Mike, Elizabeth, and Jack are nothing like my people of the same names. Felix's family is very . . . upper crust."

"And your family?"

"They're loud and down to earth."

He shot a skeptical glance across the interior of the car. "You don't seem down to earth."

She laughed. "Well . . . I *was* married to your father for sixteen years and we did live in the lap of luxury." Jeremiah wasn't in a position to judge because he wasn't exactly the poster boy for normalcy. He was born into the Camden line, a world championship race car driver, and far richer than she.

"Will I meet your Patrick, Mary, Mike, Elizabeth, and Jack today?" he asked.

"Yes. And my other siblings, too."

"You have more than three?"

"I have six. My two brothers are the bookends, with five sisters in between. There's Jack, me, Elizabeth, Margaret, Alice, and Mike."

"That's five names. Who's the sixth?"

Her muscles tightened defensively. "Her name's Isobel."

"Is that the sister who was married to Felix before you were?"

The question impacted her like a slap. To her sons, she'd always been Mom. Not the other woman. Not the sister-betrayer. Their mom, who loved them and who they loved in return. The mistakes she'd made had never been, to them, the most prominent thing about her.

But Jeremiah didn't recall any of that. If one of the few things he'd learned about her was the same thing she was known for throughout America—the scandal with Felix and Isobel—then she suddenly had no assurance that he was still on her side. "Yes. Isobel is the sister who was married to Felix before me."

"Will she be at lunch today?"

"No. She never comes to any family gathering I attend."

His forehead lined. "No? How long has that been the case?"

"Since she found out about my relationship with your father." She cleared her throat. "Isobel lives in New York and rarely comes home for visits. When she does come home, I stay away to give her a turn with the others."

"Do you communicate with her at all?"

"I haven't. But I'm working to rectify that." She'd written four drafts of her letter to Isobel so far and thrown them all in the trash.

"Anything else I should know about your family before we get there?"

"My father's life revolves around food. My mother is the happiest senile person in Maine. Jack tries to engage with his female siblings but then gets overwhelmed by us and gives up. Elizabeth is obsessed with interpreting dreams. Margaret loves gossip. Alice is eager to please. And Mike, the baby, can't get his act together and expects the rest of us to swoop in and save him."

As they neared their destination, she directed him through the final turns. They pulled up at her parents' white saltbox-style house. Like a smiling old man, it looked both weathered and friendly. It would be immediately clear to Jeremiah's sharp eyes that a lot of life had happened here, was continuing to happen here, and that the owners didn't care much about keeping the place pristine.

Weather-beaten hedges gave way to flaky exterior paint. Several children's toys dotted the front yard. The same tire swing had hung for decades from the enormous birch tree out front, whose leaves were currently bright gold.

As soon as they entered the foyer, they were met with the usual crush of people, conversations, and hugs.

Jeremiah stiffened so much that she laughed. "Jeremiah doesn't remember any of you," she said loudly. "Remember?"

"Of course he does," her mother answered dotingly.

"Have you seen any of us in your dreams?" Elizabeth asked. "The dreams of an amnesiac can provide a fascinating glimpse into the subconscious."

"Come eat!" Fiona's white-haired, eighty-five-year-old father slapped Jeremiah repeatedly on the back. "I made a casserole and the rest of these brought a dish. Big spread!"

"Dad," Mike said, "we don't have to rush them from the door to the table."

"Agreed," Fiona said. "But if we do migrate to the kitchen, we'll have more space."

"Yes, certainly," Alice exclaimed. "Into the kitchen, then. Let me get you both glasses of iced tea." She was referring to the beverage their family drank by the barrel—iced tea made from blueberry black tea bags, with a little sugar, a pinch of baking soda, and garnished with sprigs of mint.

They moved as a herd. "Jeremiah, do you really not remember any of us?" Mike wanted to know.

"No, I don't. I'm sorry."

"Not to worry, sweetheart," Fiona's mom said. "We remember you, Jude." The diminutive matriarch of the family cushioned him in one of her soft embraces.

"This is Jeremiah," Fiona corrected.

Soon they were all standing around the packed kitchen island while Alice pressed glasses into her hands and Jeremiah's.

"Meatball anyone?" Dad asked hopefully. "As an appetizer?" Without waiting for an answer, he lifted one to his mouth with a toothpick and munched hungrily.

"Don't mind if I do," Jeremiah answered, which earned him additional back slaps from Dad.

"Tell us every single detail about the things that have been happening to you," Margaret demanded.

"Yes!" the rest echoed.

Jeremiah recounted the highs and lows for them.

The O'Sullivans watched him as if he were the opening night of a long-awaited movie. In fact, this gathering had been arranged last-minute just for him. None of her siblings had brought their children or grandchildren, so the group's attention was fixed solely on her oldest son.

She'd always considered her two sons superior to her siblings' children. Frankly, it felt fitting for everyone's fascination to be centered on Jeremiah. Well-deserved for him. And, by association, well-earned for her as his mother.

The only way in which her sons lagged behind their cousins? Their lack of children. Even Alice who, Lord help them all, had a video game addict for a son and a daughter obsessed with Hello Kitty had been presented with a grand-daughter.

The moment Jeremiah finished speaking, Dad declared, "Let's eat!"

"Where are the lemon squares?" Mom asked.

"Relegated to another decade," Fiona answered. "I don't believe we've had lemon squares for dessert since 1978."

"Be sure to serve me one later." Mom beamed. "I wouldn't want to miss a lemon square."

They filled their plates and took seats at the titanic dining room table, which wasn't being asked to perform miracles today. Compared to the size and scale of their usual gatherings, this group of nine felt downright intimate. It was merely difficult, as opposed to impossible, to squeeze in a word.

"I wanted everyone to know that I'm going to be starting a new job on Monday," fifty-one-year-old baby Mike informed the group.

Mom, who couldn't remember that Mike had started and lost too many jobs to count, gasped with delight and clapped.

"Best wishes, Mike," Alice said earnestly.

The rest of them manufactured pleasant expressions.

"I hope you didn't dream about failing an exam," Elizabeth said to Mike. "If you dreamed about failing an exam, this job will be a dead end."

"No, I dreamed about jaguars swimming, actually."

"That means you need to purify your soul."

"Suzy told Heidi who told me," Margaret cut in, peering across the aging centerpiece of dried flowers at Fiona, "that she saw you at a coffee shop with Burke Ainsley two days ago. What's going on between you and Burke?"

"We're friends."

"I heard his wife wasn't at the coffee shop."

"Unfortunately, his wife passed away. He was living in Boston and just recently returned to Groomsport."

"Suzy told Heidi who told me he's a handsome man."

Burke *was* handsome. However, Fiona shrugged noncommittally, accustomed to parrying her sister's attempts at prying. The O'Sullivans at this table all had stable marriages and conventional children. She and Isobel were the only two who'd furnished the others with vivid drama.

"Anyone want seconds?" Dad asked before she'd eaten a third of her food.

"Sweetie," Mom said to Fiona out of the blue, "I'm sorry about your divorce."

Fiona's divorce had occurred eighteen years ago. "Thank you," she said solemnly.

"I know how that is. I've been divorced, too."

Startled laughter burst from several members of the family.

"Mom," Fiona pointed out, "you've been married to Dad, your only husband, since you were young. You haven't been divorced."

"Yes, I have, and it was very hard on me," Mom said.

And so it went.

The sense of belonging she found in the midst of her big, quirky family brought her peace.

She'd been the difficult one growing up. Certainly the most difficult of the seven kids. During those years, when she hadn't felt smothered by the O'Sullivans, she'd been frustrated with them. When she hadn't been frustrated with them, she'd taken them for granted. But after America had learned of her affair with Felix, and the world hated her, her family's love had instantaneously become one of the most precious things in her life.

Ever since, she'd been proving her devotion through action. She was the one who'd ensured that her nieces and nephews could afford to go to the college of their choice. She was the one who always had a job at her company or a room in her home for anyone who needed them.

The feisty will that had made her so challenging when young now made her the sibling who championed the rest, the one who bent over backward to help them, the one who always fought for their best.

After returning from the O'Sullivan family lunch, Jeremiah repeatedly tried to get a hold of Remy on her cell phone.

She didn't respond to texts and she didn't answer his calls.

It was now six o'clock and inky darkness blanketed Maine. Worried, he paced his house.

Texted her again. Nothing.

Finally, he got in his BMW and drove to Wendell's.

He waited on the front stoop for Remy to answer his knock.

At last, the door creaked open. Wendell filled the opening.

"Did you bring my delivery of chicken tikka?" Wendell asked jokingly.

"Not this time."

Wendell winked. "In that case, best not to expect a tip."

"I came by to speak with Remy. Is she here?"

"No, son. She returned to Islehaven this morning. She left your car key here and asked me to give it back to you."

Chapter Nineteen

Remy had left? Without telling him?
Denial rose within Jeremiah, mixing with confusion as it gathered force.

Gigi had arrived and so Remy had run? Why was she punishing him for Gigi's actions?

That wasn't fair, his conscience pointed out. Gigi was 1.0's issue and he lived in the body of 1.0. Also, if he'd answered Gigi's texts or calls, he could have stopped things with her before she'd taken action and shown up at his house.

Also . . . Gigi probably wasn't the only factor that had motivated Remy to go. There was also Remy's desire to return to her island and her work, his dead ex-wife, his amnesia, and the complication of their kiss.

Still. Why had she gone without telling him? That hurt. His body was struggling to metabolize the fact that she was no longer nearby on the mainland. She was the only person he cared about deeply, and she'd left him behind.

"Here you are." Wendell handed over the key to the Cobra.

"Thanks." Jeremiah started toward the classic car. "I'll be

back soon to pick up the BMW."

"No hurry. Next time, please bring a side of mint chutney with my order."

Jeremiah didn't have it in him to respond with a smile. All the enjoyment had drained from the day. From the town.

Even when they hadn't been together, knowing Remy was in the area had calmed him and, at the same time, given him something to look forward to. She was the color in his days. The rest of his life felt like shades of beige compared to her.

He steered his Cobra toward Appleton.

He wanted to be what Remy needed because she was everything he needed.

He'd been reading up on recovery from sexual trauma. Memories that interrupted the present, like the memory that had interrupted their kiss, were called "intrusive thoughts." Apparently, they could be a frequent struggle for survivors.

Additionally, he'd learned that the culture pressures those who've suffered sexual trauma to keep their stories hidden because their stories are "messy." But it only makes things worse when people are told to cover up the wound with things that won't fix it—like silence, new hobbies, new relationships. It's best for survivors to learn to ask for what they need.

Remy had asked him not to pursue a physical relationship with her and he'd respect that request. If someone was going to add a physical component to their relationship, it would have to be her. Until then, he'd wait while she gathered trust in him. But how was she supposed to gather trust in him if she was on Islehaven and he was here?

It was joy, pure joy, to lose herself in her art again. Even if, or maybe because, losing herself in it had proven more difficult than ever after returning home.

Yesterday Remy had disembarked at Islehaven's harbor, Leigh had given her a lift home, and she'd done some hasty unpacking. Then she'd zipped herself into a jumpsuit and turned on crashing classical music. She'd been chagrined when she'd confronted the state in which she'd deserted her current piece. It was in its adolescent phase—a gawky, awkward time. Not the best stage for a parent to jump ship.

At first, she'd tried to immerse herself in what she'd initially envisioned for the wood. A goblet, belonging to a coalition of cosmic princesses. When they sipped from it, it gave them the power to spin galaxies.

She'd taken up the ten-inch wood rasp she used for smoothing her sculptures . . . then failed to tap into her powers of concentration. Over and over, her connection to the imaginary narrative fractured and her thoughts wandered away from the vessel and the princesses and back to Jeremiah, the Camdens, Alexis, and Wendell.

When her dinner alarm had sounded, she'd thrown in the towel with disgust.

Upon locating her phone, she'd seen she had texts and missed calls from Jeremiah. They'd been concentrated close together.

While reading and rereading his texts, she'd eaten frozen chicken adobo with veggies and ancient grains. Which, after the fresher food she'd had in Rockland, tasted awful.

She'd pondered how to respond and eventually sent a reply.

REMY

I decided to come home to Islehaven. Call when you want to talk about it.

She'd expected him to call right away. However, he had not.

By this morning, she'd arrived at a place of genuine irritation with him. Yes, she'd said to call when he was ready to talk about her leaving. But he *still* wasn't ready? He was reacting to her departure from the mainland with surprising indifference. He'd led her to believe she meant something to him! Yet . . . no call. No return text.

She'd skipped her morning walk and yoga in favor of rushing straight into the distraction work provided. Without her permission, her imagination morphed. The goblet was no longer the possession of princesses but belonged to a singular cosmic prince. He lounged disdainfully on a silver throne. He had a lean torso, sandy hair, and charisma. The ladies in waiting were either cowed by him or infatuated with him. Only one blond peasant had the bravery to stand up to him. He began to straighten in his throne, his focus intensifying on her, as she gave an impassioned speech detailing why his ability to spin galaxies must be harnessed for good.

That daydream had stuck.

Just like old times, she startled when her phone let her know the lunch hour had arrived.

Emerging from the music and absorption of her work, she was surprised to realize that a storm was rolling over her cottage. Great booms of thunder. Screeching wind. Torrential rain. When had that started?

She peered out the kitchen window at the twisting trees, microwave whirring as her meal circled around and around inside it.

Strange how oddly empty the house felt now that she was here alone again. She'd lived here for six years. And only shared this space with Jeremiah for ten days. Yet his imprint remained in every single room. She hadn't washed the sheets last night because the wonderful scent of him mixed with the scent of her soap had been all over them. He'd had the nerve—the nerve!—to turn her blessed solitude into solitude tinged with loneliness—

A knock, loud and decisive, rapped against her front door.

She jumped.

"Remy?" came a muffled but easily recognizable voice.

Jeremiah? Her heart sprinted off the blocks. She crossed the living room and opened the door.

The water dampening his hair and face only made him more beautiful. Behind him mayhem raged—lightning striking the ocean in feral zigzags.

"Uh . . ." she said dumbly, having trouble making sense of this.

He stepped inside.

The wind pushed against the door, and she had to shove it closed, cutting off some of the violent noise.

He wore a gray sweater and jeans beneath a khaki coat. "Remy," he said in a deceptively conversational tone, "I think you might've forgotten to mention to me that you were returning home."

She blinked. "No indeed. I didn't forget. I made a strategic choice not to mention it."

"Why?"

"Because I didn't want to argue about it. Also because I'm not obligated to run my decisions by you." She pushed her shoulders back. "Why are you here?"

"Because this is where you are." He looked her straight in the face while gently extracting an inch-long curl of wood from her topknot. "If this is where you are, then this is the only place I want to be."

Her imaginary ladies in waiting collapsed onto chaise lounges in romantic delight, their hands on their chests.

"Would it be all right with you," he said, "if I move back in?"

Heat flushed up her neck. "Absolutely not." It had been one thing to host him when he'd been weak and incapacitated. But now that he was brimming with strength? No.

"I'll sleep on the blow-up mattress in the office," he suggested.

"*Absolutely not.*"

"Okay. I'll stay with Leigh."

"Leigh? Leigh's house is . . . rustic." That was the most charitable way to phrase it.

"You think I'm too pampered to hack it there."

"After seeing your house, I think you're too pampered to hack it anywhere other than the Ritz-Carlton."

"Leigh's house is near your house. So, I'll like it."

"How long are you intending to stay?"

"As long as I want."

She tossed out her arms. "You can't just invite yourself into Leigh's house and stay on Islehaven for as long as you want. It's too much to ask! Even more importantly, there are *numerous pressing questions* that need your attention back in Groomsport right now."

"Screw those questions. This is where I feel the most peace."

"You have to go back."

"No, I don't." A molasses smile curved his lips as the air crackled. "I'm not obligated to run my decisions by you." He'd turned her earlier statement back on her.

She spluttered. This was insane.

She wanted to kill him. She wanted to kiss him. She wanted to kill and kiss him. She earnestly *did not want* a break from him, but she *should* take a break from him for her sanity. She needed to immerse herself in her work and get back in touch with herself and get over him. How was she supposed to do any of that when he was around?

"I'm retired from racing," he said. "I have money. I can do whatever I want."

"You're crazy."

"This from the woman who makes sculptures inspired by magical women living in the Black Forest?" he asked with affection.

"How did you get here in this weather?"

"I have two boats. The *Camdenball* and the other one. I brought the other one here." He shrugged. "Then I convinced a lobsterman to serve as my temporary chauffeur. He's waiting outside."

She yanked open her door. Droplets spattered her leg. "Take your delusions to Leigh's house."

"I'll meet you here tomorrow when your dinner alarm goes off. I'll provide the food."

"Don't bother. I have frozen meals. And they're delicious."

"See you then," he said lightly, striding out.

With a cry of exasperation, she kicked the door closed behind him.

⛵

Leigh's house was worse than rustic.

When he'd gotten into the car with the lobsterman, he'd texted Leigh and offered to pay her for the privilege of staying with her. She'd immediately said she'd love to have him as her houseguest, as he'd expected she would. Between Remy and Leigh, Leigh had always been the one sensible enough to like him.

Because it was Saturday, she wasn't out on the boat but at home. They'd driven to Leigh's place, he'd paid the lobsterman, and now he was running through pounding rain to her front door.

Leigh met him at the threshold with a hug stronger than a chiropractic adjustment.

Inside, he set down his suitcase and looked around. She kept it tidy, but it appeared to have been last updated in 1985. Leigh gave him a tour of her pastel time capsule. It was so dimly lit that Jeremiah had to squint. And it smelled strongly of seafood. Not in a good way.

"Don't even think about flushing the toilet or running the sink when the shower's going," Leigh warned when they reached the bathroom. "Won't be good for any of us. Oh, and don't plug the tub. I keep this plug here as a memento of when my kids took baths when they were small. But, these days, if we fill the tub with water, it's likely to fall through the floorboards, which are half-rotten."

"Gotcha."

Back in the hall, she toed a bucket a few inches to the side so the rain dripping through the roof plunked into its center. "Here's the spare bedroom." She gestured to it.

Jeremiah entered a room wallpapered in a graying print of tiny tulips. The pink-and-white-striped bedspread had been turned down to showcase eight heart-shaped accent pillows. "Thank you for letting me stay here."

"Ayuh. More than glad to have you, especially at the rate you offered to pay. Best not to tell the locals the amount. They'll accuse me of highway robbery."

After seeing the place, the amount did seem like highway robbery. But like a rookie negotiator, he'd thrown out the sum before seeing the premises. It didn't matter. He wasn't paying for the quality of the accommodations. He was paying for proximity to Remy. "It's our secret."

Leigh's blunt features creased around a grin. "You look great. You're all healed up since the last time I saw you."

"Yeah."

Her baseball cap slanted to the side as she cocked her head. "Did you follow Remy back here?"

"I did."

"Are you two a love match?"

"So far I haven't been able to convince her to give me a chance as her boyfriend."

"Remy is very . . . sincere in her opinions. I admire that about her."

"So do I."

"But sometimes that means she's sincerely wrong. Like when she decided it would be best to avoid romance." She pushed her hands into her sturdy pants. "I, for one, think it's good you're in her life. Are you going to try to win her over?"

"Yes. By waiting to see if she'll make the next move."

Leigh didn't look impressed. "You planning to live in my spare bedroom for the next thirty years?"

"You know, right, why I have to go at her pace or nothing?"

"I do know why, yes." She thumped him on the shoulder. "I'm surprised she told you. She wasn't a fan of yours at all at first."

"I wasn't a fan of hers at first, either. You were the one I immediately liked."

"Because I got you drugs."

"Because you're the best woman in the world."

"Want to change your mind about Remy and date me instead?" she joked.

"Yes. Deal."

She laughed her barking laugh. "Ayuh, you charmer," she said as she walked off. "Ayuh."

Chapter Twenty

Jeremiah arrived on Remy's doorstep the next night as promised.

"No one's at home!" she yelled in response to his knock.

He didn't bother answering, just set down the large bag of food he'd brought and tested the knob. Locked. He used the knuckles of both fists to tap out the most annoying beat he could invent.

After three and a half minutes of that, she responded by turning up her music so it drowned out his tapping.

He tugged on the sill of the picture window. It lifted beneath his grip. Lax security around here. He stepped through the window into the living room. Remy was nowhere to be seen.

Bobbing his head in time to the music, he arranged the food on the kitchen counter in an assembly line.

When she finally did walk in several minutes later, wearing overalls and a white long-sleeved undershirt, her hair everywhere, she stopped short when she saw him. "How did you get in?"

"Window. Is this how you welcome everyone who brings you free food?"

"No. This is simply how I welcome you when you and I both know you should be on the mainland at the moment, dealing with . . . stuff."

"I don't want to be there when I can be here, sleeping on the bed in Leigh's spare bedroom, which is as uncomfortable as one of those planks they use when water-boarding enemies."

The edges of her lips tweaked up. "I warned you."

"I had a *bucket* in my room last night for catching the rain. Sadly, the single bucket was optimistic, seeing as how it indicated Leigh thought there was just one leak."

She eyed the food. Baked fish. Potatoes. Green beans. "Is that sourdough bread from the mainland?"

"Yep."

They filled their plates and were soon sitting in the places they'd occupied at her table before his chest infection had rushed them away.

Pleasure, deep and still as a forest pond, settled over him. Since she'd pulled him from the ocean, he hadn't belonged anywhere as much as he belonged in this seat in this house.

In coming here, he'd had to pause his hypnotherapy and psych appointments. It wasn't that he'd lost his hunger to get his memories back. He hadn't. It was just that this—Remy—mattered more.

"Mm," she murmured as she chewed her first bite.

It felt warm in here, so he unbuttoned the gray flannel shirt he had on over a white T-shirt. "Mm?" he asked.

"Mm," she confirmed, nodding.

It took him a minute to remember what she'd told him about the inspiration behind her work in progress before they'd left here. "Are you back to work on your cosmic goblet?"

Immediately, he was rewarded when her face lit up. "Yes. It's speaking to me and I'm starting to glimpse the path forward."

He listened with interest as she talked about "cutting away what didn't belong" and "revealing the essence" and "allowing what it wanted to become to guide the way."

"I'm glad it's coming along well. I think you're a brilliant artist," he said honestly. "Since you won't let me buy the Emiline piece, please let me buy the goblet."

"No."

"Yes."

"It will go to the person who's destined to have it."

"Whatever the destined person is paying, I'll pay twice that."

"No!"

"Fine. Triple, then."

She laughed. "No. I need a certain amount of money to support myself, but I'm not driven to amass more than that."

"Are you driven by sentiment? The cosmic goblet is the piece you've been working on since I met you, so it's our piece. I'm the person who's destined to have it."

"Jeremiah." She paused her eating. "You are not getting your way in this. In fact, if you could accept that you aren't going to get your way in general—in so many areas—you'd be much less of a handful."

"I'm sure that's true."

Daintily, she set aside her fork and dabbed her lips with her napkin. She rested against her chair's back and considered him.

"What?" he asked.

"I'm wondering if having you for a neighbor is going to derail me."

"Please explain."

"I came home because I wanted to return to work. But I *also* came home to put distance between us. Your arrival removes that distance."

The statement sliced him like a small, sharp blade. "Why do you want to put distance between us?"

"So many reasons."

"List them all and I'll try to keep track."

"You are too . . . much for me. I thrive on simplicity and privacy. But there's none of that to be had in your orbit."

Before her rape, she'd lived in a big city, had a life filled with relationships and people. But after one of those people betrayed her and the courts yanked away her hope for justice, she'd fled here. If he had to guess, he'd say her art, plus the simplicity and privacy of her life, were crutches. They didn't actually bring her security any more than did the fame and success and money crutches he'd clearly pursued in the past.

"Also," she said, "and this is embarrassing . . . . I'm becoming very, um, *drawn* to you physically. At this point, it's hard to be in the same room with you."

"I feel the same."

"But physical attraction is a minefield for me. You're setting off mines left and right. Every day since our kiss, I've had to face one awful memory of Gavin or another. I realize that's in part because I probably pushed those memories down. Facing them will likely prove healthy in the long run. Even so, you . . ." She sighed, looking conflicted. "You make me want more kisses and my judgment's telling me that might be safe but I'm afraid it's not. Because there's no way this thing between us will lead to a happy ending—"

"Try me and see."

"—So then I doubt my judgment."

It was hard for him to contain the protectiveness and

tenderness he felt toward her. "If your judgment's telling you it would be safe to kiss me, your judgment's right."

"My judgment told me it was safe to kiss Gavin."

"It wasn't your judgment that failed you that night, Remy. It was him. Only him. If I'd been dating a woman, invited her into my home, and kissed her, it would not be my judgment's fault if she then physically attacked me. She'd be at fault. That's it."

"You're right." She scooted back a few inches from the table, scratched the back of her neck.

He leaned forward. "I'm sure there's a lot of context that went into the verdict Gavin received. Legal reasons why it went the way that it did. But you and I both know that he *was* guilty. You weren't. You did nothing wrong. Your judgment was sound. Your judgment *is* sound."

"Maybe so. Regardless, I don't want the complexity that dating you would require. I'm not ready. It's too scary."

Remy had spent years proving her bravery to herself. He could see by her paleness what it had cost her to confess that something was too scary for her.

Tears gathered on her lower lashes and the sight of that was a blow to his lungs. He wanted to take Gavin's neck in his hands and squeeze.

Her chair screeched as she jumped to her feet. "I need air. Do you need air? It's too stuffy in here." She disappeared outside, leaving the door hanging open.

He didn't want to crowd her, so he gave her two full minutes. Then followed into the night. The sun had set almost forty-five minutes before, and it was nearing full dark. He stopped beside where she stood on the rocks of the cliff that dropped to churning black waves. She'd crossed her arms over her chest—a slender figure with long hair whipping.

The wind was raw tonight. It penetrated his clothing, chilling his skin and bones.

"Is there anything I can do to bring Gavin to justice?" he asked in a low tone that barely cut through the sea air. "If there is, I will do it. I will go to any lengths to see that he pays for his crime."

She glanced across at him and he saw a flash of fierce gratitude before she turned her profile back to the ocean. "There's nothing that can be done at this point. He was tried for raping me and acquitted. The only way he can be tried again in criminal court is if he does the same thing to another woman, which is utterly sickening. He's out there free, and as long as that's true, other women are at risk." Several locks of hair slanted across her face. She disentangled them from her lips, then held them in her fist.

"Could you file a civil suit?"

"The clock's run out on that option. Technically, I could have done so over the last six years. I didn't because that would have meant dragging it all back out. Rehashing everything. And for what? They might have ruled in his favor again. But even if they hadn't, he'd simply have had to pay me money. I don't want his money."

Remy had learned firsthand that the world wasn't full of rosy sunsets. Yet she still hoped and smiled and contributed.

She turned and walked back to the house. Inside, she opened a cupboard in the kitchen and pulled out a liquor bottle. With hands that had gone white from the cold, she plunked down shot glasses on the counter, then filled them both to the brim with tequila.

"How come you didn't share any of this with me back when I was begging you for alcohol and drugs?"

"Because drowning sorrows in liquor is a terrible idea," she said. "A flaw. I do not recommend it."

"How often do you drown your sorrows in tequila?"

"I don't allow myself to do it very often at all. But tonight's the time."

Good. He could use tequila.

Using the tip of her pointer finger, she slid one of the glasses in front of him. They clinked the rims together. "Cheers." They downed the fiery drink.

She gave a whistle and a gasping laugh.

"I want to stay on Islehaven and sleep on the water-boarding plank," he said. "You want distance. So let's hash out terms."

"What's your offer?"

"I'll join you for your morning walks and yoga sessions on the weekdays. Then stay out of sight. Then bring dinner in the evenings."

"The walks are fine but it's a no for the yoga sessions. Most of the yoga poses require me to point my butt toward the ceiling."

"That's not a dealbreaker for me."

"Hard no."

"Fine."

"You can bring dinner but only on the five weekdays."

He assessed her, chin to chin. "Agreed."

⛵

He's a magician, Remy thought later that night when she reluctantly parted from Jeremiah and padded toward her bathroom.

She'd plainly listed the reasons why she wanted distance from him. And those reasons had been so valid! But he had a way of making her want him more than she wanted all the sensible things she should value more.

He was smart, ridiculously enjoyable to look at, and *good*. Good in a way her soul recognized.

The spell he cast was a powerful one.

Even now, her skin was flushed. She felt both drained from the difficult emotions of the evening and giddy.

No doubt it would have been better for her if she could have stuck to her guns and insisted he return to the mainland. But she hadn't insisted.

He would leave eventually. Maybe even soon. His memories would come back, he'd be reunited with himself, and he'd leave. She might survive that so long as she did not *under any circumstances* come to rely on having him around.

The following morning, Jeremiah met Remy on her front deck, and they followed an overgrown path to Restoration Point. They were admiring the view of the small, uninhabited islands off the coast when his phone alarm went off.

She looked at him inquiringly.

"Your yoga session is supposed to start in five minutes," he announced.

"You're setting alarms on your phone now for my schedule?"

"I know how you like to stay on track."

"If yoga is starting in five minutes, then I'm very much off track. It's a twenty-five-minute walk back to my house."

"You're a terrible influence on me." He grinned.

"You're the one who's a terrible influence! I'm never late for yoga."

On Tuesday, he ensured she was back at home after their walk right on time.

On Wednesday, classical music greeted him when he

arrived at her house for dinner. She didn't respond to his knock, so once again he let himself in through the window.

He went to her studio to alert her to his arrival—but stilled in the doorway, transfixed. She was busy carving. Creativity hovered in the air even more powerfully than the scent of wood. Her hair was high on top of her head. One section had escaped, and she'd thrust it behind her ear. Another tendril fell against the delicate skin at the back of her neck.

When her phone alarm sounded, she glanced up, then shrieked at the sight of him as if he'd materialized from thin air. "Jeremiah! Are you trying to give me a heart attack?"

"No. I'm trying to feed you dinner. It's quitting time."

"*What?* It can't be."

"It is." He found her phone on the floor in the corner and showed her the time.

She gaped at the screen, clearly wondering who had stolen her day. "I need twenty more minutes."

Graciously, he left her alone. She repaid him for his cooperation with a leisurely dinner. They talked about big things and inconsequential things. She explained the latest disappointments regarding her search for Marisol. He explained his disappointments regarding his search for clues about Alexis. They ate lobster. They laughed.

Simply watching her fascinated him. Her emphatic gestures, the fire in her eyes, her expressive face.

On Thursday night, they had dinner with Leigh at Leigh's house. Jeremiah and Remy worked together to make clam chowder, sourdough bread, and a dessert of chocolate pudding.

Leigh entertained Jeremiah by recounting what it had been like to grow up in Maine. The Islehaven of today was a difficult place, but according to her it was as luxurious as a diamond bracelet compared to the past.

"He's a good housemate, you know," Leigh said to Remy,

indicating him. "I can see why you kept him as long as you did at your house."

"I kept him at my house out of sheer necessity. Not because he's a good housemate."

"He cleans up after himself and then some," Leigh said. "Plus, he's a great conversationalist."

"You're giving me a big head," Jeremiah drawled.

"He also had quite an impressive career there," Leigh continued as if Jeremiah hadn't spoken. "I don't know anything about Formula One racing but the things he's achieved speak to his work ethic. And determination."

"Or my vanity," he suggested, "and thirst for recognition."

Leigh gave him a look that asked, *What are you doing? I'm trying to talk you up!* "I don't believe for a minute that you're motivated by vanity and recognition."

"Oh?" Remy said. "Speak for yourself."

"I've been talking too long." Leigh rose from the table, which contained only their empty pudding bowls and glasses. "Don't move a muscle. I'm going to clean things up since you two cooked." She lowered the lights by fifty percent, which made their surroundings look fifty percent better. "With a decent sound system and dim lights, you can replicate a lounge. That's what my ex-husband and I used to do. We'd make our own homemade lounge. I'm going to do the same for you two now."

"I'm not one to go to a lounge even when I'm in a place where such a thing exists," Remy said.

Leigh tapped on her phone until the song "I Just Died in Your Arms Tonight" flowed from it.

"Jeremiah and I aren't really the dancing type."

"Dancing is romantic," Leigh stated.

"Yet Jeremiah and I aren't engaged in a romance."

"You two are going to dance. This is my house and that's

the way it's going to be." Leigh herded the two of them into position.

Jeremiah, who was more than happy to dance with Remy, held himself still, looking down at the top of her head. Remy placed her hands on his shoulders near his neck in the classic middle-school dance style. Her body was positioned as far away as possible from his, yet the feel of her hands on him caused his breath to freeze.

When she looked up at him, he saw glimmers of silver in her irises. Freckles sprinkled across her nose. Two were grouped close together underneath her lower eyelashes on one side. Her pulse beat in her throat and he could smell her shampoo.

"You two. Honestly." Leigh moved his left hand to Remy's waist and his right hand out so that his bare fingers wrapped around Remy's. She set Remy's free hand on his shoulder. "Closer now."

Remy stepped within a few inches of his chest. The small gap between their bodies snapped with voltage.

Leigh returned to her phone to increase the volume of the song.

"You okay with this?" Jeremiah whispered to Remy.

"Yes."

"You'll let me know if that changes?"

"I will."

"Dance," Leigh encouraged, shoving pieces of furniture out of their way. They danced on a thousand-year-old carpet that Jeremiah believed was woven out of nothing but dust. "Ayuh. That's it. I'll leave you to it while I clean. I don't want either of you quitting until five songs, minimum, have passed." She disappeared into the kitchen.

Remy's waist was smooth and firm beneath his touch. It was hard to think. "When we agreed on terms regarding me staying on Islehaven," he said hoarsely, "we didn't discuss weekends."

"At the time of our agreement, I intended we'd go our separate ways on weekends. That will give you the opportunity to return to Appleton. Which, of course, you can do anytime. You don't have to wait for the weekends."

"I don't want to go back to Appleton. I want to spend my weekends with you. What do you typically do on Saturdays and Sundays when you're not nursing strangers with broken ribs?"

"I work," she confessed.

"In that case, I'm offering an anti-work weekend. I'll plan something for us to do on Saturday. You plan something for Sunday."

"For the whole day or just part of the day?"

"Just part. Activities lasting between two and five hours." If he asked for too much, she'd balk.

She was smiling dreamily, mouthing the chorus.

"Remy? Do you say yes?"

"What am I saying yes to?"

"Weekends with me."

"Hmm?"

Gotcha, he thought.

During the middle of the day, when Remy worked on her sculpture, Jeremiah spent his time on three things.

One, figuring out how to get ingredients for their dinners. Islehaven had no grocery store. Either you planned in advance and brought food with you when you arrived. Or you placed orders with a grocery store in Rockland and they loaded your order onto a plane. Or you bought items directly from Islehaven residents. Lobster, halibut, tuna, redfish, and more could sometimes be had off the dock. Bakery items could sometimes be had out of the house of a woman named Hilda.

Two, he continued to investigate Alexis's death. He'd just finished a master spreadsheet based on the worksheets that had come in from the conversations Jude, his mother, and Anton had completed. They'd all reported that the people they'd spoken with had been forthcoming, except for one. Fiona had said a friend of Alexis's named Skye had been reluctant to share anything with her. Jude recommended Jeremiah follow up with Skye at a later date, when back stateside and when more of his memory had returned.

Three, he worked on Remy's truck without her knowing. She was oblivious to the noises he was making thanks to the music she played, which suited him fine. He wanted her to have more reliable transportation. But he didn't want the lecture she'd give him if she knew he was repairing her truck without her approval.

On Saturday, Jeremiah steered the two of them to a neighboring island. They anchored in a bay rimmed with pines and hiked to the island's peak. When they reached it, Remy threw out her arms and turned in a circle. She was dressed in a parka, insulated leggings, and duck boots. The cold had turned her cheeks pink. She seemed to love her view, but it wasn't half as good as his. Back on the boat, they ate lobster salad sandwiches on crunchy rolls while the boat rocked them gently in the current.

The next day, Remy booked them massage appointments. They went to the home of someone named Samantha, who was also the local mailwoman and hairstylist. She'd set up a portable massage table in her kitchen that smelled like peanut butter. The table creaked loudly when Jeremiah lay stomach-down on it.

"Not to worry," Samantha said uncertainly. "It'll hold."

He had a hard time relaxing because he kept expecting the thing to crash to the ground. Also, her cats kept walking by on the counters, eyeballing him. Also, Samantha wasn't very strong, so the massage didn't feel great. Then again, if she pushed downward with any additional force, he really might crash.

As he and Remy walked from Samantha's house to Remy's truck, he looked across at her and pronounced, "Best massage I can ever remember having."

Remy had learned her lesson. Jeremiah would arrive on time for dinner and if she allowed herself to get so carried away in her work that she lost track of time, she'd pay for that mistake when he suddenly appeared—shocking her senses with his gorgeousness. One needed to prepare oneself for the onslaught of Jeremiah.

On Monday, Halloween, she outsmarted him by setting her dinner alarm ten minutes earlier than usual, then hurrying to the nearest mirror to check her appearance. She hadn't given a thought to her looks in years. But yikes. She was glad she'd checked.

She removed wood chips from her clothing and a stain from her chin. Returning to the studio, she positioned herself so that she was facing the room's doorway.

Once again, he was punctual. He showed up looking like the wind had raked loving fingers through his gold-brown hair. He'd taken to wearing the warm clothing necessary for autumn on Islehaven, yet it was clothing from a Camden closet. Upscale. Tonight, a flannel such a dark blue it was almost black, a waffle-knit shirt underneath, jeans that fit so well they should have been outlawed.

"Quitting time?" he asked.

"Quitting time," she agreed.

A smile hovered in his eyes as he watched her approach.

Jeremiah had a way of making her notice tiny details. The quality of the overhead light as it fell against his cheekbones. The gemlike shade of his eyes.

"Hello," she said when she was just inches away.

"Hello."

And there it was—desire thickening the atmosphere between them. It had become a constant presence. Heavy and languid at times. At other times sharp.

"I missed you," he said.

They'd only been apart since this morning's walk.

"A lot," he added.

She released a shaky exhale.

He scrutinized her. "What're you thinking?"

She slid her hands into her jumpsuit's pockets. "I'm thinking it would be a lot simpler to be around you if you were easier to resist."

His lips curved. "It would be a lot easier if you *didn't* resist."

Heat swirled in her abdomen. "The other night at Leigh's? When we danced?"

"Yeah?"

"I liked it. It didn't frighten me. So ever since then, I've been wanting to . . . ."

"To?"

She shrugged. "Be close to you like that again, I suppose."

"What do you suggest?"

She wet her lips. Her imagination conjured up an image of what she honestly wanted to do—press him against the hallway wall and make out with him. "I'm not sure. I don't know what kind of closeness I'll be able to handle."

"Why don't you test it and see?"

She gave him a questioning look.

"I volunteer myself. I'll remain still. And you can experiment with the level of closeness you're comfortable with."

"Really?"

"Do I have reason to worry you'll take advantage of me?"

"No."

"Then yes. Really."

She *yearned* to touch him. She'd love having carte blanche to explore, though that would come with the cost of awkwardness and uncertainty. Was she brave enough to try what he was suggesting? "You arrived two minutes ago. We haven't even eaten."

Humor tugged at his mouth. "You don't have to wine me and dine me first."

"I can trust you not to make a move?"

"Yes."

"And you won't be grumpy with me when I stop?"

"I promise you that I won't."

The invitation he was giving her felt like someone had thrown open the doors to a shop full of wood-carving tools and told her she could take all of them she wanted for free. Too delicious to turn down. "Then . . . yes," she said. "I'll take you up on that offer."

"Excellent."

"Now?"

"Now is good for me."

Chapter Twenty-One

"Where should we . . . ? Hmm." Instinctively, she patted her pockets the way she did when looking for her phone. As if she was going to find the answer to how to handle this situation in the pockets of her jumpsuit.

She glanced around her studio. Then went digging in her hair and fished out her glasses, setting them aside. She couldn't very well place Jeremiah on her worktable like a slab of mahogany. He was quite tall! How could she position him and herself so this would be as un-embarrassing as possible?

It was rapidly becoming clear that some level of embarrassment would be unavoidable. Closeness was vulnerable by definition. More so because she was extremely rusty at physical interactions with men.

She made her way down the hallway. "How about if you half-sit, half-stand against the table here?"

Right away, he leaned most of his weight on the table's edge. He looked outwardly relaxed—boots planted apart, hands wrapped around the table's rim—yet she sensed his coiled anticipation.

He was sublimely masculine but not threatening. He'd subdued his power for her sake.

"Comfortable?" she asked.

"Yes. You?"

"As comfortable as someone who's highly flustered can be." She laughed nervously as she neared him. "Where to start? Where to start?" She ran her focus from the top of his head down to his chest and back up.

"Take your pick."

She hesitated.

"You follow your instincts when you create art," he said, his voice like velvet on her skin. "Do the same here."

It felt much too forward and presumptuous to go right for his hair or his face, though both of those areas were screaming for further investigation. She decided on his hand. She picked up his right hand and studied it. There were veins running down its exterior, defined ligaments and tiny muscles. The inside of his wrist was paler than the top side. Jeremiah had large, capable hands. The hands of a man. The hands of a race car driver.

With barely-there pressure, she slowly glided the pad of her pointer finger from the base of his wrist along the outside of his thumb. Then traced a path up and down each finger, pausing for a split second in the valleys between.

Experimentally, she intertwined her fingers with his, pressing their palms together, then closed her eyes for a few moments to test the sensations. Her temperature was rising. Need gathered with pain-sweet force.

Eyelashes flipping open, she watched the rising motion of his chest, listened to the quiet sound of his breath. She released his hand. Placing both palms on his chest, she felt the heat and solidity of him and, beneath that, his thudding heart.

He had almost died, that day she'd found him at sea. But he was all health and strength now. Alive. Virile.

She dared meet his eyes.

He gazed unflinchingly back, causing an almighty *gong* to reverberate through her.

Gently, she turned his face to the side because it was too much to have him staring at her as she investigated him like a three-dimensional map.

Her fingers siphoned through the hair near his temple. The texture of it was slightly denser than it looked. She charted a trail around his ear and down the cord of his neck. Across a collarbone. Back to the groove at the base of his neck. Along the other collarbone.

Her air went shallow. This was ridiculously heady. She couldn't believe he was letting her do this.

She roamed halfway down his hard chest, then her hands split, trailing up both sides of his ribs, noting the lean indentations of them. He was a gorgeous man. Worthy of sculptures.

Gathering her nerve, she turned his profile back toward her and skimmed her thumb along his bottom lip.

She'd shared pleasurable intimate moments with the boyfriends she'd had before Gavin. Always, though, those moments had felt slightly rushed and her mind had been divided. Half her brain had been focused on incoming stimuli. The other half had been wondering how much or little the guy was enjoying things.

Somehow, this approach was working wonders for her. It was unhurried. No fear existed because he'd given her control. She wasn't distracted by anticipating or responding to him. Here, she was fully present, free to drink in every response of her five senses.

This was sensual in the simplest way. Mind blowing.

He had not swerved a millimeter from his promise to remain still, which stoked her confidence.

She set her palms on the sides of his face, her pinky fingers cradling underneath the line of his jawbone. In incremental degrees, she brought her profile toward his. Overwhelmingly curious. Greedy for just a quick feel of his lips under hers. Her eyelids sank closed, avoiding what she knew would be the searing heat of his eyes. Then she set her lips on his.

Firm and soft at the same time.

She moved back, putting a space between them.

It was as if an orchestra was hitting a crescendo inside her body, heart, mind. She'd known him for seven weeks. Time enough to begin to comprehend his facets. Time enough to love him.

She pressed her lips to his again in an act of discovery. The pressure was light. It was the emotional intensity that packed a wallop—

For the first time, caution flickered in her like a match lighting. The flicker wasn't born of trauma. Even so, she responded instantly. Stepping away, she let her hands slide tenderly from his face and drop to her sides. She looked toward her office, seeing nothing.

Why the caution?

Because she was starting to want a relationship with him. Persistently and stubbornly. Almost rebelliously. She'd always considered a real relationship between them as hopeless, but did it have to be?

Maybe. No? Yes? The prospect of change frightened her. A relationship would mean sacrifices. It would mean putting herself out there. She'd need to give up some degree of her safe and secluded life here. Was she willing to do that?

The sameness of the past years had kept her mental and physical health intact. While her Islehaven existence had never brought her the type of exhilaration that kissing him brought her, it did offer more subtle rewards. She knew she'd be okay doing what she'd been doing. She didn't know if she'd be okay if she risked her whole heart on Jeremiah.

"Did that upset you?" he asked. His color had risen but otherwise he looked much more unaffected by what had just happened than she felt.

"Not at all until right at the end," she told him truthfully. "That said, I don't regret a second. It was . . . revelatory."

"How so?"

"It gave me hope that nightmares don't necessarily have to intrude every time."

He seemed to consider that as he nodded. "You are incredibly beautiful to me."

She waved a hand and took another step back, unwilling to let herself internalize his words or the way he looked saying them. "You're the dazzling one. Ask anyone."

"I don't care what anyone else might say. Between us, the truth is this. You're the dazzling one."

"Well." She smiled. "You said you wouldn't be grumpy afterward and you're not grumpy."

"No. I'm not grumpy."

It wasn't easy to shake off the hormones. They were urging her to reach for him, to put her lips back on his lips. "Happy Halloween, Jeremiah."

"Happy Halloween, Remy."

She curved her hands into fists to keep them under control, then went to the kitchen and began staging dinner. Just how tricky was it going to be to re-institute normalcy between them? "Let's eat!"

He seemed to understand her wish to switch topics and began unpacking a bag of dinner groceries. "Let's eat."

· · ·

Remy had no idea what she'd just done to him.

She'd never be able to understand how much he cared about her or the depth of the effect she had on him. It had felt, leaning there against the table, as if he'd waited more than a lifetime for the feel of her hands on him. For those kisses.

It had been hard to remain motionless and, on the other hand, easy. With her history, there was no way that he'd have done anything to jeopardize her trust in him. He'd called on the self-control some said he'd once been famous for and devoted himself to watching her. He'd seen every flicker of change on her features, every shift of her posture.

Those scorching seconds had made him believe in a future for them.

They ate dinner, talking in their usual way about the usual things. Yet something new lived between them. It was as if a curtain had been pulled back, revealing unseen territory. And also on her end, he sensed, fresh worries.

After dinner, they settled on the couch together to watch a show. In the past, they'd taken opposite ends. Tonight, she sat close enough to rest her head on his shoulder. Her side was pressed to his side. He carefully—not wanting to startle her—wrapped his arm around her.

She chose a weird fantasy TV series filled with characters who had unpronounceable names. No cable here, so they watched on her computer. The show buffered every fifteen minutes or so thanks to her spotty Wi-Fi. He didn't understand anything happening onscreen.

And none of that mattered.

Not when contentment was swelling so strongly inside, filling every edge and corner of him.

Fiona sat inside the study of her fairytale house, doing a non-fairytale thing. Finishing draft fourteen of her letter to Isobel.

She'd written drafts that were pages and pages long. Drafts that contained self-deprecation. Drafts that detailed memories of things she and Isobel had done together.

She nudged her reading glasses higher on her nose and read over what she'd written this time around.

Isobel,

There was no one on earth closer to me during our childhood than you. You're entwined with my earliest years so tightly that I can't think back without thinking of you. My playmate, my teacher, my room-mate, my big sister. As soon as I was old enough to comprehend the people in my life—there you were. An integral part of my family and heart. And I repaid you, the person closest to me, with betrayal.

I want you to know that I'm sorry. Deeply sorry. I bitterly regret the actions of my twenty-three-year-old self. I was selfish and envious, and I destroyed the thing I should have recognized as one of my most valuable possessions—my relationship with you.

The total solar eclipse we promised each other we'd view together back in South America is coming to Maine in a year. When we promised each other we'd view it together, I dearly wanted to experience the eclipse with you. Now, I want to experience it with you a hundred times more than I did then.

I'm writing to ask for an opportunity to meet with

you and apologize. I realize I don't deserve that opportunity. But if you can find it within you to see me briefly, I'd greatly appreciate it. I'll come to New York whenever it's convenient for you.

Fiona

Unlike the prior drafts, this one felt right. It wasn't long but it genuinely communicated her feelings. She folded the thick piece of stationery and sealed it in its matching envelope.

Her sister Alice had always been the sibling most anxious for Fiona to reconcile with Isobel, so Alice had kept Fiona apprised of Isobel's new addresses and phone numbers over the decades. Fiona scrawled the address of Isobel's current New York apartment on the front of the envelope, then hesitated over what to put in the return address slot. It seemed likely Alice had kept Isobel informed of Fiona's addresses and phone numbers, too. If Isobel recognized Fiona's address, she might not open the envelope. So in the return slot, Fiona wrote only the address of her company's office.

Riding a wave of determination, she got in her car and drove to the post office downtown with the letter occupying the passenger seat. It was late and Groomsport had been put to bed for the night.

She pulled up to the outdoor mail collection box, rolled down her window, opened the chute. Was she going to throw up? Acid climbed her esophagus. Anxiety mounted quick and high, making her light-headed.

Weary of how long she'd fussed over the drafts of the letter already, irritated by her weakness, she grasped the letter in her free hand. Before she could second-guess, she thrust it into the chute. Out of her grip it went, down into the belly of the collection box.

There. No going back.

The following day, Jeremiah sat at Leigh's kitchen table, laptop in front of him, spreadsheet open. Jude had just sent him a text, asking how he was, so Jeremiah texted back, letting him know he was doing even better on Islehaven than he'd been doing in Groomsport. Jude stayed in contact with him regularly. The guy struck Jeremiah as having it all together, highly organized—

All of a sudden, he remembered himself and Jude . . . at a huge dining room table. In their childhood home. He was in fifth grade, his brother smaller. Pieces of paper belonging to Jeremiah's science fair project covered the table. But Jude was the one assembling the board.

Jeremiah leaned back, balancing his chair on its back two legs, sneakers crossed on the table. His thumbs worked the handheld video game he played. Jude was a lot better at this type of stuff than he was. He'd made a good bargain when he'd given Jude an unopened Lego set in exchange for sitting here chilling while his brother did all the work.

Back in the present, Jeremiah startled.

A memory.

He didn't try to force more. Instead, he simply tried to open up his brain. *What else do I know about Jude?*

In response, a few more images landed in his head like isolated droplets of water. He saw himself and Jude as kids posing for a photo in front of the Eiffel Tower. He saw himself and Jude walking into their elementary school together on the first day of school. He saw himself pushing a kid his age after that kid said something mean to Jude. He saw himself and Jude hugging goodbye when he'd moved to Europe to compete in karting.

What do I know about my mother? He pictured her as she'd looked the last time he'd seen her. And then, yes, he could recall some things. She yelled, "Dance break," and he'd looked way up at her as they'd danced to loud pop music. He saw her reading to him before bed. He saw her rushing to her feet in a standing ovation after his elementary talent show act. He remembered receiving a phone call from her. He was in an apartment . . . in Austria. His uncle was in the kitchen making dinner and his mother was on the other end of the line telling him in a cold, furious voice that his father was Max Cirillo's biological dad—

Sharp pain carved through his head, slamming the door on that memory.

He laid an arm on the table and rested his forehead on it. He breathed through the pain steadily until it decreased to a bearable level.

Pleasant memories were fine but painful memories weren't. So what did he remember about his father that was pleasant? He saw his father at the wheel of a convertible 1967 Chevy Corvette Stingray, hair whipping around his head as he drove. He remembered everyone flocking around Dad and asking for autographs when he showed up at Jeremiah's middle school. He saw Dad dressed in a gray suit, beaming at him after an F1 race.

Anton? More enjoyable memories came.

Alexis?

Nothing.

He waited, bringing to mind the different photos he'd seen of her. He expected a walking, talking, breathing memory of her to come. But nothing answered except gray smoke.

He quit trying with Alexis and went back to Jude, Mom,

Dad, and Anton. A couple additional memories trickled in. Then they all came to a stop—as if his mind had given him all it was willing to give for one day.

Which was fine. The memories were coming back just as the psychologist had predicted they would. Thank God. Finally, he was seeing the progress he'd been hoping for. Finally, his brain was issuing a payoff for all the time he'd spent waiting.

That evening Jeremiah waited for Remy—once again half-standing, half-leaning against her table.

When her music went silent, he watched the hallway eagerly.

She walked into view wearing a gray top and beige cargo pants. Hair in a messy side braid. Glasses on. Pleasure leapt into her expression at the sight of him.

"Several memories came to me today," he told her.

"They did?"

"Yeah. I remembered things about Jude, my mother, father, and Anton."

"That's fabulous news." She hugged him.

He thought that might mean he had permission to hug her back. He did so, taking care not to crush her against him the way he wanted to.

The second she leaned back, he released her. She gripped his shoulders. "Tell me everything."

He did.

She asked questions and he explained.

"So nothing about Alexis yet?"

"I tried but still nothing."

"It'll come. This is so encouraging."

Beneath her obvious excitement for him, he read sorrow in the tiny brackets on each side of her mouth. "Is something about this making you sad?" he asked. "If so, please tell me."

"What? No."

He gave her an expression that said, *I know you're lying.*

"I'm embarrassed to say anything. It's selfish."

"Tell me."

She fiddled with the collar of his brown sweater, seeming to test its weave. "If your memories are coming back, that means your days here are numbered—"

"And you'll be sorry to see me go?" He gave her a masculine grin of approval.

"I might be just a tiny bit sorry. What's a very small unit of measurement? One one-hundredth of an ounce? I'll be that sorry to see you go. The rest of me will be happy for you and wish you well."

"I've been trying to tell you all along that my memories are not a threat to us."

"But you can't be certain of that until you get them all back."

"Which is one of the reasons I want them back. So I can put your mind at ease—"

"My mind is already at ease." She spoke with so much conviction that he knew she was lying.

He stared down at her thoughtfully. "At this point, I'm not planning on leaving. It's only because I'm here with you, where I'm at peace, that I'm remembering."

"Okay, but you *will* go when it's time to go," she said firmly.

"Remy—"

She cut him off by placing a finger against his lips. "The return of your memories is a joyful turn of events. Let's leave it that way. . . ." The sentence drifted off as her vision dropped to where she was touching him.

Just like that, desire rolled in his abdomen, firing his nerve endings.

"May I?" she asked.

"You may."

Their profiles close, he heard her inhales quicken. His blood rushed with possessiveness. Hunger.

Her palm slid around to the back of his neck, warm.

She closed the distance between their mouths until there was just a fraction of an inch left. Then paused.

He stopped himself before making a sound of impatience. Instead, he merely looked at her, willing her with his eyes to kiss him.

Kiss me.

It felt like the most urgent thing in his world. The difference between life and death. He was willing to give her his house, his cars, and everything else he could think of if she would just kiss him.

She was going to back away. He needed to prepare for that—

Closing her eyes, she pressed her mouth to his.

Like a greedy man unwilling to part with a nickel, he was unwilling to give up a single sensation. He wanted them all.

His hands gripped the table hard. *Let her set the pace*, he repeated to himself over and over.

She was as strong as the wildflowers that grew on this island. Brilliant in her creativity. Rare in her individuality. The better he knew her, the more he appreciated her.

She gentled the kiss as if testing to make sure she could step back when she needed to. He showed her that she had that freedom.

With a small sound of satisfaction, she leaned her body against his.

Blazing minutes passed. Unhurried and also too fast. Perfect. Regret twisted in him when she ended it.

Her cheeks were bright. Her eyes hazy.

Come back to me, he thought.

She made no move.

"You done?" he asked hoarsely.

"I'm still deciding. You done?"

"If you are."

She resettled her braid. "If you'd like, you can put your hands on me."

He moved with so much speed that she quickly added, "I should've been more specific."

His hands stopped in midair.

"You can put your hands on my face. Or hair."

Inclining his chin, he slowed his movements. He ran his thumbs over her cheekbones, then threaded his hands into her hair. Gently, he supported the base of her head.

In answer, Remy's hands came up to grip his sweater and pull him closer.

"Okay?" he asked.

"Yes." Then she was kissing him again.

And then they were kissing each other. And Jeremiah was doing his best to put every single thing he felt for her into that kiss.

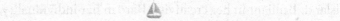

Ten days passed after Jeremiah had arrived on Islehaven. Then fifteen. His life took on a rhythm he liked. His time was his own. Remy was safe here. He was safe here. It was quiet, without pressure or demands. But *with* Remy. Hanging out with her. Holding her. Kissing her.

In time, his stress level dropped so low that his amnesia

seemed to decide it was safe to let in a wider range of memories.

He recalled many of the trips he'd taken with his family before his parents' divorce. Ski trips to Aspen. Beach trips to Turks and Caicos. Trips to visit his mother's grandparents after they'd moved to California to escape the winters in Maine.

He recalled his years at school in Groomsport and his years in the karting circuit in Europe. While other kids his age had been attending normal middle schools and high schools back in the USA, he'd been completing his classes with a tutor in between training sessions.

Jeremiah was on a walk with Remy one morning, glancing to the side at the ocean, when he remembered steering the *Camdenball* across the waves. He'd swiveled in the captain's chair and looked over his shoulder. Sitting on the deck's sofa, wearing a large hat, sunglasses, and a strapless dress . . .

Was Alexis.

Recognition bolted through him. He kept walking, slower now, on the trail on Islehaven. But he was seeing Alexis more than his actual surroundings.

She was stunning. Photos of her hadn't fully prepared him for the power of her appearance in 3D—long legs crossed, picture-perfect dark hair, one hand supporting a champagne flute.

The emotion he'd felt toward her on that particular day? Love.

Gradually, another memory rose, of when he'd met Alexis. One of the women on the team who'd handled press had introduced them. Alexis had been worldly and flirtatious, and he'd immediately experienced a jolt of strong attraction. He'd used the double barrels of charm in his arsenal.

They were snowboarding. She looked like a model in her knit cap, her hair falling down either side of her fashionable snowsuit. He saw the two of them touring Appleton. Except that it wasn't his house as he knew it now. It had been filled with someone else's furniture and art. This was when they'd taken their first look at it. From across the room, she met his eyes from where she stood listening to the real estate agent. She gave him a knowing smile that clearly communicated, *This is the one for us.*

He envisioned himself, Alexis, Anton, and Camille sitting at a restaurant table overlooking a view of the French Riviera. Alexis threw her head back to laugh. Her elegant throat was white, the three gold necklaces around it slightly tangled.

Her personality began to take shape. She'd been intelligent. Ambitious like his mother but not nearly as forthright as his mother. It had been hard to get to know who she was down deep, below her persona. There he'd eventually found kindness, insecurity, willpower, competitiveness.

He was competitive, too. But only on the racetrack. Her competitiveness had no borders. He'd come to realize it was rooted in her need to be loved and her need for security. He'd determined to give her those things.

He'd proposed with a five-carat teardrop-shaped diamond ring because that's the one she'd asked him to buy. They'd honeymooned in Fiji. The sex . . . The sex had been great—

They were standing in the bedroom of their Monaco apartment. She was wearing a negligee and screaming at him. Picking up a lamp, she threw it at his head.

On the path here on Islehaven, his head split with pain as if that long-ago lamp was connecting with his skull.

Right away, the memories of her ended.

Chapter Twenty-Two

On his eighteenth day on Islehaven, the real world came for Jeremiah in the form of a knock on Leigh's door at ten in the morning.

He straightened from his spot at the kitchen table.

Remy never knocked when she came by, so he had no reason to think it was her. Even so, he couldn't stop himself from hoping as he crossed to the door.

Felix waited on the threshold.

His father wore a suit beneath a formal wool coat. He was dressed very much like he'd been dressed the only other time Jeremiah had interacted with him—that day at the hospital.

"Hello," Felix said with relaxed ease, as if him showing up here was commonplace.

"Didn't I ask you to stay out of my life until I reached out to you?" Jeremiah's tone was more interested than accusing. Unlike at their first meeting, he did have memories of his dad now. Good ones. Some not-so-great ones.

"I was patient for a month and a half. That's a record for me." Felix arched a golden brow. "May I come in?"

317

In answer, Jeremiah opened the door farther.

Felix strode in like a king, looking around with interest. "Not your usual style of accommodation."

Jeremiah let that go. "What brings you here?"

"I'm on my way to Canada. Since I was flying past this general direction, I thought I'd stop in and check on you." He slid his hands out of his leather gloves and stashed both gloves in a pocket. "Have any memories returned?"

"Some."

"Yet you still don't trust me?"

"No. I found out you're the one who'd benefit financially from my death."

Felix smiled. "You think I tried to kill you by beating you up and throwing you over the side of your boat in order to gain your Camden family inheritance?"

"You'd benefit financially from my death," Jeremiah repeated.

"Where's a paper and a pen?"

Jeremiah nodded to the old-fashioned landline phone on the Formica counter between the small living room and the kitchen. Next to it sat a stack of Post-it notes and a cup of pens.

"Here's the website of my financial planner. Contact him." Felix wrote on the top Post-it note. "I'll give him permission to share my net worth with you. Once he does, you'll know that I have no need of your Camden family inheritance." Inserting the pen back into the cup with a rattle, he faced Jeremiah. "Any other reasons why you don't trust me?"

"Other than the fact that you cheated with my mother on your first wife and then cheated on my mother with Max's mother?"

"Everyone in America enjoys feasting on my past sins. Why should you be any different? They are, after all, very juicy sins." He appeared almost bored as he crossed to a wall and straightened a fake wood frame. "I've admitted to the world at large that I'm untrustworthy when it comes to romantic commitments. But research me even a little and you'll find that I've always taken responsibility for my actions and dealt with the consequences. Which is more than I can say for you right now. You're living out here as if you're in the witness protection program."

"I like it here."

"You're avoiding life here."

"I'm choosing how I want to live."

"And how much of this choice of yours has to do with a blond sculptor?"

"If you're asking if she's manipulated me into following her here, the answer is no. She tried to convince me to stay in Groomsport."

"I see."

His memories were returning, but he now viewed his life from a new perspective. Jonah's perspective. It was as if Jonah was still inside him, looking out at the events and people that surrounded him and helping him determine what mattered and what didn't. Remy mattered.

He didn't owe his father that explanation, however.

The silence between them grew long. Was there anything beneficial Felix could provide while he was here? "I found evidence that Alexis was unfaithful to me during our marriage." Maybe Felix could offer insight on that.

Felix's face remained impassive.

"Did you know about that?" Jeremiah asked.

"No."

"It occurred to me that maybe Alexis and I were both unfaithful. Maybe she started having affairs after I betrayed her."

"I wouldn't think so."

319

"Why?"

"Because we're alike in many ways. But we're different in one important way. I'm not faithful to women. You are. I think that's partly because you saw firsthand the damage that my infidelity did. You told me more than once that you would never do the same to anyone. You were faithful to the girlfriends you had before Alexis, and I have every reason to think that you were faithful to her as well."

"Then why did she cheat on me?"

"Alexis had many good qualities. She was beautiful and stylish and socially adept. On the other hand, she was demanding. And required a great deal of attention. Perhaps she was looking for someone else to . . . make her feel whole."

"Because I failed at making her feel that way?"

"No one could make her feel whole, Jeremiah. She was looking for something she was never going to find."

It was as if Jeremiah's history was a puzzle.

Each day, new pieces appeared, and he found where they fit. Each night, he reported the new memories to Remy.

By mid-November, two months after Remy had rescued him, many of the puzzle pieces regarding Alexis had slotted into place.

After their marriage, she'd become hard to please. She had her own work as an influencer and plenty to fill her schedule. Even so, she was jealous of his time. No matter how much of it he gave her, it wasn't enough. She'd married a man who traveled to races for a living, but sometimes she didn't want him to go. When he'd remind her she could go with him, she'd say she was sick of plane flights and hotels and hotel food.

She'd started picking fights with him. Afterward, she'd give him the silent treatment for days. Then she'd apologize, buy him presents, and wrap herself around him. Things would be mostly fine again.

Eventually, though, the bad facets of their marriage began to overshadow the good. He'd taken to reminding himself of her best qualities on repeat. Her generosity. Her chops as a businesswoman. Her ability to move smoothly in the lowest and the highest circles.

About a year and a half into his marriage, he'd happened to open Instagram on a flight home. Alexis lived and breathed social media. He did not. He'd had a few accounts from the start of his professional driving career, but the Mercedes marketing team had handled almost all of the work and time associated with those accounts. There were too many comments and tags to keep up with, plus most of it was too idiotic to bother with. He looked at it only rarely. On that flight, however, he'd typed a hashtag followed by his name into the search bar, then flicked through several of the posts that appeared.

The usual. Posts from fans. Haters. More fans. But then a picture had caused him to stop, his thumb frozen on the screen.

The picture showed Alexis with another man. She was walking with her hand on his bent arm and wearing clothes he recognized—recent clothes.

Frowning, he read the caption.

#JeremiahCamden, just checking if you know that your lady is out with some guy who ain't you.

His gut had turned into a ball of cold metal.

At that point, he and Alexis had been in a good place for a whole month. She was content. No arguments. He'd been congratulating himself, relieved. But looking at that photo it had occurred to him that he wasn't the one making her content. She was content because of this man, in the picture.

When he'd reached home, she'd denied it. An explanation had rolled off her tongue. She'd said the man in the picture was gay, an employee of a clothing brand she was partnering with on an upcoming campaign. Every word had sounded convincing.

It would have been easiest to believe her. But his instincts wouldn't let him.

He'd thought about the picture for days. He'd watched her. He'd looked through her physical things as well as her phone, computer, iPad. He'd found nothing suspicious. Which is when he'd called his father and told him he needed the name of a PI without explaining the reason why. Just as he'd expected, Felix had been able to recommend a PI. Fred Kimley.

Kimley's first report had cracked their marriage and Jeremiah's heart. He'd been shocked and disgusted. Betrayed.

Quitting, though, wasn't in his nature, just look at his driving record. He'd never have earned a square inch of success if he hadn't been so dogged, so stubbornly motivated in the face of defeat. He was loyal—which explained why he'd driven for the same team his whole career. And he was old-fashioned enough not to want to break the vows he'd spoken to Alexis on their wedding day.

She'd begged him for a second chance and—ultimately—he'd given her one. They'd seen a therapist.

There had been times, after her affair, when it seemed like everything might be okay. And times when it seemed all was lost.

If she didn't accompany him to a race, he'd wonder what she was doing while he was away, a nauseous feeling low in his torso.

They'd spent the off-season after the affair in Maine. He'd hoped downtime in one place, together, would help them.

But then in the spring of last year, she'd started going out several nights a week. She began taking trips when he was at home. Most damning of all, she'd been overly sweet toward him, suspiciously content. Grim, he'd hired Kimley a second time. While he'd waited on Kimley's report, he'd existed in the same house with Alexis—not sleeping together, not connecting. Beneath his calm façade, resentment simmered. He'd known that, if he received proof of another affair, their marriage would be over.

While he'd been waiting for the second report from Kimley, one night in June, she'd told him she was going to dinner with friends. She hadn't come home. Nor had she answered her phone. His initial reaction had been anger because he'd concluded that she was with her lover and that she'd arrive home with a slick cover story.

Once she'd been gone twenty-four hours, though, he'd been unsure how to feel or what to do. A normal husband would feel worried. He didn't feel worried, but he *was* a husband, so he'd called her friends. When that led nowhere, he'd called her family. They'd been terrified. It became clear that none of the people close to her knew where she was. At that point, he'd contacted the police.

The next morning, Jeremiah had received Kimley's second report. While the PI had been unable to name the man she was having an affair with, it was clear Alexis *had* been engaged in another affair, exactly as Jeremiah had suspected.

Later that same day, a boater on Megunticook Lake spotted her body.

He'd wanted to divorce her, but he had *never* wanted her dead. She was young and healthy. The greatest portion of her life should have been before her and that future should have been bright.

Her family had been crushed and it had been terrible to

witness their heartbreak. Grief, guilt, and confusion had submerged him. In that haze, one thing had been clear.

He did not think she'd jumped. He suspected that the man she'd been having an affair with had stolen Alexis's life.

Jeremiah had wrapped up his final season of racing, fulfilled his contract, and retired. Once the demands and adrenaline of that were behind him, he'd holed up in Monaco for months, reclusive, hiding from everyone and from his sorrow, trying to find his footing.

In time, he'd realized he wouldn't be able to move on from his troubled marriage until her killer had been brought to justice. He'd loved Alexis once, so much that he'd married her. He owed her justice. Once he had that for her, she'd be free, and he'd be free. That was why he'd continued to wear his wedding ring. It hadn't been a symbol of his love for her. Instead, it had been a symbol of his obligation to her.

He'd yet to learn the identity of her lover. Aware that he had an unknown enemy, he'd left his files in the secret room behind the liquor shelf prior to his boat trip.

He'd spent weeks before that trip and since assembling notes and hunting for clues—any clue—that would shed light on Alexis's death.

He'd come up empty.

⛵

Then one ordinary day on Islehaven . . . he finally hit on something.

This might be nothing, he told himself. Yet it struck him as strange enough to call his brother.

"Hey," Jude said, picking up right away as usual.

"Hey. I've been looking through the social media feeds of everyone in Alexis's calendar and also everyone connected to me. In each case, I've gone back to a few months before Alexis died. Then I've scanned over everything they've posted up to the present."

"Smart."

"You remember me telling you who Gigi is?"

"Yeah. The woman you were dating."

"Right. Before Alexis died, Gigi had wavy blond hair. She didn't wear much makeup and her clothing was simpler. Less sexy."

"Women change their style all the time."

"Except in Gigi's case, it's creepy because after Alexis died, her hair became long, straight, and brown. She started doing her makeup like Alexis. She started dressing like Alexis."

Jude gave a thoughtful, "Hmm."

"Do you think it's weird that Gigi entered my life soon after making herself look as similar as possible to my dead wife?"

"I do think it's weird, yes. Though the similarity of Gigi's new look to Alexis's look could be a coincidence."

"I checked to see if Gigi followed Alexis on Instagram and she did."

"Alexis was an influencer. Thousands of women copied her clothing, hair, and makeup. Perhaps Gigi was one of them."

A few moments of silence passed.

"What's your theory?" Jude asked. "That Gigi became what she believed was your type in order to snag you?"

"I don't know. Maybe?"

"It's worth looking into further. If she was in love with you from a distance, or obsessed with you, that gives her motive to kill Alexis."

Jeremiah's suspicions had gone in that same direction. "When I spoke with Gigi, she did not strike me as dangerous."

"Some of the most dangerous people don't strike others as dangerous."

Jeremiah went into motion, walking up and down the hallway of Leigh's house. "If Gigi killed Alexis so that she could have me, why would she then try to kill *me* shortly after she and I started dating?"

"Good question. That doesn't fit. Hang on a minute. I'm going to run Gigi's arrest record. What's her last name?"

Jeremiah supplied details on Gigi. Had he been mistaken to focus for so many weeks on the people Alexis knew instead of the people *he* knew?

In less than five minutes, Jude came back on the line. "Gigi has never been arrested. She's only received one speeding ticket for going forty-five in a thirty-five zone."

"Clearly, she's a killer," Jeremiah said dryly.

"There's another angle here."

"I'm listening."

"What if . . . you're not the one Gigi was obsessed with? What if the one she was obsessed with was Alexis?"

Jeremiah processed that shift. It was true that a lot of Alexis's followers had been very devoted to her. There'd been a huge outpouring of grief and adoration from them when Alexis died.

"In this scenario," Jude continued, "Gigi had nothing to do with Alexis's death. But what if Gigi was so wrecked by it that she got you to turn your attention to her just so she could punish you for Alexis's death?"

A chill slithered between Jeremiah's shoulder blades because the scenario made a sick kind of sense.

"It could be she thought that you killed Alexis?" Jude suggested. "Or that your neglect caused Alexis to commit suicide? Knocking you off was her way of getting payback for her idol."

"So then she stowed away on my boat and beat me up? *No way* she beat me up."

"You were hit on the back of the head. If she snuck up on you from behind with a bat, for example, she might have stunned you enough with a blow to your head to get in several blows to your ribs and push you overboard."

Jeremiah tried to picture it, but it felt too far-fetched.

"The fact that your attacker didn't succeed in killing you," Jude said, "points to the fact that they might have been weaker than you."

"Or an amateur at killing."

"I think we should meet with Gigi, confront her, and gauge how she responds."

Put your head down and finish the last ten minutes of work before the dinner alarm goes off, Remy told herself that evening. *Focus, and you'll soon have the reward of seeing Jeremiah.*

For the first time in years, she found herself paying attention to the time of day while working. Why? Because her life had undergone a shift. She now loved what happened at the end of her workday more than she loved the actual work.

When she finally emerged from her studio, she found Jeremiah waiting for her, exactly as she'd hoped. He'd taken up his customary position—feet planted wide, leaning against her table, wearing a navy sweater and casual charcoal pants. However, something was slightly . . . off. He looked more tense than usual.

Remy stopped a few feet from him. "What's happened?"

"Nothing to worry about. Just a potential new direction in the search regarding Alexis." He straightened away from the table and extended a hand to her, asking without words if she wanted to hold it.

She took it and they stood facing each other. Freezing wind off the ocean whined against the outside walls of her cottage.

He explained the change in appearance Gigi had undergone and the theories he and his brother were kicking around. "I think," he said, "I should return home. That way I can talk to Gigi. And now that I remember the people Alexis saw during her final days, I can also follow up with some of them in person."

He's leaving. "Of course," she said smoothly. His motivation for going was completely reasonable. The amount of loss twisting through her in response? *That* was the unreasonable part. *You knew he couldn't stay forever, Remy! You knew all along that he would go.* "You belong on the mainland."

"I belong wherever you are," he corrected.

"No. You don't."

His forehead lined. "Will you come with me to Groomsport?"

"No."

"I'd like for you to come."

"The last time I went with you there it was because you were sick. You had no memories. You needed my support then. This time you don't need me."

He looked her dead in the eyes. "I need you." There was power in the words and intensity in his expression.

She broke the contact of their hands and took a step back, thrusting her fingers into the hip pockets of her overalls. "Technically, no. You don't need me." And under no circumstances could she cave and become the needy one. If she did, she'd never forgive herself. "I have to stay here and work and you'll do just fine without me. You have friends, a large family, a whole world who adores you."

"But you are the only one that I adore."

Don't weaken, she ordered herself. "Be that as it may, you don't owe me anything. Including an explanation as to why you're going."

He gave her a look like, *What are you talking about?* "Of course I owe you an explanation."

"Again—not technically, no."

His lips flattened.

Emotionally, she was overreacting to the news that he was going. She knew it and yet she couldn't seem to tamp her internal overreaction down. It was clearer than ever in this moment that the size of her love for him made her vulnerable. He had the power to hurt her, badly. Which was *terrifying.* Perhaps best to use this opening to make her position clear to him and try to shore up her own cracks. "You're free to stay or go," she stated. "It's not as if we're boyfriend and girlfriend."

His eyebrows slanted. Obviously, he wasn't in the mood to acknowledge how noble she was being. He had a tremendously long fuse. Five times as long as her own. However, she could see that she'd now succeeded in stirring his anger and lighting that fuse. "We *are* boyfriend and girlfriend, Remy."

"You're recovering well from the amnesia now. It could be that this whole interlude—living here, kissing me—will soon begin to seem strange to you and that you'll then want your actual life in Groomsport and your actual girlfriend."

"Living here and kissing you will always seem like the rightest thing in my life because you *are* my actual girlfriend."

"I haven't agreed to that. How can I when it's so hard to imagine how this relationship could work out well for you and me?"

He scowled. "Here's how. We get engaged. We get married. But before any of that can happen, you have to commit to me enough to be my girlfriend."

She gaped at him. Engagement and marriage? "You can see yourself marrying me?" she asked incredulously.

"Yes."

It was all well and good for Jeremiah to toy with the idea of happily ever after! He was the one who could survive the end of this. He, so cavalier and popular, didn't love her so he was free to indulge his whims. "You can afford to play house on Islehaven if it suits your fancy. I can't afford that. You're—you're acting like all of this is simple when it's not."

"This *is* simple for me."

"And for me it's anything but. I'm not fancy enough or outgoing enough for you. I'm scared to leave Islehaven, but as your girlfriend I'd need to leave it often. For what purpose, though? Since I'm unlikely to fit into your world once I get there."

"I'll change my world to fit you."

"I don't believe that."

"I would do anything for you, Remy."

She thrust away a tendril of her hair. Jeremiah's blind confidence was maddening! Reckless. Foolish. He wasn't acknowledging—nor even seeming to hear—her concerns. "Alexis was basically the female version of you."

"Did you notice how badly things went for Alexis and me? That is no longer what I want."

"The Camdens represent everything I don't like, which is a huge red flag for me."

"I wish I only came with upsides. I don't." His jaw set like granite as he scratched the back of his neck. His arms dropped. "I was raised under a microscope of scandal. I've never had anonymity and I never will. My parents are difficult. My wife cheated on me. My driving ability faded so I gave up my career. Alexis died. I lost my memories. And all of that has only made me more determined to prioritize this." He motioned between them. "Us. I don't bring perfection and I'm not asking you to bring perfection."

Remy swallowed hard. Tears were stinging behind her eyes.

"I want to be with you," he said. "I have flaws. But if you'll accept those, I'll give up whatever I need to for you. Will you do the same for me?"

As upset as she was, she saw the fairness of his question. For several weeks after meeting him, she'd made numerous sacrifices for him. But since she'd returned to Islehaven, he'd made all the sacrifices and she'd made none. That wasn't how a healthy relationship functioned. Both partners had to bend and give things up for the other.

She understood that. So why was her heart drumming much too fast with panic? All these feelings were *overwhelming*. Her need to detach from them and withdraw was visceral. "What are you asking me to give up?"

"Some of your isolation and some of your control. In order to make room for me. So we can try for something bigger together."

She gestured to the cottage. "This *is* my definition of a big life. You know me well enough to know that this life makes me happy."

"I know you well enough to know that it makes you safe," he said. "But also, ultimately, empty."

Empty! Defensiveness rushed to its feet inside her like a battalion of soldiers. "That's not true. Just because a woman doesn't have a boyfriend or husband does *not* mean her life is empty."

"Your life isn't empty because you don't have a man in it. It's empty because you're hiding." His tone was forceful but level. He'd always been the more self-disciplined of the two of them. He had composure in spades and Remy wanted to tear tracks in it with her fingernails.

"This is how I healed from what Gavin did to me. What right do you have to judge how I healed?"

"I judge it because I care and because I'm angry that you're letting Gavin win."

She opened her mouth, but shock and fury stole her words. *What did he just say?* That she'd *let Gavin win.*

Was that what he thought of her? Was he busy viewing her as a beaten rabbit, quaking in her burrow while she was simultaneously viewing herself as strong and brave? That *hurt.* That cut her deeply. Believing that Gavin had won completely belittled the strides and victories she'd made. Gavin might have won in court, but he had not won. And if Jeremiah were truly on her side, he'd understand that.

She felt whiplashed by this conversation. By his romantic words followed by his accusing words. *Time to put space between you and him,* an inner voice demanded. *Better now than later. Wait and you'll be even more head-over-heels invested in him than you already are.*

"I'm asking you to take a chance on me," he said bluntly. "And I realize that's risky for you. But I'm telling you that I won't let you down. Do you trust me?"

"How can I ever trust the person who just accused me of *letting Gavin win?*"

Color rushed up his face. "Remy—"

"No. No more." She'd reached her limit and now must end this. "I think it would be best if you leave."

He remained stock-still, hectic suffering in his gaze.

She played her ace in the hole. "When I asked Gavin to leave, he didn't listen. Will you listen?"

He walked slowly to the door. After pulling it open, he turned. "I've hurt you and I'm sorry. When can we talk about this?"

"I don't know." Her voice broke. She stiffened her posture.

"But I need your assurance that you'll give me room to figure it out. I can't do pressure from you. Not through texts, not through phone calls, not through surprise appearances. If you respect me, you'll give me room and time. Okay?"

There was so much pain in his face and in her chest that she honestly *could not* bear it.

"Okay."

Then he was gone. And her view of the most beautiful man her eyes had ever seen was lost to her. Along with everything else.

Horrified, she covered her mouth with her hands and tried to comprehend how things had gone sideways so totally between when she'd finished work and now. In just a handful of minutes she and Jeremiah had traveled to opposite sides of a continent.

The dinner he'd brought waited in the kitchen. A pot— probably stew—and sourdough bread he'd somehow imported because he knew it was her favorite.

What have I done?

She'd done what was necessary to safeguard her peace, her progress, and her independence.

But there was no, *no* comfort or relief in it.

There was only deepest grief.

She'd anticipated that her romance with Jeremiah would end but she hadn't wanted it to end like this . . . in anguish so shockingly personal it struck her like an insult.

Chapter Twenty-Three

"I s Jeremiah *still* on Islehaven?" asked Margaret, Fiona's gossip-loving sister, the following evening.

"Yes." Fiona stood at her kitchen island, rattling Fritos Scoops into a bowl to go with the clam dip she'd made. Expertly, she hid the fact that her son's disappearance to Isle-haven annoyed her. When suffering from amnesia, he should be home, surrounded by his family, receiving treatment from psychologists. Instead, he'd chosen to live in the spare bedroom of a lobsterwoman on Islehaven.

Which was *so* unlike him.

Not just his living situation but the fact that he'd chased after a woman. She'd never known Jeremiah to chase a woman. Never. Not even when he was young. And why would he? He had always been the chase-ee. It was more his style to put space between himself and the women who pursued him.

But chase Remy he had. Events were making it clearer and clearer to Fiona that the blond artist held great power over him. Fiona would need to court Remy's favor because if she didn't,

Remy might take a stand against her, which in turn could pose a threat to her relationship with her son.

"It's strange," Margaret said, "that he's lingering on Isle-haven so long. Life there is so inconvenient. Is he staying because of that woman who saved him?"

"I think he's partly there for her." Fiona downplayed Remy's draw. "But I also think he likes it on Islehaven. It's relaxing. It's been a hard year and a half for him. He deserves rest."

Margaret's expression sharpened hungrily, like a mouse eyeing a morsel of dropped cheese. "Do you think he loves this woman?"

Fiona waved a hand. "No, no. She nursed him back to health after the boating accident so he feels a connection to her. They're close but it's too early to discuss love."

Their father, drawn by his sixth sense for food, bustled over and used a chip to scoop up a huge bite of dip. "Hello, girls."

"Hi, Daddy." They were no longer girls and had probably, technically, outgrown the term *daddy*. Yet they continued addressing one another in these ways because . . . tradition. It made them all happy.

He waggled his white eyebrows and scooted the bowl of dip in front of his belly. "Here's *my* dip. Where's everyone else's?" He was only half joking.

The NFL season was heating up and the O'Sullivans had gathered to watch their mighty Patriots dominate the competition in Monday night football. She'd invited the rest over, as she often did, for a football-watching party. Her home was the best, her TV was the largest, and her hostessing skills were brimming with grace.

This evening, Mom and Dad had come. As had Margaret, Margaret's husband, their adult son, the O'Sullivan baby of the

335

family Mike, Mike's wife, Burke, two of Fiona's local friends and their husbands.

"What can I do to help?" Burke asked, nearing the island.

They'd been hanging out two or three times a week, she and Burke. Fiona liked him more each and every time. "You can take this tray to the others." Fiona pointed at the chips and dip, just one of the several appetizers she'd prepared.

He bent to lift the tray—

Dad moved to block him. "Not so fast, young man. Let me get a few more bites first. This food will be as contested as a basketball lay-up once it gets out to those vultures."

"Of course, sir," Burke said politely.

"Burke?" Margaret's hungry-mouse look returned. "Are you dating anyone at the moment?"

"No."

"Who, if anyone, are you interested in dating?"

He glanced at Fiona.

She gave him a warning look. *Whatever you say, buddy, you say at your own risk.*

"I'm not interested in dating right now," Burke answered.

Fiona's man radar was excellent. If she had to bet, she'd say that Burke *was* interested in dating her. Seeing as how he'd not yet expressed that to her, there was no way he was going to confide in Margaret. When he did express his feelings to her, Fiona was prepared to let him down gently (something at which she was an expert). Afterward, she and Burke would maintain their friendship and she'd be buoyed by the pleasing knowledge that he found her attractive.

"I know several women I could set you up with," Margaret said. This was clearly a bid to gauge the truth of his disinterest in dating.

"Thanks. I'll . . . let you know if I'm in the market for that."

"If I were you," Dad said, "I'd stick with food over women. Food doesn't demand anything and it's a lot more predictable."

"Food doesn't keep you warm at night," Margaret said.

"You only say that," Dad murmured with his mouth full, "because you've never eaten chicken wings out of the oven at one in the morning."

"Dad," Fiona scolded, "that's enough for the moment. Burke, you can take the tray."

They all picked up food and drinks and followed Burke to Fiona's media room, where the others had congregated.

At present, the O'Sullivans were arguing about who served the best whoopie pies in a fifty-mile radius of here. Mainers had strong feelings about whoopie pies, LL Bean, the soft drink Moxie, Red Hot Dogs, Amato's pickles, and more.

Then Mike started listing the reasons why he didn't feel properly valued at his new job—never a good sign. Margaret's son talked over Mike because if there was a topic that bored them all instantly, it was the state of Mike's career. Mom asked about lemon bars again, five decades too late.

Fiona heard the front door open and turned with expectation toward the hall. Jude?

Yes, Jude.

But then he was immediately joined in the doorway by a second man and her happiness corkscrewed downward.

Felix had come.

All talk ceased. Her family had embarrassed themselves by fawning over Felix when he'd been dating and married to Isobel. She'd been ashamed by the way they'd idolized him even as she'd plotted to have him because she'd idolized him, too.

Then he'd betrayed Isobel with her. Afterward, she'd forced her family to accept him a second time, as *her* husband now. But that second time, the nicest thing that could be said was that the O'Sullivans had treated him with uneasy suspicion. Fiona had spent years pretending she didn't notice the awkwardness that permeated family get-togethers when Felix was present, while thinking to herself, *Look at him! He's gorgeous and debonair and mine. Who cares if this is uncomfortable!*

After he'd betrayed her, too, he'd gone from partial villain to absolute villain in the eyes of her family.

Practicality had dictated that Fiona find a way to coexist with Felix. They shared children. They lived in the same small town. They existed in the same social circle.

He was, the devil, still charming. And he was, the devil, still ruthlessly handsome. His outfit today made him look as if he'd stepped off a yacht, which was entirely possible.

Fiona had waited and waited for his looks to tarnish. They never had. He was like a Greek God—more formidable and appealing with age.

Curse him.

She *still* felt his magnetism. She still found him sexy. From time to time, she'd experience a pang of desire when he looked at her a certain way. Nonetheless, she'd known all along that they would never get back together. For one thing, she was too proud to give him a second chance. For another, he didn't want a second chance with her. He'd quickly moved on from her romantically.

Felix Camden had remained married to her for sixteen years. That was the biggest payoff she was going to get.

"Dad and I swung by Aunt Elizabeth Camden's house together," Jude said to the hushed room. "So he dropped me off here."

"Hello, O'Sullivans," Felix said. "Your prodigal family member is glad to see you as always."

"Felix!" Mom rushed up to him. "Welcome! We're

delighted you came, your honor." She hugged him. "Come eat a lemon square!"

"Look at this, Jude," Felix said, patting Mom's back paternally as if he was from the generation above her instead of the one below. "You predicted my reception would be frosty but not every O'Sullivan hates me to the core."

"My mother has forgotten that she hates you," Fiona said pleasantly. He had such towering self-confidence that the prospect of entering a hostile environment did not cause him hesitation. In fact, he almost relished it.

"Hate him?" Mom asked, scandalized. "No, no. I do not. We're so lucky to have you as part of our family."

"He's no longer a part of the family," Fiona stated.

But Mom was busy smiling up at her scoundrel of a former son-in-law. "You're a gem, Felix."

"He's gifted in many ways. For example"—Fiona counted the ways on her fingers—"in football. In charitable giving. And in thinking highly of himself. But he is *not* a gem of a husband."

Felix shot her a look that twinkled with admiration. "She's quite right."

Fiona saw Burke stiffen. He was shooting metaphorical daggers at Felix, which was surprising, given how even-tempered Burke was.

Dad took up a position just slightly forward of where Fiona stood. "It's probably time for you to go," he said gruffly to Felix.

His attempt at defending her was adorable seeing as how she didn't need help defending herself from Felix and seeing as how Dad couldn't even defend himself from sugar cravings. Dad was no match for the likes of a Hall of Fame quarterback accustomed to looking into the fiery eyes of a defensive line.

Felix's head tilted, but he was certainly not going to rise to the bait of someone so unequal to him in sparring ability. "In that case, goodbye. I think of you all fondly and wish you the best."

Fiona didn't doubt that Felix thought fondly of the O'Sullivans nowadays. He had that luxury because he no longer had to interact with her large clan. While they'd been married, he'd viewed her family as a trial to be borne.

His Irish-American ancestors—beginning with the legendary Finbar Camden—had all been shrewd with money, daring, and frequently unscrupulous. They'd become the titans of the Gilded Age back when Fiona's ancestors had been working in their factories.

Felix's interactions with his family were distant and formal. They all did their own independent, successful things, meeting up from time to time to attend graduations from Harvard or weddings held at historic stone chapels. None of them showed an overabundance of emotion nor an unseemly reliance on the others.

Felix finished his remarks with, "Go Patriots."

"Go Patriots," the room replied because a statement in support of the Patriots could never be left hanging in this portion of the United States.

Felix nodded to Fiona, gently disengaged himself from Mom, fist-bumped Jude, and disappeared.

In his wake, he left unsettled silence.

Mood killer. Half dismayed by his ability to suck the levity from a room and half entertained by it, Fiona clapped her hands twice. "All right, everyone! We've had our fulfilling little spectacle for the day. Let's get back to what's most important. Eating snacks and watching football."

Everyone concurred except Mom. "Where did Felix go?" She blinked, bewildered.

"He had errands to run, Grandma," Jude answered, enfolding her in a hug.

"But he missed the lemon squares," Mom said.

Thirty hours had passed since Jeremiah's fight with Remy.

Thirty hours. And she had not reached out to him.

He was lying on the waterboard Leigh called a bed. His body and heart were exhausted, but he couldn't get his mind to turn off. Lying on his back, he thrust a forearm under his head and scowled through the dark at the popcorn ceiling.

He'd screwed up and he was furious with himself because of it.

He knew Remy's history. He'd planned to be as patient as she needed him to be. He'd even told her, when he'd first learned about Gavin, that they could go slow, at her pace. He'd told her that.

Due to his parents' scandals and the attention that followed their family wherever they went, he'd learned control early. But the things Remy had said to him yesterday had injured him, and he'd let his control slip a few inches.

He'd been reliving their exchange over and over. His curse was that he remembered every word.

"It's not as if we're boyfriend and girlfriend," she'd said. *"It's hard to imagine how this relationship could work out well for you and me. How can I ever trust the person who just accused me of letting Gavin win?"*

He felt so much for her and he'd let all the things he felt crack some of his restraint. Like a rookie. Like a selfish idiot. He should have hung on to every inch of his restraint *because* he felt so much for her. He hadn't. Instead, he'd said what he was thinking and gambled the relationship he valued most. Then lost.

His hands formed fists. He pushed the thumb-side of both against his eye sockets.

He'd spent the day stewing with anxiety and regret.

It was embarrassing how worthless he was at doing anything—even sleeping—while in this headspace. He'd fought with Remy. That fact shouldn't wreck him to this degree. But it had. Why?

Literally . . . why?

Because I love her.

There it was. As true as his heartbeat, as clear as glass.

For several seconds, he grappled to understand himself, to take an objective look at his emotions.

Conclusion: He was completely and totally, no-going-back, no-saving-himself-now in love with Remy Reed.

How had he let this happen?

He'd let it happen with every decision he'd made after coming to consciousness in her house the day she'd rescued him. When he'd insisted she come with him to the mainland. When he'd sought her out. When he'd kissed her. When he'd followed her to Islehaven. He'd been pursuing her almost from day one without consciously understanding the depth of what was going on inside him.

He hadn't spent time weighing his feelings for Remy because he'd been preoccupied doing stuff . . . mainly trying to fix his forgotten life. With all the drama he'd been dealing with, these last months hadn't been the time to fall in love.

But love didn't care about timing, did it? He'd met Remy when he'd met her. And love had come for him when it had come for him. A person didn't get to choose when.

This was not ideal. *He* was not ideal. She'd been at her best these past months, but she'd seen him at his worst—hypothermia, injured, no memory, trying to sort out the Alexis mess.

He wished . . . Well. It was pointless to wish she could have met him at a time when he'd have been better and more lovable. What was done was done.

He loved her. And she'd kicked him out. And why hadn't he realized he loved her sooner so he could have told her he loved her yesterday? She didn't know where he stood.

What if she didn't let him back into her life and so he didn't get the chance to tell her?

Fear sliced toward him like a guillotine blade. For the past thirty hours, he'd been telling himself that surely she'd contact him. That he hadn't done anything terrible enough to deserve her breaking up with him for good. He'd shown her his character across the past few months, and he knew her character. She'd contact him. She'd give him the benefit of the doubt.

Right?

He told himself yes. Which would have been a relief if he'd been able to make himself believe it. In truth, he worried that he hadn't had enough time with her. Hadn't done or said enough to convince her to give him another chance.

Figuring out what happened to Alexis, getting his memories back, understanding how he'd ended up in the ocean . . . these were things that had value. But it was clearer to him than ever that those things didn't have nearly as much value as Remy herself. So how had he managed to lose Remy in the process of going to the mainland to chase less important things?

If needed, he could let go of all those other goals.

The only non-negotiable for him . . .

Was her.

On the fourth day after their fight, desperate to keep his body busy, Jeremiah went out on the lobster boat with Leigh. After they returned to the harbor, he walked across to the church.

He stayed for a long time, sitting in a pew, praying, thinking, struggling to find peace. There was no way he wanted to leave the island while things between him and Remy were a mess. But he didn't know how much time she'd let pass and it made no sense to wait here while she figured things out on her end. She could reach him on his cell phone just as quickly on the mainland as she could here.

He would make himself go. Tomorrow. Unless she contacted him between now and then.

She didn't contact him. And so, the next afternoon, he packed his things.

"Thank you very much for letting me stay here," he told Leigh as he dragged his suitcase into the living room.

Leigh waited by the door, prepared to drive him to where he'd docked his speedboat. "You're kidding, right? I'm the one who should thank you for staying here and paying me such generous rent." She gave him a one-armed hug that ended with a powerful thump to his back. "I'm convinced that you're a fallen angel and it's not every day I get to share my house with a fallen angel."

"Can we keep my secret identity just between us?"

She grinned. "Ayuh." Winking didn't come naturally to her, but she managed to execute a wink on her second try. "Here. I have something for you." She fished in the front pocket of her pants and held an item out to him.

His Omega watch.

"I thought you pawned that," he said.

"I hope you'll forgive me for lying and saying I had. You weren't going to rest until you had some money to your name.

But Remy and I didn't want to sell this. We worried it might hold sentimental value."

"It does." He secured it to his wrist. "My family gave this to me to commemorate my first F1 win. It's my favorite watch."

"Well good, then. It's important for angels to tell time. Wouldn't want you to be late for a heavenly assignment."

"I'll forgive you for lying about the watch on one condition."

"What's that?"

"You'll allow me to reimburse you for the cash you gave me and the clothes you bought."

She waved a hand. "We can work that out on the way to the dock."

"Now." He added her name in an affectionate tone. "Leigh."

She sighed. Once he'd opened a money-paying app on his phone, she reluctantly provided her username.

"Is it okay with you if I add at least one more zero to this number?" he asked.

"No! If you think I'm going to take more than I'm owed from a celestial being, you're crazy."

He held the door for her, then followed her toward her car.

The first time he'd left Islehaven he'd been forced to do so by a chest infection. His health was excellent now. Yet his chest was even heavier and more painful than it had been the last time.

Not because of illness. Because of something harder to cure.

Sorrow.

Remy never wanted to see or hear or think about Jeremiah Camden.

Ever, *ever* again.

Since their fight, she'd thrown herself into her art. She'd completed her goblet project, notified her sister that it was ready for sale, then pulled out a block of South American snakewood she'd had on hand for years. She often kept blocks for long periods of time, getting to know them and pondering them until inspiration struck.

This time, she didn't have the luxury of waiting for inspiration nor the luxury of the serene mind required to imagine worlds and stories. She'd eyeballed the piece for sixty seconds, pulled on her goggles, and heedlessly started carving. Bark flew. Her muscles complained. Instincts overtook her. And dark satisfaction rose.

Each time her mind tried to replay the things Jeremiah had said and the way he'd looked saying them—injured and honest and brutally appealing—she icily cut off the memories. Every thought of Jeremiah, she blocked. It was the mental equivalent of the physical blocking she'd learned to do in all those self-defense classes. Block. Block. Block.

She'd given up eating at her regimented times, walking, and yoga. All her time was spent working, power-watching *Merlin*, and sleeping. She did ensure that she was consuming the proper amount of water, because one must have *some* standards and dehydration was considerably below her standards.

Her piece was ugly in a raw, powerful way. She was going to finish it in record time, and she took savage pleasure in her productivity.

He did not have the power to rob her of her effectiveness.

She didn't need anyone. She loved her life here all alone. This was the perfect, perfect place for her. She'd chosen it. She was so very strong.

All was well.

Or . . . all *would* be well if not for the ominous and niggling suspicion at the back of her mind. She kept powering past it and refusing to confront it.

But the suspicion was this . . . .

Something deep, deep within her was drastically wrong.

Chapter Twenty-Four

T he following day, midmorning, Jude eyed his brother as Jeremiah made his way toward him through the crowd at Java Junkie. "You look terrible," Jude said.

"And you look polished. Every hair in place."

Regardless of what he looked like on the outside, Jude knew he wasn't as polished on the inside as usual. He'd started tossing and turning at night over the upcoming op surrounding Rhapsodie perfume.

No one had needed to teach him how to be responsible. That's who he was. *Responsible*. That's what flowed through his bloodstream. The op remained in its preparation phase, he'd yet to meet Gemma Clare, and already he was feeling the weight of ensuring that a legendary perfume recipe, held close for centuries, did not fall into the wrong hands. Soon, the full pressure of that responsibility would rest entirely on him.

Jeremiah settled into the chair across the table. He hadn't shaved and his hair made Jude think he'd shaken it out wet and run his hands through it once. It hadn't been trimmed in a while, so it curled at the base of his neck. His skin was too pale, his irises too bright. The hollows below his cheekbones were deeper than they should have been.

"Remy broke up with you," Jude deduced based on the evidence.

"It's temporary."

It didn't seem temporary from where Jude was sitting. It seemed like Jeremiah feared he'd never see her again. "You love her."

"Yes."

Jude sensed the stir working its way through the coffee shop in response to his brother's presence.

"Why did she end it?" Jude asked.

"I mentioned her weakness."

Jude let his head fall back. After a few seconds, he straightened. Dad and Jeremiah almost never spoke an unstrategic word. "How are you going to fix it?"

"I told her I'd wait for her to reach out to me."

Jude lifted his eyebrows.

"I had to. She's been hurt in the past. Giving her freedom is the only thing that might work."

"In that case, I hope she uses her freedom to choose you." Jude took a sip of his coffee, savoring its strong flavor.

"You ready to go?" Jeremiah asked.

They were about to drive to Portland together to confront Gigi. "I haven't finished my chocolate chip croissant." Chocolate was Jude's only indulgence. He let himself have one serving of it a day and he refused to let Jeremiah's bad mood interfere with his enjoyment.

Jeremiah glared impatiently out the window. "What's our tactic with Gigi?"

"We state our suspicions as if they're facts we can prove. I'll take the lead. You play along."

"Are you Jeremiah Camden?" asked the college-aged guy working behind the reception desk at Gigi's company. He gawked as the brothers walked up to him.

"I am."

"No way! I started watching F1 because of you. Incredible." He thrust out a hand. Jeremiah shook it. "Absolutely phenomenal driving, man. It was such a rush to watch you."

"Thank you." What had seemed odd to him when he'd had no memory—strangers identifying him on sight—he now remembered to be commonplace. "We're here to see Gigi Kaminski. Is she in?"

"Yes. Just down the hall. Third office on the right. Before you go . . . can I get a photo with you?"

"Sure."

"Wow. Thanks. This is an honor."

Jude stepped in to snap a picture with the guy's phone as Jeremiah now recalled Jude had done hundreds of times before. As his past had come back to him, so had a deep appreciation for his younger brother. The state of their mother's mental health after the divorce could have ended Jeremiah's driving career before it had begun. It hadn't gone that way because Jude had stepped into the gap with their mother and insisted Jeremiah continue. Jeremiah owed his career to Jude.

His brother was more strait-laced and by-the-book than Jeremiah. But he was also everything that was best of them.

Jeremiah knocked on the door of the third office on the right.

"Come in."

Gigi's pretty face creased with joy at the sight of him. She rose, wearing a black turtleneck and tailored plaid suit pants. "Jeremiah! What a wonderful surprise."

He introduced her to Jude.

"How's the amnesia?" she asked.

"Improving. I remember quite a bit now."

"That's great. Do you remember me?"

"I do."

"I'm so relieved!" She ushered them to a seating area in her office. The brothers chose the sofa. She chose one of the chairs.

Jeremiah recalled enough about Gigi to know that he'd viewed things as casual between them. Even so, he'd slept with her. So Gigi couldn't be blamed for introducing herself to him and Remy as his girlfriend.

Why had he slept with her?

He'd done it because his life had been flat and gray after the end of his marriage and his racing. He'd been trying to interrupt the gray with anything that provided even minutes of light or heat.

Still, he shouldn't have slept with her. Doing so hadn't been kind to Gigi because it had led her on. And it hadn't been true to himself because he hadn't liked her all that much.

"I'm glad you stopped in." Gigi crossed her legs and stacked her palms on her upper knee. "Were you in the area?"

"We drove down to see you," Jude answered, "because we know that you changed your appearance to resemble Alexis and that your first meeting with Jeremiah was no coincidence." His brother had gotten right to the point, calmly pulling the pin from the grenade.

The excitement in Gigi's face melted, leaving only alarm and concern. "I beg your pardon?" she whispered.

"Did you follow Alexis on Instagram?" Jude asked.

Her eyes had the look of a fox being chased in a foxhunt. "Yes."

"And so you knew all about her husband, Jeremiah, and, later, all about her death?"

"I did. Yes."

"I'm an agent with the FBI. Just so we're clear, I'm not here in an official capacity. I'm here as a brother. But I'll give you an insight I've learned with the FBI. In my experience it always goes more smoothly for subjects when they tell the full truth from the start."

"Okay."

"Can you tell us the truth about why you arranged to meet Jeremiah?"

"Sure, I . . ." She rolled her lips inward and bit down. "Well. Like so many of Alexis's followers, I was devastated when she died. I felt as if I knew her." Her gaze slid to Jeremiah. "And you. It was awful."

Jeremiah felt obligated to fill the pause that followed. "Yeah, it was awful."

"Months passed," she said, "and I couldn't get you out of my mind. I knew you lived close by, and I really cared about you. I . . . wanted to find out how you were doing."

"And also wanted to date him?" Jude asked.

"I mean, sure. That was my biggest dream."

"So you changed your look," Jude said, "into what you hoped would attract him?"

She blushed. "Mostly, I changed my look because I was in the mood for something new. But a small part of me . . ." She appeared to lose her nerve.

"The full truth," Jude prompted quietly.

"A small part of me *did* think that a style update might help me catch your eye," she admitted to Jeremiah.

"How did you arrange to meet him?" Jude asked.

"People I know here in Portland had posted photos of you at the Blyth and Burrows bar on social media. You clearly liked that spot, so I started hanging out there, too. Not every night," she rushed to add. "Just from time to time. When you finally walked in one night, I was thrilled. Starstruck. So happy."

"Why didn't you tell me you knew who I was and had come there to meet me?" Jeremiah asked.

"I thought that might have made me seem . . . desperate or suspicious."

"I would have felt less suspicious then than I feel now," Jeremiah said.

She winced.

"What can you tell us about Alexis's death or the injuries Jeremiah sustained on his boat trip?" Jude asked.

Her jaw lowered with shock. *"Nothing.* You think . . . I?" She leaned forward. "I didn't have anything to do with Alexis's death or your injuries, Jeremiah."

"Did you ever meet Alexis?" Jude asked.

"No, never. But I loved following her posts. She was awesome."

"Who do you think might have attacked Jeremiah on his boat?"

"I have absolutely no idea." Her eyes turned pleading as she looked at Jeremiah. "I was your girlfriend when you left on that trip. Crazy about you. I'd never want to hurt you. I only want your best."

He knew what his best was. The amnesia had made all his flaws and bad habits and mistakes clear. His best wasn't Alexis, and it wasn't Gigi. His best was an artistic woodworker who didn't want his fame or his money. Or him. That was his best.

Jude pulled his card from his wallet and passed it to her. "If you have anything else to say, now's the time."

"I've told you the whole story."

"Please contact us if anything else occurs to you," Jude said.

"I will."

They all stood.

"Goodbye," Jeremiah said, and he didn't mean goodbye in a temporary way.

"Goodbye."

As they walked back to their car, Jude said, "She didn't have any tells that indicated she was lying."

"Alexis was one of the most believable liars I ever met. I never saw a single tell and she lied to my face."

"Some liars don't have tells," Jude acknowledged. "They can train away those tendencies."

"Or they're just born with a talent for it."

"She seemed genuine to me," Jude said. "But if she was obsessed with you and wanted you for herself, she did have motive to kill Alexis."

"Yeah." He hated the idea that someone's infatuation with him could have cost Alexis her life. *God, please don't let that be the case.*

Early the next evening, when Wendell answered Jeremiah's knock, Jeremiah passed over the brown paper sack of Indian food he'd brought. "Complimentary food delivery for you."

Wendell took a whiff and smiled appreciatively. "What did I do to deserve this?"

"You're Remy's friend." Jeremiah's breath misted white in the cold air. "She told me about your search for Marisol. How's that coming?"

"We haven't found her."

"I'm sorry to hear that."

"I regret more than anything that I told Remy about Marisol. I shouldn't have done that because now Remy has her heart set on finding her."

"Right. So if you were to figure out Marisol's whereabouts, you'd tell Remy about it?"

"Oh yes. She'd be the first person I'd call."

"And, I'm guessing, you'd ask her to join you on your trip to meet Marisol. You wouldn't want to go alone . . . seeing as how finding Marisol was a project you and Remy started together."

"If I found Marisol, you bet I'd ask Remy to come with me to go see her. I wouldn't think of going without Remy." He shrugged. "For one thing, I don't drive."

"Can I get your number? I'd like to check in from time to time to see if you need more tikka masala."

"Sure. I just have a landline, you know," the older man warned. "I'm not into cell phones."

"I respect that position." Wendell rattled off his number and Jeremiah typed it into his phone. "I hope you enjoy the food." He walked backward down the front path.

"I will. Thank you."

"By the way, this is a secret delivery, Wendell. Please don't tell Remy I brought you food because she worries about your kidneys and will kill me if she finds out."

"True, true. I won't tell her."

"Just between us?"

"Yes."

Jeremiah turned.

"Have you considered driving for Uber Eats?" the older man asked.

"I'm considering it, Wendell."

As soon as Jeremiah reached his car, he left a message for Fred Kimley, PI. "I'd like to hire you to find a woman. Her maiden name was Marisol Soto and she's around the age of eighty-two."

He disconnected and sat with one wrist resting on the Shelby's steering wheel. Wendell loved Marisol and Remy loved Wendell.

He was itching to *do* something for Remy. Finding Marisol's location was the only gift she'd accept from him right now . . . if he could pull it off anonymously.

That said, he wasn't altruistic enough not to use the thing that Remy wanted to gain the thing that he wanted. If Remy returned to the mainland to help Wendell meet Marisol, then he'd find a way to see her.

Many miles to the east, Remy stood on the edge of the cliff in front of her cottage, overlooking the magnificent Atlantic. She pondered the windswept waves and cold sky.

For the first several days after The Fight, she'd remained hard-hearted and angry. But six days had passed now. Enough time for her indignation to cool and her defenses to soften. As Wendell had said, feelings were like storm fronts. This was the most violent storm front she'd lived through since her rape. It hadn't passed yet and wouldn't for a long time. But she took comfort in telling herself that it *would* pass.

Right?

She still blocked four out of five thoughts of Jeremiah out of necessity. If she didn't, she wouldn't be able to function. But there were times, like now, when she gave her mind the freedom to go there. It was sweet torture. Like scratching a bug bite that itched all the time, even though you knew scratching would make things worse.

She remembered how he'd looked standing in the doorframe of her studio, watching her. She saw him leaning against her table, his face tilted down to hers and just inches away—

those hooded eyes hot and tender. She saw him standing at Restoration Point with the sea as his backdrop.

The truth was this. Living with a broken heart day after day was awful. He'd entered her well-ordered life like a meteor. Bright, sparking heat. He'd become a source of joy, friendship, belonging, laughter. He'd been her person, *her central person*, for months.

She'd lost all that. *Jeremiah's gone* was the first thought that entered her head each morning and the last thought every night. She was aware all the time that if she'd been able to resist loving him, she'd have saved herself this. Thing was, she'd tried. She'd done her best to resist him, but resisting him had proven impossible. There'd been no resisting him then, and now that he'd left, there was no replacing him.

With the benefit of distance, she could acknowledge that Jeremiah had not said or done anything unforgiveable during their fight. He'd spoken things that had been hurtful, yes. But not unforgiveable.

And she'd made mistakes, too. She liked to picture herself as enlightened, as someone who valued each person for who they were without catering to cultural stereotypes. But she *had* stereotyped him almost from the start—as a rich untrustworthy playboy—even though his actions and words had only proved the rich part. And she'd stereotyped herself as not good enough to hold him.

Also, her decision to kick him out had likely been too extreme for his perceived crimes. She was a passionate person who felt things strongly. When her buttons were pushed and she got triggered, she reacted strongly. At the time, his going had felt necessary to her survival, so she'd ordered him to leave. But that response had been harsh. And she regretted that she'd injured him.

Admittedly, there had been some flaws in how she'd ended

things. But that didn't mean that ending things had been wrong. Now that a break had been made, no matter how clumsily, it seemed best to leave things as they were and grit it out.

Here on Islehaven, she had the two things she valued most: safety and independence. Jeremiah threatened both of those pillars. Jeremiah scared her. As miserable as she was, she suspected that she'd done the right thing when she'd picked safety and independence over him. And now she only wished those things were bringing her deep satisfaction. That's what she was owed after all she'd sacrificed. And one day, she *would* feel deep satisfaction in safety and independence again, surely.

But right now?

Right now, this life she'd protected from Jeremiah felt completely hollow without him in it.

Chapter Twenty-Five

The following morning, Jeremiah woke to an email from forensics expert Eleanor Dobbins with the subject line *Lab Results*.

He opened the email's attachment and found he couldn't interpret Eleanor's scientific terms. In the body of the email, she'd suggested that he call when he had the report open in front of him.

He did so, listening to it ring.

He'd burned the past hour sitting here in his home office, watching snowflakes fall to earth outside, consumed with thoughts of Remy. He missed her so much he ached with it.

"This is Eleanor Dobbins."

"Eleanor, this is Jeremiah Camden. I'm calling to get your take on the lab results you sent."

"Certainly. After analyzing the samples, I pinpointed two substances that are likely the most relevant."

"Go on."

"If you recall, a bottle of Native Vitality energy drink had spilled on the carpet of your boat."

"I remember."

"The stain contained the components used to make Native Vitality. It also contained potassium chloride."

"Which is?"

"Poison."

He sat more upright. "Someone put poison in my energy drink?"

"That's my conclusion, yes. Had you consumed the entire bottle, you'd likely be dead."

"Is it possible to add poison to a closed bottle?"

"In this case, I found a hole almost too small to detect with the naked eye near the screw-top of the bottle. I believe that hole was left by the needle used to puncture the bottle and inject poison into the liquid. When you unscrewed the cap, it would have behaved exactly as expected because the screw-top was not tampered with."

"I see."

"If you were drinking the energy drink while in the kitchen preparing food, and began to feel the effects of potassium chloride, that might explain why you dropped the bottle and abandoned food preparation midway through."

For the first time, he vaguely recalled setting off from Groomsport's harbor the morning of the trip. As if recalling shreds of a dream, he visualized himself going below deck for lunch. Opening an energy drink. Sliding bread into the toaster. Then . . .

Dizziness.

Jeremiah grimaced, trying to find more images in the fog.

He'd braced a hand against the wall and watched everything revolve. Fear and confusion had penetrated. He'd staggered upstairs for fresh air. The world had been swirling. Sea and sky. Sea and sky. The wrong one up, the wrong one down.

"Mr. Camden?" Eleanor asked with her flat voice.

"I'm here." He ran a hand over his mouth and jaw.

"This particular poison can be challenging to detect. Had you died on your boat that day it might have been quite some time before your body was recovered. By then, the likelihood of identifying potassium chloride would have been low."

"You mentioned that you found two substances that might be relevant. What's the other one?"

"I confirmed that the smear on the outer portion of the doorframe on the upper deck is blood. Your blood."

Think, Jeremiah. When you made it to the deck, what happened?

He'd felt worse and not better. He'd stumbled. The world had gone hazy, spinning. He pitched backward. His skull collided with the doorframe.

Pain burst over him.

He fell forward onto his hands and knees. His breath panted. He wasn't himself. Something was terribly wrong.

Where was his phone? He needed medical help.

His phone was in his pocket, then his hand. He couldn't make it work. His fingers wouldn't cooperate. Groaning, he sat on the floor, leaning against the built-in seats.

The sky was very blue. Clouds.

His whole life played before him. Not fast, like an old-fashioned cartoon made from flipping paper. But in a slow roll.

Was this the end?

No. He couldn't let that happen. Clenching his jaw with effort, he clawed and pulled until he got himself to his feet. He'd go below. To the radio—

Panic. So much dizziness.

He was losing his balance. His ribs slammed against the side of the boat—dead weight against a solid surface—knocking the air from him. Wheezing, he got himself partially upright. Then everything spun again. His center of gravity lurched

361

forward. His torso continued over the edge of the boat. Water raced up to meet him.

The cold shock of it. Heavy, freezing, thick.

Salt water stung his eyes as he broke the surface and dragged in air.

His boat pulled away.

He swam for it but couldn't reach it. It was all he could do to keep his head above the waves. He had to keep paddling. *Stay alive*, he'd ordered himself over and over. *Stay alive.*

"I noted that the refrigerator on the boat was stocked with several bottles of Native Vitality," Eleanor said. "There were no fingerprints other than your own on the spilled bottle I brought back to my lab. However, I suspect that the person who wished you harm likely injected poison into the other bottles as well. Please send the remaining bottles to me so that I can test the liquid and also the exterior of the bottle for fingerprints or any other markers of identification."

He thanked Eleanor, hung up, called Jude, and relayed what Eleanor had told him.

Jude swore softly. "We assumed you were beaten by someone, but you weren't."

"Right. There was no one on the boat but me. I hit my head. And my fall broke my ribs."

"Poison is known as a woman's weapon," Jude stated. "This makes me think Gigi."

Jeremiah prowled to his feet and strode toward the garage. "I'm going to drive to the harbor and collect the remaining bottles of energy drink."

When he reached his boat, Jeremiah made his way below deck, squatted in front of the refrigerator, and yanked its door open.

The bottles of Native Vitality were gone.

Every one of them.

Taken.

He'd definitely seen them here, as Eleanor had, the day of their visit. It chilled him to look eye to eye at the proof that someone had been here and tampered with this boat. Clearly, the same person who'd poisoned him had confiscated the other bottles. Which almost certainly meant the other bottles also contained poison.

He stood, closing the refrigerator door with his foot. He'd brought those bottles to the boat the evening before his trip. In between then and when he'd set off the next morning, someone had poisoned them. His enemy had been able to get here and away in a short window of time. His enemy had known when he was leaving. More recently, his enemy had known when his boat returned to port.

Those clues pointed to someone who lived within a few hours of here and someone who was either close enough to him to know the details of his life or was watching him from a distance.

The hair on the back of his neck prickled.

He left the boat and went to the harbor's small administrative building.

A friendly, round-faced man named Graham had been working here for as long as Jeremiah could remember. He'd always appeared to be in his mid-fifties. Still did.

"Hello, Mr. Camden." Graham greeted Jeremiah with a smile. "What can I do for you today?"

"I have reason to think someone has been on my boat. Both before I left on my trip back in September and again more recently. Do you have any video cameras that record activity on the harbor?"

His face fell. "I'm sorry, but no. It was the best I could do to persuade the owner to take our operation online." He patted his desktop monitor. "This is the most high-tech thing we have on the premises."

Disappointment tasted bitter in Jeremiah's mouth. "If you see anyone around my boat, will you record them or take photos? Then contact me?"

"Absolutely."

Outside the office, he checked his phone, then placed a call to Kimley. "I saw that I missed a call from you," Jeremiah said when the older man answered.

"Hi, Jeremiah. Yes. I was calling to let you know that I've determined the whereabouts of Marisol Soto."

"Wendell," Remy said warmly when she picked up his call while eating a microwaved lunch.

"Remy!"

It felt good to hear her friend's voice. So much so, tears pricked her eyes. She was unusually emotional these days. It was as if her torso was filled with a ball of seething orange feelings. The smallest things—a text message from her mom, a hug shared by two characters in her current novel, the sight of Leigh's sturdy face—could cause her throat to tighten. "How are you?"

"Very well."

"Are you following our organizational system?"

"To the letter!"

"The house is clean?"

"As a whistle. Listen, I have news."

"Oh?"

"A man who . . . Goodness. This is hard to believe."

"Take your time."

He paused and she imagined him marshalling his excitement to gather himself. "A man," he continued, "who works at the Serene Hollow Assisted Living Community in Monroe called me. He said that he came across the digital notice you created, the one asking for information on Marisol's whereabouts. Remy, he told me that my Marisol lives at Serene Hollow."

That was amazing and hopeful and . . . weird. An employee from an assisted living community gave Wendell details about a resident? In this day and age of strict privacy? "Really?"

"Yes! Marisol lives just forty-five minutes away from me. Her married name is Marisol Gordon. She's still alive."

"Incredible." Especially so seeing as how Remy had come to the conclusion that she was the world's worst detective after having no success helping Wendell find Marisol and no success helping Jeremiah learn his identity—

Shoot. She'd thought his name, which reminded her that she loved his name. Loved the firm *J* sound followed by those round vowel syllables. *Jeremiah.*

"The man who called me," Wendell was saying, "is a good Samaritan. Or maybe I should call him a Cupid."

"Based on what happened the last time we tried to meet Marisol, I think it would be best to call and speak with this woman. That way, you can determine whether she really is the Marisol you remember."

"The Cupid told me she's eighty-two and lived in Belfast for a time, just like *my* Marisol. This is the right one, Remy. And I don't want to call her. I want to see her, right now, with my own eyes."

"I understand, but—"

"I'm all worked up," Wendell confessed. "I've thought about Marisol for so long. We'll go see her as soon as you can get here."

"Me?"

"Yes, you. I'm not going unless you're coming with me."

Remy's heart did a spiraling nosedive. She couldn't go to the mainland. What if she ran into *him* there and he thought her lovelorn and desperate enough to have followed him? The humiliation would kill her. "I'm engrossed in my work." True. But mostly because she was escaping into it.

"I know you have work. And I know that you're busy. But you have to help me. ElderTransport only operates here in Rockland. It won't take me to Monroe."

Remy bit her lip.

"When you came to Rockland, you asked if you could stay with me and I said yes," Wendell pointed out. "Will you return the favor?"

"I already did return the favor and then some by purging your house and organizing sixty years of stuff."

"Very well. Don't do it as a returned favor. Do it for me. Please. I've worked up the courage to see Marisol. But I need you to go with me."

Remy could feel herself losing this battle. It was as if his army was swarming over hers five to one.

"Will you come?" he asked.

You have to say no, Remy! But her mouth said, "Yes."

"How soon can you get here?"

It was the Sunday before Thanksgiving. If she worked late tonight and all day tomorrow, she could finish her current sculpture. "Tuesday."

"And you'll spend Thanksgiving weekend with me? I'm going to my kids' for Christmas but they're spending Thanksgiving with their in-laws, so I'm on my own."

She, too, was scheduled to spend Christmas with family in Texas. Thus, she'd planned to proceed as if Thanksgiving didn't exist and work straight through. "Yes. I'll stay with you for Thanksgiving weekend."

"Hey, Wendell," Jeremiah said over the phone the next day. He was standing on his freezing front porch surrounded by frost and snow because he'd needed to escape the walls of his house. A person could only do so much miserable pacing. "Have there been any developments in your search for Marisol?"

"The most wonderful news! Believe it or not, we found her."

"That's great." Jeremiah pretended surprise. "Will Remy travel to the mainland to help with the reunion?"

"Yes. She'll arrive Tuesday morning and stay through Thanksgiving. As soon as she gets here, we'll drive straight to Marisol's."

"Excellent. Congratulations. I'm guessing you're planning to take Remy out to dinner Tuesday night to celebrate?"

"Ah? No . . . I wasn't. Dinner out is very expensive."

"How about you take her to the country club? I'm a member there and you can put it on my tab."

"I've never been to the country club."

"Now's the time. Order whatever you like. The most expensive food. The most expensive wine. Feel free to bring Marisol, too."

"Wine? Put it on your tab?"

"Yes. All that you want. What time would you like to eat? I'll call the club and tell them you're coming."

"I usually eat at five."

Five? Did humans eat dinner that early? The ambience wouldn't be good at five. "How about six thirty?"

"All right." Wendell seemed to know better than to look a gift horse in the mouth.

Now Jeremiah knew where Remy would be and when. He'd arrive at the club at the same time and the separation between them would be broken. "Same deal applies here as with the Indian food the other night. Please don't tell Remy that I'm behind this. She won't be happy that I'm letting you drink wine and eat rich food. You can just say one of your friends in town insisted on treating you to dinner. Deal?"

"Best deal ever."

On Tuesday, Remy led Wendell toward the reception desk of Serene Hollow Assisted Living Community at eleven o'clock in the morning. Her body was moving heavily, as if through water instead of air, because exhaustion weighted her limbs.

She hadn't slept well the past few nights after telling Wendell that she'd return to the mainland. All day today—during the choppy boat ride, while renting a car, as she navigated here—she'd felt ridiculously furtive. She kept worrying Jeremiah would catch her—like an adult catching a middle schooler in a floodlight while the middle schooler was TP-ing a house.

It was irrational. The best that could be said was that her preoccupation hadn't rendered her insensitive to Wendell's own preoccupation. She'd sensed her elderly friend growing more and more nervous as they'd neared the assisted living complex, which had made her sympathetically nervous on his behalf. Wendell had lost a great deal over the past few years. He earnestly needed something to go his way.

Wendell's tread stopped behind her as she reached the reception desk. He waited politely in his sensible shoes and trousers. He'd dared to bring out his best sweater with the nautical flags once again.

The middle-aged woman behind the desk had close-cropped black hair and an enormous bosom clothed in yellow scrubs. "Welcome to Serene Hollow," she said with an easy smile. "What can I do for you folks?"

"My friend Wendell Reeves would like to visit with Marisol Gordon."

The woman tapped on her keyboard. "I don't see Wendell Reeves on Marisol's list of approved friends and family, so I'll just need your IDs, please. Then I'll give Marisol a quick call."

"That'll be fine," Wendell replied, white-faced yet determined. "Thank you."

They passed over their driver's licenses and the woman scanned them. Was there a chance Marisol wouldn't remember Wendell? Or perhaps Marisol harbored animosity toward him and wouldn't want to see him? If Marisol turned Wendell away, he'd be crushed.

The employee dialed her desk phone, then lifted the handset to her ear.

Remy held her breath. *Please, please, let this go well.*

"Mrs. Gordon," the employee said into the phone, "Wendell Reeves is here to visit with you, and he's brought along a friend. Is it all right with you if I send them your way?"

She listened, nodding. "Yes. That's right. Wendell Reeves." More waiting. "Yes, I'm quite sure it's him. I have his driver's license in front of me." A few seconds of listening. "It *is* amazing." She winked at Wendell. "No, I won't let him leave. I'll send him right up. What's that?" A pause. "Understood." She hung up and beamed at Wendell. "She's extremely excited to see you. So excited that she asked if you could give her five minutes to work on her hair and makeup and change her outfit. Is that possible?"

Wendell's face glowed with pleasure. "Of course."

"May I get you a glass of water while you wait?" the woman asked.

Remy and Wendell both took her up on the offer. Remy watched with amusement as Wendell downed his water in one long gulp.

They went to stand out of earshot of the reception desk. "I'm sure you'd like privacy," Remy told him. "You go see Marisol by yourself. I'll wait down here for you."

"I'll need your help finding her room. I'm not good with unfamiliar buildings like these, even when I'm not shaken up. Right now, I'm shaken up. Also, I don't know what kind of . . . state Marisol's going to be in. What if she's fragile and needs a hand with walking, Remy? My balance is shot. If I tried to assist her, both of us could fall and break our hips."

"Breaking your hips would not be ideal." For Wendell's sake, Remy hoped that Marisol wasn't fragile. Or suffering from dementia. Or fighting the final stages of a terminal illness.

"You'll come with me for a few minutes?"

"Yes, I'll see you settled. Then I'll leave you to it and you can spend as much time with her as you want."

"A lifetime?"

"Absolutely. But if you're going to spend a lifetime, just give me a heads-up so I don't spend my own lifetime waiting in this sitting room."

"You betcha."

The employee provided a map that laid out the route from their current position to Marisol's apartment. The facility was large, reminding Remy of an enormous vacation condo development.

Without taking a single wrong turn, Remy cut a path through a green space that included a pool, Jacuzzi, and outdoor fireplaces. They entered Marisol's building and took an elevator to the second floor. Remy double-checked the apartment number, but as soon as the elevator doors opened, she saw that she wasn't going to need the number. A lady was waiting with a face full of anticipation halfway down the hallway. She had dark eyes cushioned in a broad face that radiated sweetness. An irresistible smile. Milk-white hair. Her rounded body couldn't have been taller than five foot two.

Her focus didn't waver from Wendell. She looked at him with outright astonishment and joy.

Purposely, Remy slowed so that Wendell could go ahead of her. She tried to be as unobtrusive as possible but really, had she been performing jumping jacks, neither Marisol nor Wendell would have paid her any attention.

Marisol gave a quiet exclamation of happiness and opened her arms. Wendell engulfed her in a bear hug. They stayed that way and Remy saw his shoulders shaking. He was crying.

"My darling," Marisol whispered. "You're really here. How did I get so lucky?"

"How did *I* get so lucky?" he asked in return, voice choked. "I never forgot about you. I just . . . I didn't think I'd ever have a chance to see you again."

"Is this a miracle?" She leaned back and cupped his face in her hands. "I was having a regular day, sitting here playing Words with Friends, and suddenly here you are. I can't believe it."

"I can't believe it either. You're the most beautiful woman. You haven't changed."

She laughed and it sounded like birdsong on a spring breeze. "I've aged so very much. But I know what you mean because in my eyes you are still Wendell. My Wendell. The same one I knew. I'd have recognized you anywhere." She gripped both his hands in hers. "Are you married? Do you have children?"

"I was happily married for more than fifty years," he said. "My wife passed away."

"Ah," Marisol murmured.

"We had two children," he said. "Five grandchildren."

"Good, good. Such a blessing."

"And you?" he asked.

Her attention searched over his face as if she needed to commit it to memory because she'd be quizzed on every detail. "My husband died two years ago. He was a wonderful man. We had my son and his daughter, then we had twins together. And now twelve grandchildren."

"Marisol," he said urgently, as if he couldn't hold the words back another second, "I'm sorry about what happened way back then. I shouldn't have let our parents come between us."

"It was my fault, too. I was scared."

"I sincerely apologize. I let you down. I—I never thought I'd have the chance to tell you how sorry I am."

"But you have."

"I'm so glad."

"I'm so glad, too. Because now I have the chance to tell you that I'm also sorry for my part in what happened. My Wendell." She lifted to her tiptoes and gave him a peck on the lips. "It's such a gift . . . a surprise, undeserved gift, to see you again. The greatest gift."

Wendell appeared speechless with bliss.

Remy felt an undeniable presence in that hallway. A presence she'd shut away years before. God's presence. And with it His love, grace, kindness, and approval. Not just for Wendell and Marisol, but for her, too.

"Thank you for finding me," Marisol said to Wendell.

"Thank you for being found," he said dumbly.

"How did you know where I was?"

"My friend Remy—Remy!" Clearly just now remembering

that she was in the vicinity, he turned toward her. Holding one of Marisol's hands, he used his other to beckon Remy forward. "I'd like to introduce you to my friend Remy Reed. When I explained that I was the saddest person because of you, she's the one who helped me find you."

"God bless you," Marisol said to Remy. "What a treasure you've given us."

"I was delighted to help. Now that I know Wendell has found his way to you, I'll be going." She met Wendell's eyes. "When should I come back for you?"

"How about two hours?" he asked Marisol.

"I expect two hours will give us enough time to decide what our plans are for the rest of the day, the week, the year." Dimples grooved Marisol's skin.

"Perfect! I'll meet you by the outdoor fireplaces in two hours." Remy hurried to the parking lot, fighting the emotion that was suddenly rising up like flood water and leaking out her eyes in wet tracks. She walked faster and faster.

As soon as she shut herself into her Kia rental car, she covered her face with her hands and cried. Great sobs. All the tears she had not cried when Jeremiah left Islehaven came pouring out. Heart twisting. Grief and loss but also the beauty of what she'd just seen.

You know who wasn't prioritizing safety and independence over love as she had done? Wendell and Marisol.

They'd let fear separate them back when they'd first fallen for one another. They'd lived a long time since, gained a lot of wisdom. And just now they'd given her a front row seat to what they viewed as important. Relationship.

They weren't trying to protect themselves. They weren't afraid of transparency and vulnerability. They were honest and they were brave.

Was she really willing to let her own fear separate her from

Jeremiah now, go numerous decades without him and then, maybe, enjoy a reunion with him when she was eighty?

No. She was not willing to go that route. Not even for the sake of excellent things like safety and independence.

Her life had changed irrevocably the day of Gavin's assault. Yet she'd believed she'd recovered as much as any survivor could. This crossroads revealed that she still had some recovering to do if she was denying herself Jeremiah when Jeremiah was what she truly wanted.

And he *was*. What she truly wanted.

He'd been right when he'd said she'd been hiding. To some degree, she had been.

So the next step forward was to quit hiding and risk all, which was the hardest step of all. Love was so thorny! So messy. It would confront her with all her demons regarding physical intimacy over and over again. It would test her boundaries and buffet her with feelings so big they'd overwhelm her sometimes.

Jeremiah came with particular challenges. Media scrutiny. Strangers who would recognize him in public places. The need for her to live at least some of the time in populated places. A heavy past so different from hers. A family and a legacy so different from hers.

She could not expect only happy days. No one could expect only happy days. There would be disappointments, things to work through, hurts to forgive and ask forgiveness for. Their relationship might end six months or six years from now and leave her devastated. Or it might last until death did them part. She wouldn't know until she tried.

There was *no* guarantee of success.

But if it came with a guarantee of success, it wouldn't be love.

Love had to be given without the assurance of reciprocity or a lifetime of security under its umbrella.

She hated to be wrong.

But the night of their fight, she'd chosen wrongly.

She'd chosen to defend herself by preserving her sheltered life. When she should have chosen him.

Jeremiah arrived at the country club that night thirty minutes before Remy and Wendell were scheduled to do so because he didn't trust Wendell not to arrive for dinner bizarrely early. He did a circuit of the restaurant first to confirm they hadn't beaten him here.

They hadn't.

He leaned against the luxurious bar directly across the hall from the restaurant hostess stand. From here, there was no way he'd miss them when they came in. He watched the time tick toward six-thirty.

He'd gotten a haircut today. He'd showered before leaving his house with the soap he knew she liked. He'd ironed his clothes.

Already, his shoulder muscles were tight with nerves because he knew he couldn't screw up again. He'd run all the scenarios, trying to figure out how to act with her tonight. He'd never in his life spent this much time thinking and planning his moves with a woman. He'd always been quick on his feet, and talking with women came easily to him. But the last time he'd seen her he'd said the wrong thing to the woman that meant everything to him.

No room for error tonight.

He was definitely going to lead with an apology. Beyond

Becky Wade

that, he planned to take his cues from her body language and words. If he saw an opening, he'd tell her he loved her—

Wendell came into view with a white-haired woman on his arm.

Jeremiah's senses went on high alert. He straightened. However, Remy did not follow after Wendell as he'd expected.

Maybe she was . . . parking the car?

Wendell raised a hand in greeting. Jeremiah nodded.

Wendell whispered something to the lady. She answered, then they separated—her toward the hostess stand, Wendell toward Jeremiah.

The older man had been transformed. He looked relaxed and euphoric. Younger. Wendell clasped one of Jeremiah's shoulders. "I'm sorry to say that I couldn't convince Remy to come."

Despair settled over Jeremiah like black smoke from a fire.

"I tried," Wendell continued. "Remy drove me to meet Marisol. Then she drove both of us to Rockland. Marisol's going to stay at the inn in town through Thanksgiving weekend. Anyway, point is, we both tried to persuade Remy to join us tonight, but she wouldn't come."

"It's all right." But it wasn't.

"Maybe you could deliver Indian food to her? I bet she's a better tipper than I am."

"Maybe. Have a nice meal."

"You betcha. I'm expecting it to be the best meal I've ever eaten. Thank you for treating Marisol and me."

"You're welcome."

Wendell and Marisol trailed the hostess into the restaurant. They were holding hands as if they feared they'd lose each other if they let go.

He'd done a good deed for them. He saw the evidence of it,

376

but his own disappointment kept him from experiencing satisfaction in it.

If Remy returned to Islehaven before he had a chance to see her . . . then what?

Resting both elbows on the bar's shiny surface, he stared down at the dark wood. Minutes passed. Gradually the thing that had always met him in moments of discouragement filtered in.

Determination.

How could he salvage this? Remy had seemed to like Jude. He could ask Jude to reach out to her. Except that would seem strange to Remy and she'd likely avoid contact with anyone in his family.

What about Anton's wife, Camille? He remembered Remy and Camille had gotten along well the night Anton and Camille had hung out with them at Appleton.

He found Camille's name in his list of contacts and sent her a text.

JEREMIAH

> Did Remy give you her number, that day at
> my place?

Thirty seconds later her reply came.

CAMILLE

> Yes! I really like her.

JEREMIAH

> Can you do something for me? Can you send
> her a text saying you'd like to see her the next
> time she's on the mainland? When she says
> she's here now, can you invite her out to do .
> . . whatever it is women do?

Becky Wade

CAMILLE

Sure. How would all of that be helpful to you?

JEREMIAH

I need to know a time and place where she'll be so I can "coincidentally" run into her there.

CAMILLE

Anton told me you guys broke up. It sounds like you're wanting to get back together with her?

JEREMIAH

Very much.

CAMILLE

I'm your ally in the cause of love. Hang on. I'll reach out to her and get back to you.

A group of four men came over and asked for his autograph and a photo. He chatted with them until his phone pinged, then he excused himself and found a quiet spot near the patio doors.

CAMILLE

I invited Remy over to my house for lunch Friday. I'm dropping the kids off at my parents' place that day, but I'll be back by 12:30. I figure you can come by while she's at the house under the guise of giving Anton something.

JEREMIAH

Perfect. Thank you.

378

Chapter Twenty-Six

Across town, Fiona was consuming the one generous glass of wine she allowed herself daily at a faster rate than usual. Typically, she savored the glassful to prolong the pleasure. This time, pleasure wasn't the goal. She needed the alcohol to steady the shakiness inside.

Burke had invited her to stop by his house after she got off work. Upon arrival, she'd found him wearing a fleece and battered jeans, watering his assortment of indoor plants. She liked his modern, three-bedroom house despite that his masculine design aesthetic was the opposite of her ultra-feminine one. Instead of manicured grass, he was surrounded by five acres of trees and a forest floor of pinecones and pine needles.

From her current position on his mission-style sofa, she could see most of the open-concept living area. Hundreds of books stocked the shelves surrounding the fire smoldering in his fireplace. Muted shades of red, dark blue, and beige melded on his Persian rug. The chair he sat in was a high-quality Eames imitation.

She got the sense that the furnishings were a hodge-podge

collected by him and Kay during the stages and locations of their marriage. Even so, the overall effect worked.

She drained the last of her wine—very sad occurrence, that —and leaned to place her glass on an end table.

"What's the matter?" he asked.

"What do you mean?"

He gave her a wise expression. "You know what I mean. Has something happened with Isobel?"

Mind reader. He was the only person she'd told about the letter she'd sent to her sister. She blamed the fact that she'd confided in him on his calm, non-judgmental personality. He was just so blasted supportive.

She rustled around in her purse, then extended a piece of mail to him.

He accepted it, examined it quickly. "This is the letter you sent her?"

"Yes."

"Unopened."

"Yes. Do you see how she wrote *refused* on the front?"

"I do."

"The post office returned it to sender. I received it today." When she'd seen the letter in her stack of mail at work, it had been like spotting a coiled rattlesnake. Fear had hit her first. Then, when she'd realized Isobel had returned it unopened, the same nausea/anxiety combo she'd felt when she'd mailed it had overtaken her. "I didn't put my name or home address on the letter. She must have recognized my handwriting."

"And we're sure she was the one who wrote *refused* on the front? It wasn't one of her family members or an employee?"

"We're sure. After all this time, I recognize her handwriting, too."

"I'm sorry." He placed the letter on the coffee table. "What are you going to do next?" He hadn't asked whether she was going to give up her quest to reconcile with Isobel. Which proved how well he'd come to know her.

"I'm not sure. I need time to strategize and regroup. I knew this process was going to be difficult. I really shouldn't be so disappointed that this first bid didn't succeed. But for some reason . . . I am." She slipped off her high heels and rubbed her sore instep. "This is a one-glass-of-wine-isn't-enough day. But don't let me have another, okay?"

"Okay."

"Can I have another, though?"

"No."

"Very good, Burke."

"Feet hurt?" he asked.

"A little."

"May I ask why you wear high heels?"

"Because I adore them. I'll be wearing high heels in my coffin."

His eyes crinkled. He curled his fingers inward a couple of times. "Give your feet here. I'll massage them."

"Really?"

"Yes."

She was wearing a wide, camel-colored skirt, which she tucked around her in a ladylike way. Propping her back on a stack of throw pillows, she rested her feet in his lap.

"What about these pantyhose?" he asked. "Do you adore them also?"

"Yes. My sheer nylons are another fashion accessory I'll be taking with me to the coffin."

Supporting one foot in his hands, he ran the pad of his thumb firmly up her arch.

"Heaven," she moaned.

His beard creased around his grin. She liked the contrast between his silvery hair and lightly tanned skin. His brown eyes communicated steadiness. In the way of men, his wrinkles didn't make him look old and tired but instead lent him character.

Fiona let her eyelids drift closed to better focus on the sensations. She heard the fire devouring dry logs and a bird's distant caw.

Burke Ainsley was more comforting than wine. He accepted all her sharp angles and so with him she felt . . . at home. For the first time since she'd received the returned letter, the shakiness inside began to diminish.

After a time, he switched feet. She said nothing, unwilling to break the spell. When she could tell he was finishing up, she cracked an eye and murmured, "Rubbing my feet goes above and beyond the call of friendship."

He wiggled the tip of each toe. "I'd like to go above and beyond friendship with you."

Both her eyes opened. So there it was. He'd finally given voice to the magnetism he felt toward her.

He regarded her with a mild expression. He didn't look anxious, he simply looked honest.

"That's very flattering," she said, "and if there's one thing I like—"

"It's flattery."

"Precisely." She brought her feet to the carpet. Sitting upright, she crossed her legs. "However, I won't suit as anything more than your friend."

"Because?"

"Because I only allow myself fun, harmless flings."

"Because?"

"Because my ex-husband sired a child with my closest friend, then kept that secret for fourteen years. I'm not inclined to dally with marriage again. Which only leaves fun, harmless flings."

"And you're not interested in having a fling with me?"

"Oh, I'm interested. But I only go for men that A) I can't take seriously and B) won't be heartbroken when I end things. My lightweight romances have all been with men who understood the deal. You, Burke, are not made for lightweight romance."

"No. But I don't think you are, either."

"Yes, I am. I'm the high-maintenance one with a wicked reputation. You're hunky Nice Dad."

"Nice Dad?" His forehead grooved. "I haven't had a child living under my roof for a long time. My daughter is now *married* to a Nice Dad. How can I still be Nice Dad?"

"That's what you were when I met you, so you'll always be that in my eyes."

"I don't want to be that in your eyes anymore."

"I notice you're not arguing the *hunky* adjective." She smiled. Genuinely, she cared about him.

"Hunky's fine. I only wish you found me hunky enough to date."

"I do find you hunky enough to date. It's just that you're cut from committed cloth. You're very . . . *good.* Certainly, much better than me."

"Fiona." He waited until he had her full attention. "I'm crazy about you, just the way you are."

The words impacted her with surprising force. They both struck at her emotions and caused tingles to cascade down her body. "Thank you. It's nice to be valued for being me."

"But you won't date me?"

"I'm sorry, no. I love our friendship, though. Until you came along, I didn't realize how much I needed another friend."

"I love our friendship, too." He surveyed her. "But I want

383

you to know that with patience and time . . . I think I'll be able to win your heart."

"One foot massage at a time?" she teased.

"Yes."

Not going to happen, buddy. She was in the driver's seat of this relationship, and she was far too smart to steer this car in that direction.

The following day, Remy hiked to a spot that rewarded her with a panoramic vista of Groomsport's harbor, the hills that protected it, and the coastline. She sat alone on the wooden bench at the outlook.

Today's sun and forty-something temps had melted the snow, turning it into drips and glimmering rivulets. The woods and the little town, which had been concealed with white when she'd arrived in Groomsport, were now not only unconcealed but also washed bright and clean.

What was that old song they'd sung at church when she'd been growing up? *It is well . . . something?*

In a flash, she recalled the lyric and melody. *It is well with my soul.*

The internal battles she'd been waging since Jeremiah left —sleeplessness, heartsickness, doubt, hurt—had left her staggering and weary. She was still catching her breath after all of that. But since Wendell and Marisol's reunion, she could say that it was well with her soul.

"God has a soft spot for those of us who feel like we've been thrown onto the garage sale pile. A giant soft spot for us," Wendell had said to her that day at his kitchen table. *"He's never closer to us than when we're beaten up, unloved, betrayed."*

As bad as things had been since she'd last seen Jeremiah, she was experiencing the truth of that. God was with her. She'd been too hurt or maybe too young to sense Him during the last storm. But incredibly, after all her years of rejecting Him, God *was* with her still. Loving her. She knew it with deep intuition.

She also knew that she needed to talk with Jeremiah. What she didn't know was when. Or what, exactly, to say. She didn't want to blunder in unprepared.

It was Wednesday. She was here until Sunday. She'd let Thanksgiving pass tomorrow, then she'd speak with him. And somehow . . . put her heart on the line? And apologize for hurting him?

You're a creative person, Remy. Think of something grand and imaginative. Or maybe that wasn't the way to go. Probably heartfelt and real was better.

SOS! Why was this so tricky?

Because it meant so much.

"Thanks for inviting me to stop by," Jeremiah said to Alexis's friend Skye on Thanksgiving night.

"Of course. Thanks for coming." She held the door and he stepped from the dark porch into a well-lit formal living room. He could hear conversation and the sound of a TV coming from another downstairs room, a room where people lived. Unlike this one.

He'd called Skye yesterday to touch base following Fiona's unproductive interview with her. Skye was the only person on the spreadsheet that Jude had recommended Jeremiah talk with once his memory returned. Skye had told him over the phone that she'd be free Thanksgiving night after her family's afternoon feast, if he was willing to stop by her parents' house. So here he was.

Jeremiah's day had been exhausting—filled with lots of people at both the O'Sullivan meal and the Camden meal. The whole time, he'd felt lonely in the midst of the crowds. Like a fraud for talking and pretending to enjoy the food when he was desolate on the inside over Remy.

"I'm glad you called me," she said. Like all of Alexis's friends, Skye was young and fashionable in an Instagram way. She pushed at her cuticles. "When your mother started asking me questions about the last time I saw Alexis, it took me off guard. I just . . . I don't know Fiona very well. And also, I couldn't remember a lot about the last time I saw Alexis off the top of my head. So I didn't say much. Then I felt badly, afterward, that I hadn't been more helpful."

"I get it. It's okay."

"A few things have come to me since, so when I heard from you, I was like, oh good, a second chance. Even though the things I remembered are really little. Probably nothing."

"What did you remember?"

"I remembered that Alexis seemed happier than usual. She was kind of . . . beaming. I commented on it and she blew it off, made a joke about how her happy glow was from the retinol she was using. But I came to the conclusion that it was you making her happy. It was just . . . that kind of glow."

A man *had* been making her happy. But that man hadn't been him.

"She mentioned how she was in the mood for night hiking," Skye went on. "She was really wanting to go and asked me if I was up for it. I told her no because I went night hiking with her once and it scared me to death. I almost broke my wrist. And that was on an easy half-mile hike. She was talking about hiking all the way to Maiden's Cliff and I was like, what? That's steep and remote. Anyway, I told her no. Then after I found out where she died, I felt guilty. Because if I'd gone with her, maybe that wouldn't have happened to her." Her expression asked for understanding.

"There's no reason for you to feel guilty. What happened to Alexis had nothing to do with your decision."

"There was just no way I was up for a hike like that. In the dark."

"I understand." He thanked her and spent as much time chatting about her life since Alexis's death as politeness demanded. They exchanged goodbyes, and he made his way to his car.

So Alexis had been wanting to go night hiking to Maiden's Cliff well before her death. Skye had turned her down. Who had Alexis found to go with her?

He hadn't discovered anything the last time he'd made a trip to Maiden's Cliff. But Skye's comments had motivated him to return.

Jeremiah reached Maiden's Cliff in time to watch the sun rise. He took a seat near the cliff's edge, his athletic clothing and down jacket keeping him just warm enough to remain stationary. The white metal cross stood over him like a still and patient bodyguard as he watched the clouds turn pale peach, then gold as the sun made its appearance. Far below, the surface of the lake glimmered a deep sapphire color.

Since the start of his separation from Remy, he'd had very little sleep, which was why he'd come here at such an early hour. He'd already been awake. A lot hinged on this day. Hopefully, he'd talk to Remy at Anton and Camille's house and, by some miracle, convince her to give him a second chance.

He looked to the left. No hikers yet today. No movement whatsoever—

A reflection of light blinked at him.

The last time he'd come here with Remy, he'd looked in the same direction and seen that same small reflective surface. There had been activity here that day, so he'd assumed the light was shining off sunglasses or a metal water bottle.

He no longer thought so because this reflection originated in the same spot as before.

Moving quickly, he followed the trail toward the reflection until the trail curved away from his target. At that point, he left the path and stomped through foliage.

The reflection was situated on an outcropping below the elevation of Maiden's Cliff. When he came to an exposed patch of land, he glanced back at the white metal cross. His elevation was about right but he hadn't gone far enough yet.

Jeremiah continued over a fallen tree and around a shallow ravine. Finally, he drew near a ledge of bare rock. Breathing hard, he pushed his way to it. A Canon camera fastened to a short tripod pointed back toward the cross of Maiden's Cliff. The sparkle he'd seen must have come from sunlight hitting its lens.

Someone was . . . photographing activity on the cliff?

A narrow footpath snaked away from the tripod into the woods. He followed it uphill. Five minutes later, the track ended at a small, scruffy cabin. Smoke drifted from its chimney and masculine junk cluttered the yard. The shell of an old Ford. A rusted-out gas pump. A steering wheel. He was willing to bet that a man lived here.

An early rising man might not mind a visit from a male trespasser as much as a late-sleeping woman.

The porch screeched beneath his weight. He knocked on the peeling door.

A few seconds later, the door pulled back to reveal a wiry seventy-something man. He wore a dingy plaid shirt and baggy corduroys. White tufts of hair stuck out in every direction from his beige face.

"Jeremiah Camden?" the man asked with disbelief.

"Yes, sir."

"Well, what do you know! *Jeremiah Camden*." His palm pressed to his chest. "I'm Gil. Gil Gilderson."

"Sorry to disturb you so early."

"What can I do for you, son?"

"I was at Maiden's Cliff just now. I looked over and saw the reflection of your camera lens."

"Yes. Does this visit have anything to do with what happened to your wife?"

"Actually," Jeremiah said with surprise, "yes. As you may or may not know, she died on that cliff."

"I know all about it. She fell to her death there summer before last. Terrible thing."

"No one has been able to give me an explanation as to what happened."

"It's mighty cold out there. Please, come inside and have a cup of coffee." He beckoned and stepped back to allow Jeremiah to pass.

The interior was as rickety and filled with junk as the exterior. But it smelled great—like coffee and bacon.

Gil led him to a dining chair, then filled a yellow ceramic mug with steaming coffee and gave it to Jeremiah. He topped off his own mug and leaned against the tile counter. "I like time-lapse photography. You know those videos you see when a flower unfurls? That kind of thing?"

"Yes."

"I set up my camera out there to capture the sunsets over Maiden's Cliff on evenings when there's no rain or snow in the forecast. Then I create a video from the photos, you see, and choose the best one of the week to put on my Instagram account. It's quite a thing! I have a whole lot of followers. Fifteen hundred of them, do you believe?"

"I do."

"They depend on me for those weekly videos."

"Were you taking photos the night that Alexis died?"

Gil regarded him sadly. "I was, yes. The police, they came to see me the very same day she was found. They had records that listed all the residents on this hill, and they made the rounds, speaking to each of us about Alexis. Detective Holland sat right where you're sitting now." He motioned with his mug, which caused coffee to slop over the side. "I told him about the time lapse and made them a copy of the video from the night of her death. They were real hopeful about it. So was I."

"But?"

"But, at the time of night when she died, it was full dark. My camera catches the light of sunset. But it's not able to see in the dark any better than you or I could. I've watched the footage myself at least twenty times. It shows darkness and nothing else. The police called me a few days later and confirmed the same thing. I'm real sorry but the video won't help you."

"Do you still have the video?"

"Oh yes. I save the recordings that are extraordinary. That one qualifies because of what happened to your poor wife. You're welcome to it. You can watch the sunset on that night, at least. Maybe there'll be some comfort in that for you."

Jeremiah had zero hope of finding comfort in the sunset on the night Alexis had died. But his heart was hammering, and his skin was raising with chills because he *did* have hope concerning the recording. "I'll take the video footage, please."

"You bet. Let me pull it up on my computer and copy it to a flash drive." He disappeared into a room down the hall.

It wasn't hard to believe that Gil and Groomsport's small-town police force had determined the footage to be unusable.

But Jude worked for the FBI.

And the FBI employed some of the foremost video experts in the United States of America.

If anyone could manipulate the video in order to reveal events obscured by darkness, they could.

Chapter Twenty-Seven

After trying and failing to contact Jude on his cell phone, Jeremiah drove to Mom's house, where Jude was staying for Thanksgiving weekend.

The house was dark and quiet, so he walked around and knocked softly on the window of the room where Jude slept. He wanted to be heard by Jude but didn't want to alarm their mother. She was not one who enjoyed being awoken on a holiday morning and not one who'd react calmy to pounding and yelling. Also, she was nosy. He didn't want her to know anything about this.

The bedroom curtains jerked to the side. Jude looked out at him grumpily, wearing pajama pants. It was rare to see Jude's hair in this tangled state.

"I need your help," Jeremiah said through the glass.

Jude slid the window frame up. "What help do you need from me at seven forty-five the day after Thanksgiving?"

"I have a video recording of Maiden's Cliff on the night Alexis died." He held up the flash drive. "The footage is dark, though. So I'm hoping you know an FBI video expert."

"I'll meet you at your car in ten minutes."

Jeremiah inserted the flash drive into the side of his computer. Jude sat next to him in Jeremiah's home office at Appleton.

The video began to play—hills and the cliff, sun in a sky dotted with white clouds.

"What time of day did the coroner determine that Alexis died?" Jude asked.

"Between ten and midnight."

"At what time does this recording start?"

"I asked Gil that and he said he always sets the camera to begin taking pictures forty-five minutes prior to sunset."

"When did sunset happen on this day?"

Jeremiah downsized the video and ran a quick search for a sunset/sunrise calendar for Groomsport.

They spoke in unison. "Eight twenty-three p.m."

"Which means this recording began at approximately seven forty," Jude said.

"Which means if we look at how long it takes from the start of the video to sunset and then fast-forward around twice that long, we'll reach the section where her death may have occurred."

Jeremiah skimmed forward that amount and hit play. Nothing but black showed on the screen.

Jude leaned back in his chair and looked up toward the ceiling thoughtfully. "I've worked with several of the examiners at the Bureau's Digital Evidence Lab. Video analysis is one of the things they specialize in and it's incredible what they can do with blurry and dark images. However . . ."

"Yeah?"

"This video doesn't fall under the purview of their caseload. There's only one examiner I can think of who has a home setup almost as sophisticated as the setup at the lab."

"His name?"

"Nathan. He's young, but he's good."

"Can you ask him to take this on freelance?"

Jude tugged his phone from the pocket of his jeans. Even though he'd been rushing this morning, his beige long-sleeved T-shirt didn't have a single wrinkle.

Jude dialed and held the phone to his ear.

"Tell Nathan," Jeremiah said, "I'll pay him triple his usual rate if he can work on this now, this morning."

"And if he can't work on it this morning?"

"For triple, he *can*."

"Hey, Nathan," Jude said into the phone. He explained the situation and Jeremiah's payment offer. "You bet. I'll trim the video so that you'll only receive the portion we're interested in."

Jude listened and then said, "Got it. I'll upload the video onto a file-sharing site now and email you the link."

Jeremiah waited, tense, while his brother wrapped up the call.

Finally, Jude disconnected. "Nathan's going to get going on it right away."

With time to kill while they waited, the brothers made themselves breakfast. Omelets, bacon, toast, orange juice, and coffee. *Good coffee*, Jeremiah thought, draining his mug. Freshly ground Arabica from an espresso machine. Yet he'd give anything, *everything*, to be at Remy's house right now, drinking Folgers.

When they finished, they worked together to load the dishwasher. Then went to the garage to check the cars' engine oil and tire pressure.

The first two times Jude's phone rang, he checked the screen and shook his head.

The third time it rang, he nodded. After he connected the call, Jude gave Jeremiah a small, victorious smile. "Yep. If you'll upload that to our shared folder, we'll take a look. I can't thank you enough for working on this immediately." More listening. Then, "Thanks, man."

They washed car grime off their hands and returned to their seats in front of the computer.

Jeremiah navigated to the shared folder.

"Nathan says he's glad I sent this over," Jude told him, "because what it reveals is messed up. His words."

They exchanged a look like, *Did we just solve this thing?*

"Nathan trimmed the new video so that it shows only the relevant activity," Jude said. "Also, he worked on clarifying one particular still frame that he enlarged. That's included at the end."

Before, the recording revealed nothing but opaque dark. Now it resembled the night-vision pieces of film he'd seen on news programs, documentaries, and movies. The landscape had a surreal quality to it—the whole thing was shades of gray and eerie green.

The silhouettes of two people—a man and a woman—came into view, walking toward the cliff holding hands. The woman carried a flashlight, and the man carried a rolled-up blanket. They were distant, grainy, and shadowed. No way to identify either of them.

The man spread out the blanket. As the woman swung to the side to kneel on it, her long hair flared out and was caught by the wind. That hair was pure Alexis. So was the way she moved and the shape of her body.

Both figures reclined. It was hard to see them clearly against the land. Maybe they were talking? Looking up at the stars? The woman rolled on top of the man.

Jeremiah winced. "It looks like my wife is making out with her lover."

"Yeah. It does."

He'd known Alexis had affairs. Still. It made him nauseous to see video of her with another man while she'd been married to him.

Even though the time-lapse video moved quickly, it was obvious they'd done a lot more than make out. Afterward, they rested against the blanket again. Then, all of a sudden, the woman rushed to her feet. Her outline jerked on clothing. Jeremiah recognized her angry, confrontational body language because he'd been on the receiving end of that plenty of times.

It seemed their conversation had taken a turn that had made Alexis mad.

The man stood, too. He was pulling on his pants, gesturing emphatically.

Alexis shoved him so hard in the chest that he almost fell before catching his balance. Her hand swung back as if preparing to slap him. He blocked her arm and they wrestled before she yanked away. She stepped back, toward the cliff.

He placed himself between her and the cliff, palms raised as if trying to back her up.

Once again, her arm reared back. This time, her hand connected with his face. She appeared to be screaming, her shoulders rounded forward, her hands in fists.

He grabbed her upper arms and shook her. Alexis kicked at his shins. He swung her around so that she was now nearest the cliff, and he was the one in the safer position. He pressed her closer to the ledge. Just inches now separating her from empty air.

Jeremiah's blood moved through his veins slow and cold. He knew the ending of this movie. She was about to die. He didn't want to see it. More than that, he didn't want it to be true. Powerlessly, he wished he could change what was about to happen.

He and Alexis had not been cut out to be husband and wife. But divorced, they could've both gone on to live full lives. That's what he would have chosen for her. He wished she'd found her way to a good, long life.

Alexis head-butted the man's throat, kicked out at him again. Clearly both of them were screaming—

Leaning into it, he stepped forward and shoved her away from him. The move was deathly successful.

Instantaneously she vanished from the camera's scope.

Jeremiah and Jude said nothing. In the silence he registered the whir of his heater and the low *chug chug chug* of the dishwasher.

Life went on for him. But not for Alexis.

Just like Jeremiah had suspected for a long time, she had not jumped. She'd been murdered and here, at last, was the terrible proof.

The long-range shot of the man's outline came to a halt. Then the video cut to the still frame Nathan had mentioned to Jude—a close-up of the man's chest, shoulders, and head.

Though pixelated and hazy, the face was recognizable for the first time.

It was Anton.

The sight drove the air from his lungs.

Anton. The name rattled around his head like a stone in a Mason jar. *Anton.* His best friend had been having an affair with his wife. The betrayal of it coursed through him like acid.

Anton and Alexis had spent more than enough time together to develop a secret flirtation. They had proximity.

They'd have been motivated to cover their tracks well because they were both married, and Alexis would have told Anton that she'd been caught in her first affair. Jeremiah had been home from racing when Alexis had taken the trips Kimley had found suspicious. When Jeremiah was home from racing, Anton was home from racing, too. And available to travel.

Anton lived in Groomsport so it would have been simple to sneak onto the *Camdenball*, first to poison his drinks and then to remove the remaining drinks. He'd have known when to do that because Jeremiah himself had kept him in the loop about everything.

All of his memories had come back now. Just in time for several memories of Anton to taunt him. The countless work trips. The times they'd laughed. The times Anton had encouraged him after a bad race. The thousands of hours Anton had spent as his physical trainer. The times Anton had functioned as a bodyguard or a press secretary. The trip to Ibiza he and Alexis had taken with Anton and Camille.

Wait. *Camille.*

Icy realization split into his consciousness. "Remy is going to Anton's house today to have lunch with Camille."

"What? When?"

Jeremiah's attention raked over the computer's screen. In his panic, he couldn't remember where to locate the time. There, in the corner. It was twenty after twelve. "I think Camille told me Remy would be there at twelve thirty." He'd intended to stop by a little after one.

"We've got to keep her from going over there."

His hands were shaking, but he managed to bring up the last text he'd received from Camille. "Yeah, twelve thirty. That's when Remy will be there." Ten minutes.

He dialed Remy. An eternity of time passed between every

ring. It went to voice mail. He dialed her again. *Remy. Once in your life, just this once, have your phone on and answer.*

Problem was, even if she had her phone on, she wasn't likely to answer a call from him seeing as how she'd asked him not to contact her. He shot her a text message.

JEREMIAH

> Anton killed Alexis. Do not go to Camille's house.

"Jude. Try to call and text Remy." If she'd blocked his number, maybe Jude could get through.

"Number?" Jude asked.

Jeremiah read out the digits. Jude punched them in and held his phone to his ear.

"Do you have your gun on you?" Jeremiah asked.

"Always."

"Let's go."

Dialing Remy again, Jeremiah sprinted toward the garage. She still wasn't answering. *Remy! Answer!*

He went straight for the Ferrari, one of the fastest street-legal cars in the world.

"Why isn't she picking up?" Jude asked as he slid into the passenger seat and Jeremiah into the driver's seat.

"She never answers her phone." Jeremiah fired up the engine, then slammed the car into gear, peeling into a reverse spin from the garage, and shooting down his driveway.

"We might get there before she does," Jude said.

Fear was carving a deep, dark well down the center of Jeremiah. He couldn't let anything happen to her.

"And if Remy's going there to see Camille," Jude added, "Anton probably won't be home."

"Except that Anton works from home now. And Camille and I . . . we arranged it so that I could see Remy by pretending

I was coming by there to give Anton something. He'll be there today because of that."

His manipulations had placed Remy at Anton's house.

Jude double-checked his handgun. "Anton may not even see Remy when she arrives. But if he does, it will be fine because Camille will be present. Also, Anton has no idea that we know what he did to Alexis."

He appreciated what Jude was trying to do—talk him down. But there was nothing Jude could say that could talk him down right now. His life was hanging on a cable over a canyon. Either it would rise up to safety. Or it would crash. "Keep calling Remy," Jeremiah ordered.

"On it."

Jeremiah wrapped both hands around the steering wheel. The speedometer climbed. He flew around a corner.

"Under Maine law," Jude said, "if we're in danger, we should retreat to avoid harm. If that's not possible, we must use the least amount of force necessary. It's only if someone attempts deadly force against us and we have no other recourse that I can defend us with deadly force."

"Understood."

"She's still not answering her phone."

"Remy," Jeremiah growled as he neared an intersection, "answer your phone." He could see no oncoming traffic, so he blew through the red light. "Keep trying."

Jude did so, repeatedly.

The air thickened with urgency. He drove extremely fast yet had the sense that he was failing. It wasn't fast enough. This was how he'd felt under hypnosis—too slow. Guilty. At fault. Desperate. Except a thousand times worse because this was real life, and this was Remy.

"Would Remy have driven herself to Anton's house?" Jude asked.

"I think so. Last time she was in town, she rented an economy car. I'm guessing that's what she did this time."

"So when we get to Anton's, we look to see if there's a car parked out front with a rental agency sticker on it. If not, we don't go to the door. We wait out of sight in the direction she'll be coming from and stop her car en route."

"And if we see that a rental car is already parked out front?"

"Then we enter the house as casually as possible. We tell her there's been an emergency. Does she know anyone who lives nearby?"

"Yes, a man named Wendell."

"You tell her there's an emergency regarding Wendell and that you need for her to leave with you immediately. We get Remy out of there. What's the name and number of the detective handling the investigation into Alexis's death?"

"Detective Phillip Holland." Jeremiah tossed his phone into Jude's lap. "He's in my contacts."

"I'm going to text him access to the shared folder so that he can view Nathan's video footage."

God, Jeremiah prayed, *please let us reach the house and see that Remy has not yet arrived. Please.* He repeated the prayer. Over and over.

They drove into Anton's wealthy neighborhood and followed a winding street downhill. Anton had spent his whole career as an employee of the Mercedes F1 team. He'd been paid well but he'd been paid even better by Jeremiah, who'd chipped in big bonuses out of his own pocket. Jeremiah himself had given Anton this house—a fact that sickened Jeremiah now.

As soon as he came around the last curve before Anton's house, he spotted a small white Kia parked at the curb.

His stomach dropped.

Chapter Twenty-Eight

"**S**low," Jude said. "Let me see if there's a rental car sticker on it."

Jeremiah slowed.

"Yeah," Jude said gravely, "it's a rental. I'm going to call Groomsport PD."

Jeremiah parked the Ferrari while Jude identified himself to the police over the phone. He explained that Anton Quintrell, a suspect in the murder of Alexis Camden, was at 312 Chestnut Lane. Potentially armed and dangerous and in the company of others. "Please notify Detective Phillip Holland. My brother and I are going in, but we need your help as soon as possible."

Remy is inside this house with the man who killed Alexis, was all Jeremiah could think, over and over.

Jude slid his gun into the back waistband of his jeans.

They set off across the deep, tree-filled lawn toward the front door.

"Look relaxed," Jude whispered sharply.

Jeremiah slowed his pace and did his best to do what his brother asked, but his face felt like a hardened mask.

The garage came into view. Its door was open and only one car sat inside. Anton's car.

"Camille's car isn't here," Jeremiah said, low.

All of the best-case scenarios—Remy not yet having arrived, Camille being here—ripped away.

Ever since Anton had moved into this house, Jeremiah had let himself inside without knocking. He followed that pattern now, turning the knob and entering the foyer. "Hello?"

"In here," Anton's voice replied.

Jeremiah cut through the sitting room overlooking the front yard. Most of the wall between the sitting room and den was open. When he and Jude reached the mouth of the opening, he saw a thousand things in a glance.

Remy sat to the side, head tilted quizzically, wearing a cable-knit sweater and jeans, hair half up and half down.

He loved her.

She was so beautiful to him, and he'd missed her so much and, at last, he was close to her. But Anton was here, too. On his feet, facing them. Outwardly, Anton's expression was calm, but Jeremiah knew him well enough to see the tension underneath.

From the position where Anton stood, he had a clear view through the windows. If he'd watched them approach, then he would have noticed the stress in Jeremiah's body language. Also, the timing and Jude's presence might have him worried. Jeremiah was here earlier than scheduled and Anton hadn't been expecting Jeremiah's FBI brother to come with him today.

"Hi." Jeremiah greeted Anton, then gazed at Remy. "Camille told me you were having lunch with her here today. I came by to let you know there's an emergency with Wendell. We need to leave."

Instantly, her features revealed concern. She rose to standing. "Is he okay?" Her face, her voice, her hair were achingly familiar.

"He will be, but we need to go. We'll drive you there."

Remy moved forward.

Anton put out an arm, barring her progress. "What kind of emergency?"

"He fell and broke his leg."

"Excuse me," Remy said to Anton, starting forward again.

Anton's fingers curved around Remy's upper arm, keeping her in place.

Hot denial scratched up Jeremiah's throat. Below that heat, though, spread freezing realization. Anton was not going to allow her to walk out of here.

"Let me go," Remy ordered.

Jeremiah met Anton's eyes. He knew just how serious and determined his former friend could be.

"Release her right now," Jude said. "And we'll leave."

"Which will make it easy for the police to take me when they get here," Anton said in a chillingly smooth, controlled voice. "I'm guessing you've already called them?"

"What's going on?" Remy asked Jeremiah.

"They've learned something about me," Anton answered.

Remy tried to jerk her arm free. "*Let me go.*"

"I can't." Anton hauled Remy in front of him, twisted her arm up against the center of her shoulder blades, and locked his other arm around her neck.

She struggled. "What? Let go!"

Glancing to the side, Jeremiah saw that Jude had drawn his weapon and was aiming.

"Easy," Anton said. "You don't want to hurt her, do you?"

"How dare you." Remy's tone was thin with pain, but also tough with anger. "Let go of me."

"I can't let you go just yet," Anton said to her. "You're my only bargaining chip." Looking at the brothers, Anton motioned with his head. "Jude, place the gun there." He indicated a side table. "Then back up so I can take it. Once I have it, Remy and I will leave."

"No," Jeremiah gritted out.

"You have my word that I won't harm her," Anton said. "Once I've put enough distance between myself and this place, I'll let her go."

"Let her go now," Jeremiah demanded.

"My only hope of getting away clean is in taking her with me." Anton twisted Remy's arm higher. She cried out.

Jeremiah died inside. His heart was rushing. His soul was screaming.

"Set your gun on the table," Anton said to Jude, louder. "Move slowly and keep both hands where I can see them."

"Fine," Jude said even though he must know they couldn't let Anton leave with Remy. "Keep calm. We'll do as you ask." Jude eased toward the side table.

"I won't let him take me," Remy told Jeremiah. "I can't let another man attack me."

"I won't hurt you," Anton said.

"You're hurting me right now."

"I have no quarrel with you."

Remy turned her distress on Jude. "I'd rather you take your chances and try to shoot him."

"We can't risk that," Jude said. "Go with him and do as he says and everything will be fine. Call Jeremiah as soon as you can, and we'll come and get you."

"*No*," Remy whispered, and the sound was like nails through Jeremiah's skin.

Jude set his gun on the table and moved away from it.

Tears tracked down Remy's cheeks.

"Back up, toward the front of the house," Anton said. "Both of you." Once they'd done so, he added, "Kneel with your hands up."

Jeremiah knelt next to Jude. Terrified. Hating himself. Furious.

Remy looked stricken—white-faced and wild-eyed.

Anton wrestled her toward the side table so that he could retrieve the gun.

Remy's shoulder muscles were screaming. But that was *nothing* in comparison to the wails of old trauma that Anton had forced up from their grave. Flashbacks of Gavin were swirling.

No to a man doing with her what he wanted against her will for the second time. If Anton gained control of the gun, they'd all be at his mercy. No to letting Anton shoot Jeremiah or Jude. No to being defenseless. No to letting it go down this way. *No.*

Jeremiah was clearly willing to sacrifice himself for her, but the truth was that she would sacrifice *herself* before she'd let Anton hurt either him or his brother.

God, she cried in the chaos of her thoughts. *I need you now. Help me.*

In response, power surged through her like a mighty wind. It blew everything away, leaving room for clarity of thought.

She understood two things in a flash. One, her body was in full fight-or-flight mode. Two, this time she was going to choose *fight.*

As soon as Anton released the arm around her neck to reach for the gun, Remy used her free hand to yank her twisted hand down. She'd practiced this maneuver dozens of times in her self-defense classes and muscle memory activated. Anton jerked forward and she drove her elbow into the side of his head, then spun and moved to press his upper body down—

He was too fast. He wrenched away just before she could gain control. Grabbing a fistful of her hair, he lunged for the gun.

Before he got there, Jeremiah connected a right hook to Anton's jaw. The force of it loosened Anton's fingers from her hair and Remy stumbled free. Jeremiah drove Anton back into the carpet. They hit with bruising force. Jeremiah straddled Anton and Anton grabbed Jeremiah's neck, hard enough to cut off his air.

"Let go." Jude stood above Anton, handgun aimed at his forehead.

Anton's hands remained locked on Jeremiah's throat. Jeremiah punched him again.

"Let go," Jude said loudly, "or I will have no choice but to fire. Three, two, one."

"Shoot me," Anton snarled.

Jude dropped to a knee and punched the center of Anton's throat. Anton's body curved inward involuntarily and Jeremiah thrust both of Anton's wrists against the hardwood floor above his head.

"And this is how we'll stay," Jude said, "until the police arrive with cuffs."

Without removing any of his force or weight from Anton, Jeremiah turned to look for her. "Remy?"

"I'm here."

"Are you all right?"

"Yes." Actually, she was on the verge of hyperventilating, as she had during her rape, but this time, *this time*, the outcome was different. This time, she was on her feet, hands balled. This time she'd done enough to give Jeremiah and Jude an opening.

Angry red marks from Anton's grip blazed across Jeremiah's neck. But he was alive. Jude was alive. She was alive.

"Remy," Jude said, "sit down, put your head between your knees, and concentrate on slowing down and deepening your breath."

She did as he asked. As if witnessing herself from a distance, she noted that she was dizzy and shaking. Her brain, heart, and history were waiting for the other shoe to drop.

It's fine, she told herself repeatedly. *That's not going to happen.*

Gradually, she gained control of her breathing. The shaking was a lost cause, nothing she could do about that.

Distant sirens reached her ears.

At the sound, Anton tried to buck Jeremiah off. Remy flinched but Jeremiah redoubled his efforts and Anton remained pinned.

"We have video," Jeremiah told Anton, "of what happened between you and Alexis that night on the cliff. We know you pushed her."

Anton cursed but said nothing more.

Several seconds later, two policemen flowed into the room, asking questions and taking control of the situation.

Relief started to trickle over Remy like a hot shower on a cold day. She remained sitting but she watched and reveled in the watching as they secured Anton's wrists in handcuffs. Jude did most of the talking—law enforcement to law enforcement. A policeman read Anton his rights, then walked him toward the front door.

They were out of sight, just over the threshold, when Remy heard Camille's voice. She was asking what was going on and she sounded distraught and scared.

Remy had genuinely liked Camille. Now Camille's life and the lives of her children would never be the same. Remy had endured a never-the-same event and she felt a wave of compassion for the woman.

All at once, Jeremiah was before her, offering a hand to pull her up. Without hesitation, she set her fingers in his. Holding hands, he led her toward the back of the house. "I'll leave you here to explain things to Camille," Jeremiah said to Jude as they passed by. "We'll meet you at the car when we're ready."

"Absolutely." Jude caught Remy's eye and gave her an admiring nod that communicated his respect.

She reciprocated. Jude had risked his life for his brother. Out of all the things she logically could've been crying over at this point in time, she suddenly wanted to cry over that. Jeremiah's brother's loyalty. It was like her emotions were out of whack, unable to distinguish which stimulus merited tears.

Jeremiah grabbed a throw blanket as they skirted a sofa, then they were through the back doors. An expansive flagstone area gave way to lawn that gave way to woods. They continued, stopping when they were out of sight of the house beneath sheltering branches of pine.

He ripped off his jacket, helped her into it, then zipped it up the front. For good measure, he wrapped the throw blanket around her.

A breeze lifted strands of her hair while he studied her. Then he gathered her against him, hugging her as if determined to give his vitality to her. She locked her arms around his lean waist.

It was a hug more secure and comforting than any in the history of hugs.

Reassurance flowed between them. Him to her. Her to him.

They stayed that way, clinging to each other without words. Together again. The physical proof that he was here with her—his solid body, his warmth, his height, his scent—was almost too glorious to process.

"I missed you so much," he finally said.

"I missed you so much, too. Does this . . . Does this hug mean that you're not mad at me?"

"I'm not mad at you. Are you mad at me?"

"No."

He pulled back so they could look at one another. His arms remained around her and hers around him. His eyes were like an exotic natural spring shot with sunlight.

"Are you really all right?" he asked. It wasn't a rote question. She could tell he wanted to know.

"Yes. You?"

"If you're all right, then so am I."

"And Wendell?"

"We faked Wendell's emergency to try to get you out. Wendell's fine."

"How did you find video from the night Alexis died?"

He explained. "Anton and Alexis were having an affair. They fought that night, and he pushed her."

"I'm glad the truth came out." With video on their side, Alexis had an excellent shot at receiving justice. Remy had played a small role in making that happen and, in doing so, earned a slice of justice for herself, too.

It felt good. It felt like vindication.

"As soon as Jude and I watched the video," Jeremiah said, "we raced over here. I was sick inside because it's my fault that you're here."

"How so?"

"I hired Kimley to find Marisol, in hopes you'd return to the mainland for their reunion."

Understanding clicked. "And Kimley posed as someone from Marisol's apartment complex and told Wendell her whereabouts."

"Right."

"In finding Marisol, you've made Wendell very happy."

"I like Wendell, but I didn't find Marisol for him. I did it for me, selfishly. Because I couldn't stand not seeing you."

He was obviously in a repentant mood, so she nodded sagely like a priest listening to confession. But inside she wasn't feeling as grave as Jeremiah looked. Quite the opposite. It was like she'd been on a teeter-totter. The altercation with Anton had been the teeter-totter seat jarring against the ground. But these moments with Jeremiah were like flying upward to the teeter-totter's highest point—exhilarating.

"He was supposed to take you with him to dinner at the country club the other night," he said. "I was waiting for you there."

"And your plot was foiled because I didn't join them for dinner."

"So I contacted Camille and asked if she'd set up a meeting with you."

"Lunch today. You planned to run into me here instead?"

"Yes. So you can imagine how I felt when I realized you were here. With a killer. And I'd organized things to make it so."

She could imagine a portion of what he'd felt. Because when Anton had her in his grip, she'd read despair in every line of Jeremiah's strong frame. Then she'd watched him kneel and put himself on the line.

Gavin hadn't even been willing to tell the truth for her sake. She had no context for a man who would risk himself for her.

"I arrived early for lunch," she said. "When I got here, Anton told me that Camille was running behind. We were chatting and everything was normal until he saw you and your brother. He went still as he watched you walk toward the house."

"He knew I was on to him," Jeremiah said with regret. "Remy, I'm so sorry."

"I forgive you," she said quickly and sincerely. Smiling, she placed her palms on the sides of his face. Her thumbs ran delicately over his cheekbones.

They stared at each other—his profile tipped down and hers tipped up. A conversation of hope moved between them. She interlaced her hands behind his neck.

"In the last few months," he said, "I've lost my whole world and gained it back again. The most important thing to me out of all of it—everything I've lost and everything I've gained—is you."

She blinked at him with wonder.

"I love you," he said. "I will love you until the day I die. No looking back. No changing my course."

Joy gusted within her. "I love you, too. I will love you until the day I die. No looking back. No changing my course."

His features smoothed with astonishment.

"I've been trying to think of a way to say that to you," she continued, "that was either grand and imaginative or heartfelt and real. But there's no better way to say that than how you just said it to me. So I'm riding your coattails."

"I want to marry you," he said bluntly. Then hurried to add, "But I realize you're nowhere near ready for that, so I'll wait and maybe one day you'll say yes. On that day, I'll have a ring and a better speech."

"This speech isn't terrible."

"I'll go to Islehaven to be near you and sleep on Leigh's torture mattress."

"You'll live there without a grocery store or a decent road?"

"For you, yes."

"And I'll expand my horizons," she said. "Maybe one day we can live at least part of the time at Appleton together."

He quirked a brow in surprise.

"I suppose your ostentatious mansion isn't the *worst* fate in the world," she conceded. "I might be able to hack it there. But only if you get rid of Dartin's art."

He grinned.

"And if we live as simply and privately as possible," she continued. "In fact, I think it would be best if you give your money away to charity."

"I'm not giving all of it away. I like fast cars."

"And freshly ground Arabica coffee and twenty-one-year-aged rum."

"I also like good food, good sheets, good clothes, and good Wi-Fi," he rattled off.

She laughed and was rewarded with his heart-melting smile as he looked at her softly.

"But mostly," he finished, "I love *you*."

Then he took her face in his hands and kissed her.

Remy's thoughts spun and their chemistry enveloped them, and in their little corner of Maine near the ocean, everything was righter than right with their world.

Epilogue

Jeremiah came downstairs early on Christmas morning hoping to catch Remy alone.

He'd joined her in Dallas for Christmas with her family, which had been great. Her dad kept introducing him to buddies who were F1 fans. Her mom and sister treated him like he was Prince William. Only one thing about their time in Dallas had been less than perfect.

Jeremiah didn't get Remy to himself as much as he would've liked.

That wasn't generous of him seeing as how her family lived far from Maine and only got to see her a couple times a year. But there it was. The greedy state of his heart on Christmas Day.

He came to a stop, barefoot on the hardwood floor at the arched opening to the living room. Remy was indeed alone. She sat cross-legged at the end of the sofa, staring into the crackling fire.

She had on a black shirt, pushed up over her delicate forearms, and the red-and-black-checkered pajama bottoms he'd once been forced to wear. Her pale hair was down—a beautiful, messy tumble over her shoulders and chest.

The tree lights glittered and Christmas music played quietly. She wasn't looking at her phone or reading or doing anything except thinking. This wasn't unusual. She often took vacations into her own mind and imagination.

He took his time, memorizing every detail of the picture she presented. She was endlessly intriguing to him. Filled with facets and layers. Feisty and tender. Practical and spiritual. Self-sufficient yet willing to let him in.

They were very different, but they were also made for each other. It was as if God had known exactly what He was doing when he'd placed Jeremiah in the water outside her cottage in range of her binoculars. Jeremiah had never loved or trusted anyone as much as he loved and trusted her. And he couldn't believe he was fortunate enough to be loved by her in return.

Every time he remembered the day that Anton had used Remy as a shield he got a cold pit in his stomach. Those images couldn't be unseen, so the best he could do was use those memories as a reminder to be grateful that Anton hadn't hurt her.

He also couldn't unsee memories of his fights with Alexis or memories of the day he'd learned of her death. One thing had gone away, though. His nightmares about Alexis. He supposed that was because they'd uncovered the truth and were working to get justice for her. Anton had been charged with manslaughter for what he'd done to Alexis. He'd also been charged with attempted murder for trying to poison Jeremiah in order to stop him from investigating Alexis's death and uncovering Anton's role in it.

Jeremiah had rewatched the time-lapse video of Maiden's Cliff. It was clear to him that Alexis had gone into one of her furious tirades. Jeremiah had always reacted to those with

415

control. Anton had maintained control for a while. But Alexis had continued to strike out at him and eventually Anton's temper had snapped the way Jeremiah had seen it snap before over the course of their years together. Alexis had pushed Anton over the edge of his tolerance. And in a moment of white-hot anger, he'd pushed her over the edge of the mountain.

Anton had nearly gotten away with it. If Jeremiah had consumed more of the drink or if Remy hadn't rescued him when she did, he would have.

Jeremiah shifted his weight and the floor let out a creak.

Remy glanced up. When she saw him, happiness illuminated her face. "Watching me again?" she asked with amusement.

"Every chance I get." He crossed to her, leaned over, and kissed her.

Right when he was losing his ability to think and breathe, she whispered, "Merry Christmas, Jeremiah," against his lips.

He pulled back a few inches. "Merry Christmas, Remy."

They beamed at each other.

"Can I open my gift now?" she asked.

"Only if I can open mine." He straightened, nodding to the rectangular, five-foot-tall wrapped box.

"Deal." She popped to her feet and retrieved her smaller, flatter box. "Me first." She tore free the paper to reveal a very amateur painting of ocean, the cliff in front of her cottage, her house, and sky. Her lips parted in delighted surprise. "Did you . . . paint this?"

"I did. I've secretly been taking painting lessons. It wasn't easy to figure out what to give a woman who doesn't want expensive, store-bought things. What you seem to like best is art that has sentimental value. So I hope this has enough sentimental value to make up for the fact that it's terrible."

She hugged it against her chest, eyes dancing. "Jeremiah! I love it. It's my new favorite piece."

"Maybe you can squeeze it onto a wall somewhere next to the rest of your crazy art."

"I'll thank you not to call my art crazy."

"Fine. From now on I'll call it eccentric."

"Open mine!"

Turned out she was a bossy Christmas gift person.

"The box has no bottom," she added. "You can lift it straight up."

He did so. Beneath stood one of her sculptures. His favorite sculpture. *"Emiline?"* he asked, grinning. "I thought you said I couldn't have it. That it wasn't for me."

"Turns out it *was* for you, after all. I'm as surprised as anyone. Can you figure out why it's for you?" Remy intertwined her fingers with his.

He had no idea. "Because Emiline harnessed her powers? And so have I because I harnessed my powers of flirtation and won your heart?"

"No." She made a *try again* gesture.

"Because Emiline has an inflated head and so do I?"

She laughed. "No! Because Emiline was brave and eventually *found herself.* You had amnesia. But you were brave, and you found yourself, too."

He tugged her against him. "Thank you."

"I'll take my thanks in a less verbal form."

"What did you have in mind?" he asked in a low whisper.

"Kiss me, Duke."

And so he did.

"For the mountains may move and the hills disappear, but even then my faithful love for you will remain." Isaiah 54:10

Catch up with Jude Camden (and Fiona & Burke, too) when Jude goes undercover as Gemma's boyfriend in Rocky Road, Book 2 of the Sons of Scandal series!

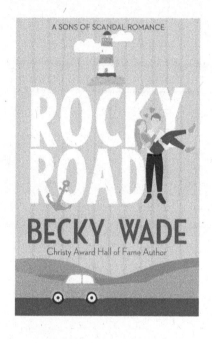

About the Author

Becky's a California native who attended Baylor University, met and married a Texan, and settled in Dallas. She published historical romances for the general market before putting her career on hold for several years to care for her three children. These days, she loves writing sweet contemporary romances filled with sizzling chemistry, twisty plots, faith, banter, and humor. She's the Christy and Carol Award–winning author of twelve novels. When she's not writing, you'll find her power-walking her neighborhood, driving carpool, eating chocolate, doing yoga, or admiring her Cavalier spaniel.

To learn more about Becky and her books, visit her website at www.beckywade.com. While you're there, subscribe to her free quarterly e-newsletter for updates about upcoming books, exclusive giveaways, and more!

You'll find Becky on Facebook as Author Becky Wade and on Instagram as BeckyWadeWriter.